"Other people,"  "have to live in this house too.

Sometimes it's not easy, but generally I manage to cope. But it's hard enough as it is without you pulling stunts like that. Do you understand?"

He'd have said anything to get the hand off his shoulder before he choked to death. "Yes, I understand. I'm sorry."

Stheno held him just a little longer; just a little too long. Then he let go, and all Gignomai could think about was breathing. "I can see why you did it," Stheno said, not at all unkindly. "In your shoes, probably I'd have done the same. But you don't have that luxury. Right?"

"Right."

Stheno nodded. A curt nod that said, quarrel over, let's not bother with grudges. "Glad you're back," he said. "I was worried."

"Stheno?"

"Yes?"

"The sword," Gignomai said. "I lost it, in the woods. Really."

Stheno frowned. "I suggest you find it," he said, "else, Father'll kill you."

"That's what I was thinking."

Praise for the Novels of
K. J. PARKER

"I have reviewed books before that I thought might someday be found to have achieved greatness...K. J. Parker is writing work after work that demands to be placed in that category." —Orson Scott Card

"Blends gritty military fantasy with the 18th-century 'island story' tradition....Parker carries the reader on a headlong gallop to the powerful conclusion." —*Publishers Weekly* (starred review)

"Imagine *Lost* meets *The Italian Job*...a masterfully planned and executed book, one that builds on ever-revealing characterization and backstory, leading slowly yet inexorably to its final conclusion." —SFF World

"It's a dark, bleak and fiercely intelligent portrait of the human condition..." —*SFX*

"A deftly paced mix that's brimming with psychological insights." —*Library Journal*

"The whole thing is brilliant—disturbingly so, since these fantasies (without a whit of magic) explore the human condition and reveal it all, brain, heart, guts and bowels, with a startling precision." —*Locus*

"Parker's intricately plotted and meticulously detailed book...moves as deliberately and precisely as an antique watch." —*Entertainment Weekly*

"An audacious, utterly captivating novel...Parker's prose glitters with intelligence and precision...one of the most entertaining novels I've read this year." —*Realms of Fantasy* magazine

"K. J. Parker is more of a hurricane than a breath of fresh air." —*Dreamwatch* magazine

"It's a splendid story, full of turmoil and conspiracy." —blogcritics.org

"As efficient and well constructed as its protagonist's well-oiled machines." —*Starburst*

By K. J. Parker

THE FENCER TRILOGY

Colours in the Steel

The Belly of the Bow

The Proof House

THE SCAVENGER TRILOGY

Shadow

Pattern

Memory

THE ENGINEER TRILOGY

Devices and Desires

Evil for Evil

The Escapement

The Company

The Folding Knife

The Hammer

THE
HAMMER

K. J. PARKER

www.orbitbooks.net

Orbit
Hachette Book Group
237 Park Avenue, New York, NY 10017
www.HachetteBookGroup.com

First Edition: January 2011

Orbit is an imprint of Hachette Book Group, Inc. The Orbit name and logo are
trademarks of Little, Brown Book Group Limited.

Library of Congress Control Number: 2010938878
ISBN: 978-0-316-03856-0

10   9   8   7   6   5   4   3   2   1

Printed in the United States of America

For Ian and Angela Whitefield and Jim Alcock,
An everyday story of country folk

Seven Years Before

When Gignomai was seven years old, his brother Stheno gave him three chickens.

"They're not yours, of course," Stheno said, "you're just looking after them. Food and water twice a day, muck 'em out when the smell gets bad, make sure the fox doesn't get them. No big deal. Father thinks it's time you learned about taking responsibility."

"Oh," Gignomai said. "How about the eggs?"

"They go to the kitchen," Stheno said.

For a week, Gignomai did exactly as he'd been told. As soon as he woke up, he ran out into the yard, being careful not to slam the door in case it disturbed Father in his study, and went to the grain barrel, where he measured out a double handful of wheat into the battered old pewter cup he'd found in the barn. He scattered the grain all round the foot of the mounting-block, filled the tin pail with water, counted the chickens to make sure they were all there and made a tour of inspection of the yard palings. One paling was rotten at the base, and Gignomai was worried that a fox could shove against it, break it and get in. He reported his concerns to Stheno, who said he'd see to it when he had a moment. Nothing was done. Two days later, something broke in during the night and killed the chickens.

"Not a fox," his brother Luso said, examining the soft earth next to the broken palings. Luso was a great hunter, and knew everything there was to know about predators. "Look at the size of its feet. If I didn't know better, I'd say it was a wolf, only we haven't seen one of them for years. Most likely it's a stray dog from town."

That made sense. Town was a strange, barbarous place where common people lived, barely human. It followed that their dogs would run wild and murder chickens. Luso undertook to patrol the woods with his gun (any excuse). Stheno told Gignomai not to worry about it; these things happened, it wasn't his fault (said in a way that made it clear that it was, really), and if you kept livestock, sooner or later you'd get dead stock, and there was nothing more to be said. That would have been fine, except that he then issued Gignomai with three more chickens.

"Try to take better care of them," he said. "The supply isn't exactly infinite, you know."

For three days, Gignomai tended the chickens as before. For three nights, he sat in the bow window overlooking the grand double doors of the hall. He was too young to be allowed out after dark, and from the bow window you could just about see the far western corner of the yard. He managed to stay awake for the first two nights. On the third night he fell asleep, and the predator broke in and killed the chickens.

"Not your fault," Stheno said wearily. "For a start, you wouldn't have seen anything from there, and it was dark, so you wouldn't have seen anything anyway. And even if you'd seen something, it'd have taken too long. You'd have had to come and wake me up, and by the time I'd got out there, the damage would've been done."

It was the same large, unfamiliar paw print. Luso still maintained it was a dog.

"You didn't mend the broken paling," Gignomai said.

"I will," Stheno replied, "soon as I've got a minute."

Custody of the remaining dozen chickens was awarded to one of Luso's huntsmen. The paling didn't get fixed. Two nights later, the leftovers from two more hens and the cock were scattered round the yard.

"We'll have to get a cock from one of the farms," Luso said. The met'Oc didn't condescend to trade with their neighbours, but from time to time Luso and his huntsmen went out at night and took things. It wasn't stealing, Mother said, but she didn't explain why not. Stheno tied the paling to the rail with a bit of twine from his pocket. Gignomai knew why he hadn't mended it: he had the farm to run, and he did most of the work himself because the farm workers were weak and lazy and not to be trusted. Stheno was twenty-one and looked like Father's younger brother rather than his son.

The next night, Gignomai climbed out through the kitchen window. He'd noticed some time before that the catch didn't fasten; he'd made a note of this fact, which could well be strategically useful, but had decided not to squander the opportunity on a pointless excursion. He took with him a horn lantern he'd found in the trap-house, a knife from the kitchen and some string.

The predator came just before dawn. It wasn't a dog. It was huge and graceful and quiet, and it nosed aside the broken paling as though it wasn't there. It jumped the half-door of the chicken-house in a single fluid movement, and came out a short time later with a dead chicken in his jaws. Gignomai watched it carefully, and didn't move until it had gone.

He thought about it. The predator was a wolf. He'd seen pictures in the *Bestiary* in Father's library, and read the descriptions in Luso's *Art of the Chase*. Quite likely it was the last surviving wolf on the Tabletop, or maybe in the whole colony. The met'Oc had waged war on the wolves when they first came here. Luso had always wanted to kill a wolf, but he'd only ever seen one, a long way away. This wolf was probably old, which would explain why it had taken to burglary; they did that when they were too old and tired to pull down deer, and when they were alone with no pack to support them.

There was no way a seven-year-old could fight a wolf, or even scare one away if it didn't want to go. He could tell Stheno or Luso, but they almost certainly wouldn't believe him.

Well, he decided. The job had to be done or it'd kill all the chickens, and nobody else was going to do it because they wouldn't believe he'd seen a wolf.

He thought hard all the next day. Then, just as it was beginning to get dark and the curfew came into force, he went as unobtrusively as he could to the chicken-house, chose the oldest and weakest hen and pulled her neck. With the knife he'd borrowed from the kitchen and neglected to return, he opened the guts and carefully laid a trail of drops of blood across the yard to the woodshed, where he put the corpse on top of the stacked brushwood. He scrounged some loose straw from the stables and laid it in the shed doorway, and found a stout, straight stick about three feet long, which he leaned up against the wall. It was the best way of doing it that he could think of. There'd be trouble, but he couldn't help that.

The wolf came earlier that night. Gignomai had been waiting long enough for his eyes to get accustomed to the dark, and besides, there was a helpful three-quarter moon and no cloud. He watched the wolf's nose shove past the paling and pick up the scent of blood. He kept perfectly still as it followed the trail, pausing many times to look up. It was suspicious, he knew, but it couldn't figure out what was wrong. Old and a bit stupid, but still a wolf. He made sure of his grip on the lantern, and waited.

Eventually, the wolf followed the blood all the way into the woodshed. Gignomai kept still until the very tip of its tail had disappeared inside; then he jumped up, took a deep breath, and crept on the sides of his feet, the way Luso had taught him, across the yard. He could smell the wolf as he groped for the stick he'd put ready earlier. As quickly as he could, he opened the front of the lantern and hurled it into the shed, hoping it'd land on the nice dry straw. He slammed the door and wedged the stick under the latch.

Nothing happened for a disturbingly long time. Then he heard a yelp—a spark or a cinder, he guessed, falling on the wolf's back—followed by a crash as it threw itself against the door. He'd anticipated that, and wished he'd been able to steal a strong plank and some nails, to secure the door properly. But the stick jammed against the latch worked just fine. He could see an orange glow under the door. The wolf howled.

He hadn't anticipated that. It was guaranteed to wake the house and bring Luso running out with his gun. Luso would open the door and either he'd be jumped by a maddened, terrified wolf, or the burning lintel would come down and crush him, and there'd be nothing Gignomai could do. He considered wedging the house door with another stick, but there wasn't time and he didn't know where to find the necessary materials. Then the thatch shifted—it seemed to slump, the way lead does just before it melts—and tongues of flame burst out of it, like crocuses in spring.

Stheno came running out. Gignomai heard him yelling, "Shit, the woodshed's on fire!" and then he was ordering people Gignomai couldn't see to fetch buckets. One of the farm men rushed past where he was crouching, unaware he was there, nearly treading on him. Quickly Gignomai revised the recent past. As soon as it was safe to do so, he got up quietly and headed for the house door. Luso intercepted him and grabbed his shoulder.

"Get back to bed. Now!" he snapped.

Gignomai did exactly as he was told, and stayed there until the noise in the yard had died down. Then he made his way down to the hall. Stheno and Luso were there, and Father, looking extremely irritable. Stheno was telling Father that the woodshed had caught fire; they'd tried to put it out but the fire had taken too good a hold by the time they got there and there had been nothing they could do. Luckily, the fire hadn't spread, but it was still a disaster: half the winter's supply of seasoned timber had gone up in flames, along with twelve dozen good fence posts. Father gave him a look that told him that domestic trivia of this nature wasn't a good enough reason for disturbing the sleep of the head of the family, and went back to bed.

Next day, Stheno went through the ashes and found the twisted frame of a lantern. Some fool, he announced, had left a light burning in the woodshed, and a rat or something had knocked it over, and now they'd all be cold that winter. It would go hard, he implied, with the culprit if he ever found out who it was. But his enquiries among the farm hands produced a complete set of perfect alibis, and Stheno had too many other things to do to carry out a proper investigation.

The attacks on the chickens stopped, of course, but nobody noticed, having other things on their minds.

Gignomai wasn't proud of what he'd done. Clearly, he hadn't thought it through. On the other hand, he'd done what he had to, and the wolf, quite likely the last wolf on the Tabletop, was dead and wouldn't kill any more chickens. That was important. The violation of the family property wouldn't happen again, so there'd be no need for him to repeat his own mistake. Accordingly, he didn't feel particularly guilty about it, either. It was a job that had needed doing, and he'd done it.

A little while later, when he thought it was all over, his sister came to him and said, "You know the night of the fire."

"What about it?" Gignomai replied.

"I was in the kitchen," she said. "I went down to get a drink of water, and when you came in, I hid and watched you climb out of the window."

"Oh," Gignomai said. "Have you told anyone?"

She shook her head. "Why did you burn down the woodshed?" she asked.

He explained. She looked at him. "That was really stupid," she said.

He shrugged. "I killed a wolf," he said. "How many kids my age can say that?"

She didn't bother to reply. "I ought to tell Father," she said.

"Go on, then."

"But I won't," she said, after an agonising moment. "He'd just get mad, and then there'd be shouting and bad temper and everybody in a mood. I hate all that, specially when it goes on and on for days."

"Fine," Gignomai said. "Up to you, of course."

"You might say thank you."

"Thank you."

"It was still a really stupid thing to do," she said, and left the room.

After she'd gone he thought about it for a long time and, yes, she was right. But he'd done it, and it couldn't be helped, and it had to be done. The only criticism he could find to make of himself was idleness and lack of foresight. What he should have done was stack brushwood in the old cider-house, which was practically falling down anyhow (Stheno was going to fix it up sometime, when he had a moment) and would've been no great loss to anybody.

Next time, he decided, I'll make sure I think things through.

The Year When

His first real command were pigs. There were fourteen of them, quarter-grown light brown weaners, and it was his job to guard them while they foraged in the beech wood and keep them from straying. He dreaded it more than anything else. The men from the farm—proper stockmen who knew what they were doing—drove them up there from the house in the morning and led them back at night, but for the whole of the day they were his responsibility, and he was painfully aware that he had no control over them whatsoever.

Fortuitously, they were naturally gregarious animals and stuck together, generally too preoccupied with snuffling in the leaf mould to wander off and cause him problems. But he had an excellent imagination. What if something startled them? He knew how easily they spooked and once that happened and they started dashing about (they were deceptively fast and horribly agile) he knew he wouldn't stand a chance. The whole litter would scatter and be lost among the trees, and that'd mean turning out the whole household to ring and comb the wood in a complex military operation that would waste a whole day, and it would be all his fault. The list of possible pig-startlers was endless: a careless roebuck wandering into the clearing and shying; a buzzard swooping down through the canopy; the crack of a dead tree falling without warning; Luso down in the long meadow, shooting his stupid gun. Or what if a wild boar decided to burst out of a briar tangle and challenge him for leadership of the herd?

The first half-dozen times he performed his wretched duty ("It's time your brother started pulling his weight on the farm," his father had pronounced. Why couldn't they have told him to muck out the goose-house instead?) he'd spent the whole day at a breathless, stitch-cramped trot, trying to head off any pig that drifted more than a yard from the edge of the clearing, an exercise in counterproductive futility. It didn't help that the beech wood was on a steep slope. Since he clearly couldn't carry on like that for any length of time, he resolved to think the thing through and find an answer. There had to be one.

In the long barn, he knew where to find a large oak bucket, which everybody else had apparently forgotten about (the farm was crammed with such things, perfectly good and useful but long since mislaid and replaced). He also knew where they kept the yellow raddle. He got up very early one morning, mixed a pint of raddle in a derelict saucepan and used it to paint the bucket, which he carried up to the clearing in the wood. Next morning, he stole half a sack (as much as he could carry — actually, slightly more) of rolled barley and took that up as well, hiding it safe and dry in the crack of a hollow tree.

The idea was simple and based on sound principles of animal husbandry he'd learned from watching the stockmen. Three times a day, he fed the pigs from the yellow bucket. He knew the pigs loved rolled barley above all things — the sight of fourteen of them scrambling over each other and scrabbling across each other's heads to get into the bucket was really quite disturbing — and he made sure that each feed was preceded by a distinct and visible ritual, because pigs understand that sort of thing. When he walked to the foot of the hollow tree, they all stopped rooting and snuffling and watched him, still and tense as pointing dogs. When the sack appeared, they started barking and squealing. As soon as he moved, holding the sack, there'd be a furious torrent of pigs round his ankles, and he'd have to kick them out of the way to get to the bucket to fill it.

A great success, whose only drawback was that it was strictly illegal—he'd requisitioned equipment and drawn restricted supplies without authority, a serious crime, the consequences of which didn't bear thinking about, but the risk of detection, given the way the farm was run, was acceptably low. He took great pains to hide the yellow bucket when not in use, and was almost excessively careful in planning his raids on the rolled-barley bin. It was, however, a significant part of his nature that he didn't believe in perfection. The system worked just fine, but that didn't mean it couldn't be improved.

The most beneficial improvement would be doing without the barley, but he knew that wouldn't work, or not for long. He could rely on the squealing of the main body of pigs to draw in any outlying stragglers in an instant, but wouldn't it be better if he could train them, by association, to come to a feeding call of his own? The stockmen did it with the cows. All they had to do was call out, and the herd came quick-shambling to them right across the forty-acre meadow. He tried various calls, but the pigs just looked at him as if he was mad. In desperation, he tried singing. It worked.

His mother had once told him he had a fine singing voice (but then, she'd told Luso that he was handsome and Pin that she was pretty). He wasn't quite sure what "fine" was supposed to mean in this context. If it meant loud, Mother's words were a statement of undeniable fact, not a compliment. He thought he sang rather well, but he was realistic about his own judgement. In any event, the pigs seemed to like it.

To begin with, he restricted himself to a few short simple halloos and volleys, the sort of thing Luso used to communicate with the hounds ever since he'd lost the hunting-horn in the river. They worked perfectly well. By the fifth note out of eight, all the pigs came running, even if the sack was still in the tree (though he knew he had to keep faith and fulfil the contract by feeding them or the whole procedure would fail). Nevertheless, he felt the need for improvement or, at least, further elaboration. He extended the halloos into verses from the usual ballads, and the pigs didn't seem to mind. But he didn't like ballads much, they were plain and crude, and the words seemed a bit ridiculous taken out of their narrative context. So he began to invent words and music of his own, using forms from his mother's music book. He made up serenades to call them, estampidas for while they were feeding (the only form boisterous enough to be heard over the sound of happy pigs) and aubades for the minute or so of forlorn sniffing and searching before the pigs managed to accept that all the barley was really gone. Gradually, as he elaborated and improved his compositions, the singing became an end in itself rather than a function of practical swineherding, and the terrifying chore blossomed into a pleasure.

For the afternoon feed of the day in question he'd worked up what he considered was his finest effort yet. He'd started with the basic structure of the aubade, by its very nature a self-limiting form — but he'd extended it with a six-bar lyrical coda that recapitulated the opening theme transposed into the major key with a far livelier time signature. He'd run though the coda many times during the day, sitting with his back to the fattest, oldest beech in the glade. A wolf tree, the men from the farm called it. It had been there before the rest of the wood grew up, and instead of pointing its branches directly at the sky, it spread them wide, like his mother making a despairing gesture, blocking the light from the surrounding area so that nothing could grow there, and thus forming the clearing which generations of pigs had extended by devastation into a glade. When the angle of the beams of light piercing the canopy told him it was time for the feed, he got up slowly, brushed himself free of leaf mould and twigs, and hauled the yellow bucket out from its secure storage in a holly clump. Three pigs looked up, their ears glowing translucent against the slanting light. He grinned at them, and lugged the bucket into the middle of the clearing. Then he walked slowly to the hollow tree and felt inside the crack for the barley sack. Two more pigs lifted their heads, still diligently chewing. He cleared his throat with a brisk cough and began to sing.

La doca votz ai auzida…

(Lyrics weren't his strong point. They had to be in the formal language of Home, or he might just as well sing ballads and, in theory, he was fluent in it as befitted a boy of noble birth albeit in exile. In practice, he could pick his way through a few of the simpler poems and homilies in the books, and say things like "My name is Gignomai, where is this place, what time in dinner?" As far as writing formal verse went, however, he hadn't got a hope, so he tended to borrow lines from real poems and bend them till they sort of fitted.)

De rosinholets savatges —

He stopped suddenly, the next phrase congealed in his throat. A string of horsemen had appeared through the curtain of leaves and were riding up the track towards him. In the lead was his brother Luso, followed by half a dozen of the farm men and one riderless horse.

His first impression was that they'd been out hawking, because he could see a bundle of brown-feathered birds, tied at the neck, slung across the pommel of Luso's saddle. But there was no hawk on Luso's wrist. Had Luso lost the hawk? If so, there'd be open war at dinner. The hawk had come on a ship from Home; it had cost a fortune. There had been the most appalling row when Luso turned up with it one day, but Father had forgiven Luso because a hawk was, after all, a highly suitable possession for a gentleman. If Luso had contrived to mislay the wretched thing…

Luso looked at him without smiling. "What was that awful noise?" he said.

There was no way he could explain. "Sorry," he said.

They hadn't been hawking. They were wearing their padded shirts, with horn scales sewn into the lining. Two of the men had wide, shiny dark red stains soaking through their shirts, Luso had a deep cut just under his left eye, and they all looked exhausted. The birds on Luso's saddle were chickens.

"Keep the noise down, will you?" Luso said. He was too tired to be sarcastic. For Luso to pass up an opportunity like this, something had to be wrong. The men rode by without saying anything. Their horses had fallen into a loose, weary trudge, too languid to spook the pigs. He didn't bother trying to hide the barley sack behind his legs; Luso didn't seem interested. Under the chicken feathers, he could see the holsters for the snapping-hen pistols. The ball pommel of one pistol was just visible. The other holster was empty.

When they'd gone, he performed the feeding ritual quickly and in silence. It worked just as well without music. When the swineherds showed up to drive the pigs back to the farm, they were quiet and looked rather scared. He didn't ask what the matter was.

Father was angry about the man getting killed, but he was absolutely furious about the loss of the pistol, so furious that he didn't mention it at all, which was a very bad sign. Gignomai heard the shouting before they were called in to dinner—that was all about the man's death, how it'd leave them short-handed at the worst possible time, how Luso had a sacred duty by virtue of his station in life not to expose his inferiors to unnecessary and frivolous dangers—not a word about the pistol, but it was plain as day from what was said and what wasn't that the real issue wasn't something that could be absolved through sheer volume of abuse. Dinner was, by contrast, an eerily silent affair, with everybody staring at their hands or their plates. When the main course was served, however, Father looked up and said, in a terrible voice, "What the hell is this supposed to be?"

A long silence; then Luso said, "It's chicken."

"Get it out of my sight," Father said, and the plates were whisked away. No great loss, Gignomai couldn't help thinking; it had been sparse and stringy and tough as strips of leather binding, and he was pretty sure he'd last seen it draped over the pistol-holsters, in which case the chickens had been laying hens, not table birds, and not fit for eating. There was rather more to it than that, of course. They'd eaten layers before, when they'd had to, and had pretended they were perfectly fine.

Next morning, early, his brother Stheno told him he wouldn't have to look after the pigs for the next week or so. He gave no reason, but Gignomai could tell it had something to do with yesterday and the chickens. He supposed he should have been pleased, particularly since Stheno didn't give him anything else to do. Instead, he felt aimless and somehow disappointed, as though he'd closed his eyes for a kiss that never came.

He wanted to sneak up to the hayloft with a book, but as usual Father had entrenched himself in the library (the place he was usually to be found). Going to the loft without a book would just be a waste of lifespan. He looked for Mother's music book, but she was propped up in bed reading it, feeding scraps of cold chicken to her cats. How slender, he thought, is the division between happiness and misery. All he needed for a day of perfect pleasure was a book (any book, so long as he hadn't read it so often he could say the words with his eyes shut), but there wasn't a book to be had, and so the day promised to be wretched.

Unless, of course, he did something desperate and illegal. Those aspects of his proposed plan of action held no charm for him in themselves. He preferred to avoid danger and keep to the rules whenever it was possible to do so. But the prospect of drifting aimlessly round the farm all day suddenly seemed unbearably dreary, and he felt as though he didn't really have a choice. He decided to break out of the Tabletop, walk down to the town and see his friend.

Breaking out was no small thing. The Tabletop, the plateau on which they lived, rose steeply out of the plain, a rectangle a mile long and a quarter of a mile wide, three sides of which were bare perpendicular rock. At the foot of the southern face, where the beech wood sloped sharply down to the river, they'd built what everybody called the Fence, though it wasn't a fence at all, but a high earth rampart, topped with a stone wall, with a deep ditch at its foot on the river side. There was one gate, the Doorstep, in the middle of the Fence, a massive thing guarded by two towers which Gignomai had never seen opened. Hired men, seasonal workers and the very occasional visitor were winched up the north face in a terrifying beam and plank cage, in which Gignomai had sworn a private oath he'd never set foot. There was, however, a third way out, the one Luso used. Gignomai wasn't supposed to know about it, but he couldn't help having a lively mind. Once he'd followed the bridlepath through the wood down to the Fence, and found that it stopped abruptly at the point where it met one of the many run-off streams that turned the lower part of the wood into a quagmire for two-thirds of the year. The stream-bed looked impossibly steep for a human being to walk down, let alone men leading horses, but he guessed it must be possible, since that was apparently what Luso and his raiding parties did.

Scrambling down it the first time had terrified the life out of him. Once he'd been up and down it a dozen or so times, he realised it could be done, safely if not comfortably, if you knew exactly where to go and where to put your feet. It came out beside the river between two giant rocks, lying so close that they looked like one enormous monumental facade, commissioned by some great emperor. The crack (you went in at an angle, where the two rocks sort of over-lapped) was so slight you'd miss it if you didn't know it was there. On closer examination, it turned out to be wide enough for a horse to squeeze through, but from only a few yards away it looked like just another facet of the sandstone wall. It was, when Gignomai came to think about it, pretty well perfect. Luso, returning from one of his frolics, could ride up the river, leaving no trail, and melt away into an invisible chink in the wall. If anybody were to stumble upon it and look upwards, they'd immediately assume that the stream-bed was unscalable, and continue their vain search for the real entrance.

As he walked through the wood, contemplating the reason for his surprise holiday, he had to assume that it was to do with Luso's raid, which he knew had gone badly. The beech wood was, he supposed, the Tabletop's most vulnerable aspect, though (needless to say) it had never been compromised in the past. Therefore, as a precaution, it had been emptied of man and pig until the fuss had died down. That made sense, but it hadn't been deemed necessary before. It occurred to him that this time, Luso might have made rather more trouble than usual. In any event, he expected to find at least one sentry on duty at the head of the stream—standard procedure for two days after a raid—and he wasn't proved wrong. There were, in fact, four.

That was awkward. He spotted them easily enough from his usual vantage point at the top of the worked-out limepit he called the Woodland Cathedral. They were some of Luso's best men (best in this context bore a rather specialised meaning: they didn't do farm work, and a lot was said about them behind their backs) and their presence tended to support the hypothesis that something bad had happened the previous day. It occurred to him that he could have used his day off rather more usefully eavesdropping on Father in the library; except that was a highly dangerous operation and, if anything, even more illegal than breaking out. Besides, it would've involved a great deal of sitting, or crouching, perfectly still, and he really wasn't in the mood.

Luso had a book called *The Art of War*. He kept it beside his bed and had let it be known that dreadful things would happen to anybody who so much as noticed it existed. Gignomai had therefore taken it as his fraternal duty to read it from cover to cover, several times, an exercise far more excruciating than any punishment Luso's rather limited imagination could ever have devised. It was a boring book, badly written and self-evidently useless (by his own admission, the author's only qualification for writing about military strategy had been twenty years as headmaster of a small provincial school), but Luso clearly set great store by it, since he'd posted his sentries almost exactly as shown in diagram C on page 344. As a result, there was a blind spot where the double trunk of a fat old split oak blocked the western sentry's view of the riverbed; not a major flaw, since they were presumably guarding against enemies coming up

the stream, who'd be visible at other points, not delinquents going
down it. As for those other points, he guessed he'd be able to get past
them by virtue of being small and skinny. He could duck down and
be covered by the overhang of the moss and ivy clusters that hung
from the stream's lower bank.

He considered the tactical position. With the blind spot in his
favour, the risk was acceptable, but only just—according to the
handy reckoner in Luso's book, something in the order of 25 per
cent, with 33 being the cut-off point. In such circumstances, the
book recommended raising a diversion. On that issue he begged to
differ. A diversion—throwing a stone, breaking a branch to simu-
late the stealthy approach of an enemy, starting a small fire—would
require activity and movement, with the attendant risk of detection.
True, the penalties for being caught crashing about in the bushes
were considerably less than those for being caught trying to break
out, but it'd still mean he'd be marched back to the house, where
he'd be given into the custody of his brother Stheno, who'd assign
him uncongenial farm work as a remedy for excessive leisure. A
one-in-four chance. He studied each of the sentries carefully in turn,
weighing up what he knew about them. Luso's book suggested that
guards could be neutralised with gifts of alcohol, either drugged or
in bulk. But Luso's best men would know exactly what was going on
if one of the sons of the farm strolled up to them with a huge jug of
beer and, besides, they could drink anybody else in the house under
the table, so it'd have to be a barrel at least.

He sighed. Stupid people shouldn't be allowed to write books, in
case even stupider people believed them.

Dismissing the book's final fall-back suggestion (picking the sentries off at extreme range with a crossbow), he resolved to take the
one-in-four chance. There was, however, no sense in rushing. He
settled down to wait for the right moment.

It came when the eastern sentry, who stood the best chance of
spotting Gignomai as he emerged briefly from the cover of the split
oak, yawned and began unwrapping a bundle he'd taken from his

pocket, which proved to be a fat slice of cheese. Perfect. First he'd
have to unwrap it. Then he'd carefully pare away the plaster and the
rind, using a sharp knife. Most likely, given the size of the slice and
the time of day, he'd cut it in two and save one piece for later. A person could go a long way while a man was busy doing all that.

The ground underfoot was dry. There was no wind, which meant
sound would carry, but the mild rattle of the stream would deaden a
certain amount of noise. He stood up, feeling a mild tingle, like that
of a two-hour-old nettle sting, and forced himself not to hurry. He
looked down at his feet (swinging his head from side to side watching the guards was unnecessary movement, and movement is what
gets you seen) and covered the first leg to the base of the split tree, in
faultless style.

Once he was safe behind the tree, his nerve failed. He couldn't
have moved even if he'd wanted to; he was sweating and he had to
make a determined effort to breathe. A detached part of his mind
commented that this was just something that happened occasionally; it didn't seem to need any particular reason, and it didn't signal
any unusual increase in the danger level. Sometimes people just
froze in the middle. This commentary didn't help much. He knew it
was stupid, but he couldn't do anything about it, which meant he
was stuck. All he could do was keep still and quiet and hope he'd pull
himself together sooner or later.

It turned out to be later—half an hour, maybe, though he had no
means of knowing for sure since he couldn't see the sun or a helpful
shadow without moving his head, which he didn't dare try. He
couldn't see the sentries, but logic told him if they'd noticed anything they'd have come looking by now. Gradually the panic thawed,
giving way to a curious sensation of grossly heightened perception.
He could hear sounds he'd never have noticed otherwise, and the
light seemed bright enough to tan skin. He really wished he was back
in the hayloft not reading a book.

From experience he knew the best way to break the spell was to
count up to some randomly chosen number. He opted for 250 but, in

the event, he moved on 187 without quite knowing why. He crossed the open patch with no bother at all, and could feel the blood pounding in the veins in his head. He swooped like a hawk into the streambed, ducked low and walked with uncomfortably long strides until he was confident he was out of sight. Then he had to concentrate.

Halfway down the stream he stopped. Normally this wasn't recommended. At that point, the gradient was so steep and the footholds so marginal you really had to get by the middle section on blind faith and happy thoughts; it wasn't a place for sitting down and taking stock. But that was what he did, almost as though his mind was exhausted and couldn't go a step further without a rest.

Not that he was thinking about anything in particular. He was processing the memory of the panic, the way you do, and half consciously running through the list of possible hazards he might encounter before he reached the bottom of the slope. Otherwise, his mind was clean and empty. He sat awkwardly on a low, sharp stone and watched the thin stream bouncing past his feet for a while. Then he stood up again, and finished the descent.

He arrived at the bottom, where the crack between the rocks opened out onto the narrow water meadow on their side of the river. Nothing to see in either direction. He lifted his shoulders, straightened his back and walked out into full daylight. As he did so, he heard in the distance the unique sound of a gunshot, a long way back in the wood.

Luso, he thought. Luso, getting dinner.

As he walked quickly down to the river, he mulled over the loss of the snapping-hen pistol. It wouldn't be the end of the world. They had six (well, five now) and even if the lost pistol had fallen into the hands of a hostile agency, it wouldn't irrevocably shift the balance of power. In terms of honour, prestige and dread it was a bad thing, needless to say. Also, it couldn't help but have a serious effect on the political situation in the family and the farm as a whole. That might not be so bad; maybe Father would be a bit less inclined to indulge Luso, which would mean Stheno would gain ground, if only for a while. On balance, most of the time, Gignomai was broadly on Stheno's side (not that his allegiance mattered a damn to anybody); not that he was against Luso, or Father, or anybody. Actually, if anybody was going to come out of this well, it'd probably be Pin, simply because she wouldn't be involved, and could therefore earn points as a peacemaker, should she choose to do so. As for the pistol itself, being realistic, it wouldn't be much good to an enemy. None of their enemies had any significant resources of powder—enough for two shots, maybe—and no balls of the right bore, and no skill to make a ball mould or more powder. It'd probably hang on a wall as a trophy for a year or two, and then Father would discreetly buy it back.

He walked—strolled, in fact, with his hands in his pockets; a gesture nobody could see, but it was important—to the riverbank, and stopped at the very edge. He was out, free and clear. In theory, he could go anywhere and do anything.

In some book, a romance of some kind which he'd read when he was too young to know that such books were to be despised, there had been a moment when the hero had stood by a river, just as he was doing now, and probably that was why he was doing it. In the book, the hero had thought about rivers, about how the water that was passing by his feet would be miles away by that evening, and tomorrow might well be tumbling into the vast and unknowable sea, mingling with that plural and singular entity that touched other shores he would never visit, places whose existence he'd never be aware of. If only a man could become water, the hero had mused, what understanding, what unimaginable clarity there must be in the common intelligence of an ocean. How bizarrely unnatural it was to be a single, isolated drop that could never join with the main.

Well, people in books thought like that, and even said that sort of stuff out loud. Father had a word for it: *melodrama*. He used it for everything he reckoned was false and just for show (that wasn't quite what it meant—Gignomai had looked it up in the dictionary) and the bit in the book was just melodrama, because people weren't drops of water, and it'd be a pretty odd world if they were. Even so.

Let the river (he cast it in mathematical form, a habit of his; he was quite good at mathematics) equal the human race minus the ancient and illustrious family of met'Oc. There was no mathematical symbol for crossing, as far he knew, so he couldn't calculate what would happen if he (x) crossed the river. Would your answer be different if you built a raft and sailed down the river? Calculate the effects necessary for proving rain falling on a fountain. He took off his boots, rolled up his trousers, and waded into the water.

On the far side, he stopped and looked back. There was nothing to see. The trees masked the Fence at this distance, and the crack between the two rocks of the Doorstep was too faint to make out. People had learned long ago not to graze cattle on the rich, fat grass of the water meadow—rather a pity; it was some of the best grazing in the colony—and the deer wouldn't come out here in daylight, for more or less the same reason. Conclusion: there is a world beyond the Fence, but nobody much lives there, which tends to decrease its attraction. It was only at this point in his mental journey that he remembered that he'd had a purpose in mind when he started out: to walk into town and see Furio.

He frowned as he began the walk. He'd spent rather longer than he'd anticipated getting past the Fence and the guards, which meant he'd really only have enough time to get to town, say hello, turn round and come back again if he wanted to stand any sort of chance of returning before his absence was noticed. Quickly, to salvage the operation, he modified the objective. He'd walk into town, buy a coil of wire (he checked his pocket; he'd brought the coin) and maybe spend an hour with Furio on the way back if there was time.

Two hours from the river to town. It was a conventional figure which people tended to accept and believe, even though it was plainly wrong. Maybe it was true if you ran part of the way, or had extremely long legs. He guessed that once upon a time the road had gone through the bog, or where the bog was now, instead of round it. Come to think of it, the bog was a man-made thing, the result of subtle changes in the course of the Whitewater caused by years of uncoordinated irrigation. The road had moved, slowly, as the bog had gradually encroached on it, but in everyone's minds the time from the river to town was still two hours. If you couldn't make it in that time, it had to be your fault for dawdling.

He always felt nervous at the first sight of the Watchtower. It meant he was rapidly approaching enemy territory—melodrama. In reality, he was approaching a place where he wasn't really supposed to be, but he'd been there dozens of times, everybody knew who he was and nothing bad had happened *yet*, although he'd never been stupid enough to wander into town the day after one of Luso's pranks before. He assumed he was tolerated because he was just a kid (that'd change soon, of course), but also, well, because he wouldn't be there unless he wanted to be, and that was the fundamental difference between him and the rest of the house of met'Oc. He had an idea that the people in town recognised this, somehow, and turned a blind eye. Also, they must know by now that he was friends with Furio, and Furio's dad was Somebody in town. (He was also aware of the fundamental difference between luck and a wheelbarrow; only one of them was designed to be pushed.)

Just as the road into town was really only a suggestion in the grass, town itself was two dozen buildings, which gave the impression that they'd been left lying about after someone had finished playing with them. One of the buildings was the Watchtower. Next to it was the livery, then Furio's father's store: the Merchant Venturers' Association. Beyond that were ten long low sheds, warehouses in which people happened to live. Beyond them, in a circle, were the pens, which covered a hundred and six acres. There wouldn't be a ship for three months, so naturally the pens were empty; nobody brought cattle into town, where they had to be fed hay at ruinous expense, until a ship had been definitely sighted. When the big salt-beef freighters came in, the pens would be full, so you could walk quite easily from one side to another across the backs of cattle too closely packed together to move. Furio claimed a boy he knew had done this. Slaughtering day, when all the animals in the pens were killed and butchered, was reckoned to be a sight to see, though Gignomai had never done so. But he'd heard the noise, right up behind the Fence.

As he passed the gate of Number One pen, he stopped. It was a tall gate, seven feet high and fully boarded in, and to it a man's body had been nailed. His face and chest were pressed against the board, his arms and legs were spread out as wide as they would go, and the nails had been driven through his wrists and ankles, with one long nail through his neck. It was how you nailed a rat or stoat on a barn door, so presumably someone was making a statement about something. The man was unmistakably dead, but there was no smell, and the flesh was still firm under the smooth skin, so he hadn't been there long. There was no blood to speak of, so he'd been dead when they put him up there. Over his head, someone had daubed CATLE THIEF in blue raddle. That made Gignomai frown. For some reason, poor spelling had always offended him. He didn't recognise the face, but he hadn't necessarily expected to. Many of Luso's men kept themselves to themselves, and they came and went.

That explained the mystery of the empty saddle, at any rate. He hesitated. If they'd taken to nailing up Luso's casualties as vermin, it suggested an unprecedented level of anger, and maybe town wasn't safe any more. On the other hand, he'd come a long way, and turning round and walking tamely home again would be an admission of defeat (though who he was fighting he couldn't say). Besides, there was a world of difference between one of Luso's men and a son of the met'Oc. The town people were realists. They didn't tend to pick fights.

He walked up to the store. The door was open (he'd never known it closed) and he wandered in.

The store was one of his favourite places. To some extent, it was the sheer number and variety of objects it contained that never failed to please him. At the farm, he knew all the things. There weren't very many and most of them had been there as long as he could remember, and a significant proportion were broken, worn out, imperfectly mended or otherwise unsatisfactory. He was pretty sure he'd be able to recognise every nail the family possessed. He knew their histories—what they'd been used for, when and why they'd been reclaimed, straightened, re-used, reclaimed again. In the store, by contrast, there was a barrel full of virgin nails with the oil still on them, also buckets with all their slats intact and their original handles, cloth in great rolls that nobody had ever worn, shovels and hammers made in the old country, by strangers, things he'd never met, things he might possibly (one day, if everything changed out of all recognition) buy, and have, and keep for his very own exclusive use. Walking into the store was like meeting a thousand strangers—better, of course, because things had no reason to dislike him because of who his father was, or what his brother had done.

Furio's dad was at the back of the store, going through a barrel of store carrots, discarding the sprouters. He looked up and saw Gignomai, and there was a moment during which he could be seen doing the arithmetic, reasons for and against being friendly. Then he smiled.

"You want Furio?"

Gignomai smiled back politely. "If he's not busy," he replied. "But I'd like to buy some wire, please."

"Wire," Furio's dad replied, as though he'd just been asked for the philosophers' stone. "What sort of wire?"

"For making snares."

"Ah." A nod of the head that implied many things: understanding, willingness to trade, and a sort of community of interests and ideas, as if to say that anybody who wanted *that* sort of wire was fine by him. "How much?"

Gignomai took the coin out of his pocket without looking at it. "This much?"

Furio's dad dipped his head. "Two yards. Just a moment."

(Gignomai had found the coin in the bed of the river the time before last. One of the farm men had identified it as a silver two-quarters. It was the first coin Gignomai had ever seen, and he had no idea what it was worth. Now he knew. It was worth two yards of snare wire—a fortune.)

Furio's dad pulled a huge spool, as big as his head, off a shelf. It was hard to believe there was that much wire in the whole world. He pulled wire off the spool and laid it alongside a series of marks on the side of the bench, then he took a pair of shears, snipped it off and started winding it round his hand.

"Do much snaring?" he asked.

"A bit," Gignomai replied.

Furio's dad looked away, almost furtively. "What do you do with the skins?"

Gignomai shrugged. "We use them round the farm," he replied. "You know. Gloves, collars, fine rawhide twine."

Another nod of the head. Well, of course you do. "Worth money," Furio's dad said, in a faraway sort of voice, as if Gignomai wasn't actually there. "If you had any spare, I mean. Any left over."

"How much money?"

"Quarter a dozen." The words came out so fast they almost blended into each other. "For squirrel," he added. "Quarter for ten for rabbits. Don't suppose you get any ermine up there, do you?"

Gignomai didn't know what an ermine was. But a quarter a dozen, for stupid squirrels. The coin, briefly but no longer his, had been a two-quarter. He did the arithmetic. Two dozen squirrel skins could, by some strange alchemy, turn into two yards of wire. Amazing idea. "No," he said, because he'd have died rather than show his ignorance. "But we've got loads of squirrels and rabbits. And hares," he added.

"Hares." A sort of awed wonder, as if they were talking about dragons. "Quarter for six," said Furio's dad, and Gignomai knew that that was a lousy price, and that Furio's dad was ashamed of himself for seeking to swindle a minor. "Sure," he said. "I can get you all the hare skins you want. We've got them like rats."

(Which was a lie, and he wondered why he'd said it. Later, he realised it was because he wanted Furio's dad to feel better about the lousy price.)

"Deal," Furio's dad said, and smiled a broad, false smile, because of the guilt. "How about hawk feathers? I could give you a quarter an ounce."

"Luso won't let me kill hawks," Gignomai said, and realised he shouldn't have spoken that name, not here. Furio's dad didn't say anything, but the smile evaporated and it was clear that business negotiations were at an end. Gignomai handed over the coin and received his wire, which he stowed in his pocket, resisting the temptation to look at it and feel it, now that it was his.

"I'll see if Furio's out back. Stay there, won't be a minute."

Furio was seven months younger than Gignomai and a head shorter. His aunt reckoned he'd been born thirty years old and he really needed to mix more with boys his own age. His mother agreed, but drew the line at the common boys in the town. They compromised by not letting him read books, which were known to be bad for a growing boy's eyesight.

"What did you bring?" was always Furio's first question.

Gignomai hadn't given it much thought. It had been an impulse to break out, so he'd snatched the first book to come to hand off his shelf. "Eustatius on the identification of waterfowl," he replied, trying to make it sound like he'd thought long and hard about it. "There's some really good pictures."

Furio's face lit up like a lantern. "Fantastic," he said. "Give it here, then."

Gignomai handed over the book, which Furio just about managed not to snatch. Instead, he looked longingly at the spine, then shoved it deep in his coat pocket and folded the flap over it.

They were sitting in the store room out the back, where the bulk goods were kept. There was just enough room to squeeze through between the stacks of barrels, crates and boxes. "I didn't know you were keen on birds," Gignomai said.

Furio shrugged. Birds—whatever; it was a book. "You're taking a bit of a chance, aren't you?"

"Am I?"

"Coming here," Furio said, "after what happened."

Gignomai nodded. "I saw," he said. "What did happen?"

Furio gave him his you-mean-you-don't-know look. He'd seen it many times. "Your lot raided the Venuti place," he said.

"Where?"

Furio waved his hand vaguely — somewhere north, south or east. "They're new arrivals," he said. "From Home. Guess they don't know about your lot."

That would explain it, Gignomai thought. "So?"

"They fought back," Furio said, reaching into a bucket and producing two elderly apples, one of which Gignomai accepted out of politeness. "Your lot killed their indentured man; they killed one of yours." He paused, lowered his voice. "People are saying they captured a gun. Is that...?"

Gignomai nodded. It was an unforgivable breach of honour to disclose such a thing to an outsider. He wasn't bothered. "Dad's livid," he said.

Furio's eyes widened and practically glowed. "My dad reckons he's going to try and buy it off the Venuti."

"Why?"

Furio shrugged. "He wants one, I guess. Or he thinks he can sell it on." Furio hesitated, and those wide, bright eyes clouded for a moment. "Were you talking to him earlier?"

Gignomai nodded. "He asked if I wanted to sell him some squirrel pelts."

A faint sigh, as though Furio was contemplating some foul habit of his father's that he'd accepted but could never quite forgive. "How much?"

"Quarter a dozen."

"He's ripping you off," Furio said, with a degree of compressed savagery that Gignomai rarely heard him use. "He'll get a thaler six for them when the boat comes."

"So what?" Gignomai grinned at him. "Mostly we just chuck them away — too much bother curing them. Everything's too much bother at our place."

"Yes, but—" Furio left off; he knew when not to start an unwinnable argument. "You should make him pay you a quarter each," he said.

Gignomai laughed. "No way," he said. "If I do that, he'll get them from somebody else, and I won't get my quarter. You do realise that a quarter's an absolute fortune to me."

Furio bit a third off his apple, pulled a face and spat it out. "He hasn't got any other sources of supply," he said. "Not regular, anyhow. On account of the only big woods in the colony belong to your lot. And nobody goes poaching up there, because of your nutcase brother."

It was an established licence between them: Furio could insult Luso and nothing need be said or done. Even so, Gignomai winced. "He wants rabbits too. And hares."

"You've got it made, then, haven't you?"

"But surely there's rabbits and hares down on the flat," Gignomai said. "They're pests, you can't get rid of them."

"Actually you can," Furio said seriously, "if you can get quarter and a half for a pelt, and you've got no other way of raising cash money." The surely you know look again. "The colony pays its taxes partly in furs," he explained. "We've got a quota. We have got to fill it or the government back Home gets stroppy." He frowned. "They make them into hats, apparently," he said. "They make the fur into felt, and then—"

Gignomai wasn't interested in hats. "Is that right?" he said. "We pay a tax to Home?"

Furio's turn to laugh. "*You* don't," he said. "We do. Which is why there's nothing furry left alive round here smaller than a deer and bigger than a mouse. Except up your mountain, of course. Which is why you mustn't let Dad screw you over the price."

"Like I said," Gignomai replied, "I'm not fussed."

"You're strange," Furio said (the words seemed to burst out of him, like grain from a rotten sack). "I can't make up my mind whether you're better than us because you're noblemen and you've got that amazing library and you talk funny, or whether we're better than you because you're so poor and you've none of you got any money and you live like peasants. It confuses the hell out of me sometimes."

"Does it matter?" Gignomai asked mildly.

Furio considered his answer carefully. He frowned and looked at his hands. "With you and me, no. Between your lot and us, of course it does. People need to know where they stand, I suppose."

Gignomai stood up, walked to the bucket and put back the unmolested apple he'd been issued with. "In that case," he said, "my guess is, probably both. We've got the breeding and the glory of the family name, you've got..." he paused, then grinned, "*stuff.* Though stuff is good too," he added wistfully, gazing at a stack of scythe-blades with the oil-black still on them. "But my father says, one of these days Home'll boot out the bad guys and we'll go back and it'll be like it was in the old days. Meanwhile..."

"Do you believe that?"

Gignomai shrugged. "No," he said. "But then, I don't know much about it."

"Nor me," Furio said. He yawned, then reached down into an opened crate and pulled out a dusty black glass bottle. "Brandy," he said. "From Home. Want some?"

Gignomai shook his head. "I had some once. Made me throw up."

"Sure?"

"Sure. Wouldn't mind the bottle, though."

Furio raised both eyebrows, then laughed until his face was bright red. "Fine," he said. "We'll pour away the fifty-year-old vintage brandy and you can have the bottle." Gignomai thought he was joking, but a moment later he'd sprung to his feet and was looking for something—a tool for opening bottles, presumably.

"No, don't," Gignomai said. "That must be worth ever such a lot of money."

"For my uncle," Furio replied. "Already paid for, in advance."

"Oh well, in that case."

On the way home, he washed the bottle out carefully in the river. The hell with Furio; a glass bottle was a treasure. The stupid cork stopper hadn't survived, they'd practically had to pick it out a shred at a time with the tip of Gignomai's knife, but it'd be no job at all to whittle a proper hardwood stopper, and then he'd have something to carry clean water in, instead of the mouldy leather bottle that made its contents taste like sick.

It rained as he crept back into the woods. Tactically, this was no bad thing, since it meant the guards would be huddling in their coats, not paying as much attention as they should, but it was a nuisance and he got soaked to the skin, something he particularly hated. Furthermore, if he turned up in the Great Hall all wet, someone might think to ask where he'd been all day, and he wasn't feeling particularly creative. The same problem would apply if he changed his clothes. It wasn't likely that anybody would notice he was wearing a different shirt, but somebody might, just this once. The obvious course of action was to dry out, but it was too early in the year for a fire in his bedroom—Father never allowed fires outside the kitchen till late autumn, even though it was often freezing cold well before then, because late autumn was when fires were first lit back Home. It had never occurred to him to change the rule for a mere inconvenience of geography. The only place on the farm where he could be sure of finding a fire was the forge. Oh well, he thought. Could be worse.

"What happened to you?" Aurelio asked, as Gignomai sat down on the second anvil and peeled off his coat.

"Fell in the dewpond," Gignomai answered.

Aurelio was too busy watching a complicated weld heating in the fire to look at him again. "Is that right?"

"I wanted to see if I could walk across on that fallen tree. Turned out I couldn't."

Aurelio nodded, and Gignomai wondered, just out of interest, how the old man knew he was lying. He thought about it, and realised he was too clean. The surface of the dewpond was filthy, but he wasn't. "You want to be more careful," Aurelio said, and Gignomai was happy to take the advice in the spirit in which it was given.

"What are you making?" he asked.

"Just fixing the bottom hinge off the middle house door."

Ah. The middle house door had been loose since spring, you had to prop it shut by jamming a branch under the one remaining hinge. Maybe that was why he liked the forge so much. Gradually, slowly, far too late but eventually, things got fixed here. It was the only place on the farm where things got better over time. "Looks tricky."

"It is," Aurelio said. "Quiet."

Gignomai knew why. Aurelio was waiting for the moment when the two pieces of iron he was intending to weld were almost melted. You couldn't always tell the moment by looking, but if you listened very carefully there was a sort of hissing noise. He heard it. Aurelio grabbed the tongs and snatched the sun-white iron out of the fire and started tapping it with a hammer. It made a soft noise, not the usual hard ring. Gignomai waited until the hinge had gone back into the fire and asked, "Did it take?"

Aurelio smiled at him. "Just about. You could learn this, I reckon."

That was a rare compliment; also impossible. A son of the met'Oc couldn't learn a trade, though there was apparently nothing in the code of conduct about not doing menial labour, such as tending pigs, provided it was unskilled. "I'd like to," he said, "but my dad…"

Aurelio laughed. "Let me think about it," he said. "Now shut your face, I need to concentrate."

The fire provided light as well as heat, and he considered sneaking indoors for a book. But he wasn't nearly dry enough yet. But then, as he reached in his pocket for the wire, which he remembered he hadn't gloated over properly yet, he found something else: a roll of paper.

"Where'd that bottle come from?" Aurelio asked.

"What? Sorry. Found it. In the woods."

Fortuitously, at that moment a fat white spark drifted up out of the fire. It signified that the metal was starting to burn. Aurelio swore loudly, hauled the work out and started whacking it with his hammer. Under cover of all that, Gignomai took the paper from his pocket and examined it.

Paper, not parchment. Very occasionally, they made parchment on the farm, when Father felt the need to write one of his letters to someone back Home. For parchment you needed lamb rawhide, skived very thin, ground and polished (or else the ink soaked into it, and Father would lose his temper). Paper, made from rags, was beyond the limits of their technology. Gignomai shoved it quickly back in his pocket, hoping Aurelio hadn't seen. For some reason the old man indulged him to a quite extraordinary degree, but there had to be limits.

It seemed to take for ever for his clothes to dry, even in the forge where it was hot enough to make your skin feel tender. Eventually he reckoned he was dry enough to pass inspection. He thanked Aurelio for his hospitality (no reply) and scuttled back to his room, where he wedged the door shut with a broom handle before taking the paper over to the window. There was just about enough light. He'd have to read quickly, or else face the frustration of waiting for dawn. He unrolled the paper. There was a lot of writing.

THINGS YOU SHOULD KNOW

He raised an eyebrow. Furio, presumably. Who else could have slipped a roll of paper into his pocket without him noticing?

Furio Opello to Gignomai met'Oc; greetings.

Every time I talk to you, I'm amazed at all the really basic stuff you don't know. Which is crazy, really, because you know all sorts of stuff I don't know. Different sorts of things. Well, you lend me books, so it's only fair. Anyway, this is some of the stuff you don't know. I hope it comes in useful.

Then a gap of a few lines. Gignomai paused to be astonished at the prodigality. When Father wrote letters, every last bit of space was filled in, and Father could write really small. The paper, he realised, was a page torn out of a ledger.

1. History of the Colony

He felt a surge of annoyance, which he quickly and ruthlessly stifled. Things you should know, indeed.

The colony was founded seventy years ago. The plan was originally to mine silver, but there turned out not to be any. However, the first settlers found beavers and other furry animals whose pelts would fetch a lot of money back home. We still pay part of our rent in furs.

When we arrived here, we didn't know the country was inhabited. The natives turned out not to be much trouble, though. They leave us alone, mostly. They don't plant crops like we do. They live off hunting and gathereing wild fruits and berries

(He frowned, reached for his pencil and corrected the spelling.)

and they move around all the time, so we don't seem to be in their way particularly. However, many people in the colony are frightened of what might happen if they decide to attack, since they outnumber us considerably. There used to be a permanent garrison here, to protect us (and keep us in order) but it was too expensive and the government at Home recalled them. Now there's just the militia, and the mayor (there isn't one) can call up any citizen for military service for a period not exceeding three months (this never happens).

2. Economy and Society

(He grinned. That was part of the title of a book he'd lent Furio last year.)

We grow all our own food here, but we have to import nearly all our tools and clothes and stuff from Home. Actually there are laws saying what we can and can't make here, to make sure we stay dependant

(The pencil again.)

on Home for everything we need, and to make sure we sell them all our meat and hides at cheap prices. We aren't allowed to trade with other countries. We supply salt beef and cured, untanned hides. My father and five other men handle all the trade between them.

    3. Your lot The met'Oc
Obviously you know all about your family

(Wrong.)

but you might find it useful to know what the people in the colony reckon they know about them, if that makes any sense.

    Your family used to be great noblemen back home, but they were on the wrong side in some war seventy years ago and had to clear out. They came here. We reckon they planned on takeing the place over. That didn't happen. There was still a garrison here then. Some people say there was some fighting. Your lot took over the Tabletop — that's what we call it, did you know that? — and made it into a sort of fortress. My dad says you have no title to it. That means you don't own it legally, with deeds and stuff.

    Your lot aren't popular, obviously, because of all the cattle stealing, but it's actually not that bad. My dad says people tollerate you because you'll protect us if ever the savages attack. Don't know if this is true. He says you're the only ones with weapons (we aren't allowed to have them) and of course you've got the guns as well as swords and pikes and bows. Dad says that all you'd have to do is fire off a gun and the savages would run away. Anyhow, that's why people put up with Lusomai. Your dad and grandad did the same thing when they were younger. Dad reckons it

doesn't actually matter that much if you just steal cattle, because people
don't really own the cattle, not like they own pigs and chickens and sheep.
They raise the cattle and get paid some money for them but they're not
theirs. It's complicated, something to do with mortgages and quit rents and
taxes. You might try telling your brother. Lay off the chickens.
My uncle says your lot will never be allowed Home.

He lifted his head and looked out of the window. It was almost too dark to read now, and he made a deliberate decision to stop there and save the rest for tomorrow. He rolled the paper up tight and stuffed it right down inside his boot, then lay on the bed with his eyes closed, trying to think of something he could give Furio that might come anywhere close to being equivalent in value. It was, of course, the most extraordinary present he'd ever been given, and incomparably the best.

He didn't deliberately set out to ration the remaining sections, but that was what he ended up doing. The next morning, he only had time to read about *Money* (twelve quarters to the silver thaler, but money of account was different) and *Geography* (the colony is just the tip of a huge island six days' sail from Home) before he was called out to help round up escaped bullocks in the cabbage field. He was sent out with the pigs before he had a chance to go back to his room, and didn't get home till dusk. The next morning, however, he made the choice to read only one section. (Most of the colony are indentured. That means they paid for their passage out by undertaking to work for the Company three days a week for fifty years.) The next morning, he was called out to feed the chickens while it was still too dark to read. When he'd finished and returned to the kitchen, Luso was waiting for him.

"Father wants to see you," Luso said, "in the library."

He tried to read Luso's face, but all he could get from it was a vague smugness; not a good sign.

"Now?" he asked.

"Now."

His conscience was relatively clear. The only major concern was breaking out, but if he'd been caught doing that, he'd have known about it straight away. He shrugged, went through to the front hall and started to climb the stairs.

Under other circumstances, the library was his favourite room. It was the biggest room in the house, with a dramatically high ceiling. All four walls were completely covered with books. The polished wooden floor was a desert. There were four old, carved chairs and a single massive table, where the rosewood box stood, and that was all, apart from a small black pot-bellied stove in the west corner. Father was sitting in the biggest and ugliest chair. It was decorated with falconry scenes in deep relief. They'd been painted once, but only a few flakes of colour remained, in the cracks and combes between the figures. He wasn't reading. On the floor beside him lay a long, narrow box, figured walnut, with silver hinges.

"Happy birthday, Gignomai," Father said.

"Is it?" Gignomai blinked.

"Yes." Father didn't smile. "You weren't to know," he went on, "we don't bother with that nonsense much in this family. But it's your fourteenth, which makes it important."

Gignomai kept his face blank and his mouth shut.

"There are certain traditions," Father went on, shifting his head a little so he was looking just over the top of Gignomai's head, as though he was talking to where Gignomai should have been at age fourteen, if he hadn't turned out disappointingly short. "At fourteen, a son of the met'Oc receives a gift of great significance."

Gignomai waited, though he could guess what was coming. Big deal, he thought.

"First, though." Father adjusted the position of his head, like a scientist with a precision instrument. Now he was looking over Gignomai's right shoulder. "It's a trifle chilly in here, don't you think? Light the stove for me, would you? I worry about the damp getting into the books."

Everything was laid out ready for lighting the stove. Inside, a neat pyramid of slender kindling. Lying next to the stove, a tinderbox, dry moss and a roll of paper.

"Light the stove," Father repeated quietly.

His own fault, Gignomai told himself, for not reading the whole thing as soon as possible. No secrets in this house. He piled the moss round the base of the kindling, cranked the tinderbox, shook the burning shavings onto the moss; he considered trying to palm the paper and slide it up his sleeve, but Father was far too smart for that, even though he pointedly wasn't watching. He held the end of the roll in the smouldering moss till it caught fire, then pushed it under the base of the pyramid. He shut the stove door and stood up.

"Your birthday present," Father said.

He went back to the middle of the room, and Father pointed at the box on the floor. Gignomai knelt down and lifted the two catches. They were beautifully made—pierced and chiselled work—and so stiff that he tore a fingernail. Inside the box, as he'd anticipated, was a sword.

"Wear it with pride," Father said. "Use it with discretion."

It was, of course, Luso's old sword. The family had eight swords, plus the hunting hanger Luso had bought from Furio's dad. Luso greatly preferred it to the sword he'd been given (this one) because it had a cutting edge. The family swords were all smallswords, thin and triangular in section. You could kill people with them, but that was all they were good for. Gignomai wondered if his father had asked Luso before taking this one back. He doubted it.

"Thanks," he said.

"You will, of course, only wear it on formal occasions," Father went on. "Lusomai will teach you how to fence. An hour a day to begin with, then two hours a day once you've mastered the basics. I expect you to practise properly."

"Yes, Father."

"Make sure you do. I'll be testing you myself from time to time." Father hesitated, which wasn't like him. Usually he spoke like someone who knew his lines by heart. "That sword belonged to my father, who had it from his uncle, Erchomai met'Oc. He was chancellor of the empire for thirty years."

Gignomai guessed that he was supposed to pick the rotten thing up at this point. He looked to see if anybody had got around to straightening the knuckle-bow—Luso had bent it, throwing it across the room in a temper when Gignomai was nine. The bend made it painfully difficult to get your hand inside the guard. It'd take Aurelio about five minutes to straighten it. Needless to say, it was still bent. Fencing lessons with Luso, Gignomai thought. What fun.

Father was waiting for something. He knew he wouldn't say what it was, because Gignomai was supposed to know without prompting or hints, and the audience couldn't end until Father was satisfied. "Thanks," Gignomai said, but it wasn't as simple as that. "Thank you," he said. "I'll take good care of it, I promise."

Either that was it or Father was getting restless. "Mind you do," he said. "Put some logs on the fire before you leave."

Gignomai waited for as long as he could—six days—then broke out again. He took the sword with him. There weren't any guards this time, the perceived threat of reprisal having faded, and he went straight to Furio's house. He thanked Furio for his gift, gravely and seriously, then asked, "How did you know it was my birthday?"

Furio looked at him. "I didn't. Was it?"

"Yes." Gignomai felt disappointed. "Well anyway, it was a great present. Thanks."

That was more thanks than Furio was equipped to handle. He looked away, keen to change the subject. "What else did you get?"

"This," Gignomai said. He'd wrapped the sword up in a big, slightly mouldy sack, to disguise what it was. "And now I've got to have fencing lessons."

Furio was staring at the sword as though he'd never seen anything like it. Well, of course, he hadn't. "That's amazing," he said. "Your family gave you that?"

He found the enthusiasm annoying. "Well, it's not really mine. I mean, Luso had it before me, but he didn't like it, so..."

"That must be worth an absolute fortune."

It hadn't occurred to Gignomai to think of it in terms of value. He couldn't imagine anybody wanting it. "Really?"

"You bet. Hey, Dad." Furio's father was passing the stock-room door. "Have you got a minute?"

Furio's father was even more impressed than his son had been. "Extremely valuable," he answered, when Furio asked him. "I'm no expert, of course, it all depends on the maker and the condition."

"It's bent," Gignomai pointed out. "Luso bashed it against a wall."

Furio's dad had drawn two inches of blade out of the scabbard. He was gazing at the patterns in the steel, the slender, semi-abstract design of wreathed foliage chiselled into the *ricasso*. He stuck his hand in his pocket and produced a lens (who on earth carried something like that about with him?), through which he stared closely at the name engraved just below the *pas d'âne*.

"Well?" Furio asked.

"At least twelve thousand," his father relied. "Could be twice that. I don't know."

"Twelve thousand thalers," Furio whispered, as if in the presence of some dark angel. "Your dad gave you a present worth—"

Gignomai said it before he could stop himself. "Is that a lot of money?"

Furio's dad laughed. Furio scowled, and said, "You know the Glisenti place? Out on the south road. Freehold. It sold last week for eight hundred."

Worth more than a whole farm — Gignomai felt slightly sick. His first thought, he realised, had been, I could get a long way away with that kind of money.

"As I said," he said, "it's not really mine, it belongs to the family."

"I'm not saying you could get twelve thousand for it *here*, of course." Furio's dad's voice had changed very slightly, and Furio was glowering at him behind his back. "I mean, nobody here's got that sort of money, and if they had, they wouldn't spend it on a status symbol. You'd have to find a merchant from Home, and of course he'd want his percentage, and then he'd probably pass it on to a specialist dealer. But definitely five thousand. Definitely."

Furio was getting angry, so Gignomai took the sword, gently but firmly, and put it back in the sack. For a split second Furio's dad looked very sad. Then he said, "If ever your family does think of selling…"

"They wouldn't," Gignomai said. "Not ever. We don't sell stuff. We keep it till it rusts, or we've forgotten where we put it."

Shortly after that, the bad thing happened, and Gignomai didn't break out again for a long time.

Seven Years After

"Do you think he'll like me?" she said for the fifteenth or sixteenth time, and Furio pretended he hadn't heard. He glanced sideways at the clock (for the fifteenth or sixteenth time). The hands didn't seem to have budged since he last looked.

"Do I look nice?" she said.

He nodded.

The clock was, of course, a joke. In a life dominated (as he saw it) by jokes, it was one of the biggest. It was the only clock in the colony, unless the met'Oc had one (and if they had, Gig had never mentioned it), and the function of a clock, surely, is to share a common truth, or at least a common belief, with other clocks. A solitary clock is the proverbial one clapping hand. No earthly good saying to someone "I'll meet you by the customs shed at ten minutes past eleven" if you've got the only clock in the country. It might have had some semblance of purpose if it had been set up in a tower in the square, but it wasn't. It lived in the back room of the store. While Father was alive, it had been on display in the store itself, but when he died, Uncle had moved it. He was afraid someone might steal it.

"Do I look all right?" she said.

"Yes, for crying out loud," he snapped. "You look absolutely fuck-ing stunning."

Also (and this was something nobody knew, except him), the clock was *wrong*. For the first sixty-three years of the colony's exis-tence, it had been carefully tended, almost worshipped, first by Grandfather, then by Father. They wound it, thirty-six turns of the key, at six in the evening every day, without fail, and once a week they advanced the big hand two minutes. Anybody looking at it could therefore rely on the information it displayed. Here, or back Home, or anywhere at all, if the clock said it was six o'clock, it was six o'clock. It was a truth that bound them together and connected them, as if by some mystical bond, with the place they'd all come from. But when Mother died and Father got depressed for a while, he'd forgotten to wind it one day, and it had stopped. He'd set it next day by the sun, making his best guess at noon, and it wasn't far out. But the link had been broken, and now the clock was a lie. Or, as Furio preferred to interpret it, a joke.

"Where's Tissa?" she asked. "She should be here by now."

"Tissa's always late," Furio replied. "Sit down, can't you? You're giving me a headache, wandering about like that."

"Charming," she replied, and she perched delicately on the edge of a table, like a carefully arranged ornament.

Which, of course, she was. By universal consensus (and it was a subject much debated), Bonoa was the prettiest girl in the colony. She was also acknowledged to be clever, a good talker; she could be relied on to laugh at jokes; she even made jokes of her own, when appropriate. She'd been the obvious choice. She was clearly pleased to have been chosen. It was just a pity she was such a fidget. He won-dered if that would matter, and decided probably it wouldn't.

The door opened, but it was only Tissa. She smiled at him. He grabbed her, gave her an absent-minded sort of a kiss and let her go. She moved away and started talking to Bonoa — you look nice, so do you stuff, a conversation to which he was thankfully irrelevant.

"He's not here, then," Tissa said.

Furio smiled at her. "Correct," he said. "How'd you guess?"

She flicked her hair away from her face. "You drag me over here to meet the legendary Gignomai and he's not here." She looked at the clock. Everybody did that, when they came in. It was remarkable how many people in the colony could tell the time. "He's late."

Furio shrugged. "Maybe he's had trouble getting out."

The girls looked at each other and, for some reason he couldn't be bothered to guess at, giggled. "Surely not," Tissa said, "not the amazing Gignomai. Didn't you tell me he can make himself invisible?"

"Or fly like a bird," Bonoa said.

"Or transform himself into a —"

"Quiet." Furio held up his hand. He'd heard a footstep outside. He scowled horribly at Bonoa, then glanced at Tissa and mouthed, *Behave.* Then the door opened.

Gignomai was soaking wet. For a split second, Furio was bitterly angry with him for not making the entrance he'd expected of him. He dismissed the anger as ridiculous, grinned at his friend and said, "You're late."

Gignomai shrugged. "Luso called an unscheduled fencing session," he replied, and while he was speaking, Furio noticed a cut above and to the right of his left eye just starting to clot. Of course, he might have cut himself scrambling through the woods. "Anyway, sorry."

"You're all wet," Furio said.

"Had to swim the river. We've taken to posting a sentry to watch the ford. I had to go a mile upstream." Gignomai shrugged again, as if wriggling out of the subject of the tribulations of his journey. He'd glanced quickly at the two girls then moved his head so he couldn't see them. "Who...?"

Furio drew in a breath, not too deep. "I'd like you to meet Comitissa, and this is Bonoa."

There was a split second when Furio was sure the whole thing was going to go horrendously wrong. During that moment, he realised that he'd been working on a mere assumption—that Gig, trapped up on that godforsaken mountain with his weirdo family would necessarily want more than anything else in the world to meet girls. On that premise he'd arranged this meeting, working long, hard and patiently. Reasonably enough he'd taken it for granted that it would be better if it was a surprise, because there's nothing more awkward than a formal blind date prearranged in cold blood. For the first time, it occurred to him that it might have been a good idea to tell Gig in advance, rather than ambush him.

Then Gignomai smiled, and Furio relaxed. Of all the components in the complex equation, the one he had least doubts about was Gig's smile—guaranteed to dazzle, stun and turn knees to water. He was delighted to see he'd been right about that. "Hello," he heard his friend say, and for the first time in days he felt the relief of not being in charge any more. Nature, he felt sure, could take its course from now on, and everything would be fine.

He froze. Gig was smiling at Tissa, not Bonoa.

Well, Furio thought, he wasn't to know. My fault, I should've said, "My girlfriend, Comitissa," or something like that. But Tissa stood up and moved just a little towards him, and mercifully Gig took the point and turned his smile on Bonoa instead. Gratefully, Furio reached out, looped his arm round Tissa's neck and hauled her towards him like cargo.

He leaned forward and whispered in her ear, "Let's get out of here."

She frowned at him, her face so close to his it was nearly out of focus. "Subtle," she said.

"Now."

He couldn't help glancing back on his way to the door. He needn't have worried; he was certain that Gig hadn't noticed he was leaving. Furio smiled. Gig was radiating charm so fiercely that he fully expected Bonoa's face to be sunburnt next time he saw her. "He's good at it," he muttered to himself, and towed Tissa out of the room.

He led her through the store onto the porch. He sat on the step and she folded neatly onto his lap. "Well?" she said.

"So far so good," he replied.

She raised her eyebrows at him. "All right," she said. "Explain."

"Explain what?"

Her oh for pity's sake look. "Why's it so vitally important for the future of the human race for your friend to get off with a girl?"

Furio tried to look blank. "Oh come on," he said. "Just think what it must be like for him."

She did her arch frown. "Did he ask you to fix him up?"

"God, no."

"Are you sure he likes girls?"

He let that one pass. "He's my friend," he said. That ought to explain everything, surely.

"You do realise Bonoa's seeing Escalo. From the mill."

"Ah." Furio grinned at her. "Not any more. She dumped him."

Her eyes widened just a little. "What? When?"

"When I told her I'd seen Escalo with Prasia."

He watched her doing the arithmetic. "That's not…"

"Maybe I exaggerated," Furio said, a little smugly. "A little bit. Actually, Prasia came to collect the flour, and I think they said hello to each other. But it got the job done."

She was staring at him. "You deliberately…?"

"It can't have been serious, or she wouldn't have dumped him just like that." He could see no need to be defensive. "Anyway, it was all for the greater good. She'll thank me for it, you'll see."

The look on her face wasn't part of her usual repertoire, which he'd taken pains to learn. "You deliberately split up Bonoa and Escalo," she said, "just so you could…" she took her time choosing the right word, "just so you could *feed* her to your friend. Don't you think that's a bit much, even for you?"

"No." He waited, but the frozen look was still there. "You want to go in there and ask? I doubt she'll be complaining. Well?"

She held the expression a moment longer, then shrugged it away. "He's nice-looking."

Furio grinned.

"All right, very nice-looking. And charming and attractive and…" She paused. "Feel free to stop me any time. You know, when you start feeling jealous."

Furio laughed, and gave her shoulder a squeeze. "You should have heard her before you arrived," he said. "*'Will he like me? Do I look nice?'* She was practically dribbling."

"I'm hungry," she said. "Let's break into the biscuits."

Between them, they ate about two quarters' worth, then carefully tapped the lid back onto the box. Hard luck on whoever ended up buying it, but Uncle would get the blame. "You only stay with me because of the biscuits," he said. "Yes," she replied, and they began to kiss.

After an interval, mostly concerned with the intransigence of buttons, Tissa said, "I wonder how they're getting on."

"You want to go and look though the keyhole?"

"Maybe they're playing chess."

"There's a chess set in there," Furio conceded. "Dad ordered six, about ten years ago. Whalebone and lacewood. Sold five, got stuck with the last one. I doubt it, though."

"Me too."

"Does Bonoa play chess?"

"She beats me."

"That's not saying anything."

She pulled away a little. "So who bought five quality chess sets?"

He grinned. "Nobody round here. He sold them to freighter captains, you know, a present from the colony. Of course they're made back Home, but whoever got given them wouldn't know that. We sell a lot of stuff to the freighter crews, but Uncle—"

He broke off. The door had swung open, and Bonoa marched past without a word. She looked furious.

"Oh," Tissa said.

Furio swore and jumped up, but Tissa grabbed his arm. "Stay there," she said, and went after Bonoa. Furio stayed where he was, not knowing which way to go. Then he saw Gignomai, standing in the doorway, peering nervously out.

"Gig," he said. "What the hell?"

"Sh." Gignomai beckoned him over. "Other way out?"

"Only if you climb through the back-room window."

"Thanks," Gignomai said, hesitated, added, "Not your fault," and vanished. By the time Furio had pulled himself together enough to follow, he found the window open and the back room empty. He closed his eyes, sat down on a crate and let his head flop forward onto his chest.

"Your friend." Tissa's voice. He opened his eyes.

"What?"

"Your friend," she repeated, "is *strange*."

He turned to look at her. She sat down beside him. "What happened?" he asked.

"Good question."

Bad answer. "Well?"

Tissa sat up straight, folded her hands in her lap. He'd always thought of it as her historian mode. "Well," she said, "according to Bonoa they were getting along just fine. You know, first date talking. She told him about her family, he told her about his..."

(That, Furio thought, I'm inclined to doubt.)

"And then," Tissa went on, "he asked if she played chess, and she said yes, so they set up the chessboard and played three games."

"Who won?" Furio couldn't help asking.

"He did," she replied, "and that's what I mean by strange, because obviously a boy lets a girl win at least one game on a first date, even if he's a Grand Master. Anyway," she went on, "she said she didn't want to play any more, and he looked a bit sad and said, so what do you want to do instead, and she kissed him."

Furio waited. Then he said, "*Well?*"

"He went berserk," Tissa said. "He jumped up, said what do you think you're doing, or something like that, so she got up and walked out." She paused, shrugged and said, "That's it." She looked at him and scowled. "Like I said. Strange."

Furio closed his eyes again. He really wanted Tissa to go away, but when he opened them again she was still there. "Yes," he said.

"Yes what?"

"Yes he's strange," Furio said. "All right?"

She sighed. "I told you," she said.

"What?"

"Doesn't like girls."

Furio massaged his eyebrows with his thumb and forefinger, but it didn't help. "Looks that way," he said, "but I don't think so."

"Really?"

"I don't know."

She wriggled uncomfortably next to him. "What other explanation could there be?"

"Don't know."

"I suppose," she said slowly, "he could have a girl up there on the mountain."

"No," Furio said. "He'd have told me. Besides, there aren't any. That was the point."

"Then it's got to be—you know." She sounded as though she was proving some mathematical calculation. "You want to watch yourself," she added.

"Tissa..."

"I'm just saying." She leaned away so as not to be in contact with him. "Think about it," she said. "He sneaks down off the mountain, breaking rules, getting past the guards, swims rivers just to come here and see you. And he gives you presents."

"He lends me books," Furio corrected her.

"Same thing," Tissa replied. "Well? Has he ever talked to you about...?"

"*What?*"

"Stuff boys talk about," Tissa said irritably. "You know."

For crying out loud, he thought. "It's not that," he said firmly, and he knew he was right. "Look."

"What?"

He hesitated. After all, it was just a guess on his part. "Don't tell this to anyone, right?"

She shrugged. That would have to do.

"I think something happened," Furio said. "About six years ago. Don't ask me what, because I don't know. But he stopped breaking out for a long time, and when he came back he was different."

Tissa raised her eyebrows. "What sort of thing?"

"Not a clue," Furio said blankly. "But whatever it was, he isn't saying and I can't ask."

"Something that's made him allergic to being kissed by girls?"

"I just told you, I don't know." He stood up, suddenly anxious to be somewhere else. "Do me a favour," he said.

Tissa let out a long, deliberate sigh. "What?"

"Tell Bonoa to keep her face shut."

Tissa laughed. It sounded more like a cough. "I wouldn't worry about that," she said. "Hardly the sort of thing she'll go boasting about."

"Just talk to her," Furio said. "Please?"

"If you like," Tissa replied. Furio realised how much he liked Tissa. In fact, he was suddenly aware that he'd made a decision about her, without realising he'd done it. "I get all the rotten jobs," she added, and he laughed.

"Well?" he said.

"What?"

"What did you think of him?"

A moment of stunned silence. Then she said, "Apart from being strange, you mean?"

"Yes."

She shrugged. "I hardly said two words to him."

"So?"

"So he's nice-looking," Tissa vouchsafed. "Which really doesn't count for much, if he's—"

"That's all?" Furio said. "Just nice-looking, nothing else?"

Apparently he'd made a mistake, because Tissa got up, told him to go to hell, and walked away. "Talk to Bonoa," he called after her. She waved a hand at him without looking round, so that was all right.

He went back inside and tidied up a bit. Then Uncle caught him—proof that he hadn't been paying attention—and put him on unpacking and degreasing a consignment of scythe blades. The job took the rest of the afternoon and he cut his finger quite badly. Tissa dropped by just before the store closed. She'd spoken to Bonoa, and as far as she was concerned, the whole miserable business had never happened. Furio kissed Tissa and she prodded him hard in the solar plexus, then kissed him back while he was still gasping for air and went home.

Luso was in a foul mood. That was bad news for everyone in the house, but worse for Gignomai because Luso tended to work out his temper in impromptu fencing lessons.

"We had one this morning," Gignomai protested.

"Yes, and you were bloody useless. So we'll go through it again." Luso frowned. "You're all wet."

"I fell in the stream."

Luso smiled at him, and he shivered. Considered objectively, Luso was extraordinarily good-looking, everybody said so, and Gignomai could see it himself. But that was Luso for you. He was a man with practically every gift, talent, quality and virtue worth having, and it wasn't as though he was actively or deliberately malicious, let alone bad or evil, he was just—*unfortunate*, their mother had called him once, when she didn't realise Gignomai was listening. Somehow, the fact that Luso could play the harp like an angel devalued harp-playing, and his good looks made you wonder if beauty was such a good thing after all.

"You're always falling in water," Luso said, hustling him across the yard into the long barn, where they used the threshing floor as their fencing ring. "Anybody'd think you've got two left feet. But you haven't."

As he spoke, he lashed out with his left fist. It was a slow punch, barely concealed. Its purpose (as Gignomai realised, too late to do anything about it) was to get him to step back smartly out of the way, thereby proving Luso's point.

"See?" Luso said. "Good reactions, pretty reasonable balance, good coordination. And yet you're for ever toppling off logs into streams. Maybe we ought to work on that."

(And that, Gignomai reflected, was the difference between them. Luso had seen him breaking out, and now he couldn't resist letting him know he knew. Gignomai would've kept the knowledge safe and quiet, for when he needed to use it.)

"If you like," Gignomai replied. He could see his sword leaning against the wall. Luso had brought it here earlier, so this lesson wasn't quite as spur of the moment as he'd been led to believe. "I don't mind."

The hard, polished clay of the threshing floor had been carefully marked out with a series of concentric rings, clearly shown up with blue raddle mixed with powdered chalk. Gignomai went and stood on the outer ring, but Luso shook his head. "Middle," he said. "We'll do voids."

Oh, Gignomai thought, but managed not to let anything show.

Leaning next to the sword was a hazel stick, the same length, about half an inch thick. Gignomai always used the sword, unbated, its point sharp as a needle. Luso used the stick.

"All right," Luso said, taking his place on the mark. "In your own time try and kill me."

That was what he always said. Once, about five years ago, after Luso had cut his bottom lip open with a swish of the stick before smacking him stupid with a blow over the right eye, Gignomai asked him, do you really mean that, about killing you? Yes, of course, Luso had said. You want to, don't you? He hadn't answered. He was still thinking about it.

Or maybe not. "If I wanted to kill you," he replied, "I wouldn't try and do it here."

Luso laughed. His face was beautiful—no other way to describe it—when he laughed. "If you do it here, you'll get away with it," he said.

"Well, I don't want to."

"That's a weight off my mind," Luso said, and aimed a fast jab at his teeth. Gignomai retreated, one step back and left. He was supposed to counter-attack in time. Luso rolled his eyes at him.

"All right," he said. "You attack me this time."

Hiding to nothing. Gignomai did his very best, and found himself walking into a slam just above the right ear that made his head swim. Luso only ever used the tip of his stick, at most the first two inches: the *stramazone* or point-flick, the only cut available with the smallsword.

"You're not trying," Luso said. "You've got to read me like a book."

"Sorry," Gignomai heard himself say, and he tried again, going in on the diagonal, lunging for Luso's kneecap. That got him a sharp prod in the face, a finger's breadth under his left eye.

"Tell me what I did," Luso ordered.

"You withdrew the front foot a full stride while raising your sword-arm and changing from first to fourth."

"Quite right. You know the move, yes?"

Gignomai nodded. "We did it—"

"You knew the move, but you thought I'd forgotten it?" Luso let the tip of the stick rest on the floor. "That's the trouble with you," he said. "You learn the moves, you get them really well, but you don't use them. You practise them as if they're dance steps, but you don't see how they fit together." He sighed. "You won't *fight*, is your problem."

Gignomai put on a remorseful face and nodded sadly, then he

drove his front foot forward, not how he'd been taught but wildly, and swung a far too wide extravagant slash at Luso's face with the sword-tip. It caught him an inch below the hairline, and for a fraction of a second nothing happened. Then blood started blossoming out of the cut, and Luso hammered the stick into the inside of his wrist, sending the sword spinning across the barn.

Gignomai froze, wondering what on earth he'd just done and, as if he were an uninvolved observer, what Luso was going to do to him next.

Luso grinned. "That was dreadful," he said. "What was bad about it?"

It took him a moment to understand the question. "Front foot?"

Luso nodded, which made blood trickle down his forehead. "Too far forward. And?"

"Too much arm."

"That's right. You wasted time and energy, and you opened yourself up more than you should've done. Apart from that," he added, wiping his forehead and looking at his hand, "it wasn't bad."

He hesitated. "Luso, I'm sorry," he said. "I don't know what I was—"

The stick swung down hard on the point of his left shoulder filling his whole body with pain. "Don't apologise," Luso roared at him. "First time in six years you've even *tried* to do this, don't you dare say you're sorry. You think I like wasting my time on you, when you can't even be bothered to *try*?"

Gignomai couldn't move the fingers of his left hand. "Fine," he said, trying to keep his voice steady. "I'm sorry I was sorry."

Luso came a long step closer. It wasn't a teaching-fencing step but a real lunge, such as Luso might make in a real fight. He was there before Gignomai realised he'd moved. "Listen," he said, and he grabbed Gignomai's right elbow, "fencing isn't fighting. You can fence better than the masters at the royal court, and one day an angry old man with a hayfork's going to stick you in the guts and kill you. Skill's a handy thing to have, but fighting's about meaning it."

Gignomai looked down at the hand clamped on his elbow. "I didn't mean to hurt you," he said. "I was sure you'd parry."

Luso let go. "For a moment there," he said, "I was proud of you." Then he walked away.

At dinner, Father noticed. "What happened to you?" he asked.

"Gig's fencing lesson," Luso replied.

Father put down the slice of bread he'd been working on. "He got past you, did he?"

"He most certainly did."

"Must be getting good, then."

"He's very good," Luso said. "He's really come on this year. Still needs to work on his single time, but we're getting there."

Father turned his head, and his eye fell on Gignomai like a firm grip, like Luso's hand on his arm. "I'm glad to hear it," he said. "It's taken you long enough."

He was required to say something but he couldn't think what. "Luso's been very patient," he said. That made Father laugh, and pick up his bread again.

After dinner, he went down into the cellar, which Luso had turned into his armoury. He was usually down there after dinner, polishing and sharpening.

"Did you mean all that?" he said.

Luso had taken the lock off one of the snapping-hens. He'd laid the screws out on the table in a sort of flattened horseshoe shape, so he'd know which one went in which hole. He didn't look up. "All what?"

"Am I good at fencing?"

Luso nodded. "Very good," he said.

"Is that just because . . . ?"

"At fencing," Luso repeated, "you'd beat anyone in this colony, except me."

Gignomai was stunned. He'd always assumed he was useless. "But you knock me around as though I was still a little kid," he said. "You use a stick and I use sharps."

"So?"

And Gignomai understood. Good, very good, but not good enough. It was, perhaps, the first time in his life he'd appreciated the difference. "Will it leave a scar?"

Luso laughed. "Girls like scars," he said. "In moderation. I've always felt I could do with one, so you've saved me a job. Or I could grow my fringe, I guess."

That seemed to be that, but Gignomai, though offered a dismissal, decided for once not to accept it. "Is there something wrong with the gun?"

Luso nodded. "Overriding at half cock," he said. Presumably that was supposed to mean something. "There's a little burr here, look." He pointed at something with the tip of his turnscrew. "It's making the sear bridge the detent. Couple of strokes with a fine stone'll put that right."

Gignomai took a step closer and looked over his shoulder. It didn't take him long to figure out how the mechanism worked. "Interested?" Luso asked.

"Not really."

Shrug. "Aurelio says you're always hanging round the forge, watching."

"It's warm."

Luso had teased out one of the components, and was drawing a small whetstone across it. "You don't approve of me, do you?"

It was such an absurd thing for Luso to say; as if the sun needed his approval before it could rise.

But he said, "I think we ought to try and get along with the other people here."

Luso grinned. "That's what Furio Opello thinks, is it?"

"He says they put up with us because if the savages attack, we'll defend them."

"Is that right?" Luso was squeezing together the legs of a powerful spring, forcing it back into place. "What a strange idea. Old-country thinking."

Gignomai didn't know what to make of that. Talking to Luso like this didn't feel right. Luso had the knack of making him feel fourteen years old. "I'd best be going," he said.

"Why?" Luso had pushed the spring back where it needed to be, and was looking at the ball of his thumb. A sharp edge had cut into it deeply. "Nobody needs you for anything."

"Do you?"

"Not really." Luso started putting back the screws. "That's the problem, isn't it? You know they only had you as a spare. In case anything happened to Stheno or me. Since we're still both alive, they're at a loss to figure out what you're for." A screw slipped through his fingers and spun onto the floor; Gignomai pounced on it and handed it over. "Exactly what is it you do all day, anyway? When you're not sneaking down to the town."

"I do what I'm told, mostly," Gignomai said.

"Yes, I know that. But you've got a marvellous gift for not being there when people are looking for you with work to be done. I don't think it's because you're idle. There's something you do. What?"

Gignomai shrugged. "I like to read."

"You like to read." Luso ran in the last screw, and pulled back the long arm, the part that held the splinter of flint. Gignomai heard it click twice—a confident metal noise, like the tick of Furio's father's clock. Then Luso pressed a lever on the other side of the lock plate, and the arm tried to lunge forward, only his bleeding thumb was in the way and obstructed it. "Apart from that."

"I do jobs around the farm."

"I asked Stheno what you do," Luso said. "He said he was minded to ask me the same question. Which made me think, maybe I should ask you directly. It's not the way we do things in this family, but I'm not morally opposed to innovation." He put the lock down on the table. "Well?"

"I do jobs around the farm. I read. Sometimes I go for walks."

"That's it?"

"Yes."

Luso laughed again. Luso was always laughing, but rarely, as far as Gignomai could recall, at anything funny. "We're going to have to take you in hand," he said. "Can't have a son of the met'Oc just drifting around aimlessly all day."

"I thought the met'Oc were gentlemen of leisure."

Luso scowled at him. "Don't be stupid," he said. "You know as well as I do, people like us are spared the necessity of miserable everyday labour so we can spend our time on things that really matter. Gentle occupations and noble pursuits."

He said it as if he meant it, so there was no point in arguing. That was where most people were wrong about Luso. He sincerely believed in something. Unfortunately, only he knew what it was.

"Stheno works on the farm. He works really hard."

Luso turned his head away. "Stheno..." He was having trouble finding words, a remarkable thing. "Stheno's had to make sacrifices, because of being the eldest. Someone's got to run the farm, because while we're stuck here in this godforsaken place we've got to eat and put clothes on our backs. Stheno sees to all that. It means he's got to miss out on a lot of better things. You should be grateful."

Gignomai could see all sorts of dangers if they followed this line of discussion. He'd been there before, arguing with Furio.

("Your family are crazy," Furio had said. "They act as though they're noblemen at court, but really you're just a bunch of farmers like everybody else."

"No we're not," Gignomai had replied automatically. Searching blind for his argument, he found the words his father relied on. "We're in exile. While we're here—"

"You're stuck here for good and you know it. Your brother Stheno knows it. He's the hardest working farmer in the colony."

"That's a good thing, surely."

"Yes, but the rest of you carry on like...Well, like you're at the hunting lodge for the summer, and wouldn't it be fun to play at shepherds and shepherdesses."

"No we don't."

"Oh, right. So it's fine for you to herd pigs, but will they let you learn a trade? Like hell they will. That'd mean *accepting*. They won't stand for it. And they treat Stheno as if he's simple or something. They're sorry for him, and they look down their noses at him.")

"I'll talk to Father about it," Luso said, and the decision was made. "There's got to be something you can do. We've just got to figure out what it could possibly be."

That remark cost Gignomai a night's sleep. He lay awake, listening to a rat busy in the thatch, and tried to come up with something. At all costs, he had to have a viable proposition to put to Father with which to pre-empt any suggestions Luso might make. He was confident Father would give him an opportunity to do so. Father was a fair-minded man on those occasions when he was prepared to take official notice of his children.

He shook his head, as if trying to throw off something horrible climbing all over his face.

What, though?

The undeniable truth about Stheno was that he was big. Luso was tall, slim and frighteningly strong, but he only just came up to Stheno's rock-like shoulder. Luso could punch a hole in a door, but Stheno could catch a six-month-old bull calf, wrestle it down and carry it on his back.

The other thing about Stheno was that he was worried. Regardless of what was happening, rain or shine, good season or bad, Stheno lived in a state of permanent anxiety, torn between the aftermath of the last difficulty and the looming prospect of the next disaster but one. When you talked to him, you knew his mind was on something, or many things else. He was gentle and kind and never lost his temper, but you were never in any doubt but that you were the least of his concerns.

Finding Stheno wasn't easy, unless you'd studied him carefully over many years. The trick was to keep your eyes open as you went around the farm and figure out where the next calamity was likely to be: a weak point in the fence where the cattle could get through; a bridge on the point of collapse; a field of corn over heavy or just starting to be pulled apart by rooks. If you wanted Stheno for something, you'd go to where the breakdown and the failure was likeliest to be, and chances were, there you'd find him.

On this occasion he was out at one of the more distant cattle sheds. One of the door-pillars, which had been giving notice for at least five years, had finally slithered out of true, and the unsupported wall had dropped, snapping the roof-tree, so that from a distance, the shed looked as though it had fallen from a great height. Stheno had got his shoulder under the lintel and was slowly, agonisingly heaving the shed upright with his right arm wrapped round a massive post which he was hoping to use as a temporary prop. If he managed it (and Stheno always managed, somehow), it'd stay propped up like that, with its broken roof and burst walls, for another six months or so until it disintegrated for good, because there wouldn't be time or resources to come back another day and do a proper job. Another disaster would have intervened by then, clamouring for Stheno's attention like a hungry child.

"Need a hand?" Gignomai called out.

"Gig?" Stheno couldn't look round. He was wrestling with the shed like the hero in the fairy tale who wrestled with Death for the life of his mother. "Get hold of this post, and when I say push..."

(It was, Gignomai decided, rather like Luso and fencing, or Luso and Stheno and strength. He had no idea if he was a good fencer or physically strong. All he knew was that he was a worse fencer than Luso and not nearly as strong as Stheno. No absolutes, just comparatives.)

It was mostly a determination not to fail that made it possible for him to drag the bottom of the giant post onto the flat rock Stheno had put there for a base, and then jam the top under the lintel, while Stheno heaved on it like someone trying to tear the sky off the earth with his bare hands. They managed it, and for quite some time afterwards, neither of them could spare any breath for talking.

"Remind me," Gignomai said, "what we use this shed for?"

"Haven't actually used it for a while," Stheno replied, "but we stored hay for the upper pastures here when I was a kid. Saved having to drag it all the way down to the yard and back again."

Gignomai did the calculations in his head: man-hours wasted, productivity squandered. "We ought to fix it up," he said.

"I will, when I've got five minutes."

(And the chances of Stheno having five minutes were about the same as Gignomai learning to fly like a bird, or the met'Oc ever going Home.) Stheno took a few steps back and gazed at the shed with sadness and loathing. "Right," he said. "What can I do for you?"

They're sorry for him, Furio had said, and they look down their noses at him. "Have you got a minute? I wanted to ask you something."

"Sure," Stheno replied. "I'm heading down to Pitland."

Pitland was a joke. It was a fifteen-acre field on a slope like the side of a house, but the soil was good and inexplicably deep—one of the few cultivable places where drainage wasn't an issue. Therefore, Stheno ploughed it every year, balancing on the edge like a fly on a wall and, when the inevitable happened and the plough toppled over, broke the traces and went tumbling down the slope, he hauled it back up again, one monstrous step at a time. Now, however, the corn was green and hopeful, and the problem was the branch of a great oak that had come down on top of the fence, shattering the rails and skewing the posts, allowing access to deer, boar and every other relentless enemy of agriculture lurking in the woods. Gignomai had been waiting for the branch to fall for years.

There wasn't time to go back for axes and saws, so they lugged the branch off in one piece, then did the best they could for the fence by tamping stones down into the post holes and binding up the fractured rails with about a mile of string. "I don't know," Stheno said, cutting round a knot with his knife. It was astonishing that fingers that big could make something as delicate as a knot. "I'd have thought it was up to you. What do you *want* to do?"

"I know what I *don't* want to do," Gignomai replied. "I want to stay well clear of the family business."

Stheno grinned. "Which is?"

"I don't want to get mixed up with what Luso does," Gignomai said. "It's not right and it's stupid, and one of these days he'll get himself killed."

Stheno looked the other way. "And I take it you don't want to work on the farm, either."

"No."

"And who could possibly blame you for that?" Stheno said cheerfully. "Not sure what else there is, though."

Gignomai took a moment to prepare himself, as though he was about to challenge God to a duel. "Ask yourself," he said, "what's the one thing we need around here and haven't got?"

"Just one thing?" Stheno shrugged. "Enlighten me."

"Money," Gignomai said forcefully. "Well, it's true, isn't it? Father talks to you. How much money have we actually got?"

Stheno frowned. "You know," he said, "that's a good question. I haven't got a clue. I know there's that rosewood box in Dad's study, I think there may be some in there, but I've never actually looked."

"Luso did," Gignomai replied quickly. "He told me. There's thirty gold angels, a dozen or so thalers and some copper. That's it. And that was ten years ago, and I'll bet you that money came from Home, when we first moved here."

"There's your answer, then," Stheno said, matching the two parts of a splintered rail. "We've got on for seventy years without it, so we don't need it. And we don't, do we?"

"That's like saying the donkey doesn't need feeding," Gignomai said, "which it doesn't, until it dies. Well, think about it. I don't suppose Grandfather came here with no more than thirty angels. I bet that box was full, and others like it. If there's only thirty angels left, it means we've nearly run out."

"False premise," Stheno said. "Start wrapping the string, will you? You're assuming we use money. Tell me what we use it for."

"I don't know," Gignomai confessed. "But that's because nobody tells me anything."

"You have your own ways of finding things out, so I'm told."

"Well, not about that. But anyway," he went on, "think about what we could do if we had some money. Stuff we could buy. New tools, materials. Can you think of anything we've got that's not flogged out and patched up?"

Stheno shrugged, like a cow dislodging flies. "What's that got to do with you?"

"We could trade," Gignomai said.

"Really."

"Yes. The Opellos would pay us a quarter a dozen for squirrel pelts. More, probably. And rabbits and hares."

"I see," Stheno said slowly. "So basically, you want to go into business as a rat-catcher."

"That's just an example," Gignomai said, making himself stay calm. "We've got a seam of top-grade clay. They haven't got anything anywhere near as good down on the flat. And have you got any idea what lumber goes for down there? Or charcoal? They're shipping in charcoal from Home, it costs them an absolute fortune, and we could supply them for a fraction of what they're paying and still make out like bandits."

Stheno raised his eyebrows. "Do what?"

"Sorry," Gignomai said, with a grin. "It's one of my friend Furio's expressions. It means we could make a lot of money."

Stheno nodded slowly. "Charcoal," he said, "is one of the monopolies. They're obliged to buy it from Home, it's the law."

"Right. And who's going to tell on them? And there's more to it than that," he went on, unable to control himself now that someone was actually listening. "The way Luso's carrying on, it won't be long before they've had enough of us and they come for us with weapons. But if we start selling them stuff, things they actually want, then they'll need us. It's not just about trade and money, it's about survival. You do see that, don't you?"

Stheno trimmed another knot. "So basically," he said, "you want to be Minister for Trade and Industry, so you won't have to muck in with your brother or me. It's an idea," he added, before Gignomai could protest, "but Dad won't have it."

"It's a good idea."

Stheno laughed. "Listen," he said. "There's a shitload of good ideas. I've had them, so has Luso. But selling them to Dad is another matter entirely. You'll never do it. Believe me, I've tried often enough."

It had never occurred to Gignomai that his brothers talked to their father. He'd assumed they just listened, received their orders and carried them out. He was, therefore, encouraged rather than put off. "I'll talk to him," he said.

He talked to his father.

That was an experience. First, there was the summons. It was delivered by his mother, who left the sewing room specially for the purpose. All she said was, "He wants to see you." No commentary or interpretation. She'd have made a lousy priestess, he couldn't help thinking. Then she went back to where she belonged and shut the door.

Next, the climb up the stairs to the library. When Grandfather built the house, he must have had their old house back Home in mind. There were three floors—five, if you counted the cellar, which was huge and these days full of Luso and his weapons, and the attic, where the servants lived in small, warm, tidy boxes (he always thought of them as being put away at night like a good child's toys). The bedrooms were on the third floor. The ground floor consisted of the kitchen, which was enormous and the only part of the house where anybody could go, the dining room and the Hall, where the family assembled once a day like a parliament in session. The middle floor was the library, with Father's study separate in one corner. Two servants went there to clean—it took them the whole day, every day—and Father lived there, often sleeping in the magnificent, rather terrifying chair that had come from the old house. What he did there all day was nobody's business. Mother had told him once, when he was young, that Father was writing the history of the family, but Gignomai was inclined to doubt that, because they made parchment so rarely. It was an acknowledged fact that he sometimes wrote letters to important people at Home, which had to be unofficially conveyed to ships' captains in town, a commission that Stheno undertook, most unhappily. If all he did was read the books, there were enough of them to keep him busy for the rest of an unusually long life. A servants' legend had it that when the met'Oc came here in three ships, one whole ship was full of nothing but books. Gignomai got into the library by the servants' stairs at noon, when Father retired to his study to eat.

Today, though, he entered the library from the main stairs, through the double doors. The last time he'd been here officially was when Father had made him burn Furio's present. He'd hated the place since then, though he still came to steal books (which always found their way back onto the shelves, no matter how carefully he hid them). Father was sitting in the Chair, his head flopped onto his chest, asleep. For the first time in his life, Gignomai wondered how old his father was.

The head snapped up as soon as Gignomai closed the doors. "You sent for me."

"Sit down," Father said. There was a book open on his lap. He marked the place with what looked like a glove, closed it and put it on the table, next to the rosewood box. "Lusomai tells me you've got nothing to do."

"That's not strictly—"

"There's an important difference," Father said, "between leisure and indolence. In our society, not working is a state shared by the very rich and the very poor. Both sections of society live, you might say, off the labour of others; by rents and dividends and by charity. You, I fear, presently live on the charity of this household. It's time we found you something to do."

"I work on the farm," Gignomai said. "Only this morning I was helping Stheno—"

His father raised three fingers of one hand, a total prohibition on speech. "Sthenomai has taken over from me the day-to-day running of the estate," he said. "That's his duty, as the eldest son. Lusomai, as second son, pursues a military career. Were we at Home, you would be reading for the House or the Temple. Unfortunately, that isn't possible, but we have all the necessary texts. You can read them here, and then, when we go Home, you can be admitted straight away without having to go through seminary."

Gignomai couldn't be sure, but he had an idea who the glove had belonged to. That made him so angry that for a moment or so he couldn't speak. But he pulled himself out of it, because there was a real and present danger to be dealt with.

"Would it be all right," he asked, "if I suggested something else?"

His father looked at him as though he was an explorer who'd brought back some strange and improbable novelty from a distant land—a bird with two heads, or a deer with a pocket in its belly for carrying its young. "By all means," he said, and rested his elbows on the arms of the chair, steepling his fingers.

"I thought," Gignomai began, and he made his speech. It was more or less the same one he'd tried out on Stheno, but with more arguments and specifics, and presented with as much of the formal method as he could remember. His father didn't interrupt and, when the speech was over, he sat perfectly still for a full minute before he spoke.

"You presented your case well," he said.

Gignomai realised he hadn't breathed for some time, but he didn't dare, not until he'd heard the verdict.

"Tell me," Father went on, "to what extent have you made a study of logical and rhetorical forms?"

Several seconds passed before Gignomai was able to figure out what his father was talking about. "I've read a few books," he said.

"Specify."

He scrabbled about in his memory for names. "Livius Secundus on Logic," he said. "Regalian on Oratory. The first six of the Ideal Dialogues."

"Excellent." Father nodded his approval. "A solid foundation, and clearly you've taken the precepts to heart and thought about them. I would be inclined to say that you will do well in the House, or you might possibly consider a career in the Law. It's not," he added with a ghost of a smile, "the most distinguished of professions—a lawyer is, after all, essentially the employee of others, you might even term him a kind of servant—but there are certainly precedents, and a good start in the Law has often led to a fine, solid career in the House. In fact, I believe I shall start you on Pacatian's *Constitutional Paradoxes* and see what you make of them. They're unorthodox, but at your age I think you're still young enough to be able to digest them without the risk of being led astray."

"So..." There was, of course, no point in saying anything. But he felt he had to, just to be sure. It'd be a great shame to change his entire life out of all recognition on the basis of a misunderstanding. "So you don't think much of my idea?"

Father looked at him and smiled. "My dear boy," he said, "don't be ridiculous. And I'm afraid I must insist that you put a stop to your forays outside the Fence. Quite apart from the danger to yourself, which is considerably greater than you seem to appreciate, there is the matter of perceptions. I would not want the people of the colony to get it into their heads that you could be, in any sense, a channel of communication between us and them. Please bear in mind the simple fact that they are trespassers on our property. I will not have their intrusion on our land in any way legitimised by your perverse curiosity." He removed the smile, and went on, "I shall talk to Lusomai, and he will ensure that no further breaches take place. You will present yourself here after breakfast tomorrow, by which time I will have put together a selection of appropriate texts. I'll have a chair and a table brought up for you to use."

Gignomai left the library through the double doors, and walked up the main stairs to the third-floor landing. His room was on the east side of the house, overlooking the stable yard. He stripped a pillowcase off the bed and stuffed his spare clothes inside—two shirts, formerly Luso's, two pairs of trousers (Stheno's, when he was very young; even so, the legs were rolled up eight inches), two pairs of socks and the scarf his sister had made him. Into the pockets of his coat he loaded his knife, two handkerchiefs (from Home—they were his but he was expressly forbidden to use them) and three unread books he'd filched from the library a few days ago, chosen because they were small enough to be unobtrusive in a pocket. He changed into his heavy boots and jammed the lighter ones he'd been wearing into the pillowcase. That, and the sword, was everything. His snares and the roll of snare wire were in the small barn, which wasn't on the route he intended to take. There'd be other rolls of wire, he told himself.

There was no reason to believe that getting out of the house would be any more hazardous than usual. After all, he'd assured Father he'd be there bright and early in the morning, and even if Father had suspected anything, there hadn't been time for him to arrange extra security, surely. Even so, he compiled a plan of action as he filled the pillowcase. From the back door, he'd cross the poultry yard to the long barn—the yard was blind to all the house windows except the kitchen, and he'd only have to be out in the open for a matter of seconds—out through the hayloft (he'd done the jump many times and knew he could manage it) and follow the thorn hedge to the orchard gate. The trees in the orchard would give him all the cover he needed, and then he'd be in Long Meadow; he could stay in close to the hedge all the way down to the eaves of the wood. Once he was safely in there, they'd need dogs to follow him, not that he'd put that past them. Probably best to make for the forest river and walk down the bed, at least as far as the logging weir.

He considered leaving a note, just in case his mother got worried, but decided against it.

Just as well he'd taken the trouble to plan ahead. There were two of Luso's men standing about in the poultry yard. That wasn't sinister in itself, but he made sure they didn't see him. As he climbed the orchard gate into Long Meadow he heard voices, which kept pace with him as he scuttled down the hedge. He heard a dog bark as he ran the few yards of open ground to the edge of the wood. Inside, he heard them again, and someone calling out instructions: "You two go on ahead, cut him off at the hunting gate. We'll skirmish the briars and the middle. He can't be too far in front." As a precaution he stayed with the river as far as Big Soak and took a deer trail west, until he could see a green glow in front of him that told him he was almost at the cliff edge. Then he followed the western edge all the way round to the Gate.

And here was the problem. The Gate would be held against him, in force. He couldn't rely on any of his usual ways of sneaking through, which depended on the guards being careless and bored. He really didn't want to have to fight, or even hit anyone over the head from behind, and besides, he had no reason to believe he'd be capable of succeeding. As he approached the Gate he could hear several voices and Luso, clearly in a bad mood. He paused to wonder how Father could have known, but that was a pointless exercise. Father knew everything, and what he wasn't told he deduced.

He faced facts. He wasn't going to be able to get past the Gate. In which case, he needed another way, but there wasn't one. To be on the safe side, he turned back and retraced his steps, venturing as close to the cliff edge as he dared go. That was risky. You could walk out of the trees and be over the cliff before you knew it, but the danger made it safer, because Luso's men knew about it too. Another way—but there wasn't one.

He realised he was in a part of the forest he'd never been before. He tended to think of it as a series of enormous rooms. This was Far West Room on his mental map, somewhere he'd never been because there wasn't anything here worth the effort of reaching. He tried to picture it from the outside, and in his mind saw a sheer white cliff, unmarked by even a single reckless tree growing out of a crack. Maybe, just possibly, you could get down off Far West Room with a lot of rope and some big nails to hammer into the rock, but he was inclined to doubt it. If there was another way (and there wasn't), here wasn't the place where he'd be likely to find it. In fact the whole chalk side of the plateau was a dead loss. He'd be much better off crossing to the east side and trying his luck on the limestone face.

He was preoccupied, therefore not thinking properly about what he was doing, therefore careless. That wouldn't have been so bad, but he was also walking noiselessly — second nature in the wood, and by now he was really good at it. So when he dropped between two fallen trees into a small briar tangle and found himself facing a pair of small, round eyes, he wasn't immediately aware of the danger he'd stumbled into.

The boar looked at him.

He was lying up, the way they do. Given half a chance a boar will run away long before you see it, and hide in one of its nests till you've gone away. But if you're walking very quietly and not thinking about what you're doing, you might just possibly disturb a sleeping boar in a nest, which will almost certainly be the last thing you ever do.

He'd frozen, which explained why he was still alive. The boar, a six-year-old with one splintered tusk, was looking at him, wondering if Gignomai was really there or if he'd just imagined him. Gignomai felt his bladder loosen; his throat was blocked like a drain and he had no strength in any of his limbs. Away in the distance he could hear Luso's dogs, which was absolutely not a good thing: dogs frighten boar, boar gets up and, as far as Gignomai's concerned, this is the end of the history of the world, a full stop and nothing.

In his left hand, he was holding the sword. A mad impulse swept over him to draw and try and kill the boar, which was out of the question, because even if he contrived to draw and level before the boar got him, all that would happen would be that the boar would run up the blade in its determination to get at him, and then both of them would die together.

Luso persecutes these things for fun, he thought. He must be mad.

Somewhere in his mind he was apologising—to his mother, father, Luso, Stheno—I'm sorry I got killed in such a stupid, stupid way. Sorry, Furio. Sorry.

The boar was looking at him, and there was no such thing as time. (It was a myth, a lie, like when he'd been very young and asked Luso where rain came from, and Luso said it was God pissing through a sieve. What a fool he'd been ever to believe that there was such a thing as time, that moments ended and new moments began, patently absurd.) He knew he couldn't move, even if he wanted to. The boar's eyes held him, frozen in place, frozen in time. Perhaps he was already dead, and this was eternity. Not that it mattered particularly. If there was such a thing as time, the next moment would be the one where he moved and the boar charged.

Then the boar moved, a tiny redirection of the head, as something made a noise behind him where he couldn't see. A dog: one of Luso's hounds. The boar had stopped looking at Gignomai but he was still frozen solid. He heard a scrabbling noise, and the ridiculous swallowed yelp that dogs make sometimes, and the boar moved.

It lunged, straight past him, and Gignomai's head moved with it, following, not from any command of his own. He saw one of Luso's hounds coming towards him and the boar bursting up out of the nest to meet it. The boar's snout was under the dog's chest, a great heave of the head and shoulders that sent the dog flying in the air. He felt blood splash his face and knew that if he was ever going to move again, it would have to be now. There was only one direction open to him. He threw himself into the boar's nest like a diver.

He hit a curtain of briars, which burst open. He felt the thorns cut his face like sawblades. His eyes had closed. He shoved his hands through the tangle and felt open space behind them—something he hadn't expected. He dug his toes in and kicked, and then he felt himself sliding on his stomach down a slope.

The sensation was too much for him, and all he could do was endure until he came to a stop. He opened his eyes, but he needn't have bothered. He tried to move his arms, but there wasn't room. He was stuck like a cork in a bottle at an unknown depth down a steep hole in the ground.

The boar would have finished him quickly, but he hadn't been able to move. He could move his legs, and a few frantic kicks shifted him a significant distance further down the hole. He heard himself yell, and the sound washed all around him like water. He knew that nobody would be able to hear him, deep in the ground like a buried man. Breathing was like lifting a hundredweight sack.

There was a decision to be made. He had to force himself to do it; so much easier just to let himself go, to slide into terror. He knew what would happen if he did that; he'd suffocate trying to breathe, or crush his own ribs, panicking.

He thought, I can't go back, but I can go forward. It's inconceivable that going forward could make things better, but if I stay here I'll die anyway. He tried to construe the hole, find an explanation for it, but he couldn't. It made no sense. He thought; I might as well kick my legs and see where the hole goes. I'm not getting out of this. It doesn't really make any odds.

He kicked, and each spasm of movement took him further than the last. His hands were still pinned hard to his sides, but he thought, Maybe if I keep going down, the hole will get wider, maybe wide enough for me to turn myself round, and if I do that, I can use my hands to claw my way back up the hole. No reason to believe it would turn out that way, but the hole was so improbable anyway that the unlikelihood of a wide spot didn't seem to matter, because none of the rules seemed to apply any more. A wide spot was no more improbable than a bottomless hole at the back of a boar's nest. He kicked very hard, and shot unstoppably forward, as if sliding on ice.

The slide ended when his head and shoulders ran into something hard. There was a long moment that consisted of nothing but pain, followed by the crushing weight of understanding. The way ahead was blocked. No wide spot, and he couldn't go forward or back.

Ironically, he could breathe quite freely, and the air was better here. He kept still and held his breath, and felt air moving against his face. He knew that meant something, but for a very long time he couldn't figure out what it was. Then it hit him like a punch in the mouth. Air was moving up the hole, so the hole must be open at both ends. It came out somewhere, and if it did, so could he. So could he, if it wasn't for the fact that the way was blocked.

He hadn't expected anger, and when it came it shocked him at first. But it felt warm and it made him feel strong. He scrabbled with his toes and found a ledge or a stone or something he could push against. All that got him was a jet of pain in his neck. He pushed again, not with muscles but sheer affronted rage (because it wasn't *fair* that the hole should be open but blocked by one stupid obstruction), and something shifted; he was pushing his nose against a hard thing. He'd have laughed if he could. His last effort had moved him a few inches, and the only thing wedging him stuck was his stupid nose.

Well, he thought. No choice in the matter, really.

There was a foothold. He found it, settled his foot firmly against it, took the decision and kicked. He heard his nose break, felt the pain (there was, curiously, a tiny interval between the sound and the feeling) and applied more pressure with his thigh and knee muscles. He moved suddenly, as things do when they're stuck and suddenly dislodged. He felt something sharp scooping skin and meat off the point of his shoulder, and then he was past that too. The next kick moved him freely, two more, and he was sliding again, gathering speed, moving fast enough for the friction to shred his clothes and burn his skin. He stopped with a jolt that hurt so much it didn't hurt at all. He opened his eyes, and saw light.

For some time it was simply too bright, and he wondered if it had burned his eyes out. But gradually it dimmed, and he could make out a dark frame to it, which he deduced must be the mouth of the hole. It was quite close — ten feet, say. He tried to breathe and realised his nose wasn't working, so he drank air through his mouth. It tasted of blood.

It took him a while and a lot of scrabbling to find a foothold firm enough to move him forward, and that was only inches. The sides of the hole were maddeningly smooth here, and his toes skidded off. But the hole was just a little bit wider and by squirming and twisting, like a drill in its slot, he managed to work himself onto his back. The roof of the hole was a little bit rougher, and he found a foothold that took him his own length closer to the light, at which point there was room for his arms to move. He laughed. He'd almost forgotten what they were for.

He twisted back onto his stomach, dug his fingernails into the sides of the hole—they were quite soft, and he remembered it would be chalk—and dragged himself into the furnace of white light. He was almost through when he realised that he'd been missing something.

The hole was pure white light, not green or brown. And there was a context, which he'd completely forgotten about.

The boar's nest had been close to the edge of the cliff. The hole at the back of the nest had taken him a long way down and—since it had turned out to be a sort of a chute, not a sheer drop—an unknown but material distance sideways, in other words, towards the cliff face. Therefore the white hole in front of him had to be a window in the cliff, and he had no idea how high up above the ground it might be.

Not to worry, he told himself (and if it was a lie he really didn't care). He edged forward until his head popped out into open air. He looked down. Directly below, he could see grass, with a tiny fringe of white chalk at the bottom edge of his field of vision. At a guess, about ten feet, fifteen at the most.

He wasn't conscious of making a decision. He heard himself say, "Oh well," out loud, and kicked hard.

There was a moment of stunned silence. Then Furio hissed, "She's a *girl.*"

He realised that he'd spoken too loudly, and everybody was looking at him.

"Yes," his aunt said crisply, "isn't she? Furio, meet your cousin Teucer."

His uncle was trying not to laugh. His aunt was pointedly not looking at him, the way she didn't look at beggars, or dogs mating in the street. Aspero and Lugano, the hired men, had somehow contrived to vanish inside themselves. They stood perfectly still, waiting for something to happen. And his cousin Teucer, newly arrived from Home, smiled at him.

"Hello," she said.

Furio made some kind of vague noise. It sounded like a grunting pig, but it was the very best he could do. "This is your uncle Marzo," his aunt was saying; Uncle grinned like a shark. "I'll show you your room," she went on, putting a hand on the small of the girl's back and shunting her towards the door.

When they'd gone, there was a moment of perfect stillness, such as there must have been at the very beginning of the world. Then Aspero and Lugano melted away, and Furio turned on his uncle like a boar facing the hounds.

"Teucer's not a girl's name," he growled. "Someone should've told me."

His uncle shrugged. "Sorry," he said. "I assumed your aunt had told you, and presumably she thought I'd told you. Anyway..."

"She must think I'm a—"

"And she wouldn't be far wrong," Uncle interrupted. "Would she?"

Furio made his words fail me gesture, a cross between scything hay and swatting a low fly. "I'm going upstairs," he said.

"Like hell you are," Uncle replied kindly. "You're going to stay right here and mind the store while your aunt and I make our guest feel at home."

Furio looked at him. Uncle was known to be unreliable where pretty girls half his age were concerned. But he laughed. "Don't worry," he said. "Your aunt'd kill me. Mind the store."

Alone with the stock, Furio tried as hard as he could to think of something else, but he couldn't. He kept hearing his own voice, over and over again, and each time he heard it, it killed a small part of his soul. Three words, three syllables, and his life was effectively over. Then, like someone testing a sore tooth with the tip of his tongue, he thought about the smile. It had been—he took a moment to compose his mind; this called for scientific analysis—it had been like one of those puzzles, where someone cuts up a picture into random shapes, and you've got to fit them back together again. The smile had been the moment when the picture emerges from the jumble. As soon as he saw it, things had started to make sense, for the first time in a long time. But that was *after* he'd said the three little words.

It was an anomaly, an equation that refused to balance, and it was making his head hurt. He pulled open a drawer and started to count the four-inch nails.

There were 107 of the four-inch, ninety-six of the five-inch, forty-eight of the six-inch round and 128 of the six-inch square tapered. He was about to embark on the four-inch square tapered when he heard boots in the porch. He looked up, and a man walked into the shop backwards.

The man was Rubrio Lucullo, a vague sort of man who appeared occasionally to buy wire and nails. He was walking backwards because he was carrying what looked like a dead body, his arms crooked under the corpse's armpits. Carrying the feet was another man, familiar face, name forgotten or never ascertained. The corpse was a hideous thing, smeared all over with blood and chalk dust.

"Clear the table," Rubrio snapped. "Quick."

Furio didn't move. "Mister Lucullo?"

"Clear the fucking table."

Furio jumped off his stool, darted round the counter and stopped in front of the long, low table on which Uncle displayed his selection of quality fabrics. He hesitated for a split second, because the stock was worth money, then dragged the rolls of cloth onto the floor. With a grunt, Rubrio and the other man hauled the corpse onto the table, straightened up and winced.

"Where's your uncle?" Rubrio said.

Furio heard him, but the words seemed to bounce off. The body on the table was Gignomai.

Rubrio repeated his question. Furio looked at him.

"Is he dead?" he asked quietly.

But Rubrio shook his head. "Get your uncle," he said. "Don't just stand there. *Get your uncle*."

The message sank in, eventually. Furio backed away a step or two, twisted round, hit his knee on the edge of the counter, and crashed through the back-room door. Uncle, he thought, upstairs. He ran up the stairs as if they were on fire, and met his uncle on the landing.

"What's all the racket?" Uncle asked.

"There's been—" He realised he didn't know how to finish the sentence. "Emergency," he said. "Man hurt. Please?"

It was one of Uncle's good times. The bad times were when he was greedy or cruel, or when he made a nuisance of himself with girls. The good times were when something terrible happened and Uncle kept his head and knew exactly what to do. That was when Furio forgave him for the other stuff.

"He's all right," Uncle said, after a long few seconds when Furio couldn't breathe. "Furio, run and get Simica. If we're lucky, he'll be home."

But Simica, who'd been first mate on a salt-beef freighter and whose head contained most of the colony's medical knowledge, wasn't home. His door was locked (he was a very mistrustful man) and his horse wasn't in the stable. Furio groaned out loud and ran back to the store. When he got there, the porch was already crowded: men from the mill and the forge and the lumber yard, several women, a few children, one sitting on the floor trying to see between people's legs. For a moment, Furio was too polite to barge through. Then he shouted, "Excuse me, please," and charged like a boar.

Uncle was peeling a strip of tattered cloth away from Gignomai's shoulder. Aunt was standing next to him, holding a bowl in one hand and a pad of rag in the other. Uncle turned his head as Furio burst in, and smiled at him.

"He'll be fine," he said. "His nose is broken and he's got some pretty nasty cuts and scrapes, and he's had a bash on the head. Simica not there?"

Furio didn't reply. He knew he couldn't just stay put indefinitely, but he couldn't bring himself to come any closer. "What happened?" he said.

Uncle shrugged. "Rubrio and Scleria here found him," he said, "down by the river. Saw it was the youngest met'Oc boy, so they fetched him here. For some reason," Uncle added, with a very slight frown. "You got any idea? He's your friend."

Furio shook his head. But the white chalk dust meant something, he knew that. Chalk could only mean the west cliff of the Tabletop: the sheer drop, from their world into ours, which nobody could possibly survive.

"My guess is, he fell off the cliff," Uncle said, teasing a shred of cloth out of the ploughed-field mess of blood and dirt. "In which case, he's the luckiest man alive. Must be a hundred and twenty feet."

Furio crossed the room and sat down on a crate, as far from the low table as he could get. He had an entire world to reinterpret, and he found it hard to believe that he was the same person who'd been in despair over saying something stupid only a few hours earlier. Very briefly he toyed with the idea that it was a punishment, but he dismissed it as far-fetched and hysterical. Instead, he experimented with placing other bodies on the low table: Uncle, Aunt, Lugano. The conclusion he was forced to troubled him.

"Are you all right?"

He looked up, and saw his new cousin looking down at him. She looked solemn and sympathetic, and she didn't affect him at all.

"Fine," he said. "Thanks."

"That man's your friend, isn't he?"

Furio nodded. "Gignomai," he said. "Yes. I've known him since we were kids."

She sat down beside him, perching like a bird on a thin branch. "Uncle Marzo says he's knocked out but he should be all right," she said, and he wondered why he hadn't noticed her there before. Probably because she was short, and Aunt had been standing in front of her. "My father was a surgeon," she said.

For the second time that day she had his undivided attention. "Do you know about...?"

She nodded. "I grew up with strangers bleeding on the kitchen table," she said. "It's all right, your uncle knows what he's doing. I watched him. He's rolled back the eyelid to see if one pupil's bigger than the other—that's a bad sign—but there wasn't anything like that. Setting the broken nose shouldn't be too much of a problem, it's not broken in a bad place. Probably just as well to do it while he's still asleep, though. It hurts like hell."

She spoke calmly, as if about ordinary things, and he couldn't help wondering what she'd seen over the years in her house where they ate dinner on a table where people were cut open and sewn back together. One thing he could be sure about. She wasn't just a pretty girl any more. He wasn't sure if this was a good or a bad thing, but he postponed the analysis and the decision.

He remembered something. "Your father," he said. "You said he *was*—"

"He died," she replied. "He caught something from a patient, and it wasn't written up in any of his books. Mother said he died of pique because he couldn't identify what was wrong." She shrugged; her shoulders were thin and sharply defined. "Mother died too, not long afterwards. I think it was consumption. So my uncle sent for me to come here."

He looked at her. "What do you make of it?"

"I don't know," she replied. "We lived in Colichamard—that's a biggish city on the coast. But we always spent the summers on my mother's cousin's farm, so I'm used to the country."

"It's very quiet here," he heard himself say. "You may find it's a bit too quiet, after the city."

She smiled. "Maybe," she said. "I don't think so. Back home, women don't leave the house much. Not our sort, anyhow. And I assume the inside of one house is pretty much like another. Actually," she added, "this one's bigger. I hadn't realised I'd have a room all to myself."

The thought that anything here could be better than Home wasn't one he'd had to contend with before. "One thing we've got here," he said, "is plenty of space. That's about all we've got here, though. Loads of space but not enough people to fill it."

There was movement at the table. They were lifting Gignomai, carrying him upstairs. He was awkward to handle, like a large piece of furniture. "He'll be all right," she said.

He stayed where he was. "God only knows what happened to him."

She frowned. "Is it true he's one of the met'Oc?"

"That's right. Youngest son. You've heard of them?"

"I heard them talking about the met'Oc on the ship. I thought they were all traitors and criminals."

When Gignomai woke up he was lying on a bed, which made him think nothing had happened. But the ceiling was different.

He tried to move, and everything hurt.

There was someone sitting next to him, a stranger, a young woman, looking at him.

"It's all right," she said.

From time to time there had been accidents on the farm, so he knew perfectly well that if someone says "It's all right," there must be something horribly wrong. He tried to breathe in and couldn't.

"Breathe through your mouth."

"Hm?"

"Your nose is broken," the girl said, and he remembered. He'd broken it deliberately, to get past the blockage. Had he really done that? "And you've got a broken rib and a nasty gash on your right shoulder. Are you feeling dizzy or sick?"

He could only see half of her, at the very edge of his vision, so he turned his head a little. "Who the hell are you?" he said.

She smiled at him. Quite nice-looking. "I'm Teucer," she said. "I'm Furio's cousin."

"He hasn't got a—"

"From Home. I arrived yesterday."

Too much information and not enough, at the same time. He remembered something extremely important. "The sword," he said.

"Sorry?"

"My sword," he repeated, and he could feel fear gushing up inside him, like filling a pitcher from a spring. "I had a sword with me. And a pillowcase."

She frowned, just a little bit. He knew what she was thinking.

"Really," he said. "It's not the bash on the head talking. I had a sword, and a pillowcase with all my stuff in it."

She didn't say anything, and he thought, No, that's right, I must've dropped them when I dived into the boar's nest. Which means...

"What are you doing?"

"Getting out of bed. What does it look like?"

"Don't be stupid."

He looked at her, then gave up. "You don't understand," he said. "I've got to go back and get it, before my brother finds it."

"A sword," she said, dismissing all swords everywhere as beneath contempt. "Listen, you've got mild concussion. If you lie still, you'll be fine. If you get up and try rushing around, you'll do yourself serious harm. Do you understand?"

She was quite possibly the most annoying person he'd ever met in his life. "Yes, fine," he snapped. "I think I'd like to go to sleep now."

She didn't move. "Good idea."

He closed his eyes, counted to 150, and opened them again. She was still there.

"You can go and look for it when you're better," she said. "Or you could get a new one."

He closed his eyes again, mostly so he wouldn't have to look at her.

* * *

When he woke up, she'd gone, and Furio was there, with his uncle sitting next to him. "Hello," Furio said. "How are you?"

"I've got to go back," he said.

The uncle (name? He knew it, but couldn't call it to mind) frowned at him. "Don't mention it," he said. "You're welcome."

"I left something behind," Gignomai said. "I need..."

Furio and his uncle glanced at each other. "Teucer did say something about a sword," Uncle said. "But I assumed you were off your head and talking rubbish."

"The sword." Gignomai nodded. "It's worth twelve thousand thalers."

Uncle's eyes swelled until Gignomai was afraid they'd burst. But Furio said, "Well, your brother'll have found it by now. They'll notice it's gone, won't they?"

"I hope not," Gignomai said. "I want to sell it."

Furio was about to say something, but Uncle grabbed his hand and crushed it. He was clearly a strong man, though not in the same class as Luso or Stheno. "Sell it?" he said.

"That's right. It's my start in life, you could say."

"What makes you think it's worth that kind of money?" Uncle asked. He'd carefully lowered and straightened out his voice, but he'd tightened his grip on Furio's hand.

"Your brother told me," Gignomai said. "He saw it."

"He offered you that much for it?"

"I wasn't selling," Gignomai replied. "Not then."

"Uncle," Furio said, but Uncle wasn't listening to him.

"But you are now?"

"They won't let him have it," Furio said loudly. "It's not yours to sell, is it? That's what you told me."

Gignomai shrugged. "I've left," he said, "and I'm not going back. That's why I need it."

There was a long, deep silence. Then Uncle said, "Where exactly...?"

Gignomai explained what had happened. When he'd finished, Furio was staring at him, but Uncle was leaning towards him with a starving look on his face. "You think there's a chance it could still be there?"

"It's a big wood," Gignomai said. "And they wouldn't know about the way down. I'm guessing it's some flaw in the chalk, and water's been trickling down there for God knows how long, and it ate away the hole I fell down. So they'd have no particular reason to look in that place, and you'd have to search hard to find it."

"Dogs," Furio put in. "You said Luso set the dogs on you. Won't they have led him there?"

Gignomai shook his head. "There was the boar, remember? It killed one of the dogs at least. Luso's probably assumed that what led the dogs there was the boar. That's what they were bred to hunt for."

"So it could still—"

"Or it might not be," Furio said firmly. "And in any case, you're in no fit state." He hesitated for a fraction of a second, then said, "I'll go."

Gignomai shook his head. "You'll never find it," he said.

Uncle nodded vigorously. "You could draw him a map or something."

Gignomai laughed. "I'll have a hell of a job finding the place again, and I know those woods better than anybody except Luso. Furio wouldn't have a hope. Also," he added, because Uncle should have, and hadn't, "can you imagine what my family would do to him if they caught him wandering about up there? Particularly if he did manage to find the bloody thing."

The door opened, and a man Gignomai only knew by sight came in. "Salio Gullermo's downstairs," he said. "Needs to talk to you about a hundred yards of twenty-gauge wire."

Uncle swore, then stood up. "I'll get rid of him," he said, and hurried out. For a while, neither of them spoke. Then Gignomai said, "Who's that obnoxious girl?"

"What?"

"That girl," Gignomai said. "Hovering over me earlier like a buzzard. Or was I imagining things?"

"That was my cousin Teucer," Furio replied. "You didn't like her."

"No."

Furio shrugged. "What the hell are you doing here, Gig?"

"I told you." Gignomai lay back and shut his eyes. "I've had it with my family. Father's decided I'm going to train to be a lawyer, leading to a career in politics. So I left."

"What do you mean, left?"

"*Left.* I have taken my leave and do not intend to return. Ever."

"But you can't—" Furio started to say, then paused. "Well, yes, you can, I guess," he said. "Won't they come after you? Say we kidnapped you or something?"

"I considered that," Gignomai said, "but I don't think it's likely. Father will decide that by doing what I've done I've proved myself unworthy of my name. Round about now, I imagine, I'll never have existed." A small scowl crossed his face and he added, "There are precedents. It's how our family deals with things."

"Your brothers..."

Gignomai shook his head. "Stheno has other things on his mind," he said. "Luso does what Father tells him, broadly speaking."

"What about your mother?"

"What about her?"

Furio seemed lost for words for a while. Then he said, "You can do that, can you? Just get up and walk away from everything like that."

"Yes. I hope so."

"Fair enough." Furio sat still and quiet for a while, then said, "What are you planning on doing?"

Gignomai opened his eyes. "Now that," he said, "is a good question. A lot depends on whether I can get that fucking sword."

"Is it really worth...?"

"Your dad thought so."

"In that case, it's worth a lot more."

"So you told me. You've forgotten." Gignomai smiled, then pulled a face. "My nose hurts," he said.

"Teucer says it's not a bad break," Furio assured him. "It should grow back straight."

"How the hell would she know?"

"Her dad was a surgeon."

"Ah." Gignomai frowned. "So she might just possibly know what she's talking about?"

"Yes. What did she *do* to you, by the way?"

Gignomai rolled his eyes. "Call it a clash of personalities."

"She's got one, you mean."

"Unlike the met'Oc women?" Gignomai smiled, and winced again. "You may have a point." He looked at Furio a little more closely. "Don't tell me you're —"

"No."

"You're lying."

"No."

"For crying out loud, Furio," Gignomai said, grinning. "You've already got all the girls in the colony sniffing round after you. Are you after the complete set or something?"

"It's not me they're after, it's the store," Furio replied. It came out so fast that Gignomai wondered if he'd meant to say it. "And my cousin's only just got here. I've barely spoken two words to her. I didn't even know she was a girl till she walked through the door." He pulled a ferocious face, which just made Gignomai smile. "Anyway," Furio went on, "you didn't answer my question. What are you planning on doing now you've made your grand gesture?"

Two days after Gignomai left the Tabletop, Lusomai met'Oc launched a raid.

Instead of heading east after he'd crossed the river, Lusomai turned south-west following the line of the logging road. Ignoring the two small farmsteads on the plain, he led his party of sixteen horsemen over the Sow's Back and down into the long shallow

Headwater valley beyond. It was the furthest he'd ever raided, and people felt safe there.

The first farm to be attacked was the Vari home, worked by a widow and her two sons. The family were in the kitchen eating their dinner when Lusomai's men kicked down the door. They beat up all three, stole three flitches of bacon and threw a sack of rye seed on the fire. They also tried to steal the geese, but only succeeded in catching one. Lusomai shot another at close range, leaving it inedible.

He then rode a mile down the valley and attacked the Pasenna farm, killing eight sheep before trying to force his way into the house. Calo Pasenna, who had helped carry Gignomai into town after finding him by the river, had been outside splitting logs when the met'Oc arrived. He ran inside and wedged the door with a bench. Finding himself unable to break the door down, Lusomai fired a shot through it, which grazed Pasenna's wife's arm. Pasenna claimed that he heard Lusomai ordering his men to set fire to the thatch. However, no such attempt was made, and Pasenna himself referred to the met'Oc raiding party "suddenly appearing out of the darkness" when he first noticed them, implying that they weren't carrying torches or lanterns. The met'Oc left the dead sheep behind when they withdrew. They'd been cut open, so that the guts tainted the meat.

After leaving the Pasenna farm, Lusomai led his party east across the valley to attack the mill and forge at Headwater Top. Senza Ferrara, the smith, claimed to have heard the shot fired at the Pasenna house; an improbable claim, since the mill was a good two miles away, but possible if the wind happened to be from the south. He left the house with his family, the maidservant and the two hired men, climbed the hill and hid in a small copse overlooking the mill tower. Lusomai broke into the smithy, stole a considerable number of tools and cut open the bellows sack. His men then used the anvil as a battering ram to smash four blades off the mill wheel before dumping the anvil in the sump pool. They cut open and scattered six full sacks of newly ground barley flour before leaving.

While the met'Oc were engaged at Headwater Top, Calo Pasenna sent his eldest son running up the valley to warn the neighbouring farms. He reached the Spetti home first, and they evacuated. In the event, however, the met'Oc bypassed the Spetti farm and attacked the Nadi house, reaching it not long after young Pasenna arrived. Lusomai's men caught Ora Nadi, his wife, mother and three daughters and the Pasenna boy on the point of leaving. They drove them back inside. One of the met'Oc raiders recognised young Pasenna and realised what he was doing there. Lusomai had the boy beaten and hung by his feet from the rafters. He stole a side of bacon and several hams, and broke up the kitchen table with an axe. When Ora Nadi tried to stop him stealing the hams, Lusomai hit him with his sword, cutting a slice off his left ear. Before leaving, the met'Oc lit a torch from the hearth and set fire to a haystack.

This nearly proved their undoing. The trapper Filio Maza, coming home from checking his snares at the top of the valley, saw the fire and hurried down to the Nadi house to warn the family that their hay was burning and to see if he could help. He saw the met'Oc ride away, guessed that a raid was in progress, and ran back up the hill, where he had the good fortune to come across the Nadi family's horse, which had bolted when the met'Oc arrived. An accomplished horseman, Maza caught the horse and rode it bareback along the crest of the ridge (the met'Oc had followed the bottom of the valley), and made straight for Blackwater, home of the Dravi family. He told Azo Dravi what he had seen. Dravi, his four sons and their three hired men armed themselves as best they could with pitchforks and billhooks, and set off in the hay cart to intercept the met'Oc at Lower Barton, assuming—correctly, as it turned out—that Lusomai intended to raid the Sanni farm and then fall back onto the Shavecross road before leaving the valley. On the way they stopped at the Razo farm, where they were joined by the four Razo sons and their two hired men.

Lusomai stole four ducks from the Sanni family, killed a pig and threw it down the well. Then, as Nadi and the Dravis had anticipated, he headed back towards Shavecross by way of Lower Barton, where Maza and his allies were waiting for them.

What happened at Lower Barton is by no means clear. All accounts agree that the ambush was initially successful. Maza's party took the met'Oc by surprise, at least two of Lusomai's men took flight immediately, and one of the met'Oc's horses was killed, either deliberately or by impaling itself on a pitchfork in the confusion. At this point, the sequence of events is disputed. The Dravi family asserted that Lusomai was the first to draw blood. Some time after the event, however, Filio Maza stated that Azo Dravi was determined to get hold of one of Lusomai's snapping-hen pistols, as a trophy or because of its monetary value. According to Maza, it was Azo Dravi who attacked Lusomai, rather than the other way about. What is not disputed is that Dravi and Lusomai fought some form of single combat, in the course of which Lusomai was stabbed in the back (giving some credence to Maza's version, though the point is not conclusive) and Lusomai cut off Dravi's right hand with his sword.

That effectively ended the encounter. The ambushers were only concerned to get Azo Dravi to the nearest house before he bled to death. The met'Oc, apparently sobered by the escalation of violence, took one of the Razos' horses and rode straight home. It's unknown whether they had intended to make any further attacks or whether they had already done everything they had planned to do. The ambushers put Azo Dravi in the cart and took him to the Sanni house, but he was found to be dead on arrival from loss of blood.

Two days later, Dravi's severed hand was found nailed to the door of the bonded warehouse in town. A gold ring worth two thalers had been removed from the middle finger.

"Your brother must be horrible," Teucer said.

Outside, the sun was bright. A stiff breeze was nagging at the awning over the shop porch, like a bad boy pulling his baby sister's hair. Gignomai shifted in his chair. It was bad enough fighting the urge to scratch the scab on his shoulder, which was itching him to death, without Teucer as well. But Furio liked her, so he made the effort.

"We've never got on well," he said. "But he's not that bad."

"He killed that man."

Yes, Gignomai thought, he did. "I very much doubt he meant to."

"He cut off his hand."

There were rules. He was allowed to say bad things about his brother, but that privilege didn't extend to strangers. "Exactly," he said. "Look, if Luso had meant to kill him, he'd have stabbed him in the eye or heart, no messing. My guess is that he was trying to knock a weapon out of his hand, and he overdid it a bit."

"A bit."

"He believes in killing cleanly." As he said the words, he realised what they made him sound like. "He wouldn't leave an animal to bleed to death, far less a human being. Those men shouldn't have tried to fight him."

"So it's their fault."

Well, yes, he thought, like someone going swimming off a beach known to be dangerous—you can't blame the sea. "They should have had more sense than pick a fight with armed men. It wasn't even as though they were defending their homes. Luso was on his way back."

Teucer gave him what he'd come to think of as her magistrate's look. Father had one quite like it, only better, of course. "Furio says you're not like the rest of them. I'm not so sure."

"Really?" Gignomai shrugged. "You can think what you like."

She let him have a second or two more of her undiluted attention, then went back to her sewing. Gignomai picked up his book, but he'd lost interest in it long ago. He'd stolen it for Furio last year, because Furio liked books with knights and tournaments and castles and dragons. But most of the characters in it were just like his family, though the author didn't seem to have realised that, or he wouldn't have made them out to be heroes.

"So why did you leave home, then?" she asked.

He felt under no obligation to reply. Good manners were all very well, but she'd set the rules by saying nasty things about his brother.

On the other hand he was a guest here. "There wasn't anything for me to do there. So I left."

"But you people don't *do* anything anyway," she said. "Unless you count hunting and hawking and fencing and all that. And they're hobbies, not a trade."

He thought of Stheno, lifting houses on his shoulders. "Whereas you're sitting there embroidering a sampler," he said. "I consider myself duly chastened."

"I do housework," she said, "and I mend clothes. I'd do a proper job if I could. I'd have been a surgeon, like my father, except it's not allowed."

He frowned. "It isn't?"

"Of course not. Women can't be surgeons or clerks or lawyers or lecturers at Temple or merchants. There's not actually a law, but there doesn't have to be. People wouldn't stand for it."

"That's at Home," Gignomai said. "I think you'll find it's different here."

She put down her sewing. "Is it?"

Gignomai shook his head. "I'm hardly an authority," he said, "but as far as I can gather, yes, it is. Furio's aunt does all the book-keeping for the store."

"That's different. That's just *helping*."

"This store's the biggest business in the colony," Gignomai pointed out, "and Furio's aunt practically runs it."

"Yes, because she's Uncle Marzo's wife."

"She runs the store," Gignomai went on, "because someone's got to, and Marzo can't manage it all on his own. Also, she's better with figures than he is. So she does the numbers while he shifts barrels. And on the farms—"

"That's different," she interrupted. "That's peasant stuff. I'm talking about—"

"What?"

"Better-class people."

Gignomai laughed. "What's so funny?" she demanded.

"Sorry," Gignomai said. "It's you reckoning you're better than the farmers' wives. My father wouldn't see there was any difference at all."

"Your father encourages his son to go out killing and stealing."

"I'm not him," Gignomai said quietly.

"No," she said. "You left home. But I don't think it's because of what you said."

Gignomai sighed. Talking to her was like walking in a swamp. When you pulled one foot out of the mud, it made the other one sink in deeper. "All right," he said. "I left home out of high-minded disgust at my family's wickedness. Will that do?"

"That's not true," she said.

"Maybe not. But you didn't like my other answer."

She lifted her head, as though she was trying to look at the end of her nose. "You should say what you mean, not what you think people will like," she said.

He stared at her, then asked, "So why do *you* think I left?"

"Because you don't get on with your father and your brothers," she replied promptly. "And because there's nothing there to do that interests you. And because you can see it doesn't make sense."

"What doesn't?"

"Your family. Living like peasants and bandits and acting like noblemen. Doing everything on the assumption that one day soon you'll be going Home, which is never going to happen, believe me. I can see that'd get to be too much to bear after a while."

"My family—" he started to say, then stopped himself. "So what are you doing here?" he said. " I know your parents died, but surely you've got other relatives at Home. Did you choose to come here?"

"Hardly." She scowled at him. He had to admit she had a pretty scowl. "But it was here or my cousins in the country. Farmers."

"So you chose a shop instead of a farm?"

"Uncle Marzo's not just a shopkeeper, you said so yourself. He's a businessman. And this colony won't always be just a dock and a few huts. It's got an exciting future, and—"

"Who told you that?"

Furio appeared in the doorway. He hesitated for a moment, as though something wasn't quite right, then sat down on the step close to Gignomai's chair.

"Your brother—" he started to say.

"Yes." Gignomai cut him off. "Quite. Can we talk about something else, please?"

"Well, no, actually," Furio said apologetically. "At least, we don't have to talk about *him*, but there's stuff you ought to know."

Gignomai thought of the scroll of paper that Father had made him burn. "Undoubtedly," he said. "Such as?"

"Uncle was talking to Uverto and Menoa—"

"Who?"

"Big men down at the harbour," Furio replied, and Gignomai was able to translate: Company agents and beef traders. Uncle Marzo's kind of people. "They were on at him about you being here. After what happened."

Gignomai laughed. "Tell them I've got an alibi. At the time of the crime I was flat on my back with bits of stick up my nose."

"Your family's not exactly popular," Furio said carefully. "Especially right now. Uncle Marzo feels…"

"He wants me out of here."

"God, no." Furio looked mildly offended. "He's worried about keeping you safe, if you must know. The Dravi boys have been making a lot of noise, about coming into town and…Well, you can guess."

"So he wants me out of here," Gignomai said pleasantly, "for a perfectly understandable reason."

"Don't say that," Furio snapped, then immediately drooped his head, as if accepting an unspoken rebuke. "Uncle doesn't let people push him around, and the Dravi boys are all talk anyhow. They wouldn't want to pick a fight with us."

Gignomai wasn't so sure about that. Whatever else the Dravis had shown themselves to be, they had to be brave men to attack Luso and his riders with farm tools. "So?" he said.

"Basically, he reckons you should stay indoors and not go outside. Probably best not to sit out here, even. If the Dravis or the Razos do come into town, they wouldn't come bursting into our house, or the store. But—well, you're pretty visible out here."

"I enjoy the fresh air," Gignomai said.

Furio shrugged. "I'm telling you what Uncle said. He's concerned."

Gignomai asked, "Why?"

Furio hesitated; then he grinned and said, "Well, I think he's still entertaining longing thoughts about your twenty-thousand-thaler sword. You know, ten per cent on twenty thousand is more money than he'll ever make selling hoe blades to farmers. But to be fair, there's a bit more to him than that. For one thing, he'd take it as a personal insult if anything happened to a guest under his roof." He shrugged, then added, "And he'd want to do his best for you because you're my friend, and he's sort of keen to be nice to me, because of Dad leaving the store to him, not me. I think he feels bad about that."

And so he should, Gignomai thought, but Furio had never seemed worried about it. Then again, Marzo had no children of his own, so the store would be Furio's eventually. "He doesn't need to get in a state about it," Gignomai said—it came out rather more unkindly than he'd meant it to. "Soon as I'm on my feet again, I'm off."

Furio looked furtively round (it was quite comical to watch), then lowered his voice. "You're still set on going back after that bloody sword."

Gignomai nodded. "And then your uncle can sell it for me, and I'll be on the next ship Home. New name, new life, money in my pocket. I can't wait, to be honest with you."

Furio looked like he had toothache. "Any ideas about what you're going to do there?"

"Haven't decided," Gignomai said. "I suppose I could buy a farm; after all, it's something I know a bit about. But I must admit, I quite fancy the idea of a factory—making things and selling them. I think I might be good at it."

"A factory," Furio repeated, as if saying the name of some magical beast. "You don't know the first thing about—"

"True," Gignomai said. "Or about buying and selling, come to that. Still, it can't be all that difficult or ordinary people wouldn't be able to do it."

A ship came in. Gignomai, who'd never seen a ship, went down to the dock to see it. Uncle Marzo got quite upset when he said he was going. There would be a great many people, Marzo said, and it wouldn't be safe. Gignomai smiled at him and said, on the contrary, it'd be as safe as a stroll in the woods. Uncle Marzo made a despairing noise and said Gignomai had better go with him; he had business to see to. Furio thought he'd given in rather too easily, and then remembered the sword. Never too early to start sounding out possible buyers.

So Furio stayed at home and minded the store. There was absolutely nothing unusual about that, but for some reason he felt resentful; he could only imagine it was because Gignomai was going and he wasn't, and of course that was a stupid thing to get upset about. Recognition of his own presumed stupidity just made him surlier, and he was quite rude to a woman who came in for a dozen pins, though luckily she was deaf and didn't actually hear what he said.

He'd been on his own for about an hour when Teucer came in. She sat down on the chair next to the stove and produced her sampler.

"I'd be better off on the porch," she said. "The light's not too good in here."

Furio shrugged. He didn't want her to go out onto the porch. "You'd do better next to the window. I'll move the chair for you if you like."

She moved the chair herself without comment, sat down again and tried to thread a needle. Furio tried not to watch her. He had an idea her eyesight wasn't anything special, close up. She was certainly patient. She tried and failed for several minutes, until Furio couldn't stand it any longer.

"Could I try?" he said.

"If you like," she said.

Furio was quite good at threading needles. His mother had always got him to do it for her. She had good eyesight, but there had been something wrong with the feeling in her fingertips due to an accident, years ago. Furio took a pair of small scissors from the counter and snipped the end off the thread, where her efforts had left it crushed and mangled. He cut it at an angle, not straight, to leave a sharp point. The needle was exceptionally fine and small. He guessed she'd brought it from Home, because it was much better than anything they sold in the store. He tried twice and failed, and felt a quite unreasonable surge of anger building up. Still, he wasn't beaten yet. He put the end of the thread in his mouth and sucked it.

"Yuck," Teucer said. "That's disgusting."

Furio looked at her. "It's what everybody does."

"Not where I come from," Teucer said firmly. "At Home, we use a little chunk of beeswax. You pull the thread across it, and it makes the thread easier to draw."

Furio was now resolved the thread the damn needle or die trying. Luckily, he managed it on his fourth try. "There you go," he said, handed it back and waited a moment for the customary word of thanks, which didn't come. He crossed the room and straightened up a row of chisels.

"So Gignomai's leaving," she said.

He remembered; she'd been on the porch. "So he says."

"You'll be upset about that."

He didn't answer, concentrating instead on getting the chisels exactly equally spaced on the shelf.

"I like him," she said, "but he's very arrogant."

Furio turned round and looked at her. "No he's not."

"Oh he *is*," she said. "Thinks he's so much better than us."

"Maybe he's right."

He'd said it to annoy her. He thought about it, nevertheless.

"Really?" Teucer said. "Well, you know him better than I do, but I can't see anything special. What's he done that's so marvellous?"

The five-eighths skew and the quarter bevel were in the wrong places. He switched them round. "Leaving home, for a start," he said.

"What's so good about that?"

"Think what he's leaving behind," Furio said.

"You said it yourself: they live like peasants up there. Anyway, I left home."

"You didn't have any choice."

"No," she replied. "That's why I'm here."

Gig's leaving, Furio thought, and she's here to stay. The wrong way round, like the chisels. "I'm so sorry," he said. "Looks like you'll just have to put up with it."

"Gignomai thinks I should learn to be a proper surgeon," she said, "like my father was."

"Does he?"

She nodded. "He says it's different here, not like Home. He says there's no reason a woman shouldn't be a surgeon or a clerk or a trader even. People wouldn't stand for it at Home because they're set in their ways, but it's not the same here. There's so few people who can do anything useful, it wouldn't matter if I was a woman if I could set bones and sew up wounds and stuff."

"Maybe he's right," Furio said.

"Of course, I'd need to read the right books," she went on. "I've got three of Father's books. The rest had to be sold, but I took the most important ones out of the box when nobody was looking. And I know a lot of it already just from watching."

Furio noticed a spot of rust on the seven-eighths bevel. He scratched it off with his fingernail. "But you've never actually done any of it."

"Father let me sew up the wounds sometimes," she said. "He said I did a neater job than he did."

"You don't mind the blood, then."

"No." She shook her head to reinforce the denial. "Really, it's no worse than the stuff in a kitchen. It's all meat, isn't it?"

"I think you'd have a job convincing people you're up to it," Furio said.

"Oh, I don't know. If your uncle hadn't been there when they brought Gignomai in, I'd have coped. And I don't think anyone would've stopped me when they saw I knew what I was doing. And once I've saved one man, word'll get about. Anyway, who do people go to when they cut themselves on the farms? Their mothers, or their wives."

"It's different on the farms."

"Not really."

Furio couldn't remember when he'd felt so strongly about wanting to be somewhere else. "Well, if that's what you want to do, good luck to you," he said. "Talk to my uncle; maybe he could send Home for the books you want. I'm sure he'd be on your side, if you share your fees with him."

Teucer didn't have to wait long for her chance to shine. Uncle Marzo had told Furio to unload a consignment of dry goods that had come on the ship. The carter had backed his wagon up to the side door, then mumbled something about seeing the smith to get his horses shod and disappeared, leaving Furio to wrestle with a wagon-load of enormous barrels. They were far too heavy to lift. Furio opened the tailgate and leaned a couple of strong planks on the wagon bed, then proceeded to dance a slow, ungainly dance with each barrel, tipping, rocking and edging it to the back of the wagon, tripping it over on its side and letting it roll down the planks. Gignomai made a half-hearted offer of help while doing his best to look frail and ill. Teucer just stood and watched, confident in the immunity of being a girl.

"Most extraordinary thing I ever saw," Gignomai was saying. "Big as a house, absolutely crammed full of stuff. I can't see why it doesn't just sink under all the weight. You'd have to be off your head to go out on one of those on all that water."

Furio paused to snatch a little breath. "It's a doddle of a run from here to Home," he said. "One day of open sea then you're hugging the coast, so most of the time you're just a gentle swim from land."

"I can't swim," Gignomai said.

"Can't you?" No reason, of course, why he should. Nothing to swim in up there on the Tabletop.

"Can't say it's ever bothered me," Gignomai went on. "But it'd be a different matter if I had to go on one of those things."

"You'll have to," Furio replied, squaring up against a barrel and heaving. "If you want to go Home. It's one instance where walking isn't an option."

"What you could do with," Gignomai observed, "is a long bit of wood you could use as a lever. In Chrysodorus' *Mirror of Algebra* there's a whole chapter about levers. Theoretically, if you could find a long enough lever and a big enough rock to lean on, you could move this whole island."

Furio scowled at him. Leaning up against one of the sheds were four ten-foot lengths of rafter, but he'd been too idle to go and fetch them, and had been regretting it ever since. "More trouble than it's worth," he replied briskly. "I just need to get my weight behind it."

He shoved a little harder than he'd intended. The barrel toppled prematurely onto its side and rolled awkwardly, sweeping away the planks. It dropped off the cart and smashed open, spilling out straw, sawdust and about a hundred shiny new spoons.

"You're probably right," Gignomai said, straight-faced. "Well, you obviously know what you're doing. I'll shut up and let you get on with it."

Furio hopped down from the wagon, grappled the smashed barrel upright, and started gathering spoons. When he'd rounded up all the fugitives, he tried to jump back onto the wagon. Somehow, he didn't quite make it. For a moment he hung in the air, as if he'd contrived to learn the secret of levitation. Then he fell backwards, landing in a tangle of limbs.

Gignomai had drawn a lungful of air to laugh with, but there was something wrong. A bright red stain was soaking through the cloth of Furio's left sleeve.

"Furio," Gignomai said, "I think you've cut your arm."

"What?" Furio looked over his shoulder and swore. He'd caught his forearm on the jagged edge of a broken barrel-stave. Blood was spreading fast, like light in the sky at midsummer dawn. He stared at it, trying to figure out what it meant.

"Let me see that." Teucer had suddenly come to life. She practically sprang at him, like a cat, dragged the sodden cloth away and studied the wound with every sign of total satisfaction.

"That's a very deep cut," she said. "Let's get you inside."

Furio looked at Gignomai, who shrugged, then allowed himself to be bustled into the store. "Gignomai," Teucer ordered, "get a bowl of water and a clean cloth."

Gignomai had no idea where a cloth might be, but he wasn't about to admit ignorance. He grabbed a large enamel soup plate from a display in the front of the store and darted into the back room, where he was fairly sure he'd find a pitcher of water. He found the pitcher, but it was empty, so he scurried out through the back door and filled the pitcher from the pump in the stable yard. That just left a cloth. He went into the back room and looked round, but the closest thing he could see was a roll of linen shirt fabric. The hell with it, he thought, and butchered a generous square out of the roll with his pocketknife.

"Where have you *been*?" Teucer had got Furio lying on the long table in the main store, where they'd put Gignomai when they'd brought him in. Furio shot him a sort of scared-resigned look. His sleeve was rolled up, displaying a long, ragged gash.

"I'll need alcohol," Teucer said. "Brandy, something like that."

It took Gignomai a moment to realise that was an order. Luckily, Furio called out, "Back room, third shelf, small wooden box with the key to the cellar in it."

The way down to the cellar was through a trapdoor in the back-room floor. It was, of course, dark down there, so he had to go back, find a lantern, find a tinderbox, reload it with dry moss, light the lantern. He could feel time passing, and for all he knew Furio was bleeding to death.

There turned out to be a whole row of brandy bottles, some clean, some very dusty. He assumed the dusty ones were for Uncle Marzo's own use, and grabbed a clean one.

He was quite relieved to find Furio was still alive. Teucer glanced at the bottle and said, "Well, open it, then."

Should've thought of that himself. It was closed with a cork and wax. He broke the wax off with his thumbnail. "Corkscrew," he pleaded.

"Box of them under the front window," Furio said.

"And I'll need a small dish," Teucer called out.

He found one, and fetched it and the bottle over to Teucer, who gave him a soul-shrivelling sort of look, and poured brandy into the dish. "Alcohol cleans metal," she explained, though more, he was sure, to show off her own knowledge than to save him from perplexity. There was a tinkling noise as something small dropped into the dish.

"Now then." Teucer turned to Furio. "This is going to hurt a *lot*, but I need you to keep perfectly still, or you'll make me mess it up."

No pressure, Gignomai thought. "What are you going—?"

"Shh." Teucer picked something out of the dish and held it at arm's length, in the direction of the window, where the light was coming from. "I'm no good at this. Gignomai, you'll have to thread it for me."

She waited for him to obey, then turned to look at him. He was standing perfectly still. His mouth was open, and his eyes were very wide. "Gignomai?"

He tried to speak, but something wasn't working properly. Teucer made a brisk, disapproving noise. "Oh come *on*," she said, "don't go all squeamish on me. A grown man like you, getting all stupid over a silly little needle."

Gignomai shook his head.

"Gig?" Furio said. He'd seen something in his friend's face, though he didn't understand it. "Are you all right?"

Teucer gave breath to a long, carefully fashioned sigh. "Men," she said. "All right, I'll have to do it." She dipped the end of the thread in the brandy, tweaked it into a point and triumphantly threaded the needle at her first attempt.

"Gig?" Furio said.

"Quiet," Teucer ordered. "Now, perfectly still." She leaned forward, the needle pinched between right thumb and forefinger, her left hand gently pressing together the lips of the wound. With a slow, even pressure, she pressed the needle point against Furio's skin.

Gignomai sprang forward, grabbed her right hand, lifted it up high, cupped her face in his open right palm and shoved her hard away from the table. She staggered, tripped and fell. Gignomai stared at her for a moment as Furio tried to grab his shoulder with his uninjured arm. Gignomai dodged, looked Furio in the face, then ran out of the store into the street.

He came back two hours later. Furio was waiting for him on the porch, his arm neatly bandaged.

"Don't ask," Gignomai said.

"Don't you tell me—"

"Don't ask," Gignomai repeated. He tried to walk past, but Furio shot out a leg to block him. "I'm leaving now. Thanks for everything. Tell Teucer I'm sorry."

"Gig, what the hell?"

Gignomai stepped over the outstretched leg and went indoors. He came out a little later holding his coat.

"You're leaving," Furio said.

"Yes."

"Gig..."

"Goodbye."

Furio watched him walk away. He didn't understand. He knew he'd just witnessed something important, but he had no idea what it could possibly be. Gignomai turned left at the corner and vanished behind the livery building. Gone, just like that.

Of course, he could run after him.

Teucer was standing in the doorway. "He's gone, then."

Furio nodded. "What the hell was all that about?"

"I don't know. Is he coming back?"

"He didn't say." Furio thought about it. "I'd be inclined to doubt it."

"Where's he going? Back to his family?"

Furio shrugged. "I wouldn't have thought so. But then, I wouldn't have thought he'd go storming off like that." He turned to look at her. "What did we *do*?"

"No idea."

He was caught. He'd seen something in her face, even though it was closed, drawn in, formal. *Oh,* he thought. Another surprise. "I didn't think you liked him," he said.

"I don't, much," she replied. "He's arrogant and self-centred. I don't think he likes me very much."

"But," Furio said.

"Yes." She sighed, as if it was something tiresome, like the milk boiling over. "I'm not sure that whether you *like* someone's got very much to do with it." She sat down quickly, as if the chair was about to be snatched away. "I think it was what he said, about how I could be a surgeon if I wanted to. As if that was an obvious thing. It hadn't crossed my mind before he said it. I'd always assumed it wouldn't be possible."

Furio turned his head and stared at the corner of the livery building, as though there was a door there through which you could go and be in the past or the future. "I guess Gignomai feels the need to believe that you don't have to carry on being what you are or what people want you to be."

She nodded. "Do you think he'll go home?"

"Probably. He's got no money, so he can't get a ride on a ship. That leaves him two choices, really: here or there. He's left here."

"I didn't do *anything*," Teucer protested with sudden fury. "You cut yourself, I stitched it up. He *said* I should be surgeon. It doesn't make any sense."

"He'll be back," Furio said. "He can't go home, and I really don't see him sleeping in haylofts." He looked at her again. She turned away. "Should I go after him?"

"That'd just make things worse," she replied. "He'll be back."

Gignomai didn't slow down until he'd passed the Watchtower, and only came to a stop when he reached the small brook that ran down from town to join the Blackwater. Once he'd stopped, he found it impossible to move.

For a long time, there was too much noise inside his head. He waited for it to die down, as he knew it would. Ah well, he thought.

It would have been nice to go Home, to get away from everything he'd grown up with, to live in a place where everybody was a stranger. He'd amused himself with the fantasy of choosing a new name for himself, as though a name was something you could put on and take off like a coat. It would've been possible with his share of the sword money.

The trouble with running away is that, no matter where you go, you have to take yourself with you. He couldn't remember who'd said that. It was either a quotation or something Luso had said, in an unrelated context, meant as a joke. He hadn't meant to scare Furio and Teucer like that. Not their fault. They weren't to know.

He looked up at the sun. Mid-afternoon, just for the record. At this time on this day in this place, I realised that I have to face up to my responsibilities. That reminded him of how he'd killed the wolf, and he frowned.

Forget all about Home, he told himself. He'd do what he had to. But this time, he'd think it through first.

It felt very strange, walking up to the Gate openly without any attempt at concealment. He could feel the arrows pointing at him long before he saw anyone.

"Hello?" he called out.

After a while, one of Luso's men came out from behind a tree. He was staring.

"Yes," said Gignomai, "it's me. Would you mind pointing that thing somewhere else?"

The guard lowered his crossbow and lifted the bolt out of the clip. Two more guards appeared on either side of him. Turning back was no longer an option.

"Come on, then," Gignomai said. "One of you's enough. Besides, standing orders say a minimum of two on guard."

But all three came with him, keeping a two-yard distance, as though he was contagious or something. They marched him to the front door of the house and told him to wait there. It was strange, being made to wait outside his own door like a tradesman.

Luso came out in a sudden explosion of movement like a boar breaking cover. For a moment Gignomai was sure Luso was going to hit him, and made the decision to stand and take it rather than try and dodge out of the way. But Luso came to a full stop an arm's length away, and all the momentum seemed to drain out of him. That was an impressive thing to see.

"You're back, then," Luso said.

Gignomai shrugged. "Looks like it."

Luso wasn't scowling or frowning or trying to look scary. He was examining him with the keen attention Gignomai had seen Aurelio the smith give to the white-hot steel, listening for it to be ready to weld. "I think I'll let Father deal with you," he said. "Come on."

Luso let him pass, then followed him up the stairs. "It's all right," Gignomai said. "I know the way." No reply. After twenty years of trying to bait Luso, he should've known better than to try.

He stopped outside the double doors of the library. "Luso."

"What?"

"There was a boar," Gignomai said. "I spooked it and it went for me. You know it's true, because it killed your dog. Right?"

Luso had a way of putting his head slightly on one side when he was interested. "So?"

"The boar was on to me. I ran. Next thing I knew, I'd blundered over the edge."

"You fell all the way?"

"Yes." Gignomai nodded vehemently. "Broken nose, cracked rib, a lot of scrapes and bruises, but that was all. I got away with it. Amazing, don't you think?"

Luso nodded slowly. "Go on."

"Some people from the town found me. They took me to Furio's uncle's place." He hesitated. "They knew we used to be friends. Anyhow, they patched me up. I'd have come back earlier, but they said I wasn't well enough."

Luso studied him, as though he was a tangle of rope and he was looking for an end. "In you go," he said, and reached past Gignomai to open the doors.

Father was at his desk, reading. He was wearing his eyeglasses. They were extraordinary things: two glass discs held together by a frame of gold wire. If you looked through them the letters on the page grew enormous. They were a great rarity even back Home. These days, Father had some trouble reading, but he only wore the eyeglasses when he absolutely had to. He looked up, over the rims of the glass discs.

Gignomai felt a firm pressure between his shoulders, and just managed not to trip over his feet as he was moved forward. He heard the doors close behind him.

"Gignomai," Father said, "you're late."

For a moment, Gignomai didn't understand. Then: Father had ordered him to present himself here to begin his studies, just before he ran away. He hadn't turned up. Therefore, he was late.

"I'm sorry," he said. "I had an accident."

"Most unfortunate. Sit down. The books you will be reading are on the small table."

Gignomai saw them, but he was looking past the table, towards the corner of the room. If the sword had been found, it would be there, leaning against the wall; that was what Father would do. Not there. He kept his face straight, crossed to the table and sat down.

"Your mother was worried about you." Father's head was bent over the book.

"I'm sorry. I fell off the—"

"Please be more considerate in future."

Gignomai took a book off the top of the pile, glanced at the spine (*Caecilius on Prosody*) and opened it. It began with a beautiful illuminated letter B and went downhill from there.

He ran into his mother on the way from the library to the Great Hall. She gave him a filthy look and walked past him without saying anything. He decided it could have been worse.

At dinner, conversation was even sparser than usual. Luso kept looking at him. Father looked over the top of his head from time to time. Mother huddled over her food and didn't look up. Stheno looked past him, the way you carefully fail to notice someone with a ghastly disfigurement. Dinner was roast wild duck. Gignomai got the bit where the bullet had passed through, smashing bones and pulping flesh.

After dinner, he announced that he was tired and was going to bed. Nobody looked up, and he walked out of the hall. Stheno, who'd gone out to check on the calves, was hovering by the stairs, evidently waiting for him. Gignomai stopped.

"Why did you come back?" Stheno asked.

Not *why did you leave.* "I fell off the edge of the world," Gignomai replied.

"Gig..."

"Seriously," Gignomai said. "I was in the woods, out on the west side. This boar jumped out at me—"

"I heard all that," Stheno cut him off (so Luso did talk to his brother sometimes). "But you weren't in the woods because you felt like a stroll."

"Well, yes, actually," Gignomai said. "That's why I was—"

"Right." Stheno made a slight movement, a small shift of the shoulders. If Luso had done that, Gignomai would have sidestepped. "And for a stroll in the woods, you took your sword."

Rather like the moment when you're stalking a deer, and it suddenly lifts its head and stares straight at you, you freeze, and everything hangs in the balance.

"It wasn't in your room," Stheno said. "When we realised you were missing, I went to see if you'd taken anything with you."

Gignomai nodded slowly. "You told Luso."

"No. Nor Father."

It occurred to Gignomai to ask why, but he decided not to. He kept perfectly still, closed, not saying anything. The met'Oc family, he reckoned, were probably better at not saying anything than anyone else in the world.

"So," Stheno said, "why'd you come back?"

"I live here."

Once, many years ago, Luso and Stheno went through a phase of playing chess. It lasted about three months, and for the first six weeks, Luso won every game, quickly and often cruelly. Then—it surprised Gignomai even now to think about it—Stheno figured out how to turn a losing game into a stalemate. For the next four weeks, he still didn't win, but he somehow contrived to draw one game in five. Then, quite suddenly, he won everything, and eventually Luso gave up and went back to playing against Father instead. Over the years, Gignomai had often tried to analyse Stheno's strategy and had never managed to pin it down. Quite a large part of it was making moves so totally illogical that Luso couldn't cope with them, but there was also a thread of tactical skill that went so deep Gignomai couldn't trace it; he only knew that it was there.

"That's not an answer," Stheno said.

"Would you rather I hadn't come back?"

Stheno ignored that. "All right," he said, "I'll try guessing. You fell out with your town friends, or they didn't want you hanging round."

"Yes, that's right."

Stheno nodded, as if to indicate that the interview was over. Gigno-mai turned away, and Stheno's hand swooped down on his shoulder like a hawk. It was so much bigger than any human hand had any right to be, and so very strong. Gignomai felt his back pressing hard against the wall. He could only breathe in part of the way; not far enough.

"Other people," Stheno said quietly, "have to live in this house too. Sometimes it's not easy, but generally I manage to cope. But it's hard enough as it is without you pulling stunts like that. Do you understand?"

He'd have said anything to get the hand off his shoulder before he choked to death. "Yes, I understand. I'm sorry."

Stheno held him just a little longer; just a little too long. Then he let go, and all Gignomai could think about was breathing. "I can see why you did it," Stheno said, not at all unkindly. "In your shoes, probably I'd have done the same. But you don't have that luxury. Right?"

"Right."

Stheno nodded. A curt nod that said, quarrel over, let's not bother with grudges. "Glad you're back," he said. "I was worried."

"Stheno?"

"Yes?"

"The sword," Gignomai said. "I lost it, in the woods. Really."

Stheno frowned. "I suggest you find it," he said, "else, Father'll kill you."

"That's what I was thinking."

"All right," Stheno said. "Tomorrow morning you go and do your studying. Soon as I've seen to the pigs I'll come up and borrow you. Urgent job — I'll think of something. You can have the rest of the morning. All right?"

"Yes," Gignomai said. "Thanks."

"A quiet life," Stheno replied. "You wouldn't think it was a lot to ask."

Luso woke him up quite some time before daybreak. At least, he woke up and saw Luso sitting on the end of his bed. It was too dark to see his face clearly, but nobody else sat motionless quite like that.

"Just wanted to make sure you're still here," Luso said. Then he got up and left, leaving the door open. Luso never closed doors behind him.

Not enough night left to make it worth trying to go back to sleep, so Gignomai got up, dressed and lit the candle. He'd intended to read (he'd smuggled *Gannasius on Ethical Theory* out of the library under his shirt; it had been on the pile of compulsory reading, but he'd found it interesting) but he couldn't keep still. He opened the window, leaned out and looked up at the sky. Too late, but not early enough.

So he pulled on his boots and went quietly down the stairs — long practice — and out into the back yard. Aurelio the smith was opening up the forge. He always started early, because it took a long time to lay in the fire and get it going properly. Gignomai didn't feel like being seen, but that wasn't a problem. He'd long ago worked out a sequence of doorways and edges that would keep him concealed in half light.

He made it easily to the barn, slipped inside and climbed up into the hayloft. It was well known as one of his places, so there was no point staying there too long. What they hadn't realised, as far as he knew, was that there was a loose stone in the back wall, a hand's span from the floor, which you could tease out with your fingernails if you were careful and patient.

He took out the stone and felt inside the cavity. The glove was still there. He'd very nearly taken it with him when he made his escape attempt; just as well he hadn't, or it'd be in the pillowcase, along with the rest of his stuff. The sword was one thing — failing to find it simply wasn't an option — but he was more or less resigned to the pillowcase being lost and gone for ever. In which case...

He put the stone back, then ran his fingertips all round it to make sure it was flush to the rest of the wall. For four months of the year, of course, it was completely inaccessible, buried deep under the winter hay, like one of those underwater cities in fairy tales.

The other thing he'd come for was lying on the floor where he'd last seen it, weeks ago. It was the broken-off head of a push-hoe, which at some time had been ground on a wheel to make it narrower (for weeding between rows of turnips, at a guess). He found it by feel, wrapped a scrap of sacking round the splintered handle end and stowed it in his right-hand coat pocket.

He stayed until the sky was light enough for him to make out the shape of the hill behind the house, then went back to his room and read three pages of Gannadius on altruism. He hid the book under a loose floorboard (force of habit; they'd found that one two years ago) and went down to breakfast.

He'd timed it well. Stheno had already been and gone. Luso hadn't surfaced yet. Father was at the head of the long, broad oak table, sitting with his head bowed over a book like a falcon ripping apart its prey. Mother was at the other end of the table, looking out of the window, her lips moving silently. Two of Luso's men were huddled in the middle somewhere, uncomfortable, eating quickly. Gignomai chose a wide open space about a third of the way down towards Father's end, close to the loaf and the wizened knob-end of a side of bacon. He hacked off slightly more than he wanted and chewed hard.

As he got up, Father took official notice of him, though without looking up from his book. "Don't be late," he said. Gignomai made a sort of respectful, non-verbal grunting noise, and went straight up to the library.

He knew he didn't have long. Fortunately, he knew where to look for what he wanted: *Lycoris on Metallurgy, Callicrates on Mechanisms, Onesander on the Practical Arts*. The dust was reassuringly thick; nobody had disturbed them since he'd last been there. No reason why they should. He slipped Lycoris in his left-hand jacket pocket, and wedged Callicrates and Onesander in the waistband of his trousers, drawing his shirt tail out to cover them. Then he sat down in front of his pile of approved reading, opened *Caecilius on Prosody*, and tried to look like someone who gave a damn about the position of the caesura in dactylic hexameters.

Father duly appeared, took his seat without looking in Gignomai's direction, put down the book he'd been reading at breakfast, picked up another, lying open and face down on the desk. Gignomai couldn't help glancing at him from time to time. All those words, he thought, all that information; it was like pouring water into sand. It all went in, through the eyes into the brain, and none of it ever came out again. Father's head was a slurry-pit into which the sum of human knowledge and experience drained away, and all that richness, too much of it, poisoned the ground so that nothing would grow there ever again. He shuddered slightly.

Stheno was as good as his word. He appeared in the doorway, looking ridiculously large, like a man in a doll's house. Father frowned, then looked up.

"Sorry," Stheno said (he always started any conversation with Father with an apology), "but could I borrow Gig for an hour or so? The weaners have got out in the kale."

Father sighed, nodded, his head dipped back to its usual incline (you could almost hear a click as it locked back into place). Gignomai jumped up, pressing his left elbow hard against his waist to trap the two books, and scuttled out of the room. As soon as the doors had closed behind him, he mouthed, "Thanks."

Stheno shrugged, and led the way down the stairs. As soon as they were outside, he said, "You're with me. The pigs really are out."

"Are they?"

Stheno nodded. "Turned them out myself. You don't imagine Father wouldn't check."

It hadn't occurred to Gignomai, but when Stheno said it, he realised it was true. How Father came to know everything, when he was never to be seen talking to servants, was a mystery that didn't bear too much thinking about. When Gignomai was a boy, he'd had a theory that Father had a magical raven who spied on the family and reported to him in the middle of the night.

Getting the pigs back in wasn't a problem, since Stheno had trained them to come running as soon as he appeared with the slop bucket. Gignomai winced when he saw how much damage they'd done in the kale patch, but Stheno didn't say anything. They put back the hurdle Stheno had taken down, and lashed it fast with twine.

"Right," Stheno said. "It'll all be my fault, so be quick."

For a moment Gignomai was tempted to feel guilty, but that was a luxury he couldn't afford. "Thanks," he said, and darted off across the yard.

There was no point getting Stheno in more trouble than necessary, so he applied the usual breaking-out protocols: close to the hedge all the way down the long meadow, through the gap at the bottom, then follow the dead ground at the foot of the wood until he got to the hunting gate and could assume he was invisible. The big danger was that he didn't know what Luso's movements were likely to be. As far as he knew it wasn't a hunting day, but Luso was perfectly capable of declaring an unscheduled day, or simply strolling out to the woods on his own with a gun and a couple of dogs. Gignomai therefore had no alternative but to consider the woods as hostile territory and proceed accordingly.

He headed generally west, keeping parallel to the main ride, which he was fairly sure Luso would follow if he was headed this way. As soon as he reached the first stream he cut away due south until he came to the deep, wet hollow where Luso had a high seat. From there he followed a stream which he knew came out on the western edge, about five hundred yards below the place where he'd met the boar. About a third of the way down the stream he heard a shot. It reassured him. It was a long way north and east, which suggested that Luso was out still-hunting for deer in the clearing by the old charcoal camp. That meant he'd be alone, so his men would be on guard at the Gate or back at the farm but not prowling about at random.

He found what he'd been looking for, a briar tangle between two fallen trees. He found the slots of the boar, very faint and eroded but still visible in a slick of dried mud. The dog's body was nowhere to be seen (or smelt, for that matter), so Luso's men had been here. It occurred to him, for the first time, that one of them might have found the sword and decided to keep it for himself. He considered the possibility and dismissed it. There might be someone somewhere brave and stupid enough to steal from the met'Oc family right under Luso's nose. By the same token somewhere there might just possibly be dragons, unicorns and similar mythical beasts, but he was pretty sure he'd never encounter one, and most certainly not here.

He found the boar's nest, and the entrance to the hole, eventually. Thinking about it, he reckoned that the boar must've been pushed back here by Luso's dogs and had stood at bay in the hole mouth, wedging its backside into the hole as far as it could go. That would account for the briars being broken down and tangled, filling the hole up and making it invisible unless you knew exactly what you were looking for. After a long, frantic search, in the course of which he lacerated his hands and arms on the briars, he found the sword, jammed down in the roots of the tangle and masked by a swathe of broken tendrils. By the look of it, the boar had rolled there. He fished it out, drew it and examined the blade. It was still straight, and the furniture was no more bent and buckled than it had been.

Gignomai sat down in the briars, not caring about his clothes or his skin, with the sword on his knees, and closed his eyes. He was exhausted, far more so than his exertions warranted. One thing, one artefact, but everything depended on it; it had been lost, and now he'd found it again. He guessed that was how it must feel when you're condemned to death, and the reprieve arrives a few minutes before dawn. He didn't bother even trying to move for quite some time. He watched blood from a scratch on his forehead trickle, out of focus, down the inside curve of his nose and drop out of his field of vision.

When at last he was strong enough to move, he got up (everything ached) and poked around for a while looking for the pillowcase. There were many good reasons for finding it: left lying about it was a serious breach of security and, besides, he didn't want to lose the scarf. In spite of all that, he couldn't summon up the energy. He told himself that if he couldn't find it, neither could anybody else. As for the scarf, well, there was precious little chance of him forgetting, so he didn't need a bit of cloth to remind him. Another shot in the distance made him look up sharply. Then he grinned. A second shot implied that the first one had been a miss. Luso did miss sometimes.

Enough dawdling for one day. He sheathed the sword, then teased the hoe-head out of his pocket, unwrapped it and used the scrap of cloth to bind up the sword-hilt. He lay down on his stomach and peered into the hole. He really didn't fancy going in there, not in cold blood, but it had to be done. He clamped the sword to his side with his left hand, reached out with his right holding the hoe, and crawled into the hole.

His eyes were open but there was, of course, no light. He felt the gentlest of touches right across his face—a spider's web he rationalised—and closed his mouth as he felt the spider running across his cheek. He wasn't good with spiders at the best of times, but he didn't have a hand free. It made his skin itch and crawl, and he couldn't be sure whether it had gone or was still there.

He moved himself by digging in with the hoe-head and pulling, keeping himself from sliding forward when the gradient was steep, drawing himself along when it was more or less level. When he reached the point where the tunnel suddenly fell away, his whole weight was thrown on the steel head of the tool. It wouldn't dig in, but it slowed him down a little, enough to stop him slithering out of control. Grit and small stones stripped the skin off the heel of his right hand, and his wrist burned with the strain of supporting his entire weight. It occurred to him that maybe he hadn't thought this operation through with sufficient attention to detail.

Then he was at the blockage. He'd thought about it many times, remembered what it had felt like when he'd squeezed himself against it. It was either a tree root (though unlikely this far down) or just a big stone. Now, here he was again. He tried exploring it with his fingertips, but in order to do it properly he'd have to let go of the hoe-head, which he didn't dare risk. When he was sure he'd come to a full stop he began twisting himself round, like a screw driven into oak without a pilot hole, until he was on his back. With the hoe he probed the darkness ahead of him, until he found a place that wasn't the blockage—stiff hard clay or chalk or something—but he could just about force the blade into it. He forced it in as far as it would go, twisted it, felt something give, levered out a chunk of something—a small wedge, presumably, but a start.

He told himself, Nothing in the world matters more to me, right now, than gouging out this hole. I must do it carefully, properly, I must not hurry, I must not just do half a job, I must not give up or panic or think about anything else. There's no rush. I have all the time in the world, and every bit of crumbly stuff I can dislodge is another bit done. I must not panic. I mustn't think about graves or the jaws of animals or any of that nonsense. There's nothing in the world except the job in hand.

He relaxed, making a point of feeling every muscle and tendon at rest, apart from his right hand on the hoe-head. He knew terror was only a breath or two away—not like the first time, when he'd been dead already and there was no hope. This time, though he'd be just as dead if he got stuck, he had the terrifying knowledge that getting through was possible, that there was a way out a few yards ahead if he could get there, and he wasn't just finding activities to keep himself occupied and take his mind off things. He knew from that experience that he could handle despair. Hope was a far more dangerous condition.

To pass the time he recited poetry: the first twenty lines of *Alphis and Eurymedon* (he despised Substantivist epic, but the relentless tumpty-tum metre had jammed it in his head when he was nine), over and over again until the words lost any vestige of meaning. He sang *"La doca votz"* and *"Can l'herba fresc,"* but his voice echoed in the tunnel, and maybe Luso was out looking for him by now. He recited the seven, eight and nine times tables, and couldn't remember what eight nines were. He summarised what he'd learned about dactylic hexameters, and tried to embody it in classical hexametric verse.

The blisters at the base of his middle and index fingers had burst, making the hoe-head almost too slippery to hold. He recited all he could remember of the met'Oc family tree. He counted backwards from five hundred.

He stopped digging. He had no way of knowing how much he'd managed to scoop out, how big the hole was, whether it was big enough. He knew there was a serious risk of getting irrevocably stuck if the hole was too small, or if he'd contrived to divert himself into another undetected blockage. The decision to go ahead was entirely arbitrary, which bothered him, but his right hand was now so cramped that he couldn't use it any more. He could lie there still and quiet for an hour or so and see if it got better, or he could go now. Life and death decision. I'll go now, he thought. I've had enough of this.

There was a bad moment when his shoulder came up against something that wouldn't shift, almost certainly a big stone. He had no purchase for wriggling back, and the original blockage was now level with his left hip, so turning round was out of the question. He twisted until he was lying on his left side, his right shoulder slightly compressed. He felt the tip of his nose (still painful to the touch) brushing the original obstruction as he eased himself along, a flex of the toes at a time. He felt the cover of one of the books jammed in his belt catch on something and tear. Then, remarkably, he was through, and sliding far too fast head-first into light.

He reached the hole mouth and couldn't stop. As he fell into thin air, he threw the sword away, so he wouldn't land on it and snap it. He hit the ground back first, and all the air was bumped out of his lungs. They were so empty that for a moment he couldn't make himself breathe in. New air and pain came at the same time. He choked, caught his breath and opened his eyes.

He was looking up at the white face of the cliff. It looked sheer and whole; he had to turn his head to find the hole he'd just fallen out of. It was barely visible, you'd take it for a shadow or a discoloration of the rock unless you knew what you were looking at. He flexed his fingers and toes, and was mightily relieved to find that everything more or less worked. His right hand, when he raised it and examined it, was a red and white pulp which he probably wouldn't have recognised as a hand if it hadn't been attached to his wrist.

Easier the second time, he thought. Well, maybe not.

The hoe-head, presumably, was still up there somewhere. He thanked it *in absentia*. A small thing, of no commercial value, judged not worth repairing by Stheno and the met'Oc, but it had brought him through the hour of his trial like the intercession of some saint. The sword was lying in the thin grass. It didn't look anything. You could have taken it for a bit of old dry wood, fallen from the edge of the canopy a hundred feet above, and the white sheen of its handle no more than silver birch bark. Mere things, artefacts, make all the difference.

He thought, Once by accident, once on purpose. Never again.

He stood up, an adventure in itself. He hadn't thought any further than this: go back, get the sword, get out again. Beyond that — beyond here, the place where he now stood — he had only a vague design, an awareness of what he had to do, a determination to make a proper job of it this time. He realised that he'd anticipated (practically relied on) dying in the hole, because good luck pushed too far turns to bad luck as reliably as any properly attested reaction in alchemy.

He walked down to the river favouring his left ankle, which he must have twisted or turned at some point. He realised he'd never been this far upstream before. He looked for a place to cross, but there didn't seem to be one; the river was fast, skimming over large rocks that sheltered deep pools. A non-swimmer with a bad ankle could slip, trying to hop from rock to rock and end up in one of those pools, or else get battered along by the current. He followed the river upstream for a while, until the pain in his leg started to get on his nerves, but the river just got wider and faster. That made him laugh. Not the best omen for someone with a head full of complex mechanisms, if he couldn't cross a river not half a mile from where he'd been born. He turned back and trudged awkwardly downstream towards his usual ford. He was nearly there when it occurred to him that if Luso was aware of his new truancy, there'd be men watching the ford from the Gate, and in his present unsatisfactory condition he wouldn't stand a chance. He turned round and limped upstream, the way he'd just come.

The hell with all this walking up and down, he decided. Time to think.

He knew there was at least one good ford upstream, because he'd heard people talking about it while he was at Furio's. The cattle drovers used it, but they were afraid Luso might ambush them there, and there wasn't (damn it, he should have remembered this earlier) there wasn't another ford for ten miles in either direction. That gave him some sort of fix. Assuming the nearest ford downstream was the one by the Gate, which he'd always used in the past, then it followed that the ford the drovers had been talking about was something like ten miles upstream from there. Ten miles limping on a bad ankle that was rapidly getting worse. Also, by the time he got there (at rather less than his usual walking pace), wasn't there a serious chance that Luso would have men there as well, if it was the only other place where the river could be crossed?

He sat down on a fallen tree and scowled at the river, which ignored him. There was, of course, a flaw in his reasoning. The drovers had been talking about places where you could cross the river with a herd of cattle. A man, even a man with a trick ankle, was rather more agile and resourceful. A man setting forth boldly to meet his destiny wouldn't need yelling at or prodding with a stick. So there *could* be another place where he could cross, which didn't mean to say there *was*.

A very small part of him was getting distinctly nostalgic for the nice warm dry library, where there were chairs to sit on and books to read. He hauled himself onto his feet, ordered his ankle to stop hurting, and lumbered painfully up the riverbank. This wasn't, of course, how it was supposed to be. When he'd resolved to go back and get the sword, he'd seen the task ahead of him, he realised, in strictly heroic terms, focusing, as any epic narrator would, on the cunning deceptions and the great, dangerous effort. The rather more mundane business of dealing with hostile geography and crossing distances was something to be glossed over with a *some time later* or an *eventually, after many travails*. The sad fact was that he didn't have a friendly poet on hand to whisk him away from the foot of the mountain and put him down where he needed to be next. Instead, he'd have to walk.

To pass the time he reviewed his options like a beggar endlessly counting the same three coins. Here on the plain, the perspectives were entirely different. By turning his head a little he could see the plateau, a neat and convenient metaphor—isolated, elevated, defended, separate. When he was up there it was all the world, and therefore any improvement in his condition could only be achieved by changing it, which (he now realised) he didn't really want to do. Leaving it was a quite extraordinary thing. It was as though he'd contrived to burrow his way out of being himself, and was now alone and free on a flat plain of infinite possibility, holding a talisman, the sword, that could turn him into something else, the existence of his choice. He couldn't help grinning, because that was just the sort of heroic thinking that he'd been cursing a little while ago. Besides, if there were heroes in his family (in spite of the history and the legends, he was inclined to doubt it), he wasn't one of them. Luso would probably do, at a pinch. Stheno had the build for it. Not me, he thought, unless it's one of those stories that begins, *Once upon a time there were three brothers.* Those stories usually ended with the two eldest brothers dead.

(If Stheno and Luso died, and Father as well, of course, I'd be... He looked back at the plateau, and shook his head. The thought of owning it, that great big enormous *thing*, was too extraordinary even to consider. Besides, would he want it? On balance, he decided, not really.)

He stopped. A flat rock stuck out into the river, with furious white water boiling up on either side of it. He could see it was slippery and sharply angled on the far side. Beyond it, he guessed, was a deep pool, almost certainly up to his chin. But it was the likeliest prospect he'd seen so far. All sorts of possible disasters occurred to him as he jumped from the bank to the rock. He could have landed worse, but there was a horrible moment when he felt himself toppling forward, and his right hand closed on empty air, and he almost toppled head first into the pool. But he managed to pull himself back (so little in it) and get himself balanced again. First thing I'll do, he promised himself, once I've made my fortune, is get someone to teach me to swim.

He stared across the pool to the far bank. If he hadn't hurt his ankle, he might have jumped it. Or he might have tried, at any rate, so it was probably just as well. Slowly, feeling extremely stupid, he sat down on the edge of the rock and lowered his feet into the pool, cringing as his shoes filled with water. He felt with his toes for a firm place, but found nothing. Metaphor, he thought, bloody metaphor again (the flat rock being the plateau, the river the possibilities of the world), and slid forward, terrified. Water rushed up over his legs and chest, into his mouth, over his eyes. His feet found the bottom. It was slippery as goose-grease.

Ridiculous, he thought, and lunged forward wildly. He staggered as the current shoved at him. His feet skidded on the slippery rocks of the riverbed and he fell, but the current kept him just about upright, as he danced furiously for a foothold. Like a fool, he hadn't thought to breathe in. There was no air in his lungs. Trying not to inhale was like trying to hold a coiled spring between his fingers. He lunged again and found a foothold. When he straightened his leg, his head pushed up out of the water. He gobbled a chunk of air, like an owl swallowing a mouse. His feet slipped again. He was unsupported, falling. His left foot landed between two rocks, twisting his bad ankle, and he hopped away from the pain. This time his right foot found a firm place, on which he balanced just long enough to swing wildly sideways. His shoulders were out of the water. He kicked at the riverbed, one foot and then the other, not even trying to stand up, just doing his best not to fall. Suddenly, unexpectedly, the bank was only five yards away. He threw the sword as hard as he could. The effort toppled him over and he landed on his outstretched hands, his face in the water but on all fours. Like this he could cope much better. He scampered the five yards, eyes tight shut, until his shoulder hit something solid, which had to be the bank. He opened his eyes again, saw a bunch of reeds and grabbed them with both hands just as his feet slipped again. He hauled on the reeds until his chest and then his waist were on the bank. Then, lacking the strength to do anything else, he rolled onto his side, which pulled his legs out of the water.

Once upon a time there were three brothers, he thought, and they came to a wide river.

He lay still for a long time. Breathing was like pushing his skinned hand against the dirt, back in the hole. If being alive hurts this much, he thought, why the hell bother?

Well, he'd learned two things. There wasn't really a secret way down off the mountain, and there wasn't really a place where you could cross the river. Instead, there were two opportunities for a bloody fool to kill himself trying. But look on the bright side, he demanded of himself. I made it, I've got the sword, I may hurt all over but I haven't broken any bones this time, and the river's washed all the dirt out of my lacerated flesh. And I'm here.

Which begged the question of where here was. A good question, probably a bit too deep for him (if he'd stayed in the library long enough to read Zosimus' *On Being and Reality*, he might have been able to answer it). In very simplistic terms, however, he was on the other side of the river, and the town was about seven miles away, north-east. Assuming he wanted to go there.

He stood up, apologising to his body for the shocking state he'd managed to get it in. He looked across at the plateau. The further away from it he went, the more of it he could see. Yet more metaphor. Fuck that. He turned round, and all he could see was the flat plain.

Some time later, he reached the dock. There was no ship.

The place was, in fact, practically deserted. There was just the one old man sitting on an upturned barrel with his feet dangling like a child's. He was looking down at his hands, and didn't look up when Gignomai's shadow fell across his face. But he said, "I know you. You're the youngest met'Oc boy."

Gignomai never understood how people he'd never met knew who he was, but he was gradually learning to accept it. "When's the next ship due?" he asked.

The old man lifted his thumb and stared at it. There didn't seem to be anything wrong with it. "Spring," he said.

"Oh."

The old man laughed. "Season's over, see," he said. "From now till spring, you can forget about going anywhere. Wind's all over the place, like the mad woman's shit."

Gignomai took a moment to parse that. "No ships at all?"

"No." Now he looked up. "You in a hurry or something?"

Gignomai shrugged. "I've got business I want to see to back Home. Look, is there anybody with a ship here who'd—?"

The old man thought that was really funny. "Nobody's got a ship," he said, "don't you know that? Term of the fucking charter, we aren't allowed any. So the Company keeps its monopoly, see? Even the fishing's owned by the Company."

No, Gignomai hadn't known that. "Nothing at all?"

"Nothing," the old man said slowly and deliberately, "with a sail, or capable of being fitted with a sail. That's the words, in the charter. It's the law."

"Fine," he said, "not to worry, I'll just have to make other arrangements."

The old man must have thought Gignomai was the funniest thing ever. "Other arrangements," he repeated, with a huge grin. "What, you going to *walk* to the mainland?"

Some time later, Gignomai thought, after many travails. But no; he'd had quite enough of doing the impossible. "Thanks," he said. "You've been a real help."

The old man was looking at his thumb again. Gignomai really

couldn't see what was so fascinating. "What are you doing here any-how?" the old man asked. "Business, you say."

"That's right. Thanks again."

So he walked into town. By the time he'd got there, he knew he wasn't going to get much further. He just made it to Furio's place. He really didn't want to pass out on the front step, because that would be sheer unadulterated melodrama, but in the event he didn't have any choice.

"You're back, then," Furio said. He was grinning.

Gignomai lifted his head. "Sorry."

"Don't be." Furio stifled a yawn. That and the way he was sitting in his chair suggested he'd been there for some time. "Glad you came back."

"The sword," Gignomai said. Furio leaned back and lifted it off the floor. "It's all right," Furio said. "It's here, it's safe. That's what you went back for, right?"

"I need to see your uncle," Gignomai said. "Soon as possible."

"Now isn't possible." Furio frowned a little. "Teucer says you're too weak for visitors. She tried to chase me out, but..."

Teucer. Gignomai raised his left hand and stared at it. Four neat, perfectly spaced little stitches. He felt his stomach contract, and he had to swallow hard three times to keep from throwing up.

"Good, isn't she?" Furio was saying. "She's forgiven you, by the way. At least, she was so thrilled to have someone to practise on. Someone who kept still, on account of being dead to the world."

Gignomai lowered his hand, letting it droop over the side of the bed so he wouldn't catch sight of it. "Please," he said, "get your uncle. She doesn't have to know."

"All right." Furio went to the door, then stopped. "You know what," he said, "for a pampered son of the aristocracy born to a life of idle pleasure, you don't half get yourself banged up."

Stheno, Gignomai thought, hoeing turnips for nine hours in the murderous heat. Pampered son, idle pleasure. "I'm an eccentric," he said. "Now will you please get your uncle."

Furio's Uncle Marzo turned the sword slowly between his fingers. "Hold on," he said, and ground away a patch of caked rust with his thumbnail. "There's some writing here."

"Where?"

"On the *ricasso*."

How come a simple merchant knew the correct nomenclature for the parts of a sword? "Is there? Sorry, I've never looked at it that closely."

Marzo stood up and turned his chair to face the window. "I can't quite make it out," he said. "Eyes aren't quite as sharp as they used to be."

Gignomai grinned at him. "In my right coat pocket," he said. "I don't know if they got busted while I was fooling about."

Marzo retrieved the eyeglasses and stood perfectly still, staring at them. "Are these...?"

"From Home," Gignomai said. "Quite old, I believe. I'm glad they didn't get all smashed up."

"I've heard of such things, but I've never seen one before."

"Try them on," Gignomai said. "The spring clip goes over the bridge of your nose. Should stay put of its own accord," he added. Marzo was holding the eyeglasses in place with both hands. "Well?"

"Amazing." Marzo tentatively let go, like a father teaching a toddler to walk, then held his fingertips up to his face. "Damn it, I can see all the pores in my skin."

"They're also quite good for reading," Gignomai said. "Go on, try it."

Marzo picked up one of the stolen books — *Callicrates on Mechanisms*, the one that had lost its cover when Gignomai got wedged in the hole. "Unbelievable," he said. "I haven't been able to see stuff that clearly for ten years."

"Must be hard in your line of work, if you have trouble reading."

"Worst thing is my own handwriting," Marzo said. "Actually, I've never seen as well as this, not ever." He took the eyeglasses off his nose but didn't put them down on the table. "I don't suppose you'd consider..."

"Selling?"

Marzo nodded hopefully.

"No."

"Ah well." Marzo laid the eyeglasses down, but didn't quite let go of them. "Just thought I'd ask."

"You can have them. As a present." Gignomai laughed, as Marzo's mouth dropped open. There was someone he never thought he'd see lost for words.

"You're sure?"

"Of course. My way of saying thank you for your hospitality."

("You're mad," Furio said later. "He'd have paid a fortune for them."

"Maybe," Gignomai replied.

"No maybe about it. He hates not being able to read. He'd have given anything..."

"Which still wouldn't be enough. But I could tell he was determined to have them, even if he had to steal them or swindle me. Now I've got a friend instead of an enemy.")

"So," Gignomai said, when he judged Marzo had had long enough to revel in his new possession. "What does the writing on the sword say?"

"Oh, right." Marzo bent close. "Hey, it's really easy with these. It says *Carnufex in civ Pol* and then a date: 973. Carnufex," he repeated.

"Oh, I know about him," Gignomai said. "My father's got a Carnufex, it's a really famous make. He gave us all a lecture about it when we were kids." He frowned. "I don't suppose he knew this one was a Carnufex too."

Marzo was turning the pages of a book he'd taken from his pocket. "Carnufex," he said. "Flourished AUC 962 to 981, premises in Foregate, value range A plus." He turned to the back of the book, then whistled.

"You've got a book of sword values?"

"Heirlooms, antiquities and objects of virtue," Marzo replied, showing Gignomai the cover. "Got it from a freighter captain year before last. God knows what I thought I'd ever need it for."

But Gignomai thought of Marzo walking out onto his porch each morning and looking in the direction of the Tabletop, that treasury of wonderful things from another place and time, and had a fairly shrewd idea. After all, one day the met'Oc might push their luck too far, and whoever was there to loot the ruins would need a buyer. Fair enough, he thought. People die, things move on. "What does the book say it's worth?"

Marzo hesitated; then maybe he felt the unaccustomed pressure of the spring clip on his nose, prompting him to be grateful and honest. "In good condition, thirty-eight thousand." His voice was a whisper, like an old woman at prayer.

"So let's knock off a third for the damage," Gignomai said briskly. "That's, what..."

"Twenty-five thousand, three hundred." Marzo said immediately.

"And you'll probably have to go halves with your buyer," Gignomai said calmly, "and I'll go halves with you. Say twelve thousand for round numbers. Deal?"

"I haven't got twelve thousand thalers," Marzo said.

"I know." Gignomai shrugged. "There isn't that much money in the entire colony. On the other hand, I'm stuck here till the spring, I can't go home, and everything I own is lying on that table." He paused for a moment, then said, "I'm sure we can come up with some sort of arrangement, don't you think?"

Marzo looked at him blankly. "You can stop here as long as you like," he said. "No charge. I thought you knew that."

"Because I'm Furio's friend?"

"Yes."

Gignomai nodded. "Let's just say I don't like being beholden.

Anyway," he added quickly, "I'm not planning on staying here. No offence, but I'm not comfortable here."

Marzo kept his face straight. "I imagine it's not what you're used to."

"You could say that," Gignomai replied. "For one thing, the roof doesn't leak. For another, I don't have to share my living space with my lunatic brother. I didn't mean comfortable in that sense." He stopped; he hadn't meant to say any of this. "I mean, I'm not comfortable being in the colony. Or up there on the hill. I want to go somewhere *else*."

"Where?" Marzo was looking at him. "There isn't anywhere."

"Yes there is. Outside."

He could tell that Marzo was forming a diagnosis: bang on the head, exposure, and when had he last eaten? "You can't," he said. "There's the savages."

"Who've never done us any harm," Gignomai replied levelly. "Actually, I meant to ask you about them. What do you know?"

"Very little, now you mention it." Marzo frowned. "I mean, they're..."

"Savages." Gignomai nodded. "Which means, not like us. But I'm not like you, and we seem to be able to get along without violence."

"They're afraid of us, that's why."

"Hardly." Gignomai smiled at him. "How many men in the colony? Two hundred? And no weapons, thanks to the government back Home."

"There used to be a garrison."

"Years ago," Gignomai pointed out, "before you were born."

"Not quite," Marzo said. "They left when I was a kid. But—"

"They may be savages," Gignomai said, "but they're not blind. I expect they can count. And there's thousands of them, and I'm prepared to bet they've got weapons."

"Not like ours."

"We haven't got any. Apart from that," he nodded at the sword, "and Luso's box of toys, and the snapping-hens. If the savages wanted to wipe you out, it'd take them a day. But they haven't, not in seventy years."

Marzo shook his head. He looked unhappy about the turn the conversation had taken. "Because we keep ourselves to ourselves," he said. "Only for that reason. If you go trespassing on their territory…"

But Gignomai smiled. "You know," he said, "that's more or less what my mother used to tell me. Don't even think of leaving the Tabletop, she said. They hate us, the people in that town. You set foot on the plain and they'll tear you apart. You know what? She was wrong. Admit it," he added, with a gentle grin, "you haven't given the savages a thought in years."

Marzo scowled at him, then nodded. "You're right, of course," he said, "once I'd given up hope of ever being able to sell them anything. They're no use to anybody and they don't bother us. They might as well not be there." He ran a hand through what was left of his hair. "But that's a whole different matter from going and living with the buggers," he said. "For one thing, they don't even stay put."

"Nomadic is the word you're looking for," Gignomai replied. "And I don't want to go and live with them."

"But you said—"

Gignomai shook his head. "I said I don't want to go back to the Tabletop and I don't want to stay in the colony. Since there's no ship till the spring, that just leaves Outside. That's a far cry from going to live in a cart with the savages."

Marzo shook his head. "As I told you," he said, "I haven't got twelve thousand thalers; there isn't that much money in the country. What did you have in mind?"

"Lumber," Gignomai replied promptly, "and provisions and some tools and other stuff. All things I know you've got."

"What for?"

"What for?" Furio asked.

Gignomai lay back on the bed. His head was hurting, and he

found it hard to think. "My future," he said. "Basically, what I want to do when I grow up."

"Gig…"

"All *right*." Gignomai sighed tragically and sat up, wincing as his head twanged. "This colony," he said, "it is a disaster."

"I wouldn't say that," Furio said mildly. "It's not bad here. There's worse places."

"How the hell would you know?"

"From what people say," Furio replied, pouring water into a cup. Gignomai waved it away; Furio drank it himself. "Men off the ships."

"You've talked to them?"

"They talk to people in the town; I hear it from them. Come on, it's not evidence in court, but I get the general idea. Compared to a lot of places, it's not so bad here. Specially for us," he added, with a slight grimace. "Running the store, I mean. We're pretty much top of the heap."

"Heap's about right," Gignomai said. "This is a terrible place. Nobody's here because he wants to be. You know that, don't you."

Furio looked at him. "I want to be here," he said.

"You were born here. So was your uncle. Ask him why his father came here."

"I know about that," Furio said. "He got into debt back Home, it was prison or the colony. I think he chose quite well, in the event."

"Better than prison, yes. But he didn't choose to come here, he was *sent*. That's why he stayed, and that's why you can't go Home. Even when your uncle sells the sword and makes his fortune, he's stuck here."

Furio grinned. "I don't know about that," he said. "He reckons a few thousand could buy us all out of here, and then we'll be—"

But Gignomai shook his head. "He's dreaming," he said. "You think that if money could buy you out of this shithole, my family'd still be here? We've tried all that."

"You haven't got any—"

"We've got friends at Home who have. Well, we used to have friends. It's been so long. I know Father's still trying, I read some of his letters, but the people who used to be our allies have forgotten about us. Understandably."

Furio sighed. "All right," he said, "it's a dump. So what?"

"It needn't be," Gignomai said (and either his headache had suddenly gone or he was too engaged to notice it). "It could be anything we like."

For a moment or so, Furio didn't understand, and Gignomai began to wonder if he'd overestimated his friend's intelligence. Then Furio said, "That's just plain stupid."

"Is it?"

"You can't just take over a whole—"

Gignomai shook his head. "Who said anything about taking over? I'm talking about..." He hesitated. There was a word, but he wasn't quite sure it was what he meant. "Independence."

"Oh, come *on!*"

"Think about it." He hadn't meant to shout, but as it turned out, it had the desired effect. Furio closed his mouth and looked straight at him. "What's wrong with this place? Not the land, not the climate, not the savages. It's this stupid, useless weight you've got to carry around with you all the damn time. Indentures, monopolies, tariffs, the Company practically owning everything. You've got seventy farms raising beef that nobody here gets to eat, and you aren't allowed to make so much as a spoon; you're forced to buy it all from Home at extortionate prices. You're all stuck here, by law, but a bunch of people you've never met five hundred miles away dictate how you all live. You can't have weapons, so you have to put up with my appalling family beating you up and stealing your chickens." He paused, and made himself say the next bit. "You don't think the people back Home couldn't have put down the met'Oc fifty years ago, if they'd wanted to? No, they left them there to keep *you* people down. To give you someone on your own doorstep to hate, so you wouldn't think about who's the real cause of all your troubles. They're screwing you lot into the ground, and you're all so dead you just let them do it. That's why it's a dump, Furio. That's what's wrong with it."

He could see Furio keeping his temper like a calm stockman restraining an unruly steer. "So what do you want?" Furio asked quietly. "Revolution? Fighting in the streets?"

Gignomai laughed; he couldn't help it. "Don't be bloody stupid," he said. "There's nobody to fight. That's what's so pathetic. It's so simple, don't you see? You don't need a civil war. What you need—"

"Well?" Furio snapped.

"A factory," Gignomai said, and Furio just stared at him. "Just a big shed, basically, next to a river, for choice, so you can have a waterwheel for your motive power. Forges, a lumber mill. Make the stuff people here need so they don't have to buy it from Home. That's it. That's all it'd take."

"But it's against the—"

"Law, yes. So fucking what? Furio, people here don't want much, but what they do want, they *need*. Tools, household stuff, clothes. Things you can't live without, just *things*. But the trouble is, things matter, things make all the difference in the world. I learned that," he added, "going back for the sword. Or take those eyeglasses I stole for your uncle. They make the difference between him being half blind and being able to read. Just two glass discs and a bit of wire, and it's changed his life. *Things* are the only difference between us and animals, Furio, and we can *make* them, out of trees and plants and bits of brown stone you can pick up in the marshes. And we can turn this dump into a good place to live, and nobody'll have to fight anybody else."

Furio just looked at him, till Gignomai was tempted to say something just to break the silence. But then Furio said, "Home won't let us. It's against the law."

"Ah." Gignomai grinned. "That's the whole point—it isn't. Not if we don't do it here. Not if we do it Outside, where Home's got no authority."

"That's rubbish," Furio said. "If people buy the stuff, they're breaking the law too."

"Difference of scale," Gignomai replied calmly. "You can send fifty men to close down a factory, but you'd have a real job on your hands going round every farmhouse in the colony confiscating illegal spoons. No, all that'll happen is the farmers won't send quite so much beef to the docks. Result? The Company won't send us trade goods, assuming that'll bring us to our senses. But it won't, of course, because we won't need their stuff any more. Eventually, the Company'll decide this operation isn't cost effective and they'll get their beef somewhere else. And then we'll be left alone—exactly what we want."

"They'll find out," Furio said, "about the factory."

"In time, I guess they will," Gignomai said.

"And then they'll send soldiers."

"Not if the factory's under the protection of the savages." Gignomai waited for an objection, but none came; Furio was too stunned to say anything. "A war with the savages is exactly what Home doesn't want. They'd have to send a regular army, hundreds of men, horses, supply chains. Ruinously expensive, and always the risk of a disaster if their army got wiped out. A government could fall because of something like that. They don't know anything about the savages. They wouldn't want to get into a situation that could go really bad on them."

"But what makes you think...?"

"Easy." Gignomai smiled. "We pay rent. We make stuff the savages want and give it to them, and all they've got to do is let us sit on a tiny corner of their land. Come on, Furio, it's perfect. The colony gets rid of Home, everybody gets the stuff they need—even the savages, so they're doing well out of it. Everybody gains, nobody gets hurt. What could be better than that?"

Furio was still looking at him, which made his hands itch. He wanted to smack the absence of convinced admiration off Furio's face. "Nobody here knows the first thing about making things."

"Wrong." Gignomai pointed at the table. "See those books there?

Everything you need to know. Including scale diagrams and lists of materials."

Furio looked at the table. "Just three books."

"Yes." Gignomai grinned. "You can add them to the list of things that make all the difference. Give me those books and five men who can saw a straight line and we can build a factory."

He could see Furio didn't believe that, not entirely. But instead, Furio said, "Fine. So why the hell would you want to do all this?"

That question. He gave the only answer he had. "I'm a met'Oc," he said. "We do big stuff. Or we used to," he added, "before we got stuck here. And this is the only big stuff to be done in this place, unless you're Luso and you equate achievement with a row of heads stuck on pikes. So, I want to do it."

"All right," Furio said with a sigh. "Don't tell me." He got up to leave the room, but Gignomai called him back. "Furio."

"What?"

"If the world is a book, are you the hero, or just a walk-on part?"

Furio opened his mouth, then closed it again. "You've read a lot more books than me," he said.

"All right, not a book, a story. Is it about you, or are you just in it?"

Furio was standing with one hand on the door latch. He stayed still and quiet for a surprisingly long time. "I think I can see where you're making your mistake," he said. "You think people've got to have a purpose. You're getting people muddled up with things. Which is odd, coming from you."

"Furio—"

"Things have a purpose," Furio went on, not letting him interrupt. "Some of them, anyhow. Things made by people, at any rate. People..." He shrugged. "You don't agree."

"I don't think I was put here to be a means of turning wheat into shit," Gignomai said.

"You see? Even when you're trying to argue your side of it, you can't help thinking in terms of purposes. "Why *do* you want to set up a factory, Gignomai? Just for mischief, or is it because you've got some big deep idea in the back of your head somewhere?"

"What else is there to do around here?"

The news that the youngest met'Oc boy had run away from home again led to a mild, slow-moving panic. Some farmers drove their cattle home from the outlying pastures; others, figuring that Luso-mai would attack homesteads as he'd done the last time, put their stock out, boarded up their houses and moved their families and possessions into remote shepherds' huts and sheilings. There were several angry meetings. Some farmers wanted to fight, the way the Dravis had done, while others pointed out what had happened to Azo Dravi and maintained that fighting was the worst possible thing they could do; much better to clear out and let Luso burn a few hay-ricks if he felt he absolutely had to. Nothing was decided, and the fighting faction stormed off to barricade themselves in their houses. In town, where many people anticipated Lusomai would attack, there was rather more enthusiasm for coordinated resistance. Gimao the corn chandler announced the formation of a Committee for Public Safety, with himself as chairman, and signed up a dozen householders, but when he tried to organise a sentry-duty roster, he found that nobody could spare the time from their other commit-ments. He did manage to persuade the town clerk to give him per-mission to block the three main approaches into town with overturned wagons, but since nobody was prepared to lend the Committee so much as a dog cart, the initiative came to nothing, and the clerk absolutely forbade Gimao to use rocks, chains or barrels instead of carts, on the grounds that such obstructions couldn't readily be cleared away when not in use, which would lead to obstruction of legitimate traffic.

Lusomai didn't attack. Pickets posted to observe activity near the Gate (two poor-relation cousins of the Dravis and their friend from town) reported hearing several shots in the woods and may have seen a man moving about up there. Their observations were of limited use, however, since they were all under age and had to promise their parents to be home before nightfall.

Instead, Gignomai's father sent him a letter. It appeared one morning nailed to the front door of the store.

> *Phainomai met'Oc to Gignomai met'Oc; greetings.*
>
> *You will find enclosed with this letter a formal notice of disinheritance.*
>
> *I have prepared and will, in due course, forward to the Court a duly notarised copy for registration in the Temple Register. I have also made the necessary alterations to my will. Kindly accept this letter as proper notice of such alterations, pursuant to section 46 of the Wills and Testamentary Dispositions Act AUC 897.*
>
> *In consequence of the said disinheritance:*
>
> *1. Notwithstanding any trusts, benefices, appointments and settlements already made (all of which are hereby declared void in respect of you), you will receive no family property at my death.*
>
> *2. You will forfeit membership of the College of Augurs, the College of Arms, the Noble Brotherhood of the Invincible Sun, the Worshipful Guild of Knights Domestic and Errant, the Order of Agesilaus and the Order of the Headless Spear, together with all rights, privileges, rents and properties appertaining to such memberships.*
>
> *3. You are hereby dispossessed of the priesthood of St Sergius Without the Gate, and the stipends and honours relating thereto.*
>
> *4. You are hereby deprived of the benefices and advowsons of the subdiocese of Athanasia Foreign.*
>
> *5. You are hereby deprived of your seat on the Greater Council, the Lesser Council and the Council of One Hundred, and of all privileges, rights and expectations thereto pertaining.*
>
> *6. You have forfeited all real and personal property held or situated at the premises usually known as the Tabletop, and you are forbidden to enter the said premises at any time and for any purpose whatsoever.*

7. *You are hereby deprived and relieved of all rights and duties of Attendance, Audience, Fealty and Judgement pertaining to your rank as a hereditary knight of the Imperial Court.*

8. *You will within seven days of receipt of this notice pay in full the cost of your induction and registration in the aforementioned Colleges, Orders, Priesthoods, Councillorships and other said offices. Should the said debt remain unpaid at the expiry of the said term, the sum in question will be registered against you as a statutory debt in the ledgers of the Imperial Court.*

You have dishonoured your family, offended your brothers and gravely disappointed me. As a last act of forbearance I have decided to take no action against you in truancy under the Families Act AUC 907. I have forbidden the mention of your name in this house.

Kindly acknowledge safe receipt and due service of this notice.

"I didn't know you're a priest," Furio said.

Gignomai took the letter back, folded it and tucked it inside the front cover of Onesander. "Was a priest," he replied. "Yes, we all are. Or were. It's like all that other garbage; stuff from Home. We lost it all, of course, when we got thrown out and came here, but naturally Father acts as though it's still all real; he..." He paused. "He refuses to acknowledge the legitimacy of the confiscation order, is how he puts it, I think. Anyway, none of it matters."

Furio wasn't sure he believed that. "What's an advowson?"

"The right to appoint a new priest to a temple when the old one dies or retires," Gignomai replied promptly, as if he was being tested. "The incoming priest pays you money, so it's worth having. Also, you can appoint someone who'll do as you tell him, so it's valuable politically. I think I had four of them." He grinned. "Lucky me. Actually, that's one of the less obscure ones. I never did find out what the Order of the Headless Spear's supposed to be about, and it wasn't in any of the books. What you've never had you never miss, right?"

Furio didn't want to say anything, but he felt he had to. "Your father's a nasty piece of work," he said. "All that stuff about—"

"He's not, actually," Gignomai said mildly. "Back Home, he'd have either been a great and distinguished scholar or First Citizen; both, quite likely. Here, he's an eagle in a chicken coop. I'd feel sorry for him, but he'd think that was degrading."

Furio knew he'd said the wrong thing, but it was too late to do anything about it. "You never told me his name," he said.

"Didn't I?" Gignomai was looking out across the porch, to where the Tabletop would be. "It's a family name, of course. They all are. Also a joke at his expense."

That was meant to be a cue. "Is it?"

Gignomai nodded. "All our names mean something, in the old language. Like, Sthenomai means 'I am strong.' Lusomai means 'I will be set free' or else 'I will be unleashed.' I'm 'I become,' which I hope I'll live up to one day, though the way things are going I'm inclined to doubt it. Phainomai means 'I seem.'"

"Oh," Furio replied. It was the best he could do.

"The joke," Gignomai went on, still staring at the skyline, "is that it's ambiguous. Phainomai followed by the present participle means 'I seem to be and I really am.' Followed by the infinitive, it means, 'I seem to be but I'm not really.' There's even a little verse to help you remember which is which."

He took a breath, and recited, "*Phainomai on quod sum; quod non sum phainomai einai.* Which everybody learns with their grammar when they're seven, or at least they do back Home if they're people like us. Anyhow, Grandfather must've called him that on purpose, because when he was pleased with Father he called him On, and when he wasn't he called him Einai. Father told me that himself when he was teaching me reflexive verbs." He lowered his head, looked down at his hands, moved his left hand so he wasn't looking at the stitches. "Just the sort of thing that'd really screw you up as a kid, I'd have thought, but it's what passes in our family for scholarly wit."

Furio felt an urgent need to change the subject. "What's this notice of disinheritance thing he mentioned?"

"It's on the back of the letter," Gignomai replied. "Supposed to be on a separate sheet, but we can't spare the parchment. Which sort of sums the whole thing up, really."

"And you can really do that? Cut someone out of your family, like they never existed."

Gignomai nodded. "I don't think it's been done for about two hundred years," he said. "But I think it's nice to keep these quaint old traditions going."

Gignomai insisted on acknowledging receipt, as his Father had asked him to. He asked for a sheet of paper and the loan of Furio's hunting bow and an old, cracked arrow. Then he trudged out to the Tabletop, waded across the river, walked up to the foot of the Gate and shot the arrow as far as he could make it go, with the paper tied to the arrowshaft.

("So what does your mother's name mean?" Furio asked him.

"Oh, nothing. Girls don't get names that mean anything, they're just to sound pretty."

He was lying, as it happened. His mother's name meant "loyal." His sister's was "gift from the sun," because she nearly died at birth.)

Furio slept on the ground floor, in what had been a stockroom in his father's time. Teucer had his old room now, up at the top of the house, under the western eaves. One thing about his new room (sometimes an advantage, sometimes not) was that every time someone battled with the front door, which stuck badly in wet weather, he woke up.

He jumped out of bed, grabbed the long stockman's coat that Uncle Marzo had taken in part settlement of a bad debt, dragged it on and ran out onto the porch, just in time to see Gignomai setting off down the street. He ran after him and caught him up at the livery corner.

"Where are you going?" he demanded.

Gignomai looked at him. "Hello," he said. "You're up early."

It was just starting to get light. "So are you."

"Long way to go," Gignomai replied. "See you this evening."

Furio scowled at him. "Would it kill you to wait three minutes while I put some clothes on?"

"Why would I want to do that?"

"You're going to meet the savages, aren't you?"

Gignomai froze for a moment, then nodded. "There was a man in the store last night saying they're back at their camping ground by the lake. Seemed too good an opportunity to miss."

"I know," Furio said. "I heard him too. Stay there. I'll just be a few minutes, I promise."

"What makes you think...?" Gignomai started to say, but Furio had run off. He walked on, quickly, as far as the little bridge across the mill race, then stopped.

Furio was a quick dresser; he could do most things quickly, if he had to. He ran home, threw on yesterday's clothes and ran back, pausing just for a moment at the corner (he's noticed, Gignomai noted, that I walked on and then stopped). "Right," Furio said briskly. He had a scarf wrapped round his neck and his hands were thrust deep in his coat pockets. Gignomai, who never felt the cold, found that mildly amusing.

"There's no need for you to come," Gignomai said.

"I'm interested," Furio replied. "I've never even seen a savage before."

There's a degree of merit, Gignomai thought, in the graceful acceptance of the unavoidable. "Now's your chance, then," he said. "Just be polite, that's all."

It was a long walk, but mostly on the flat, for which Furio was grateful. He belonged to the school of thought that holds that a walk is at best the result of a foul-up in the transport arrangements, and he ran out of breath quite quickly on hills. There was no reason why Gignomai should be aware of that, and he wanted to keep it that way. "You're serious about this factory idea," he said.

"Of course."

"I thought it might just have been, you know, thinking aloud."

"I do that too. But yes, I'm serious."

Furio shrugged. "You never told me why."

"Didn't I?"

Conversation dried up after that, and they reached the river in silence. Then Gignomai said, "It's all right, we don't have to cross it. We can just follow the bank, and there's a bridge just before we reach the lake."

Furio blinked. "How do you know?"

"Luso has maps. I should think they're accurate; he drew most of them himself." Furio noticed he kept looking at the scarf. "He sends men out to walk from one landmark to another, counting their strides as they go. He read about it in a book, but it seems to work."

Sure enough, there was a bridge. Who had put it there, or why, Furio couldn't imagine. It was right on the edge of the colony's land, much too close to the savages' country for any of the local farmers' taste. They hadn't seen cattle grazing for quite some time.

For some reason, Furio had been expecting a visible indication: a wall, a fence, something of the sort, but there wasn't anything like that. It was only when he stopped and looked back towards the bridge that he realised they must be outside the colony by now. Quite suddenly he felt uncomfortable, a sort of fear of heights feeling. Gignomai was walking slightly faster.

"What are we looking for?" Furio asked.

"Your guess is as good as mine. Smoke would probably be our best bet, or recent wheel-tracks."

In the event, it wasn't either of those. Out of a dip in the ground that neither of them had suspected was there, two men suddenly stood up.

"I think we've—" Furio whispered.

"Quiet."

They could have been identical twins. Both were tall and (to Furio's eyes) painfully thin. They had dark skins, a deeper brown than ordinary sunburn, and wore long pocketless coats that nearly reached the ground, made out of some kind of felt. Neither of them was obviously armed. One of them was frowning slightly, as though what he was seeing didn't quite make sense.

"I have no idea," Gignomai said quietly, "what language these people speak."

Furio felt a pang of anxiety. That point hadn't occurred to him. Obviously, it hadn't occurred to Gignomai either, and Furio was surprised about that.

Gignomai took a step forward. The two men immediately took an equivalent step back—like fencers, Furio thought—but they didn't seem unduly alarmed. The one who'd frowned now had his head slightly on one side.

"All right," Gignomai said softly. From his pocket he took a tin cup—Furio recognised it as part of the stock—and laid it slowly on the ground. Then he stepped back two paces, and Furio did the same. The men just looked at him. Nothing happened for the time it takes to gut a fish. Then the two men talked to each other in a low whisper, and one of them beckoned.

"I think he wants—" Furio said.

"Shh."

The men turned their backs and started to walk away, quite slowly; Furio got the impression that that was their customary pace. He stooped to retrieve the cup before following them.

They walked in dead silence for what seemed like a very long time, until they reached the shore of the lake. A large covey of ducks rose up in front of the two men, who took no notice. Maybe they're deaf, Furio thought, because anybody normal would've jumped out of his skin.

From a distance, the camp looked like the docks on loading day. There were four or five huge pens, crammed with cattle—much smaller than the breeds Furio was used to seeing, and with long, curved horns that drooped below shoulder height before flicking upwards again. There were tents, not very many, and three neat rows of carts with felt canopies. As soon as they crossed the skyline, people came flooding out of the tents and stood watching, perfectly still and dead quiet.

"Well," Gignomai whispered in his ear, "you wanted to come."

"I did, didn't I?" Somewhere, a dog was barking. It was the only noise. "What's wrong with these people? They're just —"

"*Quiet!*"

Their two guides didn't say a word, and the crowd divided to let them pass, their faces all wearing the same bemused, quizzical expression. Not the slightest suggestion of fear.

They were only a matter of yards from one of the tents, whose flap was still closed, unlike all those around it. One of their guides cleared his throat, a most refined sound that reminded Gignomai uncomfortably of his father. After a moment the flap was lifted aside, and a very old man's head poked round it. He was bald, slightly darker than anyone they'd seen so far. One half of his chin was smooth, the other half wet and covered with white bristles, suggesting he'd been interrupted in the middle of shaving. For a moment, he stared blankly; nothing like the uniform gaze of the crowd. Then his face split into an enormous grin.

"My dear fellows," he said, and his accent and pronunciation made Gignomai's father sound like a ploughman, "what a wonderful surprise. Do please come inside and have some tea."

"When I was very young," the old man said, "I was abducted."

He said it as though it was nothing at all. A young woman poured tea into three pale, thin white cups. They were extraordinarily delicate, like cups made of rose petals.

"I can't have been more than seven years old at the time," the old man went on, picking up his cup and nibbling the surface of his tea. "It was just after the first ship arrived. I was down on the beach gathering seaweed—we pickle it, you know, it's very good for you and quite delicious if it's done the right way. Five men suddenly appeared from behind a rock and grabbed me. I'd never seen so much as a rowing boat before, of course."

There were dried yellow flowers floating in the tea. Furio didn't know if he was supposed to fish them out or eat them.

"They took me back to the ship and put me in the hold, along with the barrels and the sides of bacon. It was quite dark and I was terribly frightened, but there wasn't anything I could do. I suppose I was down there for five or six days. Once a day a man came and gave me a piece of bread—I'd never had bread before—and some water in a bowl. It was too big for me to lift, so I had to lap it up like a dog. But anyway," he added, with a sweet smile, "they set sail, heading for Home, and once they were out of sight of the shore they let me come up on deck. I suppose they were worried I might jump overboard and try and get back to my people. I couldn't swim a stroke, of course, but they weren't to know.

"Anyway," the old man went on, "that's how I came to live in your extraordinary city for ten years. I think the idea was that I would learn your language and then teach you mine, as well as telling you everything about the country. I managed the languages well enough, but needless to say I couldn't tell them very much about anything they wanted to know. After all, I was only a little child. How on earth could I be expected to know how many men of military age there were in the caravan, or what sort of weapons they had? Besides, my people don't fight."

"Excuse me," Gignomai interrupted, "but what does that mean? You don't have a standing army?"

The old man chuckled—a warm, dry sound. "My dear fellow, we don't even have a word for war. We use the same word to mean fight, shout and sulk. We have a long and well-preserved tradition of oral history, and I think there's been something like six murders in the last three hundred years—something like that, anyway. Not very many. It's quite simply something we don't do.

"Now, then." The old man sat up a little straighter on his stool. Furio and Gignomai were sitting on a carpet on the ground. "Once I'd helped them with their language studies and they'd finally got the message that I couldn't give them any military secrets, I was handed over to the met'Alp family, as a gift." The old man paused, but his face didn't change. "Quite the novelty I was, as you can imagine, the little savage boy. Of course, the met'Alp were the most delightful people and they treated me extremely well. I was sent to school with their own children, and nobody was ever cruel or unkind to me. A matter of honour, you see: I was a guest, and a stranger, and to all intents and purposes an orphan. So I learned to read, and studied the approved curriculum for the sons of gentlemen, and I found it all most congenial and pleasant. In fact, I was heartbroken when on my seventeenth birthday Machomai met'Alp told me I was to be sent home to my people, as a sort of ambassador. And of course," the old man added with a slight smile, "I was entrusted with a private message for your grandfather."

It took Gignomai a moment to realise who the old man meant. "My...?"

"Oh yes." The old man nodded vigorously, so that his earlobes shook. "I'm right, aren't I? You're the youngest met'Oc. Let me see — Gignomai. I've seen you before, you know," he added, with a distinct note of affection in his voice, "though of course you wouldn't have seen me. You were herding pigs in the woods, up there on your mountain top." Gignomai opened his mouth, then closed it again. The old man laughed. "You don't notice us coming and going," he said. "Even your brother, the mighty huntsman. One thing my people do know about is how to keep quiet. It's considered a great skill."

"What was the message?" Furio demanded. Gignomai scowled at him, but he didn't seem to notice. The old man looked straight at Gignomai when he answered.

"Naturally I never had an opportunity to read the letter itself," he said. "However, from what I'd gathered during my time in the met'Alp house, I would assume that Machomai met'Alp was planning on raising a rebellion in the eastern armies, with a view to marching on the capital and staging a coup d'état, and he wanted to enlist your grandfather's support. Your great-grandfather, you will recall, won his most glorious victories on the eastern frontier, and at the time we're talking about, a substantial number of men who'd served under him would still have been in the ranks. In any case, I delivered the letter. Your grandfather was most affable to me. We sat and talked for quite some time about city news and the latest plays and books. I have no way of knowing what his reply was. I would assume that nothing ever came of it."

"And then you went home," Gignomai said.

"Ah yes." The old man smiled. "I was, of course, utterly desolate. I felt as though I had been stranded among barbarians, with whom I had nothing whatsoever in common. The discomfort, the squalor—" He laughed. "But the young are nothing if not adaptable. I went before the elders of our people and delivered the message the government and the trade guilds had composed."

"And?" Furio demanded.

"Ah." The old man nodded slowly. "Perhaps I should tell you a little about the way my people view the world. It differs in many respects from your own. When I came home, I found it ridiculous and despicable. Now, I must confess, I have changed my opinion. In fact, were it not for the fact that I know it to be based on at least one false premise, I would accept it wholeheartedly and be a true believer, because, quite honestly, it makes so much more sense than the version I know to be true. You can have no idea how frustrating it's been."

The old man drank a little tea, then went on, "My people, to put it bluntly, don't believe that your people exist. As we see the world, there are other—realities, I suppose we could call them. Unfortunately, your otherwise excellent language simply doesn't have the *words*, and even if it did, it lacks the subtle refinements of syntax and grammar that ours has. I fear I would be unable to give a satisfactory account of what we believe, simply because in order to do so I would need to employ tenses and moods of the verb which your language lacks, and use the neutral definite article followed by the active future participle to convey an abstract which is also a substantive, and in your language that simply can't be done. To oversimplify dreadfully, however, we believe that your people are merely echoes in time and space of people who are dead, or possibly people who have yet to be born. Not ghosts. Though there are heretics among us who maintain that you are lives who have been dislocated from the cycle of reincarnation. We acknowledge that you are solid, flesh and blood, capable of both active and passive interaction with our reality, but you are not of our time, quite possibly not of our world in any meaningful sense. To this we attribute the fact that when we speak to each other, neither side can understand what the other says — the concept of other languages, you see, isn't one that my people recognise, since they have been isolated here for so very long."

The old man sat perfectly still and quiet for a while, staring into his empty teacup, looking so sad and solemn that Gignomai didn't quite dare to disturb him. Then he sighed. "To put it bluntly, they didn't believe me. Their explanation was that I had suffered some kind of spell or enchantment as a consequence of trying to make contact with the — well, with your people — and I had slept for ten years in a cave somewhere. There are precedents in our folklore. I imagine it seemed far more likely than that I had actually spoken with your people and lived among them, been taken away by them on one of their extraordinary ships and visited the place they come from. I should mention that in the past, known lunatics, mystics and visionaries have made similar claims, though of course that was long before your people arrived here. In any case, they weren't the slightest bit interested in the message I had been sent to deliver — offers to establish diplomatic relations with a view to establishing trade, furs and pelts for manufactured goods. They were extremely kind to me and sympathetic, but they wouldn't listen. They tried all manner of remedies to cure me, but whenever I tried to explain, or to engage their interest with fascinating tales of the wonders of the distant land, they seemed so uncomfortable and embarrassed that I quickly gave up. Accordingly, for the last fifty-three years I have pretended that I was indeed mad for a while, but have since made a full recovery. But it's been hard," he added, closing his eyes briefly. "I was so terribly afraid I'd forget, you see. And I wouldn't have been able to bear it; like a particularly beautiful dream, that fades away as you wake up and leaves you in tears. So, when nobody's near, I talk to myself in your language, just to keep it fresh in my mind. And I have this."

From inside his thick felt coat he produced a book. Its cover glistened with grease from the felted wool, and it was tied shut with plaited rawhide. "I must confess," the old man said, with a wicked grin, "I stole this, from your grandfather's library, when I went to deliver Machomai's secret message." He hesitated, then held it out to Gignomai, who took it and glanced at the spine. The gold leaf had worn away but the impressions of the letters were still just about legible: *The Angler's Oracle Vol XIV.* Gignomai laughed.

"So that's where it got to," he said. "Ever since I was a kid, I've wondered about that. We've got all the other volumes, but there's a space on the shelf. Not that anybody's ever read it, as far as I know."

The old man looked at him gravely. "I have read a page of that book every day for fifty-three years," he said, "just to remind myself what words look like. I won't pretend," he went on, "that its content has been much use to me. It consists of a detailed analysis and comparison of the various types of fly-fishing rod offered for sale by the seven principal makers in the capital a hundred years ago. I can recite most of it by heart. Indeed, I have in fact done so, at times of great trial and stress. My children believe I become delirious and gabble nonsense. They make me drink herb tea and inhale the steam of special infusions to clear my head. But I carry on reciting quietly under the blanket."

Gignomai gave him back the book. He tucked it away in his coat with the dexterity of long practice.

"You mustn't feel sorry for me," the old man said. "I have eight sons and fifteen grandsons, and our flock is as good as any in the Commonwealth. I am a very old man by our standards; they attribute my great age and ridiculously good health to my having been touched by the supernatural, for which reason they treat me with great respect. And I have made all of them promise that on the day when representatives of your people approach us, appearing to seek to make contact, they would bring such representatives straight to me—as they have done, I'm delighted to say. And that," he added, sitting up straight and clapping his soft hands together, "is all I have to say about myself, and thank you for listening so patiently. Now, what can I do for you?"

Furio looked at Gignomai, whose eyes were fixed on the old man. Gignomai said, "How much do you know about me?"

The old man smiled. "Very little," he said. "I know that your eldest brother runs the estate, and your brother Lusomai has responsibility for its defence; your father pursues his scholarly interests. You are, if I may be frank, at something of a loose end. I gather that you have left home, and I imagine you have some project in mind for providing yourself with a suitable occupation. That is what I'd expect from a son of the met'Oc."

Gignomai laughed. "You're not far wrong," he said. "I want to ask permission to build a factory, here on your people's land."

The old man looked at him in silence for what seemed like a very long time. Then he said, "Permission. Yes, I suppose that's the way you would go about it. It would be in accordance with the proper construction of the duties and privileges of a guest. I apologise for being surprised. I should have had faith in the sensibilities of a true gentleman."

Gignomai waited for a moment, then asked, "Does that mean yes?"

The old man smiled. "If it were up to me to decide, then of course it would. But you see, I have no—authority." He'd had to search his mind for the word. "I'm not in charge here. Nobody is. I'm afraid we have no chieftains or leaders, or laws for that matter. We've never seemed to feel the need, which I guess goes to show how primitive we are."

Furio said, "You mentioned a council of elders."

The old man shook his head. He was still looking at Gignomai, as though Furio wasn't there, or was too insignificant to matter. "When we have a problem we can't immediately deal with, the old men come together to discuss it and offer their advice. Nobody's obliged to take it if they don't want to. But they generally do, because it's usually good advice. What I mean is, you can't ask permission because none of us can give it. And besides, they wouldn't understand you, and if I offered to translate they'd make me a strong pot of herb tea and suggest I lie down for a while. No, I am greatly impressed by your courtesy and honoured that you chose me to ask, but what you suggest simply can't be done."

Gignomai's eyes widened. "I can't build a factory."

The old man looked deeply distressed. "I do apologise, I've expressed myself badly. Of course you can build your factory—later you must explain to me why you want to, I'm sure it'll be fascinating—simply because none of us will make any attempt to stop you. I imagine we'll ignore you completely and give you and all your works as wide a berth as possible. What you can't do is ask our permission. Nor can your courtesy in asking be properly acknowledged, for which I am truly sorry, since it represents a grave discourtesy on our part. I hope you will bear in mind what I have told you, and forgive us."

Gignomai leaned forward. "You're sure about that," he said. "They won't mind. I mean, they won't try and stop us."

"I can guarantee it," the old man said. "It wouldn't ever occur to them to try."

Furio said, "But we'd be stealing your land."

The old man frowned slightly, as though Furio's voice was an unworthy thought inside his own head which he regretted. "I don't think my people would understand the concept of stealing land," he said. "It'd be as fanciful to them as stealing the sky. We hold that you can't own anything that four strong men can't lift. That's our tradition, at any rate, it's not a law. Besides, what use would anything that heavy be to anybody?"

"He's a snob," Furio said.

They hadn't spoken much on the walk back. Gignomai had been lost in thought, and Furio had been seriously annoyed about something, though he hadn't been sure what. The answer only came to him as they climbed over the post and rail fence that marked the boundary of the Palo farm, second in from the edge.

"Yes, he is," Gignomai said, with a mild grin.

"You think it's funny."

"Well, yes." Gignomai stopped to get a stone of out his boot. "I guess the incongruity—"

"He hardly said a word to me. He acted as though I wasn't there. Just because you're a bloody aristocrat—"

"Be fair," Gignomai said mildly. "The poor man's been away from his own kind for fifty years."

"They weren't his own kind," Furio replied angrily. "His own kind were all around him, milking goats."

"As far as he's concerned, I'm his kind," Gignomai said. "In his mind, he's some sort of poor relation of the met'Alp who got shipwrecked on a lonely island populated by savages."

"*He's* a savage."

Gignomai shrugged. "I don't think so. In fact, none of them are. It's just a word we use so we don't have to bother trying to understand strangers."

Furio didn't answer. When Furio let an argument go by default, it was usually a sign that he'd taken offence. Really, Gignomai told himself, I ought to deal with that before it turns into a problem. But he couldn't summon up the necessary energy.

"Short cut," Furio said (they were the first words he'd spoken for some time). "If we follow this track down into the combe, we can cross the Blackwater and save having to cross the moor to the ford."

Furio's short cuts were legendary in his family, but Gignomai decided to agree on diplomatic grounds. "Good idea," he said, and followed. It was a steep, awkward descent, and he didn't complain.

"Looks like you can build your factory, at any rate," Furio said, when they finally made it to the bottom. "That's if you believe all that stuff he told us."

"It sounded plausible enough," Gignomai said. "He had no reason to lie to us."

Furio went quiet again after that, and then his short cut went bad, and they were too preoccupied with finding out where they were to do any more politics. It was only when they were finally back on the road they'd left earlier that Gignomai said, "You don't think it could be true, do you?"

"Think what's true?"

"What the old man said," Gignomai replied, wondering why on earth he'd asked the question, but he hadn't been able to help it. "About—well, about his lot living in a different world, our past or their future or whatever it was."

Furio was in front of him, so he couldn't see his face. "Load of rubbish," Furio said. "Well, obviously."

"I guess so," Gignomai replied. "The way he meant it, at least."

"Look, can we please stop talking about that crazy old man?" Furio protested loudly. "He's clearly as mad as a calf in springtime, and obnoxious, bigoted and rude into the bargain. If I'd wanted to be patronised and put in my place, I could've stayed home with Teucer and saved myself a walk. Also," he added, before Gignomai could say anything, "I think I've just spotted a serious flaw in your grand plan."

"Really? Do tell."

"This factory of yours." Furio had lengthened his stride, and Gignomai was having to make an effort to keep up. "Who do you reckon's going to be doing all the work? I was assuming you meant to hire some of the savages, but if they're all like that lot, you can forget about that."

"Interesting idea," Gignomai said. He was aware that he was

using what Luso called his obnoxious voice, but so what? "I suppose you could train up completely unskilled men to do skilled work, if you had the time and the resources, and then you wouldn't have to pay them nearly as much. On balance, though, that's a bit too ambitious for me. I think I'll just hire tradesmen from the colony."

"Oh, right." Furio was being obnoxious back. That made him feel a little better. "You seriously believe skilled craftsmen'll walk away from their lives just because you ask them to."

"No, of course not," Gignomai said. "You're going to ask them."

"Me?"

"You do want to be involved in this, don't you?"

There was a moment of dead silence, during which Gignomai perceived his mistake. It hadn't occurred to him to ask Furio if he wanted to join him. Why not? Because (don't lie to yourself, Gignomai, it only makes things worse) he didn't really want him, but on the other hand, many of the assumptions he'd been working on were based on Furio being in it with him—such as recruiting workers, selling finished goods. Why had he made those assumptions? Because he'd taken it for granted that Furio would insist on joining him and a refusal would cause bitter offence, so he'd shaped his plans accordingly. The chore of actually asking had been lost sight of along the way, and now Furio was livid with him because he hadn't been asked.

"I suppose so," Furio said quietly.

"Good," Gignomai said. "I wouldn't dream of doing it without you. For one thing, I don't know the first thing about buying and selling."

"You don't know the first thing about making things. Or building sheds."

"Ah," Gignomai said cheerfully, "there you're wrong. I've helped Stheno botch up any number of fallen-down sheds and outhouses. And building them properly from scratch has got to be easier than waiting for them to collapse and then trying to fix them. We only do it that way round because we love making things hard for ourselves."

Furio laughed. "That's one family trait you've inherited, then," he said. "So, what's the plan?" He sounded completely different now — like the girl after the boy's finally proposed. "You really think you can build the shed on your own?"

"Stop calling it a shed," Gignomai replied austerely. "It's going to be a thing of beauty. There's a picture of it in Gobryas' *Mechanisms* —"

"How can there be a picture if it's not been built yet?"

Gignomai frowned. "A picture of how it'll look when it's finished," he said. "Also plans and elevations, a cutting list, schedule of hardware, the lot. The whole thing, in fact, reduced to words, and I copied it all out before I left. All I'll need to do is follow the instructions and it's as good as built."

Furio shook his head sadly. "Maybe that old fool was right," he said. "Maybe you do live in a different world from the rest of us."

No money changed hands, partly because nobody had that much in silver coin. Instead, Marzo extended a line of credit at the store to Galermo, who ran the lumber mill. In return, Galermo took Gignomai's cutting list and transformed the words and numbers into cartloads of sawn, planed wood, a small piece of magic that greatly impressed the people of the colony and left Gignomai extremely thoughtful. The work was hindered to some extent by the defection of three of Galermo's men, a third of his workforce, who announced they were quitting and refused to say why or what they were going to do instead. They left their homes in the middle of the night and didn't come back. There were similar disappearances at Derio's forge (two journeymen) and Carzo's wheelwright's shop (a tradesman and an apprentice). Marzo was rumoured to have loaded three wagons to axle-bowing point with food and dry goods, but nobody could be found who would admit to having taken delivery. Young Furio was seen riding round the country looking preoccupied and calling at houses where he wasn't a regular visitor, and the met'Oc boy who'd been staying at the store vanished completely, though this was reckoned to be no great loss. If anybody was inclined to speculate about it, the logical conclusion was that he'd gone home again. On the positive side, Luso met'Oc had been quiet for as long as anyone could remember, and it was assumed that he was busy with the woodcock season. Someone reported having seen the savages breaking camp and heading off to wherever it was they went, but that was normal and not worth mentioning. The only other rumour with any substantial degree of entertainment value was a wild story about Aurelio Tazane who'd run away from the colony thirty years earlier to work as a smith for the met'Oc. Someone claimed to have seen him, late at night, going into the store with a heavy bag in one hand and a great sack on his back. This news was of interest to the Colamela brothers. There were two of them, but thirty years ago there'd been three—the youngest had died in mysterious circumstances shortly before Aurelio Tazane left home, and the two survivors declared that they were extremely interested in talking to him about the matter. However, if Tazane had visited the store he wasn't there when the Colamelas called there, and nobody would admit to having seen him.

The next anybody heard of Gignomai met'Oc was when he turned up one night on the doorstep of Calo Brotti, who farmed the shallow valley between Greenacre and the Goose's Neck. Calo was eating bacon and beans in the kitchen with his wife and son when someone hammered on the door. Calo hadn't been expecting anybody, but his wife told him he'd better see who it was.

"I'm Gignomai met'Oc," the tall, pale young man said. "Mind if we come in?"

He slid past Calo, making it plain that permission was a mere formality. Four men came in with him: two of the sawyers from Galermo's mill, and two others Calo had never seen before. The strangers had their coats unbuttoned, though the night was cold. They had long-bladed stockmens' knives tucked into their belts.

Calo stepped back out of the way. Gignomai said, "I'm sorry, I should've known you'd be at dinner. But this won't take a minute."

At this point, Calo's wife melted away. His son stayed where he was, in spite of a ferocious scowl from his father.

"What the hell do you want?" Calo said.

Gignomai smiled and sat down. The two men Calo didn't know edged round the table until they were standing directly behind his son.

"I'll get straight to the point," Gignomai said, reaching across the table and helping himself to a slice of cheese. "About six years ago, you got hold of one of my brother Luso's snapping-hen pistols. I have absolutely no problem with how you came by it, but I'd like to buy it from you."

Calo glared at him, but he seemed not to notice. "I already said no to your father," Calo said.

"Really?" Gignomai nodded. "Well, that's understandable. If you don't mind me asking, how much did he offer you?"

Calo hesitated. He was trying to work out a complex problem of geometry in his mind. It involved the carving knife lying next to the side of bacon, the knives in the strangers' belts, Gignomai and his son. He ran the calculations twice but the answer was the same both times. "Not enough," he said.

"Evidently," Gignomai said. "Look, I'll tell you what I'll do. You say how much you want for it, and then we can haggle."

One of the men from the lumber yard didn't look too happy about what was going on, but he was well back by the door, and couldn't be included in the calculations. There was a back door, but it was barred and bolted; there'd be no time. "It's not as though I'm in any hurry to sell," Calo said.

Gignomai shrugged. "I imagine you're aware that just having it is a criminal offence," he said. "If the harbour master and his men came by and took it off you, you'd get nothing for it."

Calo didn't think much of that. He knew the Portmaster, and the two elderly brothers who worked for him because they weren't good for anything else. "Who says I've still got it?" he said. "Might have sold it already."

"I don't think so," Gignomai replied. "And it's a small house. I expect we could find it in a minute or two if we looked."

Calo noticed a small pool on the flagstones, just under his son's chair. He prided himself on his stubbornness, but pride was a luxury and luxury was a sin. "You make me an offer," he said.

Gignomai smiled. "All right," he said. "How about six barrels of white flour, fifty pounds of bacon, twenty pounds of imported nails and that harrow you've been to the store twice to look at but can't afford?"

Calo haggled a little, but mostly from force of habit, and to salvage a little of his self-respect. Besides, as he told his son some time later, it wasn't as though the stupid thing was any good for anything. There wasn't even any fire-powder to go in it.

The harrow and the rest of the agreed price were waiting for him outside the door first thing next morning, when he went out to feed the pigs. There was also a bottle of fine white brandy and a pair of new store-bought boots.

Calo told his neighbours that the met'Oc boy had called to see him, but was uncharacteristically evasive when they asked what the purpose of the visit was. They couldn't help noticing his beautiful new boots (nobody could remember the last time he'd had new footwear) but made a point of not mentioning them.

The place Gignomai had chosen was a narrow water meadow, where a wooded hill dropped steeply down to the river. It had, he maintained, more or less chosen itself. The river would provide power by means of a large undershot wheel for which he had plans and diagrams in his book, and in due course they'd be able to ship out finished goods on barges, which would be quicker and easier than road haulage. The wood was one of the few stands of timber not controlled by the met'Oc (when he told Furio that, it was apparently without irony). He didn't say what he intended to use the steepness of the hill for, but he gave the impression that it was bound to come in handy for something.

For the time being, however, it was a nuisance. The lumber carts had to come down it, and since there was no road, they had to build one. Felling trees in the wood wasn't an easy business. Mostly it was birch: thin tall straight trees crowded closely together, starving each other of light, so that nothing grew on the forest floor apart from a light cover of stunted, knee-high holly. Cut down a tree, or rather cut through it, and it had no room to fall. Instead, it flopped against its neighbours, its upper branches slotting into theirs like lovers embracing, and had to be laboriously worked free by pulling it about with ropes. The gradient made it painfully hard to drop a tree where you wanted it to fall, and none of the men he'd recruited from the colony had any experience of that sort of work. All Gignomai knew about it was what he'd learned from helping Stheno, and on the half-dozen occasions he'd done that, he'd been scared of getting crushed by falling lumber and hadn't been paying proper attention.

At the end of the first day, everyone was quiet. The men were tired and sullen. They were craftsmen, who'd been through the misery of a traditional apprenticeship so that they wouldn't have to do general field labour, and they clearly weren't thrilled at the prospect of sleeping in tents, even the rather fine ones (government surplus) from Marzo's store. Gignomai sat apart, staring into the darkness between the trees at something nobody else could see. Furio assumed it was a golden dawn and a brilliant sunlit future for the colony, or else he was worried about wolves. Furio himself stuck it out for an hour, then announced he was going home.

"What?" Gignomai said, swinging round.

"I'll walk back to town," Furio explained. "It's all right, I'll be back again at first light."

Gignomai looked at him, analysing him. "What did you tell your uncle?" he said.

"Just said I was going to be helping you out for a few days," Furio replied. "I thought there'd be less risk of a fuss if I sort of broke it to him in stages."

"Tell him tonight," Gignomai said. "Get it over with."

That sounded like a direct order. Furio walked back in the dark (he wasn't used to night walking). About halfway home it occurred to him that Gignomai had no business giving him direct orders, even if they were sensible as this one was. On the other hand, the breaking-the-news-in-stages idea was really just cowardice, and when he thought about it, he decided that it was pretty much essential that someone should be in charge of the venture, or it would rapidly collapse into a chaotic mess. It was Gignomai's show, Furio told himself and, besides, I definitely don't want to do it. So, direct order, to be obeyed.

"Where did you get to?" Teucer asked, as he limped into the kitchen and kicked off his disgustingly muddy boots. "We expected you for dinner."

"Got held up," Furio mumbled. "Where's Uncle?"

She twitched her head towards the back stockroom, where Uncle Marzo often sat up in the evenings, doing the books. "Be careful," she said. "You and your friend aren't his favourite people in the world right now."

Uncle Marzo greeted him with a muted snarl—where had he been, they'd been worried. That was just preliminary sparring, of course. Marzo had been adding up the cost of the supplies he'd given to Gignomai.

"It's not just the value of the stuff," he said, rubbing his eyelids with forefinger and thumb. "It's the fact that everything I give him I can't sell to paying customers. And we've only got so much stock, and it's months till the next ship. I'm going to have to draw a line somewhere, or we might as well lock the doors till spring."

"Tell him," Furio said, "not me."

"He's not here," Marzo replied. "You are. You're going back there tomorrow, right? You tell him. I'll carry on sending the food and basic provisions, but that's it."

"Fine," Furio said. "I'll take him the sword when I go back in the morning."

Marzo lifted his head and scowled at him. "Like hell."

"If the deal's off..."

"He's already had seventy-eight thalers' worth of stuff," Marzo said. "We can't just write that off, it'd break us."

"Remind me," Furio said. "Twenty-five thousand, wasn't it, or was it thirty?"

"That's in the future," Marzo snapped, "that's not now. Right now, I'm down to my last two barrels of square-head nails. Also we're running low on rope, saw blades, rosin, flux—"

"You haven't given Gig any rosin. Or flux."

"No, but I've traded them for his sawn lumber. And shirt cloth. I've been paying for his bacon and flour with that. Sixteen ells a barrel, which is extortion. And he's only just started. How long's it going to take him? Do you know that?"

Furio was completely still apart from his hands, which were squeezed tightly together. "Once he's set up and making things, you'll have all the stock you can sell. That's the whole point."

"Sure," Marzo growled. "And when's that going to be? He hasn't given me a date."

"Ask him," Furio said, "not me. I'm going to bed."

Furio stood up, but made no move towards the door. "Keeping him in food and tools is one thing," Marzo said. "Financing his hobbies is another matter."

"What's that supposed to mean?"

Marzo reached for a cup, standing next to a half-empty bottle of cider brandy. "He used my bacon and my flour," he said, "not to mention a harrow worth six thalers to buy something off Calo Brotti."

"What?"

"Calo wouldn't say," Marzo replied. "But what the hell would he have that your pal would possibly want? Couldn't be anything for the grand adventure. My guess is it was a falcon or a hunting dog, some sort of aristocratic crap like that."

"Where would Calo get—"

"I don't know, do I?" Marzo shouted. "That's not the point. The point is, the supplies are supposed to be for the factory."

"The supplies," Furio said quietly, "are part payment on the sword, which is worth more than this whole colony put together. You might care to bear that in mind. And Gig can't be doing with hunting and falconry, he told me so. That's Luso's stuff and he doesn't want anything to do with it."

Marzo looked blankly at him for a moment, then grinned. "You know," he said, "your pal may say he can't stand his brother, but I reckon those two've got more in common than you think."

"You don't know anything about him," Furio said, and left the room.

Uncle Marzo was right, of course. It had always been there, but ever since Gig had left the Tabletop it had been growing stronger. He couldn't call it a resemblance, because he knew nothing about the rest of the met'Ocs apart from what Gig had told him, and in the circumstances his evidence was unreliable. A tendency? Playing with words.

He sat on the porch and looked out into the dark street. Fifty yards away, there was a light in the upper window of the livery; he couldn't be bothered to speculate about what it signified. He considered the resemblance or the tendency. He'd always been aware of it, of course, but he hadn't really thought much about it until they met the crazy old man at the savages' camp. The old fool didn't once look at me, Furio told himself, only at Gig. I might as well not have been there. No, amend that. Maybe that's how the aristocracy treat their servants. They're aware of their presence but they don't talk to them or look at them unless they want something, and if a man shows up with his valet or his groom, you wouldn't talk to the servant in the master's presence, it'd probably be appalling bad manners or something. The old lunatic treated me like I was Gig's servant. Quite likely assumed I must be. Like talking to like. Of course, the old man was off his head—hardly surprising, given his life story—but Gig...Gig accepted it. He wasn't offended, he didn't think it was funny, assumed I'd accept it too. The tendency. The met'Oc running all the way through him, like the core in an apple. Running away from home didn't mean he'd changed. Basic fact of life: no matter how far you run, you always take yourself with you.

Not that it mattered. Did it? No, because it had always been there, the tendency, and Furio had always been aware of it, and it hadn't mattered before. It only registered with him now because...

Why *was* Gig doing all this? Furio had assumed it was because he was bored. He'd been planning to leave the colony, go back Home under a false name, but there wouldn't be a ship till spring, so he'd found something to do. Maybe — it was plausible. The scale of the thing didn't signify. A met'Oc wouldn't concern himself with the fact that he was turning the world upside down for his own amusement, and anything small and trivial wouldn't be sufficiently entertaining. But there were problems with that hypothesis. The factory was a long-term project. If Gig still intended to get on the spring ship, he'd leave before the factory was in full swing and having its dramatic effect on the colony; he'd miss all the fun. Besides, he'd have wasted at least part of his share of the sword money (though there'd be so much money he'd hardly notice). But what other reason could there possibly be? All that stuff about revolution, independence, freedom without bloodshed. Well, big concepts and big dreams and changing the world for ever were all very met'Oc. In fact, he could just imagine them taking enormous delight in Home losing a profitable colony. Serve the government right for banishing a noble house to a distant, barbarous land. Not a primary motivation, perhaps, but distinctly plausible as a secondary one.

The light in the livery window went out, and Furio treated it as his own curfew. He went upstairs to bed and found he was too tired to sleep.

When he arrived at the factory site next morning, he was stunned to find that the road was finished. It had only been light for an hour or so.

"We started early," Gignomai said cheerfully, leaning on his axe.

Furio saw that both his hands were bound with cloth—blisters. "And we finally figured out how to drop a tree against the lean, so it doesn't get hung up in the branches. All you do is..."

Furio didn't pay attention to the explanation, which was complex and involved technical terms he didn't recognise. When it was over, he said, "You seem pretty cheerful. All of you," he added, looking round. "Yesterday I was convinced they'd all leg it during the night."

"Ah." Gignomai beamed at him. "I had an idea. Your fault, actually."

"My—"

Gignomai nodded. "You scuttled away back to your nice clean sheets and left me with them," he said. "No option under the circumstances but to make conversation. I ended up making them all partners."

Furio tried to repeat the word, but it came out as a splutter.

"Junior partners, of course," Gignomai reassured him. "Very junior. Each of them gets one per cent of the net profit. It's all right," he added, "it's no big deal."

"Really."

"Really. If we do well, they get rich; if we don't, they're no worse off. They love the idea, naturally. They reckon that come Independence, they're going to be the new merchant aristocracy. Well, you can see for yourself," he added. Furio had to admit the point—a dozen big trees felled and cleared in a couple of hours suggested a degree of enthusiasm that hadn't been evident the previous day. "And what's eight per cent to you and me? Fleabites."

Furio was counting in his head: eight per cent. But aloud he said, "Did they ask, or did you offer?"

"I offered," Gignomai replied. "If they'd asked for it, I'd have told them to go to hell."

"I see. And this was all my fault."

As a road, it had its drawbacks. Quite soon, when the rain started to fall, it'd be too soft for carts; they'd get down the hill easily enough, but not back up again. ("But that's fine," Gignomai said. "Once we've got the lumber and the provisions down here we won't need anything else before we've built a raft, and then we can fetch stuff in by river.") Even so, it was something they'd set out to do and achieved, ahead of time and without quarrels or bloodshed. They spent the rest of the day levelling the ground for the main shed—hard, miserable work, but Gignomai personally set a ferocious pace, and the men felt obliged to keep up.

"It's what Stheno does," Gignomai explained. "Half the time you want to cut his throat just to make him slow down, but come the finish, when you realise how much you've got done in a day, you feel so good about it you don't mind. And it's how you feel at the end that matters."

Furio wasn't quite sure what to make of that, so he made an excuse and found something to do on the far side of the site. As he worked (thumping stones into the ground with a heavy wooden post; nature hadn't equipped him for arduous manual labour) he ransacked his mind for the thing that was bothering him, something Gig had said earlier that hadn't quite made sense.

Eight. Eight per cent.

Well, Lario, Senza and Turzo formerly employed at the sawmill; Ranio and the fat man whose name he hadn't managed to learn yet, from Derio's forge; Pollo and the boy (Areno or Arano) from the wheelwright's shop. Seven. But Gignomai had distinctly said eight per cent.

He rested the log against his shoulder and looked at his hands. There were soft white bubbles, like the ghastly pale mushrooms that grow in marshy ground, at the base of three of his fingers. Nobody ever got blisters working at the store. He felt in his pocket for a handkerchief to wrap round them, but couldn't find it. A few yards away, Pollo the wheelwright and the useless boy were on their knees in the deep wet leaf mould, carefully positioning a flat stone they'd fished out of the riverbed. I should feel guilty, he thought, I'm not pulling my weight, I can't keep up, I shouldn't be here. That made him think about the savages—dead, or not born yet, shouldn't be there, either way, and therefore, by the exercise of logic, weren't there. A reasonable explanation that made sense of the world, which just happened to be wrong.

That made him think about the met'Oc, who had no place here, and Gig, who had no place with them any more, no place anywhere else, so—eminently practical, supremely met'Oc confident—he was building a brand new place just for himself, in the gap between the colony and the savages. And why not?

He tried clenching his hands like claws as he gripped the post. It didn't help.

When it was too dark to see what they were doing, Gignomai called a halt for the day. Someone got a fire going. Someone else drifted down to the river to fill a pot with water. Furio waited until Gignomai had finished talking to, encouraging, cracking a joke with each of the partners in turn (the junior partners, but the term had stuck in his mind now). Then he sat down beside him next to the fire and asked, "Gig, where's Aurelio?"

Gignomai was trying to ease the boot off his left foot, but it was too sodden with sweat and damp to move. "What?"

"Aurelio. That's his name, isn't it? The blacksmith from your place. Didn't I hear he'd run away and joined you?"

Gignomai was giving his boot his full attention. "You wouldn't catch Aurelio running anywhere," he said, "not with his trick knee."

"Gig?"

"Joining us later," Gignomai said. He made a last, desperate, heroic effort and the boot came free. "Wouldn't be much use to us at this stage of the operation," he went on. "And if he did his back in lugging tree trunks about, he wouldn't be fit for the work only he can do."

But there were two other smiths: Ranio and the fat man. "Right," Furio said. "I just wondered."

"You were doing the maths," Gig said, with a grin.

"Yes."

"He'll earn his share," Gig said. "You know, I think I'll leave the other boot where it is, rather than kill myself trying to shift it. After all, I'll only have to put it back on again in the morning."

When he got back to the store, Furio went straight to the back store room. As usual, there was an open bottle of white brandy; today, a quarter full. He sloshed brandy over his blistered hands and winced sharply.

His aunt had left him some dinner (mutton stew in a bowl covered with a dishcloth). He devoured it so quickly that later he couldn't remember having eaten, then limped out to the porch. Teucer was there.

"Good day at work?" she asked.

He wasn't in a Teucer mood. "Fine," he said. "We're making excellent progress. Gignomai's turned the operation into a partnership."

"Equal shares?"

"Not quite."

She shrugged. "It's a really stupid idea," she said. "As soon as Home finds out, they'll send a platoon of soldiers and shut you down. You'll be lucky if you're not arrested."

Furio turned his head. There was a light in the upper window of the livery. "Unlikely," he said. "For a start, they won't have a chance to find out till the spring ship comes, by which time we'll be up and running, and people will have started getting stuff from us — cheaper, better stuff than they get off the ships. Uncle Marzo will be raking in money from his end of the deal, and the farmers who'll be buying the stuff won't be in any hurry to squeal to the government. And if they do find out, we're not on colony land. They won't risk a war with the savages."

"You quoted all that from memory," she said. "I'm impressed."

He felt a little surge of anger, partly with her, partly with himself (though "risk a war with the savages" was the only *direct* quote from Gignomai). "You lay off him," he said. "He's my friend."

She yawned. "I think he's getting bored with you."

"Thank you for sharing your opinion with me." He shivered, like a horse trying to dislodge a horse-fly. It didn't get rid of her. "I expect you're frozen, sitting out in the cold night air. You'd be better off indoors in the warm."

"I've got my shawl," she said equably.

He remembered how he'd felt the first time he saw her. Hard to believe, now that he knew her better, and a valuable warning against judging by first impressions.

"He's up to something," she said abruptly. "And he's going to drag you into it, and you'll be sorry."

He made himself laugh. "Is that based on hard evidence, or your unique insight into human nature?"

"You don't have to listen to me if you don't want to. But you know I'm right."

"You're just miserable," Furio snapped. Then inspiration prompted him to add, "You're down on him because he doesn't fancy you. Well?"

She shrugged. It was her best gesture, and he guessed she knew it. "What I think about it isn't the issue. You're angry because you know I'm right."

The proper course of action would have been to go inside and leave her there. Instead, he said, "Up to what?"

"I don't know. You should, you're his friend. Think about it. Why would he have a secret scheme and not tell you about it?"

"He doesn't have a secret scheme. Unless you count liberating the Colony."

"That's not a secret," she replied imperturbably. "That's just something he hasn't told everybody about yet. Well, they'll have to know, won't they? You can't have a revolution and not tell people."

"You have a wonderful imagination," Furio said. "You ought to try and find something useful to do with it."

She gave him a sad, sweet smile, stood up and went into the house. In the distance, a fox barked. The light had gone out in the window of the livery.

*   *   *

The hardest week of his life, no question about that. He'd appropriated a pair of gentlemen's kid gloves from a box of fancy goods Uncle Marzo had bought sight unseen from a ship's captain and regretted ever since. They quickly wore into large holes, but they protected his hands from the worst of it. The partners noticed him wearing them, of course, but he never managed to find out what they said about him when his back was turned. He tried his very best to be useful and occasionally succeeded. Gignomai didn't talk to him much, he was far too busy, issuing orders, setting the pace. The partners didn't say things about him when his back was turned. Of course, Furio reflected, that's one of the marks of your true nobility: leadership, leading by example, never asking the men to do something you can't or wouldn't do yourself.

"Where did you learn to saw a straight line?" he asked Gignomai, on one of the rare occasions when they talked.

"Here," Gignomai replied. "Had to, no choice in the matter. I got Senza to show me once and made sure I took it all in. Actually it's not hard, once you've got the hang of it."

Furio couldn't make a saw do what he wanted it to no matter how hard he tried. "I thought you had to be brought up in the trade from childhood," he said. "That's what people've told me."

Gignomai grinned. "Well, they would," he said. "They want you to pay them for doing a job you can do yourself."

At some point Uncle Marzo lost his wonderful eyeglasses, the ones Gignomai had given him, the ones he'd stolen from his father. Uncle had the whole house and store turned upside down, but there was no sign of them. A homeless man who sometimes did odd jobs at the livery was suspected, since he'd come in the store at some point, but when he was looked for he couldn't be found.

By the end of the week, the front and rear frames were in place. Furio hitched lifts to and from the site on lumber carts, which at least saved him the misery of the long walk. One of the carters was furiously angry with the three partners who'd deserted the sawmill.

He yelled at them each time he set eyes on them and had a hammer thrown at his head for his trouble. Another carter wanted to run away and join the project, but Gignomai told him gently that they weren't hiring right now. Empty flour and bean barrels went back on the carts at night. There seemed to be an awful lot of them, and Furio thought about Uncle Marzo's dilemma. He'd heard people talking in the store about how much stuff was going out to the met'Oc boy's wild venture, and how there was bound to be a short-fall—higher prices to start with, and most likely shortages to follow. Two or three men from the colony found their way out to the site and asked for work. Furio reckoned Gig was right to send them away; either they were known to be no good or hiring them would cause trouble with their families. Besides, as Gig pointed out, the work was coming along just fine. They didn't need anybody else.

One night he waited for the livery window to light up, then walked silently down the street to the corner. He'd climbed into the livery many times when he was a boy, using the stunted sycamore tree as a handy leg-up and hauling himself up onto the roof by the guttering. Time had passed, of course. He weighed more and was rather less flexible. There were a couple of nasty moments, as branches groaned and slates came away in his hand. He made it, though, and decided he had two weeks of grinding manual labour to thank. He was cer-tainly fitter and stronger than he used to be. It was just a shame that everything hurt all the time.

Once he was on the roof it was easy. The back eaves overhung the hayloft door; it was no trouble dropping down onto the loading plat-form, where men stood to fork up the hay, and of course the hayloft door wasn't barred. He opened it as carefully as he could, but the faint creak of the hinges sounded like a scream in the quiet dark. He left the door slightly ajar, and crawled over the hay until he could look down onto the main area of the top floor.

The light came from a big brass lamp on a strong-looking table. Behind it stood a man. Furio could only see the top of his head, which was bald and garlanded with wisps of thin grey hair. The man was bending over a solid, heavy-duty bench vice, a rare and expensive item that Furio had last seen in Uncle's back store, lying on a bed of straw and still in its grease from the foundry. Clamped in the jaws of the vice was a small metal thing, too small to make out but shining with the harsh white gleam of newly cut steel. The man was working on it with a round file, slowly, carefully, a few strokes then stop, examine, measure with calipers. There were at least a dozen files lying on the table, also a couple of small hammers, cold chisels, two frame-saws with thin blades like wire. There was something else, which Furio didn't recognise, about eighteen inches long, steel and wood, wrapped in cloth. From time to time the man took the metal thing out of the vice and compared it with something else, another small metal thing that lay beside the vice when he wasn't using it. At one point he clamped that thing and the thing he'd been filing in the vice together, back to back, presumably so he could use one as a pattern for the other. The smell of cut steel was strong enough to make itself noticed over the hay.

The man took the thing he was working on out of the vice and held it up to the light. As he did so, something on his face sparkled, and Furio knew where Uncle's eyeglasses had got to.

The next day he took Gignomai aside and asked him, "Why is Aurelio camping out in the livery?"

Gignomai looked at him. "What?"

"Your man Aurelio," he said. "The blacksmith. What's he up to in the livery?"

Gignomai was holding a hammer in one hand and a pine shingle in the other; he had a nail between his lips. He slid the hammer into his belt and spat the nail out into his hand. "I don't know what you're talking about," he said.

"Ah," Furio replied. "Only someone's been staying at the livery. He's been there a few weeks now. And he's got a workbench in there and a bunch of tools, and he's doing some kind of fancy metalwork."

"Is that right." Gignomai frowned slightly. "Well, he's nothing to do with me." He located the shingle against the uprights and positioned the nail, jamming the shingle in place with his elbow. "What makes you think it's Aurelio?"

"I just assumed," Furio replied. "I wouldn't know, I've never seen the man. Where is he, anyway?"

"He got sick," Gignomai said. "So he's out at the Lascio farm in the long valley. They're some kind of off-relations."

Furio nodded and went back to work. In consideration of his skill and ability with a hammer and a nail, he'd been given the essential and uniquely responsible job of piling up shingles in stacks of twenty. That wasn't right, he thought. Hadn't Aurelio left the colony in a hurry as a young man, on account of some bother over a girl that left one man dead and another a cripple, and weren't the victims supposed to be members of his own family? In which case, his relatives would doubtless be delighted to see him, but not the other way round. It was possible that time had healed the wound, but not likely. Good-quality grudges were treated like heirlooms in the colony, where the desire to draw blood was never far from the surface, but rarely found a solid enough pretext. When the news of Aurelio's defection had broken, come to think of it, there had been a certain amount of excitement and speculation about his whereabouts. Rasso at the livery was, however, a good friend of Uncle Marzo and deeply in his debt.

He's up to something, she'd said, *and he's going to drag you into it.*

He dropped an armful of shingles and scowled at them. He asked himself if the warning had come from anybody else, would he be less reluctant to consider it? The answer had to be yes, which tormented him like an unreachable itch. On the other hand, Gignomai was his friend, had been ever since they were kids; he'd repeatedly broken out of the Tabletop just to visit him, which was no small matter. Besides, what secret could Gig possibly have that he wouldn't want to share with his oldest, his only friend? Surely Gig knew that there was absolutely no chance he'd betray Aurelio to his family, not even by an inadvertent slip of the tongue. And in any case, why would Aurelio be hiding dangerously in town, rather than here at the site, where his relatives and other enemies wouldn't dare come after him?

I ought to ask him, he told himself. It was more of a rebuke than a decision. If he needed to ask, he couldn't be sure of getting a straight answer, and more than anything else he dreaded creating a situation where Gig lied to him and he knew it was a lie. It would be one of those places you can't get back from, and he didn't want to think about the inevitable consequences.

Velio Fasandro had been helmsman on a beef freighter until a falling spar crushed his back and rendered him more or less useless, at which point he was promoted to harbour master of the colony. Most days he sat on a barrel on the quay, watching seagulls. In the falling down wooden shack that constituted the harbour office and de facto seat of colonial government he had a slate, on which he scratched the names and due dates of incoming shipping with a nail, which lived in a hole bored in the door frame specifically for that purpose. He had no calendar or almanac, so the dates were somewhat detached from relevance, but so long as the sky was clear he could guess the time of the month more or less adequately by the phases of the moon. Besides, Marzo at the store always told him well in advance when a ship was due. Not that it mattered terribly much. He was always at his post, on his barrel, and when a ship came in, all he had to do was take official notice of it, scratch its name off his slate, and stay out of the way while it was unloading.

On the day in question, therefore, when he saw what looked disturbingly like a mast on the horizon he assumed it was a product of his failing eyesight and looked the other way for an hour or so. When he looked back again, however, it was palpably a mast, with a ship under it, heading straight for the line of buoys that marked the only safe road into the harbour.

He sat perfectly still, wondering what it could mean. In twenty-three years, he'd never known a ship to be blown off course or forced into the colony by bad weather. Only ships for the colony came close enough to be forced in there; there were no other destinations. Also, it didn't look right. Colony ships were brigs or galliots, fat as pigs and painfully slow, or fly-boats, the great long cattle barges that looked like floating islands. This one—he broke the crust on his memory and fished out the word ketch—twin-masted, square-rigged on the foremast and fore-and-aft on the main, stepped well aft, light, fast and nimble, a hundred tons burden, if that; as much chance of seeing something like that in colony waters as finding a duchess in a laundry. Unless, of course, it was a government boat. Velio Fasandro believed in the government in the same way some country people still believed in the Little Folk, and expected about as much good from them. Still, who else could it possibly be?

He studied it carefully for a while. If it really was the government, someone should be told. Who, though? He thought about it, and came to the unpleasant conclusion: himself. He was, after all, the only public servant in the colony, paid (whenever anyone remembered) out of harbour dues, in theory entrusted with the full delegated powers of the central authority. In which case...

Quickly, he put that thought out of his mind. If the government had come here, it wanted to talk to somebody important, which could only mean Marzo at the store, Rasso at the livery or Gimao the chandler. Marzo was closest. Velio stood up, took one more look at the ship (it was getting bigger every time he looked at it, like a monster in a nightmare) and hobbled up the quay as fast as he could go.

"Can't be the government," Gimao the chandler protested, lengthening his stride to keep up. "They've forgotten about us. They don't even know we're still here."

Marzo didn't bother to answer. The government didn't feature anywhere in his personal bestiary of possible threats from the sea. The Company, on the other hand, was a horrible possibility at all times. He managed to sleep at night because he'd always told himself that the discrepancies and anomalies in the accounts he sent them as their duly appointed agent were too slight and trivial to justify the bother and expense of sending a ship, and the captains of the regular ships were his friends and all, in one way or another, in his power. But the possibility that the Company's never blinking eye might some day rest on him and decide to make an example lived always with him, like an arrowhead buried in an old soldier's chest, gradually creeping towards his heart. He glanced sideways at Rasso the liveryman, who winced and looked away.

Velio had caught them up by the time the ship crossed the harbour mouth. They silently rearranged themselves so that Velio was at the front, and watched as a boat pulled away from the ship's side. Six men in some kind of uniform were at the oars; there was a canopy at the back, so they couldn't see who else was on board.

We could kill them, Marzo thought, and row them out with rocks tied to their legs, and say they died of fever. But their friends on the ship would want to know more, it'd all go wrong and then we'd really be in trouble. Besides, what was to stop the Company sending another ship, and another one after that? He couldn't really face the prospect of filling up the bay with murdered men. Quarantine? A sudden outbreak of plague, which meant they couldn't possibly land? He reckoned he could pull it off, but the other three... He dismissed the idea and tried to stand up straight, as the boat pulled up to the steps. One of the oarsmen stood up and threw a rope, which nobody moved to catch. Then Rasso nudged Velio in the back, and Velio shuffled over to the rope and made it fast to an iron ring, half rusted through. The canopy curtains opened, and...

Dead silence, as the two strangers made their way up the steps. They moved slowly and awkwardly, because of their ludicrously unsuitable footwear. The woman was wearing knee-length black boots with thumb-long heels. So, for that matter, was the man.

"Hello," the man said. "Could you possibly tell me who's in charge here?"

He was an extraordinary creature. For one thing, he was tall. The only human being any of them had seen whose head was that far off the ground was Luso met'Oc, and the resemblance didn't end there. The only word, Marzo said later, was beautiful, though you couldn't really say that about a man, could you? But he had long hair, like a girl (or Luso met'Oc) and long, delicate hands, which somehow didn't seem out of place with his broad shoulders and heroic chest. He was dressed from head to foot in brown buckskin, cut in the most jaw-droppingly exotic style, with apparently meaningless brass studs all over in a pattern, and slashes in the sleeves so that the white shirt underneath poked through—that had to be deliberate, but why would you do it?—and more pockets than the average family had between them. The woman was dressed exactly the same—in *trousers*—and her hair was the same length and colour, and she really was beautiful by any relevant criteria. They were about the same age (Furio's age, Marzo thought, but they might as well have been a different species); they could almost have been twins, except the woman came up to the man's armpit.

Marzo suddenly realised that nobody had answered the man's question. "I'm Marzo Opello," Marzo said (it sounded like a dreadful thing to have to own up to), "I run the—" No, wrong. He reconsidered quickly. "I'm the Company agent."

"Ah." The man frowned slightly. You could see him weighing the matter up in his mind, and deciding to be magnanimous and to forgive. "Permission to come ashore."

A stupid little voice in the back of Marzo's head insisted that he really ought to ask their names before he gave them permission, though of course it wasn't his to give. He ignored it. At the same moment, it dawned on him that whoever these gorgeous creatures were, they weren't the government or the Company. A tiny part of him couldn't help wishing they were. Better the devil you know than the gods you don't.

At that point he had to move out of the way. The men from the boat were bringing up luggage—a trunk so huge that two of them could barely manage it, followed by another, followed by a third. The men disappeared, with the dogged, energetic air of men who have lots more heavy lifting still to do. Marzo dragged his eyes away from the trunk and said, "Of course, yes," and stopped. If he carried on talking, he'd have to ask them who they were and what they wanted, and although he desperately wanted to know, he couldn't bring himself to ask.

The man was smiling at him. He had the sort of smile you vainly wish you could be worthy of. "Do you think you could point us in the direction of the inn?" he said.

"There isn't—" Gimao started to say, but Rasso trod on his foot. "You're welcome to stay with us," Rasso said. "As our guests."

Idiot, Marzo thought, but it was too late to say anything. Fortunately, the man smiled and said, "Oh, it's not for us. We've got a tent." He made it sound unbelievably exotic, like a tame gryphon. "But my men here will need billets."

"There isn't an inn," Marzo said, looking down at his feet. "But there are farmers who'll put up men from the ships, if that's all right." He took a deep breath and said it; it felt like diving into a frozen pond. "What are you here for, exactly?"

The man and the woman looked at each other. Then the woman said, "We've come to visit our cousins. Maybe you know them," she added, "the met'Oc."

Her voice was like drowning in honey. "Oh yes," Rasso said. "We know them. They live..." He hesitated; presumably he'd just looked down and noticed he'd walked off a cliff. "Up country a way."

"Ah." The man smiled again. "Is it far?"

Yes and no, Marzo wanted to say. "Not very far," Gimao said. "About three hours' walk."

The man frowned. The woman looked both distressed and disgusted. Intemperate use of the W word, Marzo guessed. "Rasso here can let you have horses," he said quickly.

Yet more luggage: hat-boxes, musical instrument cases, writing-slopes, a huge sack with poles sticking out of it (the famous tent, presumably), a double sword-case, boot-boxes. Very occasionally, Marzo saw tradesmen's lists from home; one of the beef captains knew he liked realistic props in his dreams. The most recent one he'd seen had been five years old. He rapidly priced the growing barricade; nearly a hundred and fifty thalers just for the containers. The thought of what was inside them made his throat dry up. "Will you be staying long?" he asked, but neither of them seemed to have heard him.

A small crowd was gathering: children, mostly, a few women, two or three old men with nothing to do. In an hour or so, Marzo thought, the whole town will know. He wasn't sure why that worried him. He heard the man say, "Horses would be an excellent idea, definitely," and realised that Rasso hadn't moved. He trod on the back of his heel, which woke him up. He nodded twice, bowed awkwardly, walked three paces backwards, turned and fled.

Now there was an awkward silence, the sort that sucks unguarded remarks out of you. Marzo heard himself say, "Actually, the youngest met'Oc boy is a guest in my house," just as his rational mind resolved not to admit to any connection whatsoever. Too late. The woman looked interested and the man turned his head, smiled again and said, "Excellent. Perhaps we could meet him, and he could show us the way."

"Unfortunately he's not at home right now," Marzo said. "He's..." Words failed him completely. The hole he'd dug himself was so deep, so sheer-sided that he could see no way of getting out of it other than feigning an epileptic seizure. Gimao (presumably trying to help) said, "He's working out in the savages' country," before Marzo's furious glare cut him short.

The man and woman looked at each other. "How fascinating," the man said. "Is that far?"

"Oh yes." Marzo snapped the words out like a man drawing a knife. "Several hours, and in the opposite direction."

"Never mind," the woman said. "We'll just have to call on him another day." She glanced at the man, then added, "You've all been most kind but we really mustn't hold you up any longer. Thank you so much." It took Marzo a moment or so to translate that into *go away*, but as soon as the message went home he felt a surge of relief. Gimao didn't seem to have figured it out for himself, so he grabbed him by the elbow and kept a firm grip as he started to back away, towing him like a horse pulling a barge. As he turned his back on them and started to walk away, he heard the man call out, "Thank you!", but decided he was deaf and hadn't heard it. He realised he'd left Velio behind, but it was too late to go back for him now. Besides, Velio had nowhere else to go, and he didn't matter anyway. As they passed Velio's shed, they met Rasso hurrying along leading two horses: the not-quite-dead-yet mare and the gelding Teucer called the Anatomy Lesson, because you could see most of its bones. Welcome to the new world, he thought, and bolted for home.

"And then they rode off towards the Tabletop," the old woman said, "like they were the king and queen off hunting." She shook her head, sad and wise. "Just what we need," she added. "More of them."

Furio had kept his head down during the narrative, which (stripped of commentary) had given him little more than he'd already gathered from his uncle. He detached himself discreetly from the group and set off for the factory site.

When he got there, they were raising the roof-tree, and nobody could spare the attention to notice that he'd got there, or was late, or had important news. After a while he was yelled at to come and pull on a rope, which he did to the best of his limited ability. Apart from that, he played no part in the operation. At midday the job was done, and Gignomai allowed a rest and a small barrel of cider to celebrate. Furio saw his chance and darted over to him when he moved away to study the diagrams in his book.

"Yes, I know," he said, when Furio gave him the broad outline. "The carters told me, when they brought up the last lot of shingles. You didn't happen to hear a name, did you?"

Furio confessed he hadn't. "Nobody asked," he said.

"Oh." Gignomai shrugged. "Well, I expect Father'll be pleased. I reckon they're in for a shock, though. I don't imagine our place is quite what they'll have been expecting."

Furio waited for something, anything else, but apparently that was that. Gignomai was engrossed in his book. The diagram, pale brown lines on yellow vellum, nearly translucent, bore no resemblance to the skeleton of the shed that he could see, but Gignomai seemed happy enough with it. If he hadn't been, everybody within earshot would have known about it. He looked tired, Furio thought, but somehow larger; as though he'd walked out of one picture into another, but with no reduction of scale. Furio had never seen Luso, let alone Stheno, but he could imagine them quite clearly by looking at Gig and splitting him into two parts, the one who heaved great big beams about and the one who gave orders.

When he got home that evening, there had been no further sightings. As far as anybody knew, the strangers had ridden towards the Tabletop and the world had swallowed them up. Their luggage — the pile of trunks and boxes that had come ashore with the boat — had gone on a cart to the Heddo farm, where the six oarsmen had been billeted. According to the best intelligence, they'd taken over an empty barn and closed the door, and all that could be heard from outside was low voices, too soft to make out words. The ship was still bobbing in the harbour, where the keenest-sighted boys from the town were working shifts. So far they'd seen about a dozen men and the thin smoke from the galley fire. One boy claimed to have seen light flashing off a bronze tube on the rail of the castle. He was known to be imaginative, but a bronze tube could be a telescope (Marzo vouched for the existence of such things; he'd actually handled one, courtesy of a friendly captain) or a rail-gun — nobody quite knew what that meant; it was some kind of warlike jewellery or accoutrement worn by warships — and Rasso's uncle said his father had seen one once, when a frigate called at the colony in the early days. They couldn't quite make out whether Rasso's uncle was referring to the gun or the ship, and it was too much trouble to press the point. In any event, telescopes and rail-guns were both unbelievably exotic items, and the thought that the strangers might own one made them seem even more magnificent and unreal.

A week went by, a roof appeared on the shed, the cradle for the waterwheel was well under way, the town boys had stopped watching the ship and the strangers were, as far as anybody knew, still up at the Tabletop. Rasso was deeply concerned about his horses, on account of which no actual money had yet changed hands. The six oarsmen still hadn't left the barn: food went in and a chamber pot was emptied out back twice a day, but otherwise they might as well not have been there. The colony stopped holding its breath, and some people began to wonder if the strangers had been real, or just a dream shared by a small number of otherwise rational people.

Gignomai didn't seem interested, and Furio was rather relieved. Not so long ago, when he'd come back from the Tabletop with the sword, all that had been keeping him here was the lack of a ship. Now there was a ship, totally unexpected, owned by relatives of his who surely wouldn't begrudge him a lift back to civilisation. Or would they, now he'd been formally disowned? But the strangers had never seen Gignomai, so if he gave them a false name, or went direct to the captain and offered to work his passage—if he really wanted to be on that ship when it sailed, he'd have found a way. Instead, he was pointedly taking no notice. That, Furio felt, had to be a good sign.

Early afternoon, and they were nailing blades to the frames of the waterwheel, while Gignomai and one of the smiths negotiated over some technical problem to do with bearings for the main shaft. No cart was expected that day, so Furio was surprised to see one bouncing down the road through the trees. It was worn and rutted now, after all the use it had been getting, and the cart was being tossed around like a rat caught by a dog. When it reached the foot of the hill, Furio saw it carried two passengers: a man and a woman.

He nearly dropped his hammer into the river. The man was tall even sitting down. His hair was long under a tall, stiff hat with a very narrow brim. The woman wore what looked like a sailor's bad-weather cap, except that it seemed to be made of blue silk. When the cart stopped and she jumped down, he saw that she was wearing *trousers*.

He wasn't the only one to have noticed. Work stopped. Nobody spoke; everybody looked. Both the man and the woman were dressed in identical close-fitting suits of green buckskin, with high tasselled brown boots. Both of them had swords—like Gignomai's—hanging from their belts. The only difference between their outfits, in fact, was the man's broad dark green sash, into which something had been wedged: a short club, or a hammer.

Gignomai marked his place and closed the book. He hadn't been sure this would happen, and though he'd spent a certain amount of time trying to prepare his mind, he hadn't managed to come up with a coherent strategy. There was too much he didn't know, and it would be counterproductive to lay plans in the absence of data.

When he saw them, he had to make an effort not to smile. He recognised the outfits at once. There were clothes just like them in an old trunk back home. They'd belonged to his grandfather and grandmother, so clearly fashions hadn't changed much. They represented a City bespoke tailor's idea of practical, hard-wearing apparel for well-bred adventurers, inspired by a famous description of a hero and heroine in a popular romance about three centuries old. The velvet-covered buttons were, he decided, a particularly nice touch. You never knew when the glint of sunlight on gold or silver might give your position away to an enemy. The only thing that was different was the man's sash, and that was explained when Gignomai caught sight of a wooden ball with a steel finial sticking out of it. He knew the pommel of a snapping-hen when he saw one.

Oh well, he thought, and straightened his back as he stood up and turned to face them. "Hello," he said. "Are you looking for me?"

"Cousin Gignomai," the man said. No doubt in his voice. The

family resemblance, presumably. "I'm delighted to meet you at last. I'm Boulomai met'Ousa, and this is my sister Pasi."

Father would have been proud of him, under other circumstances, because he had no trouble at all visualising the offshoot of the family tree that linked the met'Oc to the met'Ousa. Third cousins, and a long way back. The visit, therefore, wasn't just social.

For the first time in his life, Gignomai was glad he'd been made to learn the formal first salutation: front leg straight, back leg slightly bent; head dipped but *not too much*, unless you want to be taken for a tradesman; slight movement of the right arm, left hand tight to the chest; look pleasant, but whatever you do, don't smile. He performed it better than he'd ever done when he was being drilled in the nursery, because this time it mattered. A faultless greeting from a man in labourer's boots and a torn shirt would say more than words ever could.

They replied in kind; slightly more fluent, as you'd expect, but with no trace of hesitation, so that was all right. Clearly Gignomai wasn't regarded as a clownish country cousin. "Come and have some tea," he said, his voice successfully bright and cheerful. "You'll have to rough it, I'm afraid."

"We don't mind," Cousin Pasi answered (she had a nice voice, but it reminded him of someone else, and he shivered). "All part of the adventure, isn't it, Boulo?"

Gignomai noticed that there wasn't so much as a trace of mud on the practical, hard-wearing adventurers' boots, with their inch and a half heels. He was pleased to see that Arano from the wheelwright's had taken the hint and stuck the kettle on the fire. The handful of tea he'd stolen from Marzo Opello's storeroom, wrapped in a twist of paper torn out of an old account book, was going to come in handy after all.

Cousin Boulomai was agreeably quick to get to the point, almost before the tea was cool enough to drink. "The fact is," he said, "we've made ourselves a little bit too unpopular back home."

"I have, he means," Cousin Pasi interrupted.

"It was both of us," Boulomai said, and his tone of voice was a marker for a long story later, if Gignomai had earned it. "Anyway, we decided it might be a good idea if we cleared out for a while, till things have sorted themselves out. And we were at a bit of a loss where to go, and my uncle Ercho—Erchomai met'Andra, he'd be your second cousin once removed—said, why not go and visit the met'Oc? So we threw a few things in a bag and, basically, here we are."

Gignomai nodded pleasantly. "That's your ship out in the harbour?"

"Mostly," Cousin Boulomai replied. "We had it from our uncle Sphallomai when he died. I think some met'Alla cousins have something like a one-eighth share, but I don't think they're all that interested. Really it's just a pleasure yacht, not a business proposition."

Gignomai had heard about the bronze tube, which sounded a bit big for a telescope. Sphallomai would be Sphallomai met'Autou; Father had written him letters. He decided to let it pass, but keep his ears open. "Well," he said. "I gather you've met our lot. Presumably they told you, I'm not exactly in favour up there these days."

Cousin Pasi, interestingly, pressed her lips together, and her eyes were quite wide open. Cousin Boulomai did a kind of elegant half shrug that Gignomai had seen Father use on informal occasions. "We had sort of gathered," he said, "but these things happen. My dad threw me out when I was eighteen, but now we're the best of friends."

"I got a formal notice of disinheritance," Gignomai said. "I'm no expert, but I think that can only be overturned by a motion of the House."

Cousin Boulomai raised an eyebrow. "Can you still do those?" he said. "I thought they went out with trial by combat."

"Still legal," Gignomai replied, "as far as I know. Not that it matters, since all our property back Home's been confiscated anyway, and what we've got here really isn't worth having. But if you want to be on good terms with my father, you'd be better off not knowing me."

Boulomai shrugged. "We choose who we're on terms with," he said. "And obviously, a private family quarrel is none of our business."

Gignomai took a moment to consider them. He only had a moment; any longer, and it'd be obvious what he was doing. He covered the hiatus by dropping the tea into a tin jug and pouring in water from the kettle.

Young sprigs of the nobility in self-imposed exile. From what she'd said, she'd done something, but he'd be prepared to bet her brother was mixed up in it too. They'd had time to go to the very best outfitters and be measured for their adventurer outfits, so presumably they hadn't escaped from the Guard by jumping out of a window. It was reasonable to assume they still had money at Home, contacts, the ability to get things done there even if they couldn't go there themselves. And the ship, of course. In all the many alternatives he'd contemplated, he hadn't included the possibility of a privately owned ship. It could, of course, change everything. But he knew better than to let one component, however fascinating, assume undue importance. Precipitate action was still to be avoided. Killing them and taking the ship, for example, would cause far more problems than it would solve, and besides, they hadn't done him any harm. A lot would depend, of course, on what they intended to do.

"So," he said, "will you be staying long?"

They looked quickly at each other. "We rather thought we might," Cousin Boulomai said. "To be honest with you, it's not like we've got an infinity of choice. Not for a while, at least."

Gignomai poured tea into three enamel cups. "It's not as though I've got anything to compare it to," he said, "but my impression is, compared to Home, this is a pretty desperate place, unless you were thinking of setting up a cattle ranch. Or are your plans a bit shorter term?"

Cousin Boulomai reached out for his cup. "We'd be interested in a good investment opportunity, certainly," he said. "Preferably," he added, sniffing the steam in the approved manner, "something that isn't too closely connected with Home, if you see what I mean. Seizure of assets is a distinct possibility."

His sister nudged him in the ribs, a small movement that Gigno-mai wouldn't have seen if he hadn't been looking for it. "Boulo worries," she said. "But, yes, we do need to think about earning a living."

Gignomai had been wondering how much they knew about him. Now he had a pretty good idea. "Well," he said, "far be it from me to promote myself, but I believe that what we're doing here has quite a good future. Of course, I would say that."

"Tell us about it," Boulomai said.

"Oh, it's quite simple and mundane," Gignomai replied. "As you probably know, the Company has an import monopoly here. We're forbidden to manufacture finished goods, and everything we use has to come in on a Company ship. Basically, they pay us in pots and knives for the ridiculous quantities of beef we ship out. That and the rent, or tax or tribute or whatever you like to call it, more or less covers everything the farmers here can produce, over and above their own subsistence. It's a rotten system, and we plan on doing something about it."

Boulomai pursed his lips. "Very public-spirited of you."

"Quite. And it's a living for me, since I've been thrown out, and not without a certain slight amusement value."

"If there's a monopoly," Cousin Pasi said, "aren't you breaking the law?"

Gignomai grinned at her. "Not yet," he said. "As I'm sure you know, this isn't colony land. This is the territory of the Rosinholet, who were here before our lot arrived, and we're under their protection, so colony law doesn't affect us. We'll only be illegal once we start selling things to the colonists. In any case, there's no garrison here and no customs office; I gather you met our entire civil service when you landed—the rather dazed-looking man sitting on a barrel," he explained. "As far as colonial government's concerned, he's it. I'm not saying they wouldn't send in a platoon of soldiers if they find out what we're doing but, really, who's going to tell them? It's in everybody's interest to keep quiet."

Boulomai digested this for a moment or so. Then he said, "Won't they notice, though? I mean, presumably your people will stop sending cattle."

"Not altogether," Gignomai said, "just gradually less and less. We've still got the taxes and the rent to pay, remember. But it's a question of cost effectiveness. If all we send is the value of the tax and the rent, pretty soon it won't be worth their while maintaining their fleet of expensive cattle transports. They'll reach a point where they start losing money, and then they'll pull out."

"Won't they wonder why there's so much less beef being produced?"

Gignomai nodded. "They may do," he said. "In which case, we sing them a lot of sad songs about disease and spoilt hay harvests and rivers running dry. Farming's a precarious enough business at the best of times; it won't be hard sounding plausible." He paused to sip his tea. It tasted revolting, but his cousins had drunk theirs without any sign of discomfort. Father had said once, in an unguarded moment, that what he missed most was tea, and the next day Luso had sent a man to burgle the store. "This colony is only a very small part of the Company's business," he said. "I found some figures in one of my father's books. The vast majority of their land and stock holdings are in the south-eastern provinces; we're just a sideline." He sipped a drop more tea. It got better as you got used to it. "At one time, of course, they had great plans. There's plenty of room out here, after all, so there's unlimited scope for expansion. But they could never raise the necessary manpower. People just didn't want to come here unless they absolutely had to, and the sort of people they could force into coming weren't the kind who make useful, productive farmers. We're an experiment that failed, luckily for us."

He stopped. The cousins waited to see if there was going to be any more, then shared another quick glance. "It sounds like it could well be the sort of thing we had in mind," Boulomai said. "How long before you're up and running?"

"Ah." Gignomai put down his cup. "That depends. At the rate we're going now, not till the spring. It's the same basic problem, you see: manpower. Even if I had the resources, I couldn't just go round the farms recruiting. It'd cause a problem—not enough people left at home to do the work—and I'd make myself unpopular, and then who'd want to buy my stuff? People want cheaper tools and table-ware, but not if it means they're left short-handed on the farm. You see, it's not like Home. There are no superfluous people here. That'd be a luxury we couldn't afford. So I'm condemned to being a small-scale operation, at least until we're shot of the Company and people actually start getting to keep some of what they produce. And that's a long time away."

Boulomai nodded slowly. "I take your point," he said. "But you also said, it depends. That implies there's an alternative."

"Well." Gignomai looked down at his hands for a moment. "Let's see," he went on, "your ship's got a crew of, what, twenty?"

"Eighteen."

"Eighteen," Gignomai repeated. "Now, either you send your ship home, which I don't think you really want to do, or else you've got to feed and house those men while you're here."

"That's not really a problem," Boulomai said. "We're not entirely destitute."

"Quite," Gignomai said. "But—well, I'm no expert, heaven knows, but I'm guessing that a ship's crew's got to include a fair number of skilled men: carpenters, sail-makers, probably men who can do a certain level of metalwork."

"I imagine so," Boulomai said.

"There you are, then," Gignomai replied cheerfully. "There's your investment in return for a reasonable share of profits. Besides, at this point in the proceedings we don't particularly need skilled men, just pairs of hands. Once the factory's built, they can learn from my people. Actually, we'll all be learning together, so really it won't make much odds." He paused, shrugged slightly, looked away. "Anyway, it's an idea," he said. "If it's not the sort of thing you had in mind, that's fine."

"We'll give it some thought," Boulo said. "It sounds quite splendid, but I suppose we should be grown-up and sensible and not rush into anything. Besides," he added as an afterthought, "we really ought to ask the men what they think about it."

Lumen Tereo, as she then was, married Ciro Gabela on the day they both turned nineteen. At which point, the colony breathed a sincere yet wistful sigh of relief. No question but that Lumen was the most beautiful girl the colony had ever produced, and one of the kindest, sweetest-natured and hardest-working. She was a living contradiction of every grandmother's assertion that a pretty face, as opposed to sterling virtues, meant nothing but trouble. With Lumen safely married, life could get back to normal, lesser courtships could be resumed, and young men who'd dared to dream were at liberty to settle for second best, which they did, in droves.

Four years and a baby daughter later, Lumen Gabela was still the prettiest. Now, though, she was making an entirely different kind of trouble. Her house was the cleanest and tidiest in the colony; disapproving old women who went to call on her came home and started scrubbing floorboards. Nothing was wasted in her kitchen or storeroom, and guests declared that her pigs' knuckles on pickled cabbage was a dish fit for a great house back Home. As for Ciro Gabela, he seemed to go though life in a sort of daze, and when men asked him what it was like, he just shook his head and refused to say anything.

Midway between the Gabela and the Heddo farms was an old linhay. It wasn't much — four walls and a roof, with a partition down the middle — and nobody was quite sure who owned it. But Ciro Gabela and Lio Heddo had always been good friends, so there wasn't a problem. Each stored his hay for the upper pastures on his side of the partition, and when the thatch needed seeing to, they did it together.

When the strangers arrived, Lio Heddo was the first man to offer a billet for their six oarsmen. He later said that they'd promised him a thaler a week, which he never received. The men stayed in the barn where they'd been put and, to begin with, talked to nobody. Later, when Lio's son Scarpedino began taking them their food, they loosened up a little, mostly because Scarpedino took to hanging about for hours by the door. They spoke to him—*go away*—and when that had no effect, they allowed him to come in and sit with them for a few minutes while they ate. They'd been cooped up in the barn for several days by that point. Scarpedino said they seemed to spend most of their time playing chequers, on a board made from an old sheet of tin torn off a derelict feed bin, using pieces they'd whittled from a broom handle. He went to the store and spent his entire fortune, half a thaler, on a scrimshaw chess set that had come as part payment for a ship's captain's booze debt. He took it to the men and taught them the game, which his parents played occasionally. Thereafter, it was next best thing to impossible to get any work out of Scarpedino. He spent all his time with the strangers' men, and refused to say what he did there, or what the men were like, or what their employers' plans were.

Two days after the strangers went to visit Gignomai met'Oc, Lumen Gabela went missing. Ciro Gabela assumed she'd been called back to her father's house on account of sudden illness or the like. The Tereo house was a day's walk east, and Ciro had a batch of young bullocks to dehorn. He waited for three days, heard nothing, and walked to the Tereo house. They hadn't sent for Lumen, or seen anything of her.

When he got home, he found Lio Heddo and a few neighbours waiting for him. Lio had found Lumen's head buried in the hay on his side of the linhay. The head appeared to have been cut off with an axe found lying in the grass twenty yards from the linhay door. The tongue had been torn out, and there were other disfigurements. There was no sign of the rest of the body.

Ciro had to be taken home; two old women from the Paveta house stayed with him. Nobody had any idea as to what should be done. Lio Heddo and his neighbours held a brief, rudimentary parliament outside the linhay, and resolved to send the youngest Paveta boy to town, where somebody was bound to know. Whether anybody was aware at this point that Scarpedino was also missing is unclear.

A barely quorate town meeting deputised Marzo Opello from the store, in spite of his many and passionately expressed reservations. He left his wife and niece in charge of the store, since Furio refused to take leave from the factory project, recruited Rasso's two youngest boys as his general staff, and drove out to the Gabela house in a donkey-cart, with the Rasso boys following on their ponies.

Once he'd installed himself in the Gabela house he officially convened a commission of enquiry, following the forms and procedures set out in a book someone had found in the customs shed, left behind when the garrison was withdrawn. Since Ciro was still too ill to be questioned, he sent one of the Rasso boys to the Tereo house, where Ciro's movements were confirmed: he'd been to see them, just as he'd said. Unfortunately, as Marzo quickly realised, that proved nothing. To judge from the state the head was in, Lumen Gabela had been dead for some time. It seemed overwhelmingly likely that she'd been killed shortly before Ciro noticed, or claimed to have noticed, that she'd gone missing. Marzo questioned the Heddo family about the axe, and Lio Heddo freely admitted it was his. It had belonged to his grandfather, but nobody had used it for a while because the head had come loose and they had a better axe anyhow, so it had been put in the barn, to be fixed some rainy day.

Marzo asked how long Scarpedino had been gone. Lio admitted he didn't know. They saw so little of him these days, it was hard to keep track. Before Lumen's disappearance? Lio shrugged. But that was beside the point, surely. There were six men living in the barn where the axe had come from; they were strangers, sailors, nobody knew the first thing about them. The facts, Lio didn't need to say, spoke for themselves.

At this point, a procedural problem arose. Marzo insisted that the regulations allowed him, as duly appointed investigating officer, to enlist such able-bodied men as he chose for a posse, with a view to interrogating the six men in the barn. Lio Heddo objected that

Marzo's appointment was at best irregular and quite possibly entirely illegal, that he only had Marzo's word for it that there was any such regulation (Marzo had brought the book, but none of the Heddos could read) and that, in any case, Lio must himself be a suspect in the case, which disqualified him for posse service. Similar objections were raised by the Pavetas, the Otizzi and the Scilios, the only other families in the district. Marzo pointed out that he was unarmed, whereas the men in the barn might well not be; also, there were six of them, all undoubtedly skilled dockside fighters, whereas Marzo hadn't been in a fight since he was eleven years old.

Scao Otizzi suggested that the person most likely to be able to control the men was their master, the stranger, last heard of at the factory site. Marzo sent one of the Rasso boys back to town, where Furio reported that the strangers had gone away and he didn't know where they were now. He assumed they'd gone back to the met'Oc, on the Tabletop.

Marzo drove back to town and convened a town meeting, rather better attended than the last one. Quoting verbatim from the book, he asserted his right to enlist a posse. The meeting held that he had such a right, but since the town was outside the district in which the crime had been committed, he couldn't enlist any of them — it had to be neighbours — and Marzo should go back to the Pavetas, the Otizzi and the Scilios, and insist. Marzo refused. At this point, Estimo Fano the cooper suggested from the floor that Marzo should ask for help from the met'Oc.

The suggestion had the effect of silencing the meeting for some considerable time.

"I'm serious," Estimo said. "Why not? They've got men and weapons up there, they reckon they're nobility, better than us. About time they did something for the community."

"You must be joking," Marzo said. "You want me to go up there and ask Luso met'Oc —"

"Why not?" Estimo repeated. "He won't eat you. After all, you're in business with that other met'Oc boy. Practically makes you family."

"Gignomai met'Oc's been disowned," Marzo pointed out. "Because he's friends with my nephew, I'm the last person they'll do a favour for."

It was at this juncture that Marzo, and the rest of the meeting, realised that Marzo had, by shared assumption, taken on himself the job of ambassador to the met'Oc. Rasso quickly proposed a motion formalising the appointment, which was passed by an overwhelming majority (Marzo Opello voting against).

"We can't do this," Marzo continued to object, even though the vote had been taken and minuted. "For one thing, the met'Oc are outlaws. Asking them for help would be—I don't know—treason, or conspiracy or something."

"Who says?" Rasso replied. "Where's it actually written down that the met'Oc are outlaws?"

"And anyway," Jano Velife the well-sinker pointed out, "the book says, the posse's got to be drawn from the district where the crime happened. You look at the map, you'll see the western edge of the Tabletop's just inside the district boundary." He grinned. He wasn't the sort of man who could easily disguise his emotions. "That makes them neighbours for the purposes of the statute."

Marzo, meanwhile, was thinking hard. "Better idea," he said. "Young Gignomai's got a parcel of men working for him these days, and they've got all manner of axes and adzes and sharp pointy things. And God knows, he owes me a favour."

Furio relayed the message; Gignomai replied that he'd have to think about it.

Meanwhile, events at the Heddo house had moved on. Because the Heddos had stopped sending food to the barn (because nobody was prepared to get that close), the six oarsmen had forced their way into the house and helped themselves to bacon, flour, pickled cabbage and beer from the store room. Lio Heddo had sent to town demanding justice, not to mention protection from further assaults. In the meantime, he'd moved his family out to the Paveta house.

Furio brought back Gignomai's considered reply. He would like to be able to help, but he and his partners were artisans and business-men, not soldiers. If they wanted someone military, he recommended his brother Lusomai, who positively enjoyed that sort of thing.

Marzo had a great deal to say about Gignomai when the town meeting reconvened. When he'd finished, he was reminded of the existing motion, *requiring* him to go to the met'Oc. A further motion was passed entrusting him with extraordinary plenipotentiary pow-ers for the duration of the crisis. Nobody was quite sure what that meant, but everybody agreed that it ought to be enough to get the job done.

Ever since the strangers' visit, Gig had seemed preoccupied, distant, more so than ever. Having given it some thought, Furio was moder-ately certain he'd figured out why.

Almost inevitable, he thought, as he passed nails to Turzo, who was nailing plates to the blades of the waterwheel. She's the first girl of his own age and class he's ever seen, apart from his sister, and she's pretty enough, if you like them small and pointy. Fair enough. It had always been obvious that town girls, let alone country girls, didn't interest him. Furio couldn't help grinning when he thought how noble he'd been prepared to be, at first, when it became obvious Teucer preferred Gig to him. But Gig wasn't going to waste himself on a colonial. Cousin Pasi, on the other hand, was his own sort—he'd noticed the change in Gig's vocabulary and syntax when he'd been talking to her—and although she might be in some sort of trouble right now, she had a rich and powerful family back home, so what-ever the trouble might be, it would probably blow over.

Was that what the met'Oc had thought, seventy years ago? he wondered. Had they arrived here in bespoke buckskin adventurers' outfits, with best-quality tools and equipment in hand-polished rose-wood cases, bearing the trade labels of the finest City makers?

In any case, Gig's intentions and ambitions as far as his pretty cousin was concerned were none of his business. But he needed to talk to him about Marzo.

"Furio," think of the devil, "leave that, I want you here."

Furio grinned at Turzo, handed him a fistful of nails and scrambled down. Gignomai was leaning against the rim of the wheel, wiping sawdust out of his eyes. Furio noticed he'd skinned his knuckles which were bleeding, but Gig didn't seem to have noticed.

"Your fucking uncle," Gig said.

Oh, Furio thought. "What's...?"

Gignomai shoved a piece of paper at him. Furio glanced through it, cursed his uncle under his breath, and handed it back. "I'll talk to him," he said.

"You bet you will." Gig looked tired more than anything else. "You tell him we made a deal; all the supplies I need till the job's done. I don't construe that as meaning what he thinks he can spare when he's in a good mood. All right?"

Furio counted to five under his breath. "That's not what he's said," he replied calmly. "If he's run out of planed shingles and nails—"

"One, I don't believe him," Gig snapped. "Two, if he hasn't got them in stock, he'd damned well better go out and get them from the lumber mill."

"Nails—"

"Someone's bound to have a few spare barrels of nails; it's just a case of getting off his backside and finding them. I can't have used every last four-inch nail in the colony."

Actually, Furio thought, that was a distinct possibility. "I'll talk to him," he said. "But please—"

"It's in his own interest anyway," Gig went on, as though to himself. "The sooner we're done, the sooner he can stop feeding us. If we're stuck here sitting on our hands for want of a few lousy nails, he'll be the main loser. But I suppose he's too thick to figure that out."

Furio breathed out through his nose. "My uncle isn't stupid," he said.

"He is, though." Gig frowned, as though aiming for perfect precision. "Cunning but stupid. Cunning is pulling one over on someone in a deal. Stupid is thinking you can cheat someone you regularly do business with and not pay for it in the long run. That's your uncle."

It was a valid summary of Uncle Marzo's life in commerce, but that was beside the point. "Do you mind not abusing my relatives?" Furio said angrily.

"Why not? I say worse about mine. Sorry," Gig added quickly. "Not your fault. But please, talk to him, will you? I really don't want to have to fall out with him, not when we're so far along."

Furio calmed himself down, like reining in a fractious horse. "That might not be so easy," he said. "You see, Uncle's not going to be at home for a while."

He explained. Gig stared at him, then shook his head. "Talk him out of it, for crying out loud. Really. I said some nasty things about your uncle, but he's not a bad man. People like him ought to stay away from my brother."

Furio winced. "I don't think he's got any choice. The meeting—"

"Screw that," Gig said sharply. "What's the worst they can do to him? Luso's perfectly capable of sending him home in a box, or with his tongue cut out, to teach him manners. My brother's a bit old-fashioned in his views, I'm afraid. You should know that by now."

That was the end of the conversation. Gig was called away, and Furio didn't have another chance to talk to him. On his way home, he thought about what Gig had said. He was puzzled. Gig had said a lot to him about his brother over the years. The mental picture he'd formed was of an unpleasant man, arrogant, violent, potentially dangerous in certain circumstances, but not a lunatic. Furthermore, those old-fashioned views were surely Uncle's best protection. A met'Oc wouldn't kill or torture a guest under his roof. But Gig had been quite emphatic.

Maybe he had his own reasons, Furio decided. After all, if anything happened to Marzo...

No, that didn't work. If anything happened to Uncle Marzo, Furio would inherit, and the future of the project would be assured;

in fact, it'd be better off. If Gig was as cold and calculating as he was making him out to be, it'd be to his advantage if Luso murdered Uncle Marzo. Not that he could make himself believe that. But why would Gig exaggerate the risk posed by his brother?

He decided not to say anything to his uncle that evening. As it turned out, he didn't get the chance. Marzo had gone by the time he got back. The house was painfully quiet. Teucer was the only one who spoke during dinner. She let it be known that she thought the idea of walking into the Tabletop alone and unarmed was insane, practically suicidal. She blamed Gignomai. The least he could have done, after all the hospitality he'd enjoyed and the goods and services he'd received, was to have gone with Marzo and intercede for him. Furio tried scowling at her across the table, but she managed not to look at him all evening.

The next day, Furio arrived at the site later than usual (the result of losing a boot in the boggy patch on the near side of the river). When he got there, he found the entire workforce clustered round an enormous fire with at least a dozen cartloads of charcoal, burning under what looked like an upside-down clay bell. He had no idea where it had come from or what it was for. He asked Ranio, the ex-blacksmith, who looked at him as if he was crazy.

"We're pouring the hammer," Ranio said.

That simply didn't make sense. "What hammer?"

Ranio shook his head and walked away. Furio looked round for Gig, and saw him heaving on a long lever sticking out of what looked appallingly like the backside of a cow. When he got closer, he realised it was a bellows, made from a whole hide with the hair still on. He couldn't recall having seen that either, but it must have taken a lot of time and work to make.

"What, this?" Gig said. "Here, you take over for a bit. I'm shattered."

Furio reached up. He was only just able to get his hands on the lever. "I'll do my best," he said doubtfully. "But..."

"We stitched up the hides last night," Gig went on. "Ranio forged the nozzle a day or so back. We carry on working, you see, when you've gone home."

Furio couldn't spare the breath to reply to that. He found he could bring the lever down by hanging from it with his feet off the ground. Pushing it back up again was backbreaking.

"We made the mould last night, too," Gig went on. "And the cupola. Baked them overnight in the embers to get them dry enough for the pour. Stick with it," he added, "I'll be back in a minute."

A minute proved to be a very long time. Each stroke of the lever sent a jet of air into the heart of the fire, which responded with a four-foot-high plume of flame, as though there was a dragon lurking in there somewhere. The base of the clay bell was starting to glow. Furio could see a channel — cast-iron guttering, which he'd last seen on the eaves of the store — leading to a pit. Each time he pulled the lever, a wave of heat washed over him, making his skin tingle.

Gig came back. He had that stone-cold worried look on his face; a very bad sign. He shouted something to Ranio that Furio didn't catch, apparently got a reply, and stepped back out of the way as the hidden dragon let out another spurt of fire. Around him, all the partners seemed to be busy, though Furio had no idea what any of them were doing.

"Right," Gig shouted suddenly. "Here we go. Furio, one more pull. The rest of you, stand well back."

He didn't follow his own advice; the rest of them did, sprinting like lumberjacks out of position when the tree splits. Furio hauled the lever down, let go, dropped to the ground and curled up into a ball, as a surge of hot air, moving fast enough to hit like a punch, swept over his head. As a result, he couldn't see what was going on. But he heard a roar not made by voices, and a terrifying hissing and cracking noise like branches breaking. It sounded as though something had just gone dangerously wrong.

Apparently not. A voice he didn't recognise yelped with pure joy, others joined in. He heard Gig yelling, "Keep back, it's still hot," then several more deafening cracks, then a rushing hiss that drowned out all other sound for three or four heartbeats. Then silence. Feeling extremely foolish, Furio uncurled and opened his eyes.

He couldn't see anyone. Then Gig walked towards the pit, with a long pole in his hands. He poked savagely at something inside the pit. Whatever it was, it delighted him. His face split into an improbably broad grin, and he called out, "It's all right, it's fine." There was a chorus of whoops and yells. Apparently, it hadn't been a disaster after all.

They had all sorts of fun and games getting it out of the pit. When they eventually won the battle, the end result proved to be a monstrous grey rectangle, impossibly heavy. At this point Ranio (who appeared to be the hero of the hour) took pity on Furio and explained.

"That's the head," he said, "for the drop-hammer. The bit that goes up and down."

Furio nodded dumbly. What drop-hammer?

"We had to cast it in one shot," Ranio went on, "and of course, we hadn't a clue, it was all guesswork, plus something he'd read in his book. I told him, you'll never get it hot enough to pour but, fuck me, he did."

Light was beginning to dawn. "You melted iron?"

Ranio beamed at him.

"That's impossible," Furio said.

"Yes," Ranio replied. "They can't even do that back Home. But he said it says how to do it in the book."

Furio remembered something he'd been told — he hadn't been listening — about how iron was worked. You heated up ore in a huge furnace, and when the rock was really, really hot, iron dribbled out of a hole in the bottom. But it was filthy, full of bits of rubbish, because no furnace ever made could get it hot enough to flow clean. Then you let the dribbles cool and forge-welded them into lumps big enough to be useful, and the more you worked it, the cleaner it eventually got. But nobody could cast iron in a mould.

Gignomai could, apparently.

He walked over and looked at it. A dark grey brick, four feet long, a foot high and wide. It'd have to be pretty clean or it'd shatter; rubbish inside the metal would make it weak. He turned away, and found Gig grinning at him.

"What do you reckon?" Gig said.

"Why didn't you tell me?"

That seemed to take Gig by surprise. "It's not my fault if you don't take an interest," he said. "Anyway, that's that done. Tomorrow we'll pour the anvil. Then it's just a matter of making up the frames, and there's a diagram in the book for that. It was the bellows that swung it; double-action, you get twice the blast, which means eight times the heat." He stopped, and grinned even wider. "Come with me," he said. "You'll see what I'm on about."

Gignomai's office was the back of a covered wagon, on the bed of which lay scraps of paper, a steel ruler, sticks of charcoal sharpened to fine points and a book. Gignomai turned a few pages, then held it out to Furio. It made no sense: line drawings, a fantasy in abstract geometry, annotated in brown ink in an alphabet Furio didn't recognise.

"Ah," he said. "I see."

Gig laughed. "Of course you don't," he said. "That's the old language. Stesichorus' *Instruments*, from Father's library. This is one of only six surviving copies. I don't suppose anybody's read it for five hundred years, except me."

"But it worked," Furio said.

"Well, of course," Gig replied. "They knew what they were talking about, back then." He sat down on the tailgate, suddenly exhausted, as though all the strength had been emptied out of him. "There's a popular fallacy," he said, "known as progress. People honestly believe that as time passes, we get smarter and better. Bullshit," he said, with a snapped-off laugh. "Six hundred years ago they were doing stuff we wouldn't dream of trying now. And then people back Home, who should know better, tell you that Stesichorus is all nonsense, because he talks about doing stuff that simply can't be done. But nobody's tried, not for centuries."

"Except you."

Gignomai shrugged. "It's one of the advantages of being exiled to the last place God made," he replied. "Deprived of the advantages of a decent education but with access to the old books, I did the unthinkable and read them assuming them to be true. Back home I'd have had professors telling me it was all drivel. Different world, you see. Just like the old savage said."

It took Furio a moment to realise he'd heard that last bit right. "You mean the old man we talked to?"

Gignomai nodded. "The more I think about it," he said, "the more I'm inclined to believe his people have got it more or less right. Not literally, of course," he added, as Furio's face went defensively blank. "But they're a damn sight closer to the truth than we are. There really are different worlds, and they exist side by side, and the trick is, being able to move from one to another. Like Stesichorus," he went on (he was talking to himself). "Like the old man said— someone from the past, long since dead, everybody ignores him because they know he isn't really there, but he knows how to pour iron, and it worked. Or my lot." He looked up, and his face changed. He smiled. "Ignore me," he said, "I'm drivelling. The thing is, we did it. We made the hammer." His smile was warm and happy, but it made Furio's skin itch. "If we can do that, we can do any bloody thing."

After considerable internal debate and soul-searching, Marzo drove to the Tabletop in the donkey cart. He'd been torn between that and one of Rasso's horses. The donkey cart was his, therefore his loss if it got wrecked or stolen. On the other hand, he always suffered agonies the day after riding horseback.

He crossed the river at Long Ford and drove up the far bank to the place where Luso's men had been seen to disappear on previous occasions. Nobody had ever dared get in close enough to see exactly where they went when they melted away into the rock. He drove up and down a few times but couldn't see anything. He was making a fool of himself. He got down, tethered the donkey to the stump of a tree, sat down on the ground and waited.

He must have fallen asleep. He was woken up by the toe of a boot digging in his back. He looked up, and saw a young man, tall and skinny, standing over him.

"Scarpedino," he said. "So this is where you've got to."

Scarpedino Heddo, the boy who'd disappeared at roughly the same time the murder took place. Now why would a bright young man, heir to a good farm, take it into his head to run away and join up with the met'Oc?

"Got lost?" Scarpedino said.

"Not at all." Marzo tried to make himself sound polite. "I'd like a word with Lusomai met'Oc, if that's possible."

"You want to talk to the boss." Scarpedino grinned at him. "No chance."

"No offence," Marzo said, through a frozen-solid smile, "but that's not for you to say, surely."

"Listen." Scarpedino knelt down and put his face an inch or so from Marzo's, but he didn't lower his voice. "We've got no quarrel, you and me. You piss off back to town while you still can, all right? You go bothering Master Lusomai, you may not get the chance."

Marzo fought to keep his voice from breaking, and narrowly won. "I wonder what Master Lusomai's going to think when he finds out you believe he needs protecting from the likes of me. Maybe he'll be touched by your concern. Or maybe not."

Scarpedino stood up and performed the most expressive shrug Marzo had ever seen. "Your choice," he said. "Don't blame me." He nodded to whoever was standing behind Marzo's back, and darkness fell, rough and quick. It smelt of stale cheese and bread mould, and Marzo guessed the other guard had shoved his lunch bag over his head. Strong fingers dug into his shoulder. He allowed himself to be guided by them, onto his feet, then stumbling forward. He hoped someone would remember to feed the donkey, but he wasn't confident about it.

He had a great opportunity, but he didn't manage to learn the art of walking blindfold. He kept banging into things, stumbling, getting hauled upright and shoved along. It didn't help that they were walking uphill rather faster than he'd have chosen. Marzo disapproved of uphill at the best of times, and this wasn't one of them. He tried to calculate the distance, but since he had no idea how far he was going, it was a futile exercise. After a while he gave up asking for a chance to stop and rest, because he couldn't spare the breath. The pain was mostly in his chest and the calves of his legs, but not exclusively so.

After a very long time, a pressure on his shoulder brought him to a halt, which made him happier than he could ever remember being. He wanted to sink down and go to sleep, but the grip of the fingers kept him perfectly still and upright. He heard knuckles banging on a door, then muttering, a lot of it, then silence. He stood and waited for a long time. It was so much better than walking.

The fingers moved him on at last, not far this time. Then another stop, and a downward pressure that folded him neatly at the waist. He hoped there'd be a chair. There was. Then he felt the bag being pulled off over his face, and the world flooded with light.

"Marzo Opello," said a voice in the middle of the glare. "I'm Lusomai met'Oc."

Oh God, Marzo thought. He blinked. There was a dark shape that could just be someone's head. "Thank you for seeing me," he mumbled.

"What can I do for you?"

The dark shape was sharpening up. He closed his eyes and opened them again. "Would you mind bearing with me just a moment?" he said. "I'm a bit..."

"Yes, sorry about that," said the voice. It was light and clear, like honey, but sharp as well. "New guard, a bit over-zealous. I'll have a word with him later. Would you like something to drink?"

"Yes, please," Marzo said quickly. The voice made a sound like very distant laughter. A moment later, he felt a cup—no, a glass—pressed into his hand. He gobbled it down. It burnt his throat.

Foul stuff, the worst kind of moonshine, made by someone who hadn't got a clue.

"Thanks," he said.

"Better?"

He could see the face quite clearly. A strong face, young, handsome, topped with wavy golden hair. Bright blue eyes. And, of course, a marked family resemblance.

"How's my brother, by the way?" Luso asked. "Seen anything of him lately?"

Marzo shook his head. "He's not staying with us any more," he said.

Luso nodded. "Up to something in the savages' country, I gather," he said, and sighed. "You know, I've spent years keeping the peace between my brother and my father. This time, I'm not sure I know what to do. Still, I keep trying." He looked away, snapped his fingers. The glass was taken from Marzo's hand, and came back a moment later, refilled. "That's not why you're here."

"No," Marzo said.

"It's about young Heddo, I suppose."

Marzo wished he had more time to think. "I imagine so," he replied. "Maybe you can tell me. You see, we don't really know what happened. I'm guessing you might."

Luso's eyes opened wide, then he grinned. "I see," he said. "But I guess the Heddo boy's being here's told you what you need to know. He did it—killed the farmer's wife, I mean."

Marzo decided not to say anything.

"Naturally," Luso went on, picking up a glass of his own, "you won't have heard his side of it."

"He's got a side?"

Luso laughed. "Oh yes. He reckons the woman had been messing him around for ages: leading him on, teasing him, playing games. Boring for her, stuck in the house all day with her husband away in the fields, and she'd got used to having men sniffing round after her. Young Heddo reckons he'd had about as much as he could take, and he got mad and killed her. All very sad, but not entirely his fault."

Marzo put his feelings into the fist he was clenching on his knee rather than his face or his voice. "He cut off her head," he said. "Did he tell you that?"

Luso nodded. "He said he made a rather feeble attempt at getting rid of the body," he said. "He has nightmares about it, apparently; keeps half the men in the bunkhouse awake." He sipped his drink, appearing to savour it; he must have a tongue like saddle leather. "I'm not going to pretend he's a lily-white innocent," he said. "Not many of them about in the best of circumstances. My people are a fairly rough lot or they wouldn't be here. But I think we ought to be practical. If I let you take him back, what are you planning to do with him?"

Marzo blinked. "We haven't really given it any thought," he said.

"Well, of course not, you've only just found out he did it. But you knew someone did it. What did you have in mind? A rope over the nearest tree?"

Marzo shivered. "Hardly," he said. "I suppose we'd have to hold him in custody till the spring, then send him Home on the ship for trial."

Luso shook his head. "That's a lot of fuss and bother," he said, "and that's assuming the ship's captain would agree. Big assumption. Fact is, you people aren't geared up for serious justice. No reason why you should be—you live quiet lives, which is a good thing."

"Thank you," Marzo said, because he felt he should.

"Justice," Luso went on, "is a fancy name for public revenge, as opposed to murder, which is what they call it when an individual does exactly the same thing. End result's the same: a dead man who was alive and healthy an hour or so ago, a dead body which is no earthly use to anybody, when he could be doing some useful work. Never could see the sense in it myself. But around here, justice simply isn't *practical*. Well, is it? You don't have a prison, you quite naturally baulk at playing executioner. Don't get me wrong, it does you credit. No, what matters isn't justice, or revenge, they're luxuries for city folk back Home. What matters here, where we are, is making sure it doesn't happen again. Practical, you see. Agreed?"

"I suppose so," Marzo said quietly.

"Well, of course," Luso said. "Now, I can't really let you take young Heddo back with you, because I've accepted him into my service so I'm obligated. The rest of the men would be furious, for one thing. What I can do, and I think this is the best solution all round, is to give you my personal guarantee that he won't be allowed to leave the Tabletop. If he does, I'll string him up myself. You have my word on that. Net result, more or less the same as if he's locked up in a cell somewhere, except that with me he'll have to make himself useful. Mucking out horses, carting water, scrubbing the tack-room floor: hard labour, for life." He grinned. "Justice, you might say. Well? What do you think?"

It felt as though the bright blue eyes were picking him apart, like a woman's fingernails unpicking stitches. "It's not really up to me," Marzo heard himself say. "But I can put it to the meeting."

But Luso was shaking his head. "Not what I heard," he said. "Extraordinary plenipotentiary powers for the duration of the crisis, isn't that right? Means it's most certainly up to you and nobody else." He drank the rest of his drink and poured another from a tall stone bottle. "Now, I'm suggesting to you that the course of action I've outlined is sensible, practical and reasonable in the prevailing circumstances. Always got to consider the circumstances. Very few people have the luxury of living their lives in a vacuum. Also, it's not as though you've got a choice, unless you were thinking of coming back here with a posse and trying to take him by force, which I really hope hadn't crossed your mind. Also, I'll throw in compensation, say a hundred ells of good cloth for the widower. Also, I'm asking you as a personal favour to me. Well?"

Marzo looked at him. It was like staring at the sun. He heard a voice that must have been his saying, "Could you make that a hundred and fifty ells?" and cringed.

Luso laughed, a big noise, like horsemen crossing a bridge. "I offered a hundred ells," he said, "because a hundred ells is all we've got to spare. I can't offer any more, so take it or leave it. Anything they may have told you about the unlimited wealth of the met'Oc is almost certainly wrong. Or I could write you a bill of credit on our bank back Home. Completely worthless, of course. Father says we've got millions there, but it's frozen. We can't touch it, neither can the government. Crazy." He sat down on the edge of a table, indescribably elegant. How could a human being make a simple movement so beautiful? "The thing is," he went on, "I'm a practical man. I keep the peace. No, don't laugh. It's what I do. I spend my life keeping the peace, that's my job. I keep the peace here between my father and the rest of us. I keep the peace in the colony as a whole." Marzo must have lost control of his face for a moment because he frowned at Luso. "You hadn't realised that," Luso said, "I'm disappointed. Still, I don't do it to be appreciated. Think about it, will you? By and large, there's no crime in the colony, no violence apart from the occasional domestic, hardly any petty theft, even. You know why? Because every no-good piece of rubbish in the colony comes up here, is why. I collect them, and I keep them in order. Once in a while I take them out raiding, and we steal a few head of cattle—no great loss, they belong to the Company, not real people. I have to do that, or they'd get fractious and out of hand. Also, my father reckons we need men-at-arms, guards, whatever you like to call them, to keep us safe from our enemies." He shrugged, a big movement, a flow. "I wouldn't know about that," he said. "Maybe we've got enemies at Home who might turn up one day and want to cut our throats. Maybe it's to protect us from your people in the town. Don't ask me. That's politics—my father handles that side of things. He just tells me we need men-at-arms, and I do as I'm told. And I keep the peace. You're looking at me as if I'm mad, but it happens to be true. There's peace, isn't there, by and large? Well?"

Marzo nodded.

"You don't think it just happens," Luso said. "It doesn't grow up out of the ground, and the stork doesn't bring it." He leaned forward a little. Marzo wanted to move, but couldn't. "All I'm asking is that you do a little bit to help me do my job. You go back to town, tell them the matter's been dealt with and there won't be any more trouble. You're the smartest man in the colony, everybody knows that, and if you say it, they'll listen. I'll do my part and keep young Scarpedino on a tight leash, where he belongs. And if it works out, I can guarantee there won't be any more cattle raids for a good long while. You can give them your word on that, and when it comes true they'll remember who fixed it. They respect you, and with reason. You're better than them, because you're smart." He smiled, spread his hands in an attractive gesture. "I think it's a blessing in disguise, what's happened. It's about time we opened a dialogue, and I'm glad to have had a chance to get to know you and establish a working relationship. The main thing is that basically we're on the same side. We want to keep the peace. That's what matters, isn't it?"

Marzo couldn't help remembering the old story about the king who tried to negotiate with the sea. He won: the tide went out. Then it came back in again. "Of course," he said.

"And you'll make them see it that way?"

"I'll do my best."

"Of course you will." Luso stood up suddenly; the interview was over. "Now," he said, "I expect you'll want to be getting back. The store doesn't run itself. I appreciate you taking the time to come here, and if there are any more problems in the future, you come and see me. And I'd like you to accept this" — he put his hand in his pocket, drew it out and opened it — "as a small token of appreciation."

Lying on his palm was a large brooch for a man's cloak: gold filigree, with a lump of amber the size of a thumbnail. Marzo tried very hard not to think what it must be worth. Slowly he reached out and let Luso drop it into his hand. "Thank you," he said, in a very small voice.

"Pleasure doing business with you," Luso said. "If you see my brother, give him my love."

When Marzo eventually got back to the cart (bag over his head all the way, but at least it was downhill this time) he found the donkey munching contentedly out of a fat nosebag. Say what you like about the met'Oc, he thought, they know how to treat a guest. And it's not every day an ordinary man finds himself being terrified, threatened, outmanoeuvred, reasoned with, beguiled, convinced, flattered and bought, all in the space of an hour or so.

He pinned the brooch to his coat before he drove home — on the inside, where nobody could see it.

When he got home, they told him what had happened.

Ciro Gabelo, the dead woman's husband, had taken his wife's death badly. For several days he stayed in the house drinking his way through the winter supply of beer and cider. When it ran out, he asked the neighbours who were looking after him for some more. They told him they thought he'd probably had enough, which sent him into a rage. He chased them out of the house with a knife, which they interpreted as absolving them from their duty to the bereaved. They went home and barred the door.

Ciro stayed indoors for a day, and left the house very early the next morning. He went to the Heddo farm. From the toolshed he took a muckfork and a beanhook, then kicked his way into the barn, where the six oarsmen were staying. They weren't there. So he went to the house (which the Heddo family had abandoned when the oarsmen came looking for food, after the Heddos cut off supplies) and found them in the kitchen, playing draughts. It seems likely that none of the oarsmen had any idea who he was. He killed the man who opened the door to him with a single thrust of the fork. Its tines got stuck in the man's ribcage and he couldn't pull it out, so he let go of it and went for two men sitting at the kitchen table. He killed one of them with a blow to the head; the other one warded off his attack with his left hand, losing two fingers. Two of the survivors ran out by the back door. The third, who'd been slicing bacon with a folding knife, took a lunge at Ciro, who dodged, kicked him in the back of the knee and hooked him through the shoulder as he fell. He then tried to finish off the man whose fingers he'd just severed, but he slid under the table where Ciro couldn't reach him. This made him furiously angry. He finished off the man who'd tried to knife him, then crossed to the fireplace, flicked a couple of burning logs out of the grate and kicked them under the table where the last survivor was hiding. It was probably at this point that he realised two of the oarsmen were missing. He abandoned the man under the table and ran out of the back door, yelling at the top of his voice. Presumably he searched the farmyard and the outbuildings, but the men were long gone. They had in fact run out into the orchard and hidden in an overgrown lime kiln at the far end. Eventually, Ciro went back to his house, where he was later found hanging from a rafter.

Marzo was silent for a long time after he'd heard all this. Then he said, "Where are they now?"

"The oarsmen?" Rasso the liveryman looked mildly guilty. "They're here, in the cellar, tied up. That niece of yours insisted on patching up the man's hand. We told her not to bother—"

"They didn't do it," Marzo said, in a dull, flat voice. "It was Scarpedino Heddo. The strangers had nothing to do with it."

Everyone suddenly went quiet and thoughtful. Then Stenora the horse doctor said, "Are you sure?"

"Yes," Marzo replied irritably. "I had it from Lusomai met'Oc himself. Scarpedino's run off and joined the met'Oc. I saw him there. The strangers weren't involved in any way."

Gimao the chandler, who'd been sitting perfectly still wearing a stunned look, frowned heavily. "I heard Scarpedino'd been spending time with them," he said. "I dare say they put him up to it."

"Don't be bloody stupid," Marzo snapped. "Lusomai said Scarpedino and the Gabelo woman had been playing some sort of nasty games for some time. Seems like it got out of hand, and that's all there is to it. And now we've got this mess to deal with."

That didn't go down so well. "You can't blame Ciro Gabelo," Rasso said. "He assumed—"

"He was a bloody fool," Marzo cut in. "Does anybody know where those two offcomers have got to? They'll have to be told."

"Aren't they up on the Tabletop?"

Marzo shrugged. "I didn't see them, but it wasn't as though I was given a guided tour. Still," he went on, "I guess the met'Oc probably know where they are. They aren't going to be happy about this."

"So what?" Stenora said. "Even if the oarsmen were innocent, it's not our fault, what Ciro did."

"I'm not sure people like that are going to see it in those terms," Marzo replied. "Of course, it helps that Ciro's dead."

There was dead silence for a moment. Then Gimao murmured, "Do you know what you just said?"

Marzo closed his eyes and sighed. "You know," he said, "if this is what high public office is all about, you can shove it. What I meant is, since the man who did the killings is dead, we aren't going to have the aggravation of those two demanding justice, which would've meant either handing over Ciro Gabelo or refusing and risking a goddamned war. You do realise, don't you, that this is a really bad situation. I'd be glad of some help, if it's all the same to you. I don't remember volunteering for any of this."

Another silence, longer and gloomier. Then Gimao said, "Don't look at me. I'm not getting involved."

Marzo didn't bother to reply. "Rasso? You were there when the ship came in."

"What the hell's that got to do with anything?"

"Those two flowers of the nobility know you," Marzo replied. "And it's your turn. I've done enough."

Rasso looked terrified. "You want me to go and tell them."

"I take it you're not volunteering." Marzo laughed. "No, you're right. I've already been up there, I guess I'm it." He rubbed his eyes with thumb and forefinger. It had been a long day. "Fine," he said. "I'll go back, and I'll talk to them. I'll see if I can make a deal. But if I can," he went on, "it's binding on all of us, agreed? I don't want a murmur out of any of you or anybody else. Otherwise you can find some other idiot."

Nobody spoke. He could feel them waiting for it to be over, and the oddest thought crossed his mind: I despise them. My friends and neighbours, known them all my life, and I wouldn't give spit for any of them. They're just not...

Practical. Not practical men. Not like some.

"That's fine," Gimao said timidly. "You go ahead and do whatever you think's best. We'll all be right behind you, no problem about that."

Marzo nodded (and it was as though he was looking into a mirror, and seeing there a man who kept the peace). "That's settled, then," he said. "Now, if you wouldn't mind, I want to get out of these wet boots and have some dinner."

They didn't hang about. When they'd gone, Teucer brought him a plate of bread and cheese; they hadn't known when to expect him back, so they'd already had dinner. Displaying unusual tact and sensibility, she put the plate down and withdrew quickly.

Marzo ate slowly — he was too tired to be hungry — and between mouthfuls figured out a plan of action. It was fairly horrible, but he hoped it'd do. Then he took his boots off and propped them up in front of the fire to dry, at which point, Furio arrived home, took one look at him and said, "Uncle? Has something happened?"

"You again," said the guard.

Marzo nodded. "That's right," he said. "Have we got to do all the business with the bag?"

"Yes."

"Fine." Marzo closed his eyes, and the bag went over his head. "Take it a bit slower today, would you? Last thing I need's a twisted ankle."

This time, Luso was dressed in what Marzo took to be his hunting outfit. It must have been the very best quality, eighty or so years ago, but now it was mostly darns and patches. It looked like what the strangers had been wearing, and Marzo guessed it must have come from Home.

"Always delighted to see you," Luso said, "but I wasn't expecting you. How can I help you?"

It was easier, Marzo found, if he looked at the floor or the wall a few inches above Luso's head. He recited the facts as quickly and plainly as he could.

"Thank you," Luso said quietly. "I'm grateful to you for coming straight to me."

Marzo made himself look at him. "It's a mess," he said, "and I don't know what to do. I was hoping…"

Luso smiled, and Marzo felt a weight lift off him. "These things happen," he said. "Don't look so sad," he added. "It's not the first time, won't be the last. The main thing is, we're here talking to each other instead of organising raiding parties." He perched on the edge of the table, the way he'd done yesterday. "You're right in assuming my cousins will be angry," he said. "The crew of their ship are, naturally, under their protection, and they have an obligation to see justice is done. Fortuitously,"—later, Marzo made a mental note to remember that word in that context; so much better than they way he'd said it—"the man who killed them is himself dead, which relieves us of the need to do anything about him. On the other hand, it complicates matters. Justice, you see, has got its own sort of twisted arithmetic. Justice demands that for every crime there should be a punishment. If the obvious party to be punished is unavailable for some reason, you've got a problem. Complicated, of course, by what people feel is expected of them."

Marzo didn't like the sound of that. "These people…"

"My cousins," Luso said. "Distant cousins, but we are related, yes. Also, for the purposes of the rules of conduct, they're our guests, therefore de facto members of the household, which unfortunately makes it my problem. Well," he added, with a faint grin, "it doesn't have to be a problem. That's where your help would be greatly appreciated."

"What can I do?" Marzo asked.

Luso edged forward a little. "I think this is an interesting moment in the history of this colony," he said. "All sorts of bad things are happening, which makes it dangerous, but on the other hand, we've got two key assets: you, and me. Don't know about you but I think we're getting along pretty well. I think we can sort this out. Do you?"

Marzo hesitated, then nodded.

"Splendid," Luso replied. "All right, here's the deal. We forget about what we agreed yesterday—scrap it completely. Instead, we set off my man Scarpedino's offence against the three dead men. Wipe the slate clean, start again. I believe I can square it with my cousins, if you can handle your people. I'm sure you can."

Marzo felt a wave of panic sweep over him. He did his best to put it aside. "I think so," he said.

"That's grand," Luso said. "That's what I call a sensible approach. Actually, it works out quite well. It gives my cousins an opportunity to be magnanimous, which stands them in good stead with us. We'll have to find a way to make it all right with the rest of their crew, but you can leave that to us. Really, there's no desperately pressing need for them to know the exact truth of the matter, if you see what I'm driving at. Main thing is to put it all behind us as quickly as we can. Agreed?"

Marzo waited for a moment or so before saying yes. It occurred to him that Luso somehow knew that the deal they'd just reached was the deal he'd come here to suggest. Certainly, it did feel rather like their minds worked in a remarkably similar way. Or maybe that was what Luso wanted him to think. Not that it mattered particularly, yet.

"I think," Luso said, standing up, "this calls for a drink. No, not the family stuff," he added, to someone in the background that Marzo couldn't see. "The bought stuff."

Marzo recognised it as soon as he tasted it. He had half a case of it left, stored carefully behind a stack of empty crates in the back cellar. Which reminded him...

"Ah yes," Luso said, when he'd mentioned it. "Good point. Is the wounded man fit to travel?"

"I think so."

"Splendid. Best thing would be if you sent them up here, and we'll take care of them. Get them out of your way, before there's any more trouble."

Marzo hadn't thought of that, and shivered. He ought to have thought of it. Entirely possible that the three survivors might want some degree of revenge or justice. Then it occurred to him to wonder how he was supposed to send them. What if they didn't want to go?

"I'll have my cousins write a letter," Luso said, before he could raise the question. "Do you think you could arrange transport?"

It was a small colony and Furio had lived all his life at the store, where sooner or later everybody came. A face he'd never seen before was, therefore, a remarkable thing.

The man was there when he arrived one morning. He was unpacking tools — a hammer, half a dozen files, a steel square — from a canvas bag. He looked up as Furio approached, but didn't appear to have seen anything to interest him. He was tall, thin and dressed in cloth that hadn't been bought in the store; Furio knew every single bolt they'd ever stocked.

"From the ship," Gig told him, when Furio managed to snatch a moment of his time. "My cousins have decided to invest in the project. Very big of them."

Suddenly there were new faces everywhere. It was disturbing, like living in a dream or a different world. But the newcomers worked hard and brought new skills, or were better than the colonials at old ones. There were two smiths, employed full time in straightening horseshoes and forge-welding them lengthwise to form the long bars that would make up the drop-hammer frame. Three carpenters were building a machine out of oak beams; Gig called it a lathe, for making the pulley wheels and bearings. Half a dozen more worked on the hammer-head and the anvil; they'd been stonemasons, Gig explained, and knew how to square up stone blocks with chisels, and there wasn't a world of difference between that and chipping flat surfaces on blocks of iron. Furio tried to work out exactly how many of them there were, but as soon as he thought he'd arrived at a definitive total, a new man appeared out of nowhere and he had to recalculate. He couldn't help wondering how on earth Uncle Marzo was finding food for all these men, let alone supplies and materials, but it had become a subject he didn't dare discuss either here or at home.

The hammer seemed to grow during the night, like a strange kind of giant mushroom. Gig had two shifts running—the glow from three furnaces and a dozen forges was enough light to work by. Parts were fabricated in daylight and assembled by firelight. So far, a thousand scrap horseshoes had gone into making the two upright beams of the hammer frame, also discarded wheel tyres, hinges, bolts, hooks, scythe blades, axles, practically every piece of rusty junk dragged out of barns and briar patches right across the colony. They'd been heated up, hammered straight, welded into bars, folded, welded again, folded again, welded lengthwise to other bars. There was a machine for twisting strands of wire together into rope. Furio had no idea who'd built it. It was there and running one morning, with one stranger turning a handwheel and another feeding it three lines of wire. Meanwhile, the shed that would house the hammer was being built up round it, like an eggshell forming around an already hatched chick. They couldn't put the roof on, Gig said, until they'd dropped the hammer-head down into the frame, but he wasn't going to wait till the hammer was finished before building the shed. Another team were rigging up the gear-train that would take off power from the waterwheel and run the hammer and the sawbenches. It was like watching a child with no skin growing at a monstrously accelerated rate.

The faster the thing grew, Furio found, the less he had to offer. By now he'd proved quite conclusively that he was no carpenter, metal worker, joiner or mason. He could lift one end of something, so long as someone explained slowly and clearly exactly what was expected of him. He could drive in relatively unimportant nails. He could pick things up and carry them; he could be trusted with a certain degree of unsophisticated sorting into piles. But he was slow, tired too easily, lacked initiative, didn't seem to have the knack of working efficiently with others—not for want of trying, maybe as a result of trying too hard. There was one job he knew he could do well—quartermaster and supply clerk—but whenever he suggested it Gig didn't seem to hear him or quickly changed the subject, and he guessed this was because Gig suspected him of spying for his uncle. An illiterate off the ship got the job instead, and did it very well using a system of tallies notched into bits of stick with a penknife.

Among all the new faces, there was one old face he kept looking for but never seemed to see. Aurelio, the met'Oc smith, hadn't shown up yet, although a light no longer showed in the livery window. It was possible, of course, that the old man had repented and gone back to the Tabletop—certainly, no reason why Furio should've been told if this was what had happened—but he doubted it somehow. So far, in spite of the furious pace and demanding nature of the work, nobody had left and gone home as far as Furio could see.

One day, when he'd had enough of carrying fifteen-foot planks from one side of the site to the other (he didn't know what they were for, or why they couldn't have been offloaded in the right place to begin with) he looked round to make sure nobody was watching, then walked quickly away into the woods. If anyone had seen him, they'd assume he was going for a piss, but it was hardly likely anybody would spare him even that much thought.

He followed a deer track for a while until he came to a hollow, rising steeply on the far side. He could still hear the incessant chime of hammers and a few faint, irritated voices, but at least his ears weren't ringing. He climbed to the top of the rise, sat down on a fallen tree trunk and simply enjoyed being there, for quite a long time.

The crack of a twig in the hollow below brought him back. He looked down and saw Gig, walking purposefully, carrying a rag bundle. He'd already opened his mouth when he decided not to say anything. He wouldn't hide or anything stupid like that, but he wouldn't announce his presence, either. Not, at least, until he'd seen what Gig had with him so carefully wrapped up.

He knew what it was as soon as it came out of the cloth, though he'd never actually seen one before, but he'd heard Gig talk about them and other people had described them. It was about eighteen inches long; a wooden curve with an iron pipe let into it, and an iron plate mounted on one side. On the plate—he wasn't quite close enough to see clearly—some iron thing like a bird's head and neck, rearing up over some other iron thing like a flattened thumb. A bird's head—hence the name, the snapping-hen. Gig had said it was called that because when the hammer flew forward and struck the flint against the steel, it looked like a chicken suddenly stooping to peck. He'd imagined it all wrong, of course, but now he could actually see one he could appreciate the similarity.

Gig pulled something from his pocket. It was the pointy end of a cow's horn, with a wooden stopper in the tip. This stopper pulled out, apparently, and as you withdrew it, you tilted the horn back, as though you were trying not to spill something inside it. In fact, the stopper was also a measure. He watched Gig pour a sort of black sand out of it into the open end of the iron pipe. Then he hesitated, not knowing what to do. Furio grinned. If Gig put the snapping-hen down so he could put the stopper back in the horn, the black sand would spill out of the pipe, likewise if he put down the horn. What he needed, obviously, was a third hand. He eventually solved the problem by gripping the stopper in his teeth and sticking it back in the horn that way. Then he dropped the horn on the ground and fished around in his other pocket until he found something else: a small round nut, or stone, except it was silver-shiny. Then he froze again, confronted by some new difficulty. Then he popped the silver ball in his mouth while he went back once more to his pockets and dug out an inch-square scrap of linen rag. This he stretched over the open end of the tube, like the cloth you put over a jar of jam. He leaned forward until his nose was practically touching the tube, and gently spat the silver ball on top of the cloth stretched over the open hole. Next he pressed the ball with his thumb until he'd sunk it into the tube mouth.

(I'll bet Luso doesn't do it this way, Furio thought, or if he does, we've clearly overestimated the threat he poses.)

Next Gig looked round for a bit of stick. It had to be the right size. After quite a while he eventually found one, and used it to shove the ball further down the tube. He seemed quite concerned about this stage of the operation. Furio guessed it had to go all the way down to the bottom, or something bad would happen. Then the cow horn came out again. Gig pulled back on the bird's head until it clicked, then pushed the flattened-thumb away from him. It hinged forward. Under it was a hollow, like the bowl of a very small spoon. He unstoppered the horn, half filled the spoon with black sand and pulled the flattened thumb back to where it had originally been. There was a repeat performance of putting in the stopper; the horn back in the pocket; then...

Gig stood quite still, holding the snapping-hen, not apparently doing anything. It wasn't fear exactly, though if he'd been in Gig's shoes, Furio would've been petrified, because all manner of bad stuff happened, apparently, if you made a mistake getting the snapping-hen ready. Not fear; as far as he could tell, it was a kind of unwilling-ness—the dog that doesn't come back when it's called, the horse that won't come to the halter, the child who won't come in to dinner. Gig looked for all the world like someone who was about to do some-thing he didn't want to, but had to, but didn't want to. It crossed Furio's mind that a friend, if Gig had one, would probably go down there and talk to him to see if he could help. Of course, he stayed where he was.

Then Gig pulled the bird's head back a little further, and there was another click. He looked round—something to shoot at, pre-sumably—then raised the snapping-hen at arm's length, as though he was trying to get it as far away from himself as it would go. When his arm was straight, he stood quite still.

There was a click, as the bird's head pecked, and a hissing noise. A little round ball of white smoke lifted off the side, followed by a rushing boom, like thunder in a small room. Furio saw Gig's hand lift, like a smith swinging a hammer. There was white smoke everywhere, a whole cloudful. And that, apparently, was that.

He saw Gig slowly lower his arm, look carefully at the snapping-hen, then stoop and lay it down on the ground. He walked over to the place he'd been pointing at, but Furio couldn't see what he leant forward to examine. He watched him look for quite some time, but he didn't seem to have found anything.

Many and various were the outcomes he'd contemplated, but this hadn't been one of them — not a clean miss, at five yards. Clearly it was harder than it looked.

He knelt down and prodded the leaf mould with his finger. It'd have had to make a hole, a big, deep one, and if he could find the hole, at least he'd know by what margin he'd failed to connect. Even so — a stump the size of a man's head, at five yards, and he'd missed it. Terrific.

Still, it worked, and that was the main thing. The fact that a bow and arrow would get the job done in a quarter of the time (and you might even hit something) and with infinitely less fuss was neither here nor there. He was conscious of having taken another step on a long road. It was a cold feeling, but there was a degree of intellectual satisfaction, such as a scientist might feel at the conclusion of a successful experiment. Not what he'd been expecting, but never mind.

He took a moment to listen. He could hear the hammers, the saws, voices. It wasn't the same as being there, where he was part of it or it was part of him. It occurred to him that he could simply walk away, choose a direction and keep walking until he came to a place where he felt like stopping, and be rid of it all, now, before it closed in on him and swept him away. The urge to do just that was so strong that he could barely keep his feet, but then he thought, No, don't be ridiculous, this is what you *want*. You started it. Besides, it's all gone too far now.

There was something heavy in his hand. He looked, and saw the snapping-hen, which he'd completely forgotten about. All that, and he couldn't even hit a tree stump. Hardly what you'd have a right to expect from the harbinger of the end of the world.

He picked up the oily rag and wrapped it up carefully, making sure that the hammer and frizzen were properly concealed now that there were men on the site who might well recognise a snapping-hen if they saw one. Really there was only one direction, back the way he'd just come to rejoin the main road. Or maybe not; there was one faint possibility...

"I'll be gone for a few days," he told the foreman (Dacio, the ship's midshipman; a good, solid man who never thought unless he had to). "Keep them going on the hammer, that's top priority, and if there's time, get them started on the belts for the overhead shafts. And check all the incoming consignments against the materials book. I'm starting to have my doubts about Marzo Opello."

Dacio didn't actually salute, but the effect was the same. He'd been in the navy before he signed up with the met'Ousa, and although that had been several years ago, he was taking a long time to recover. "Leave it to me," he said confidently. I might just do that, Gignomai thought, but you wouldn't like it if I did.

He nearly managed to forget to take the snapping-hen, but at the last moment he noticed it, when he was rummaging in his trunk for his spare boots. He looked at it for a while, then stuffed it into his knapsack. It was too long to go in sideways, and he had to leave the barrel end sticking out of the top. He packed the powder flask as well, and the patches, and the spare flints, and the bag of balls; like going away on a visit with your wife, who insists on taking every damn thing with her.

He left just before first light, not that that meant anything any more. The night shift still had some time to go. They were fitting the bearings for the overhead shaft, which meant a lot of men standing still holding lanterns while the fitters checked tolerances with the gauges that had been so much trouble to make. It was a good time to leave, while they were busy. He felt painfully guilty, like an absconding husband.

By the time the sun was up he was clear of the woods, following the course of the river. It seemed a logical thing to do, because a large body of people with grazing animals wouldn't go far from water, would they, and as far as he knew there weren't any lakes or big ponds. Sloppy logic, of course. He didn't actually have the faintest idea where they'd gone, in which direction, at what speed. He was walking out into the wide empty world with a heavy pack and food for three days, on the offchance of bumping into them.

He followed the river for two days, then stopped. He'd started out with romantic notions of living off the land — shooting a deer with the snapping-hen, maybe — and cramming his mouth with the legendary nuts and berries with which the wilderness is supposed to abound. So far he'd seen one bush laden with unidentified glossy black berries which were almost certainly poisonous, and one hare, about a quarter of a mile away, which ran off when he moved. He had enough food to get him back to the site, or he could keep going and trust to luck. Also, his feet hurt.

He turned back, walked for half a day and found them. Either he hadn't noticed them on his way out, which was hardly likely, or they'd come in across country, making for the river, after he'd gone on. That was also fairly unlikely. The sheer size of the spread they made — two thousand sheep, a thousand goats, ambling along as they grazed — meant they were very hard to overlook, and the outlying edges of the spread were several hours ahead of the main body. It would be like an entire country sneaking past you in the dark.

Of course, he thought as he walked towards the camp, they may not be the same lot. Could be a completely different tribe or sect or whatever, and I can't speak the language.

But he kept walking, and when he was about half a mile from the camp, scattering the more adventurous goats, two men suddenly stood up out of the grass in front of him. They wore the same strange long coats as the ones he'd met before, and stared at him in roughly the same way. He smiled at them and kept going.

The language problem meant he couldn't just find someone and ask, "Excuse me, which way to the lunatic's tent?" which robbed him of any semblance of the initiative, so he was mightily relieved when a man and a woman approached him, stopped, looked at him, turned round and walked back the way they'd just come. He followed them right into the middle of the camp. They didn't look round once.

There were plenty of women, not many men. They were uniformly tall and thin, with high cheekbones, long faces, long necks, broad bony shoulders standing out through the thick rough cloth of their practically identical coats. They looked at him, didn't move, studied him as though he was a puzzle, for the solving of which no valuable prize was offered. His guides walked past them without a word and weren't acknowledged, as if non-existence was contagious and they'd caught it from him. His nerve was just about to give way when a face appeared in the fold of a tent curtain—a huge grin with a pair of wide eyes balanced on top.

"My dear fellow!" the old man yelled. "Yes, over here. Quickly!"

Gignomai wasn't sure he liked the "quickly." He darted across, and a huge hand on a thin wrist shot out, grabbed him round the knuckles and dragged him into the tent. The hand was warm and soft, like a woman's, and compellingly strong.

"Sit down, please," the old man said, as he yanked the curtain back in place. "You shouldn't..." he hesitated, then went on, "I am most awfully pleased to see you again, but really, you oughtn't be here, you know." He was still standing. He peeled the curtain delicately aside, glimpsed through, and turned it back. "Sit down, sit down," he said. "Please, do make yourself at home."

There was only one stool. Gignomai sat on the floor, which was covered by a thick, dusty carpet. "I'm sorry," he said. "If it's going to make trouble for you."

The old man shook his head so fiercely that Gignomai was afraid he'd hurt his neck. "Oh, you don't need to worry about that," he said. (Gignomai thought. About something, but not that?) "As a lunatic, I'm privileged and therefore immune to censure. You…"

"Am I in danger?" Gignomai asked.

"What? Oh, no, of course not. They wouldn't dream of harming you; they don't believe you exist. Now then, what can I offer you? Tea? My granddaughter has just brewed me a fresh pot. Or would you prefer milk?"

"Tea," Gignomai said, and the old man, active as a locust, dodged past him and came back a moment later with two tiny, exquisite translucent white bowls. Gignomai mimed sipping, then put his bowl carefully on the ground beside him.

"Now then," the old man said, perching on the stool like a big bird on a wire. "How may I be of service?"

Now that he was here, after the gentle melodrama of his arrival, the request sounded absurd. But it was the question he'd come to ask. "I'd like to ask a favour, if I may."

"Of course. Anything within my power."

"Do you think I could come and live with you, here, till the spring?"

The old man's eyes opened very wide indeed. He opened his mouth and closed it again three times before he spoke. "Naturally I would like nothing better," he said. "Merely to sit and talk, in a decent language, with a cultured man, about books and pictures and normal civilised things, is the most wonderful thing I could possibly imagine."

"But," Gignomai said.

The old man nodded sadly. "We understand each other so well," he said. "But it's impossible. My family, my neighbours…"

"Wouldn't allow it."

The old man looked solemnly at him. "There would be no

violence, you understand," he said. "For the reasons stated. No, I imagine what would happen would be that the rest of them would break camp very quietly in the night and go away, and keep going faster than we could follow. I can walk quite briskly even now, but not fast enough to keep pace with the carts. They would keep going until they were quite sure we were no longer following. This is a very big country, and one place is very much like another. I'm terribly sorry," he said. "I wish it were otherwise."

Gignomai smiled at him. "My fault for asking," he said. "Might I ask why? As far as I know, there's no history of bad feeling between our people and yours."

"Perfectly true," the old man said. "Apart from my own abduction—which I most certainly don't regret—there has been no bad feeling, because there has been no contact whatsoever. But please, answer me this. Why on earth would you wish to leave the company of civilised men and seek to live among savages?" He hesitated as the implications of the question struck him. An appalled look crossed his face, and he added, "Please, if the question is indiscreet..."

Gignomai laughed. "I haven't murdered anybody, or done anything like that," he said. "But things are happening here, and I'm not sure I want to be involved."

"Even though you set them in motion?"

Gignomai blinked. "How do you know?"

The old man smiled gently. "My dear fellow," he said. "More than anything else, I have time to think. I have thought about little else since you first came. You wanted to build a factory on our land; you asked permission. I know from my time in the old country that factories are forbidden in charter colonies because of the monopoly. A man seeking to build an illegal factory, taking care to do so outside the jurisdiction, whatever his motives may be, is bound to cause a great deal of trouble, sooner or later. My guess is that your project nears completion, the prospect of the concomitant trouble oppresses you, and naturally enough you are contemplating flight, escape from your own creation. The fact that you have actually come here, rather than merely imagining yourself doing so, suggests to me that whatever you have in mind is rather more momentous than a mere violation of commercial and civil law." He shook his head, a wide sweeping gesture that brought his jaw to his shoulder. "I do wish I could help. But probably it's for the best that I can't. This great and noble work you have undertaken—"

"It's not like that," Gignomai said quietly. "It's more sort of personal. An indulgence, really."

The old man looked at him, head slightly on one side. "But for the good of the people, surely."

"I want justice," Gignomai said sharply. It wasn't what he'd been planning to say. "Doesn't always do anybody any good," he said. "But it's what I want."

"Are you sure of that?" The old man was peering at him, as if trying to see through a keyhole. "Just now you wanted to run away. You wanted to come and live with the savages."

Gignomai laughed abruptly. "That'd be justice for me," he said. "I suppose I was being selfish. Tell me," he went on, shaking himself, like a man coming in from the rain, "what exactly do your people believe about there being different worlds? It sounds good, but when I try and think about it, I can't quite get a grip on it. How does it work?"

The old man smiled. "A civilised man's question," he said. "I'm afraid we don't think like that. It doesn't have to work, that's just the way it is. We'd never met strangers before. We were born and grew up in a world with a finite number of human beings. By the time a man died, it was entirely possible for him to have met *everybody*. We saw you, and we didn't recognise you. Therefore, you couldn't conceivably be human—not like us, at any rate. But you looked human, you acted more or less as humans do. We drew what seemed to be the only logical conclusion. You were humans in another phase of existence—dead, or not yet born. I told you this."

Gignomai nodded. "You did. But it set me thinking. You see, when I lived up on the hill, there were only a very few people: my family, the hired men, a few women servants. I came to realise there were more people down below, on the plain, in town. I wanted to meet them, but for some reason it wasn't allowed. That's when it all started to go wrong. And surely, that's more or less what happened to you, except I ran away and you were kidnapped. That's why, when you said about different worlds…"

"Ah." The old man shrugged. "The hill, the plain and beyond that, the savages. The further away from home, the more barbaric, the less human. But when I was furthest from home, I was among my own kind. It's here that I'm out of place. Put yourself in my position: I was snatched up by the gods and taken to heaven. Then they brought me back to live a long life among strangers." He thought for a moment, then said, "If you feel uncomfortable here, why don't you wait for the spring ship and go Home? You could be yourself there. You could…" He paused, and licked his lips. "You could take me with you, as your servant. I could clean your boots and wash your clothes and scrub the floors of your house, I have seen all these things done, I could do them. And I would be there, not there. It's all I could possibly want."

Gignomai stared at him. Then he said, "I can't go Home. You've convinced me. It's a different world. I'd be dead there or not yet born. Like my father is here. I read a bit of his history of our family once. We shouldn't be here at all. We never did anything wrong."

"Neither did I," the old man said calmly, "and my punishment was to live in heaven."

He said it in such a sad, serious voice that Gignomai wanted to laugh. He managed not to, and reached in his pocket. "Here," he said. "I thought you might like this."

The old man stared at the book as though it was the most wonderful thing. He reached for it, then hesitated, as though he was afraid it would burn his hand. "Go on," Gignomai said. "Really." He felt the book pulled from between his fingers, and for a split second was tempted to snatch it back. "It's nothing special, I'm afraid," he said.

"Just a selection of late Mannerist lyric poetry: Pacatian, Numerian, that sort of thing. From my father's library."

Originally, at least. He'd stolen it years ago to give to Furio, and stolen it back the last time he stayed at the store. He'd examined it and found the two pages he'd gummed together near the end hadn't been separated, so clearly Furio hadn't liked it much either.

"For me?" the old man said. "To keep?"

Gignomai nodded. "But not a gift," he said. "A trade."

"Of course. Anything."

"Fine. I'll need food for three days to get me home."

The old man jumped up and clapped his hands. Immediately, a woman stepped through the tent curtain. She looked straight through Gignomai as though he wasn't there. The old man barked a command at her, and she vanished.

"And I'll need a goat," Gignomai said.

The old man gave him a bewildered look. "Certainly, of course. A male or a female? What age?"

"About so big," Gignomai replied, moving his hands apart. "Oh, and one more thing. I'll need you to pass on a message."

The old man frowned, but the call of the book was too strong. He opened it, glanced quickly down at the page, then shut it again. "This is the most wonderful—"

"You're welcome," Gignomai said abruptly. "Well, I figured it'd make a change from reading about fishing rods. Personally, I can't stick Numerian at any price, but then, I always liked the Literalists best. At least they rhyme."

The woman reappeared with a sack, which she dropped on the floor before disappearing again. "That's my food, presumably."

"Quite so. Dried meat, cooked rice, dried fruit. Excellent for long journeys."

Gignomai, who'd rather have eaten worms than cold cooked rice, dipped his head in gratitude. "Thank you for seeing me," he said.

"My pleasure, my dear fellow. My very great pleasure."

They left the tent, and the old man said something to somebody, and straight away a boy appeared leading a fine yearling she-goat on a bit of string. Gignomai looked round. There were at least thirty people watching, mostly women. He put his knapsack on the ground, loosened one strap and hauled out the snapping-hen in its cloth bundle. He looked back at the old man.

"Ever seen one of these?" he said, as he peeled back the cloth.

The old man was staring. "Yes," he said.

"Splendid." He slipped his fingers round the grip, and used his left hand to move the hammer to full cock, leant the frizzen forward to make sure the priming powder hadn't fallen out, then eased it back into battery. "I'm sorry," he whispered to the old man. Then he levelled the muzzle of the snapping-hen about six inches from the goat's forehead. At that range, even he couldn't miss.

The goat slumped, as though the bones had been magically extracted from its legs. It twitched a couple of times, but that was just the muscles relaxing. Gignomai looked at it through the clearing smoke, and beyond it to the circle of faces. The silence was so hard, so brittle he wasn't sure he'd be able to break it just by talking.

"Be so kind as to tell them," he said (his voice came out thin and squeaky), "that if they want the power of the dead and the not yet born, I'll be happy to give it to them. Any time. No charge." He tried to put the snapping-hen back in his pack, but it slipped through his fingers and fell on the ground. He had to stoop and pick it up. Not very impressive, he thought.

The old man's eyes were very wide. "My dear fellow," he said.

"You promised," Gignomai said. "I'm sorry. But you do want the book, don't you? And you did promise."

The old man closed his eyes for a moment; then he said something loud and clear, in a firm, carrying voice. "Your exact words," he said. "I only wish—"

"Thanks," Gignomai said. "I can find my own way out."

The rice was soapy and the dried fruit revolting. He threw the dried meat away, and watched a crow swoop down on it, peck at it a couple of times and fly off, croaking angrily. He tore strips off the cloth the snapping-hen was wrapped up in and tried to bind up his blistered heels, but couldn't get the strips to stay in place. He couldn't help feeling it served him right.

He bypassed the site and walked straight into town, arriving just before noon. That suited him. He knew Marzo always went through the books about that time. The side door wasn't locked. It never was; he'd stolen the key on his third visit, and nobody knew how to make a new one. He went in quietly and found Marzo in the back store room. He looked up as Gignomai entered, and scowled at him.

"If you want Furio…"

"No," Gignomai said. "I'd like a word with you, if you can spare me a minute."

Marzo didn't look well. He'd lost weight, and his skin looked as though it had been handed down by an older brother. There was a quarter-empty bottle at his elbow.

"If it's about the biscuits I can explain," he said.

Gignomai made a mental note. "Don't know what you're talking about. I just dropped in to give you something. A present. Token of my appreciation."

For some reason, that made Marzo wince. "There's no need," he said. "Really."

"Fine." Gignomai shrugged. "If you don't want it, drop it down a well." He slipped his knapsack off his back, rested it on the table and unbuckled one strap. "I seem to remember a while back hearing that you wanted one of these."

He laid the snapping-hen on the table and flicked off the wrapping. Marzo looked at it, then up at him. "Is that…?"

"Yes," Gignomai said. "Genuine City-made snapping-hen, by Cioverto, about a hundred years old. Used to belong to my brother Luso, but he lost it. You tried to buy it off Calo Brotti, but he wouldn't sell."

Marzo reached out, hesitated, then allowed the tips of his fingers to rest on the lock-plate. "How much do you want for it?"

"Present." Gignomai grinned at him. "Gift. Free. Nothing to pay. Oh, and it's not much use without these," he added, dumping the powder-horn and the bag of balls on the desk beside it. "Don't ask me how you make it go bang. I assume it works, unless Brotti played around with it and broke something."

"I wasn't planning on using it," Marzo said.

"That's all right, then," Gignomai said. "Hang it on the wall. It'll look nice there, over the fireplace."

Marzo drew his fingers away, slowly. "Are you sure?" he said. "It's got to be worth a lot of money."

Gignomai laughed, a sound like a breaking stick. "Who'm I going to sell it to around here?" he said. "If Luso catches me with it, I suspect I'll get rather more than a stern talking-to. The same goes for you, of course. Unless you had it in mind to give it back to him. He'd be ever so grateful, I'm sure." Gignomai buckled the strap on his pack and wriggled it back over his shoulders. "Anyway, that's up to you. Your pistol, you do what you like with it."

Marzo's hand had drifted back; he was gripping the stock, looking like he was holding a red-hot bar. "Thanks," he said. "It's incredibly generous of you."

"It's just a thing," Gignomai replied. "And you don't own something like that, it comes and stays with you a while, like the aunt nobody can be doing with. I'm glad to be rid of it, to tell you the truth."

Furio didn't turn up till mid-morning, and he went straight to where Gignomai was supervising the raising of the hammer-shed roof.

"I'm leaving," Furio said.

"Right." All of Gignomai's attention was on the roof-tree, as it swung into place on a long-beam crane. "How long will you be gone for?"

"For good. I'm quitting. I'm going home."

"Hold it!" Gignomai yelled. The roof-tree froze in mid-air, like a bird hovering. "Say that again."

"I'm quitting. I've had enough. Besides, you don't need me here. I'm in the way half the time."

Gignomai sighed. "Fetch it down again," he called out. "We'll try again later. Right," he said to Furio, grabbing his elbow and hauling him along with him as he walked towards the office cart, "what the hell is that supposed to mean?"

Furio jerked his arm free. "You heard me," he said. "I've got better things to do with my time, you don't need me, other people do."

"Of course I need you." Gignomai looked straight at him, but then his eyes flicked in the direction of the crane. "We started this whole thing together. We're partners."

"So are all of them," Furio said, waving his arm vaguely towards the shed. "Difference is, they're doing something useful. At least, I'm assuming it's useful. Since I don't actually know what the hell it is you're up to here, I can't say for sure."

"Calm down," Gignomai said. "Have a drink, pull yourself together. This isn't like you at all."

"I don't want a drink." Furio took a step back, a bit like a fencing move. "I'm not my uncle. And I don't need to pull myself together. Either you tell me what you're really doing here or I'm going home. Is that clear enough for you?"

Gignomai leaned his back against the side of the cart. He looked worn out, but that was nothing new. "I honestly don't know what you mean," he said. "You know perfectly well what all this is about, we talked about it. Bloodless revolution, a future for the colony, and for both of us. All right," he said, rubbing his eyelids with forefinger and thumb, "right now, maybe you're not exactly of the essence, if you see what I mean. You're not a time-served carpenter or smith, neither am I. I'm sorry if it's been a bit boring for you."

"That's not—"

"But," Gignomai went on, as if he hadn't heard him, "we're pretty close to completion on the building works. It won't be long now before we finally start making and selling things, which is where I really will need you—you and nobody else. If you walk out on me now, I'll be completely screwed and you'll have wasted all the time you've already put in. You can see that, surely."

Furio shook his head. "Sounds good," he said, "but not in fact true. All this"—another wave at the shed—"is a sideshow, it's a blind, it's cover for what you're really doing. And either you can tell me what that is, or I don't think I can be here any more. Come on, Gig, for crying out loud, I'm not that stupid."

Gignomai looked at him. "I have absolutely no idea what you're talking about," he said.

"You haven't? Fine." Furio took a step forward this time. Gignomai didn't move. "Where's your friend Aurelio, and what's he doing? He's not in the livery any more. Did he finish what he was doing, or did someone else see him there, so you had to move him somewhere else?"

"Aurelio," Gignomai repeated. "You mean my father's smith?"

"You know perfectly well."

Gignomai shrugged. "I heard he'd left the Tabletop," he said, "but I haven't seen him. You're saying you saw him in town? In the livery?"

Furio felt his fists clench. "Why were you trying out the snapping-hen? Planning on shooting someone?"

"Oh, that." Gignomai grinned at him. "That's nothing. I'd gone to a lot of trouble to get it, and I wanted to see if it works. Actually, I haven't got it any more. What would I want with it anyway?"

"You haven't got it."

"No." Gignomai yawned—genuinely, Furio decided, probably just a sign of how tired he was. "As a matter of fact, I gave it to your uncle."

One of those sentences that have perfectly good words in them but don't seem to make sense. "Why?"

"He wanted it. Tried to buy it off Calo Brotti, but he wasn't inclined to sell. I got hold of it, and I reckoned it'd be good politics. After all, Marzo's had a lot to put up with lately. Thought I'd show him he's still loved and wanted. You ask him, he'll show it to you, I expect. That's all there is to it."

Furio shook his head slowly. "I thought we were friends," he said. "That's the only reason I'm here. I'd have done anything for you, you know that. But if you're going to lie to me, I might as well go home. Sorry," he said, "but that's it."

"Furio," Gignomai said, but Furio was already moving. He paused to look up at the crane, then speeded up, taking long strides to get him out of the clearing. He maintained the pace most of the way up the hill, which he wouldn't have been able to do a month or so ago. At least he'd gained something from the experience.

Teucer was on the porch when he got back to the store. "You're home early," she said, laying down her book on the empty chair beside her. "Something wrong?"

"I walked out," Furio said.

"You've left?"

"Yes."

"Good," she said, and picked the book up again. She'd got it upside down. "Uncle's gone out," she said. "I don't know when he'll be back."

"I wasn't looking for him particularly," Furio said. For some reason he was reluctant to go inside. The porch seemed a good compromise, for now.

"He said he needs four barrels of malt fetching up from the cellar."

"Later." He sat down beside her. "What are you reading?"

"Leothymus on fractures," she replied. She turned the book the right way up. It was just possible she'd been looking at a diagram. "It's a bit out of date, but there are some useful things in it."

"Where'd you get something like that?"

She looked at him over the top of the page. "If you must know, it's from the met'Oc library."

"Gig gave it to you?"

"No."

Furio waited, but either she didn't want to tell him or she wanted him to beg. He wasn't in the mood. "You were right," he said.

"Quite likely. What about?"

"Gignomai's up to something, and he won't tell me what."

"Mphm." She turned a page. "So what upset you? Him being up to something, or him not letting you join in?"

Furio looked away. She wasn't the only one who could avoid giving answers. He sat still for a while, and then a question came into his mind. He had no idea where it had come from, or why he asked it. "You really liked him didn't you?"

"No."

He did still and quiet again. It was quite some time before she said, "All right, yes. But not any more."

"Why not?"

"He's up to something," she said.

"Doesn't that just add to the mystery?"

"It did," she said. "But you can get sick of it quite quickly. I think he's dangerous."

Furio thought about the snapping-hen, but Gig had given it away. "What makes you say that?"

"He's planning something big," she said, "and he really hates his family, which wouldn't matter so much if he wasn't so like them."

"He went back to talk to the savages," Furio said. "I don't know why. Do you think that had anything to do with it?"

She marked her place in the book with a dried leaf. "Why else would he go there?"

"And he gave the pistol to Uncle Marzo."

"I know." She stood up. "He's hung it on the wall, in the back store room. He keeps looking up at it when he's working, like it's trying to read over his shoulder. I'd better go in now," she said. "Your aunt wants me to cut up cabbages for pickling. Shall I tell her you're back?"

"Might as well," Furio said. "I think I might stay out here for a while."

She smiled. "If you go in, she'll have you shifting barrels."

"I'm definitely staying here, then."

He sat there for a long time, until it was starting to get dark, and Uncle Marzo came walking up the street. Furio explained that he'd come home. Uncle Marzo looked pleased, and didn't ask why. "You might be interested to know," he said, kicking his boots off in the porch, "those two strangers rode past me as I was coming home. I'd guess they're on their way to the factory."

Furio shrugged. "They'll be company for Gig," he said. "His own kind. He'll like that."

"Your brother Lusomai," Cousin Boulomai said, "is impossible. He refuses to do anything. To begin with, he fobbed me off with excuses about bad timing. Then he promised he'd negotiate with the town mayor."

Gignomai grinned. "Marzo Opello isn't a mayor. He isn't anything. He runs a shop."

"Well, there you are. Lusomai tried to make me believe he had some sort of actual authority. And then, after keeping us both hanging about all this time, he comes straight out with it and says he's done a deal and the matter is closed. Well, I'm not going to stand for it. I have the men to consider."

Gignomai looked over his shoulder. They were boarding in the sides of the hammer shed. "I have to say," he said, "your men don't seem unduly bothered about it. I asked them. These things happen, was the general consensus. And the man who did it hung himself, so it's over and done with."

"Not as far as I'm concerned."

"I can understand why you feel so strongly about it," Gignomai said, lifting the bottle. Boulomai shook his head, and Gignomai put it down again. "It's a pretty fundamental question of honour, and if this was Home, I can see, you'd have to take steps. But this isn't Home, it's a charter colony precisely one notch up from subsistence agriculture in the middle of nowhere. We simply can't afford to have blood feuds and private wars. If we did, there wouldn't be enough manpower left to do the work and feed everybody. Luso's just being practical."

"Oh, I don't think so," Boulomai replied. Gignomai made a mental note, he was one of those people who gets quieter the angrier he gets. Sign of a serious man, in most cases. "He doesn't mind disturbing the peace when he fancies a bit of excitement, but when something significant happens, he's as quiet as a mouse."

Gignomai smiled. "You got the keeping the peace speech, then."

"Several versions of it," Boulomai said, "all amounting to the same thing, and I have to say, I wasn't terribly impressed. I happen to think there are times when the peace isn't worth keeping, not when there's something like this at stake. Four of my men have been murdered. I want justice."

Gignomai was looking over his cousin's shoulder, trying not to be too obvious about it. He would have liked to have been there when the final board was nailed in place, but instead he was here, trying to handle this other matter. "What did you have in mind?" he said.

Cousin Boulomai scowled. "It's awkward, I know, because of the confounded man hanging himself. Otherwise it'd be straightforward. Back Home—"

"At the risk of repeating myself, we aren't Home. What did you have in mind? Money? I'm afraid there isn't enough of it in the colony to pay compensation at Home rates."

Boulomai shrugged. "In that case, it'll have to be something rather more basic. And it's not just the murder," he went on. "There's the way they were treated. Those people just stopped feeding them. If they hadn't taken matters into their own hands, they'd have starved. You can't expect to treat people like that and get away with it."

"Fair point," Gignomai said. "And the people who did that are still alive, of course. But you have to admit, no actual harm came of it."

"That's entirely beside the point," Boulomai said, and Gignomai got the impression he was rapidly running out of patience; not a commodity he was well provided with at the best of times. "The point is, your brother's basically told me to shut up and get lost. So I've come to you."

"Me?" Gignomai shook his head. "I'd love to be able to help, but I'm afraid I have no influence whatsoever with Luso or any of them. Quite the reverse."

"That's not what I meant," Boulomai said. "I'm turning to you as a man of power and influence in this community. Your family up on the hill won't help me. I believe you should."

Gignomai was silent for a very long time. Then he said, "Power and influence. No, I don't think so. Sorry, but that's just not the way it is."

"You're being modest," Boulomai said. "You're a met'Oc, every bit as much as your brother. And you command rather more men. In my book, that's power and influence."

Gignomai poured himself a drink but didn't drink it. "I was under the impression they were your men," he said. "Most of them, anyway. The rest of them aren't fighters. You can take my word for that. Talking of which, if it comes down to manpower, you're the one with the most boots on the ground. If you're dead set on making something of this, you really don't need me."

Cousin Boulomai keeping his temper was an impressive sight: rather like a volcano, Gignomai speculated, the day before an eruption. "This isn't my country," he said. "If I started throwing my weight around, I'd have the colonists and your brother on to me, sure as eggs. In fact, I'd venture to suggest it'd be about the only thing guaranteed to bring them together with a common purpose. You, on the other hand..."

"I'm sorry." Gignomai stood up. "I sympathise, really, but I live here, I can't go starting wars, not if I want to sell these people cheap farm tools. I'm not pretending to justify my behaviour, I'm simply explaining why I can't help you. I'm sorry. Get Luso to do something, do it yourself or let the matter drop. Leave me out of it."

Boulomai rose gracefully to his feet. He looked as though he'd practised in front of a mirror. "I'm sorry you feel that way," he said. "I thought we had certain values in common. I apologise if my misapprehension's caused you any embarrassment."

They stood a shoulder's width apart. Gignomai said, "Does this mean you want your men back?"

"I don't know," Boulomai replied. "I don't think things can go on as they are. But I'll have to think it over. I'll let you know what I decide."

He walked away, back to the tree under which his sister was sitting, demurely reading a book. They exchanged a few words, then mounted their horses and rode away. Boulomai hadn't said where they were going next.

Two days later, a boy galloped up to the store on a black pony. He scrambled through the door. Furio was behind the counter, laying out bolts of cloth. He recognised the boy as the youngest Heddo.

"Got a message for Marzo Opello," the boy said.

"He's in the back," Furio replied. "Stay there. I'll ask if he can spare you a moment. Is it important?"

"Tell him he's got to come out to our place, right now," the boy said.

Much to Furio's surprise, Uncle Marzo didn't argue. He asked the boy what it was all about, but got no answer. He'd been told not to say anything, just bring the mayor.

"That must be you," Furio said.

Marzo nodded unhappily. "I guess so," he said.

They got out the light cart, which Furio's father had acquired in a moment of folly under the impression it was a chaise. They had to drive rather faster than they'd have liked to keep up with the boy and his pony. "Any idea what this is all about?" Furio asked, shouting to make himself heard.

"No," Uncle Marzo replied. "But if it's the Heddos, you can bet it's trouble."

The boy took them straight to the door—the front door, which nobody ever used. There was a hole in it, about five feet off the ground, roughly the width of a man's thumb. Both of them noticed it, but neither of them said anything.

"Bullet hole," Desio Heddo said. "That's what it is. Look." He opened his enormous hand and showed them a grey disc, about an inch across, tapered, like a lens. "Dug it out of the wall opposite the door. Here's the mark, see."

The hole looked like the mark you'd make if you'd dug a pickaxe into the plaster. Marzo took the grey disc and scratched it with his thumbnail. Soft. Lead.

"Middle of the night," Heddo said. "Me and the wife upstairs, fast asleep. Just as well. If we'd been in the parlour here, we could've been killed. See? Right above the settle, where I always sit. He knew that. Tried to kill me."

Marzo frowned. "You're saying whoever did this knew you always sit on the settle there."

"Looks like it," Heddo said angrily.

"So he must know you quite well, then."

"Must do."

"In that case, he'd know when you go to bed." Marzo leaned forward and poked his little finger into the hole in the wall. "That's a hell of a punch those things must have," he said. "Clean through a solid oak door and enough wallop left to dig a half-inch hole."

"Makes me go cold all over just thinking about it," said Heddo, who didn't look cold at all. Quite the reverse. "I reckon he must've come spying through the window, seen where we sit. Then he comes back at night and tries to kill me. At night, see, so nobody'll spot him."

"If you're right," Furio said thoughtfully, "the man who did this would have to be quite a good shot. Wouldn't he?"

Heddo shrugged. "Guess so, I don't know anything about that stuff. But everybody knows Luso met'Oc's handy with a gun."

Marzo winced. "You think it was him."

"Well, who the hell else would it be? Who else has got one, for a start?"

"Me, actually," Marzo said.

Heddo stared at him, then seemed to dismiss the revelation from his mind. "What I want to know is," he said, "what're you going to do about it."

Furio and his uncle drove home in silence. When they reached the edge of town, Marzo said, "I'm going to have to put a stop to this mayor thing. It's getting on my nerves."

"It's a sign of respect," Furio said.

"Like hell."

"So what are you going to do?"

"Me? Nothing."

"But you said..."

Marzo pulled up outside the store, climbed down and unhitched the horses. "Put 'em away for me, would you?" he said. "I need a drink."

He went indoors, into the back store room, and opened a drawer of his desk. From it he took the cloth bag full of lead balls that Gignomai had given him. He laid one ball on the desk, with the lead disc from Desio Heddo's wall next to it. Then from another drawer he took a rosewood box, a treasured thing, which had belonged to Furio's father. From the box he took a pair of fine brass scales. He laid them flat, put the ball from the bag in one pan and the disc in the other, and lifted them by their fine brass chain. They swung wildly, as scales do; then they settled down. There was a needle at the fulcrum, pointing to a scale calibrated in grains. There was a five-grain difference, that was all. He laid them down again and held the grey disc close to his eye. Punched through an oak door into a wall, five grains' worth of lead could easily have been shaved off. The edges of the disc were thin, like foil, and ragged. He took another ball from the bag and weighed it against the first one. Difference—two grains. So five grains, in context, was nothing.

He frowned, then crossed the room and looked carefully at the snapping-hen, hanging on wires from two nails. There was dust on the barrel and the stock. He lowered his head a little and sniffed the muzzle, but he couldn't smell anything. Someone had told him once that burning gunpowder had a sort of rotten-egg smell. Not this one, then.

He sat down and poured himself that drink. The met'Oc used to own a pair of snapping-hen pistols. Lusomai met'Oc lost one of them, which came into the hands of Calo Brotti, who sold it to Gignomai met'Oc, who gave it to Marzo Opello, who stuck it up on the wall. That left another one, presumably still in the hands of Lusomai met'Oc.

Marzo's hand shook a little as he drank. What he didn't know about snapping-hen pistols would fill a large book. For one thing, did all snapping-hens have the same diameter barrel, allowing the use of the same size ball? It's in the nature of lead spheres that if two of them weigh the same, they must be the same diameter, meaning they'd fit down the same-size barrel. He remembered the book of fancy antiques and their values. He dived to the shelf, pulled it down and flicked through the pages.

A gentleman's matchlock fowling piece, thirty-six inch barrel, burr walnut stock with silver inlay, lock by Raiddo, bore twelve to the pound.

He had no idea what that meant, so he looked it up in the glossary at the back: twelve lead balls of the right size to fit the barrel would weigh a pound. That in itself implied that not all barrels were the same diameter. Of course, the gun in the book was for shooting birds. There weren't any snapping-hens listed.

He closed it and put it back. How many of these things in the colony? One, this one. One belonging to Luso. One, at least, belonging to the stranger Boulomai. Unless all snapping-hens had a standard bore size, which on balance he was inclined to doubt, the bullet Heddo had prised out of his wall must have been fired from Luso's gun.

He poured himself another drink. The stuff didn't seem to work quite as well as it used to. If Luso, the self-styled keeper of the peace, had shot a bullet into Heddo's door...

That needed thinking about. He poured a third drink but let it sit quietly on his desk. Boulomai and his sister had been up at the Tabletop, that was an established fact. Boulomai was the employer of the murdered oarsmen, but Luso had given Marzo his word that he'd sorted all that out. If the ball had come from Boulomai's gun, then the likely explanation was that Luso had overestimated his diplomatic abilities and Boulomai had decided to take matters into his own hands. But that didn't seem to fit. Marzo had only met them once, of course, but the two semi-divine beings he'd encountered at the dock had struck him as the sort of people who believe that a thing worth doing should be done properly—as witness the carefully tailored adventurers' outfits, the fully manned ship, the huge pile of luggage. If Boulomai was good and angry enough to go to war over a matter of honour, would he restrict himself to making a hole in a door at a time when it was fairly certain that nobody would be hurt? Marzo considered the question as the third drink slid down, and thought, Probably not. More likely, he'd have had his men nail the door shut, then set fire to the thatch.

If the ball had come from Luso's gun, however, the sequence of events made rather more sense. A shot into a door in the middle of the night is a gesture. Luso, whose idea of keeping the peace was rounding up all the bad men in the colony and occasionally turning them loose to steal cattle, was rather more likely to deal in gestures, if that was what it took to get a whining cousin off his back. And a gesture with no harm done was a perfectly acceptable thing, if it kept the peace.

Peace, Marzo reflected, as essential as air, food and water, because how could you possibly live any sort of a life without it? Presumably Boulomai met'Ousa thought the same way. He had to keep the peace among his ship's crew, whose colleagues and friends had been murdered. Being a stranger, and a guest of the met'Oc, naturally he would apply to them for justice. Lusomai met'Oc had therefore struck a deal with the town, to keep the peace, but he'd misjudged the business. So, to keep the peace, he'd made an empty show of violence, using the snapping-hen, an instrument ideally suited to the purpose. Result: honour satisfied, justice done, and everybody who'd been alive this time yesterday was still alive, and Heddo had a conversation piece in his door which he'd undoubtedly show off proudly to everybody in the district.

Marzo looked guiltily at the bottle and left it where it was. What are you going to do about it? he asked himself. I'm going to be practical, Marzo replied, I'm a practical man. And the next one who calls me mayor goes home in a wheelbarrow.

Desio Heddo told his neighbours that he'd reported the attempt on his life to mayor Opello, and had been promised justice. Any day now, he said, the mayor would be raising a posse, with a view to going up there and teaching those bastards a lesson. When one of the Adesco brothers, who'd never liked the Heddos anyway, pointed out that it was Desio's son Scarpedino who'd done the murder that caused all the trouble, Desio hit him in the mouth with the handle of a hay-fork, knocking out two teeth. The next day, a large section of the Heddos' northern fence was broken down, allowing fifteen of Desio's eighteen-month bullocks to stray into the Sagrennas' water meadow. The Sagrennas, citing damage and unauthorised grazing, refused to let Desio have them back unless he gave them four loads of hay by way of indemnity. Desio refused angrily, claiming that the Adescos had smashed down the fence to get their own back for the two teeth. All three families were inches away from bloodshed when someone had a bright idea. Let's all go into town, he suggested, and let the mayor sort it out.

In the morning, they ran the drop-hammer for the first time. It worked perfectly for about an hour, then broke a shaft. Gignomai declared that this was much better than he'd anticipated, and supervised the stripping of the gear train. It was a simple fracture, the result of a cold spot in a weld. It would take most of the afternoon to fix.

In the afternoon, Cousin Pasi came to see him. She appeared through the trees on a white palfrey, led by a single groom. She wore a dark green hooded robe. It was like something out of a fairy tale, which was presumably the desired effect. The groom was Scarpedino Heddo.

Gignomai was up to his elbows in black grease, aligning the bearings on the overhead shaft. "Leave it," he said, "I won't be long." He wiped his hands on his shirt, and went down to meet her. She'd brought a tiny lightweight folding table, two cushions, a bottle of imported wine and two glasses.

"Your brother Luso and I are getting married," she said.

Gignomai nodded. "That's why you're here, I assume."

She smiled. "Luso told me you're sharp," she said. "That's right. When did you guess?"

Gignomai raised his glass in a formal toast. "Why?" he asked.

She shrugged. "Really it's the only logical course of action," she said. "I did consider Stheno, but..."

"Quite."

"And your father agrees with me," she went on. "He feels Luso would be the more appropriate choice. Strength of mind were the words he used. I think I know what he meant by it."

Gignomai put the glass down. "So," he said, "what exactly did you do, back Home?"

"Oh, that." She flicked a strand of hair away from her face. "I sort of killed someone."

Sort of, Gignomai noted. He couldn't help admiring the choice of phrase. "Who?"

"My husband. He was impossible," she went on, frowning a little. "Oh, he drank and he gambled and he was a lout and he chased the maids and generally carried on, but I could put up with that. He wasn't any worse than my father, and I've always got on well with him. No, what finally put the lid on it was when he decided he wanted to play at politics. I warned him, he'd get into all sorts of trouble, but he never listened to me, of course. And then he got indicted for some ridiculous conspiracy, and I knew that as soon as they pulled him in and started putting pressure on him, he'd lose his nerve and say anything they wanted him to, and then there'd be an almighty mess. I really didn't want to get sent into exile with him, so I put a little something in his drink. Really, it was the best thing for everybody under the circumstances. Unfortunately, my father-in-law made a quite appalling fuss about it—he simply refused to believe his precious son was mixed up in any nonsense. He made out I wanted Phero out of the way because of some stupid affair, but that had been over for months anyway. Boulo tried to sort him out, but poor Boulo's not the sharpest needle in the cushion and he made rather a botch of it. Father-in-law went to the Court and laid a formal charge of murder, so Boulo and I thought it'd probably be just as well if we cleared out. Ironic, really: I killed Phero so I wouldn't end up in a place like this, and here I am."

"How awful for you," Gignomai said pleasantly.

"Quite. Well," she went on, "we really didn't have the first idea about where we were going to go. Boulo said we should head for the Republic, because at least it's civilised there. He's always wanted to see Vesanis, of course, he does so love the theatre and music, not to mention Vesani actresses. But I told him, bearing in mind the nonsense poor Phero was mixed up in, Vesanis was the last place on earth we could go: it'd look like he and I were in it too, and then we'd be officially outlawed and all the money would be seized, and then where would we be? So he suggested coming here."

Gignomai nodded. "So you could marry Luso."

"Or Stheno, or you. We weren't too bothered about details. People still think quite highly of the met'Oc back home, you know. You're considered to have taken a principled stand, and several good families think you were rather hard done by, though naturally that's not the sort of thing anyone says unless it's strictly among friends.

But" — she shrugged, and sipped her wine, absorbing a tiny amount
of it — "after all, I've got to marry somebody, and really, there's not
an infinity of choice, unless I marry outside the Families, which I'd
really rather not do if I can help it." She smiled. "Boulo tried to persuade me that some of the older Vesani houses are practically
respectable, but he's such a romantic. In time, all this nonsense will
blow over, and then I'd be stuck abroad for ever and ever, married to
some clown with longer hair than me, spending all my time going to
the opera. No, Boulo had to admit it eventually, the met'Oc were
the logical choice. So here we are."

Gignomai nodded slowly, as though it all made the most perfect
sense. "Luso's quite happy with the idea."

She mock-scowled at him. "Yes, of course he is. I mean, who's *he*
going to marry otherwise? No, he's perfectly delighted with it."

"Do you like him?"

She grinned. "Actually, I do. He's so *fierce,* it's such a refreshing
change from poor dear Phero. Of course Phero couldn't help the
way he was made, and with that awful father of his he turned out
much better than anyone could have expected. But he wasn't up to
much. People used to say he was so soft you could've spread him on
fresh bread. Luso's quite different. I think we'll get on famously."

"Quite possibly," Gignomai said politely. "Does he know? About
your first husband, I mean?"

She nodded. "He laughed," she said. "Made some joke about having to be very careful about eating what was put in front of him. I
think your father was a bit alarmed at first, but he's a practical man,
he knows a good deal when he sees one."

Gignomai smiled. "Oh, I'm sure he does. The deal being, Luso
inherits when Father dies, because he's the one capable of producing
a legitimate heir, meanwhile, the met'Ousa will do everything they
can to see to it that we can go back Home and get our property
back. You'll end up as the wife of the met'Oc, and we'll get away
from this place. Ideal."

"Thank you," she said. "We think so. Of course, there's a lot of detail to sort out first, and it's so difficult in the circumstances, without proper valuations, or even knowing what you'd be likely to get back and what's gone for good. But in any event, it's got to be better than pining away in Vesanis. It's so hot there, all year round, I think I'd go out of my mind. Boulo doesn't feel the heat, of course. He's lucky."

Gignomai sat up a little. "Well," he said, "I hope it all works out for you, and I wish you the very best of luck. Not sure what any of this has got to do with me."

She gave him a rather sweet smile. "Oh come on," she said. "You're Luso's brother. You're family."

"Not any more," Gignomai replied quickly. "And I've got a piece of paper to prove it."

"Oh, I think we can sort that out," she said mildly. "Luso's very keen to get you back. In fact," she went on, shifting just a little, "he's sort of made it a condition of the agreement."

Gignomai frowned. "Go on."

"Well." She looked away a degree or so. "Bluntly, he won't marry me unless your father revokes the disownment. I'm with Luso," she went on. "I think it was an awful thing to do, and if Luso wants to use the wedding to put pressure on your father, I'm all for it. Luso's very fond of you, you know. He says it's been very fraught up there since you left, and he's been trying to think of a way——"

"Luso always agrees with Father," Gignomai interrupted. "He always does as he's told."

"He keeps the peace," she said. "And really, you can't blame him for that. Someone's got to, in every family. My mother's made a career out of keeping my father and Boulo from tearing each other to bits. And Luso's very good at it. You've got to admit, you're not the most docile family in the world."

Gignomai didn't say anything for a while. Then he said, "You still haven't told me what you want from me."

She pursed her lips. He got the impression she disapproved of the request she was about to make. Presumably he was meant to. "Like I said, the dowry terms are still being sorted out, but Boulo thinks it's almost certain that he'll need to ask you for his men back. As I understand it, your father wants them to add to his garrison or standing army, or whatever you like to call it."

"Luso's gang."

"Yes, if you like. Your father feels that your family needs more footsoldiers. And the fact that they're from Home really appeals to him. He reckons that means they'd be better than the local material."

"And Luso agrees with him."

She made a nothing to do with me gesture. "Back Home it's considered unforgivably gauche for the bride to take an interest in the settlement negotiations. I'm just passing on the message."

"And Cousin Boulomai sent you instead of coming and talking to me himself."

"I wanted to talk to you anyway." She gave him a hard, cold look. "I had this silly idea you might like to get to know your future sister-in-law. Please forgive me if I've inadvertently breached some local protocol."

Gignomai lifted his hand in the minimum possible apology. "The thing is," he said, "I'm not sure they'd want to. They've fitted in here really well, made themselves useful, they're excellent workers and they seem to like the idea of what we're trying to do here. If they want to stay, I honestly don't see how I can make them go."

"I'm sure you can think of something," she said. "Anyway, that's the request; what you do about it is entirely up to you. The other thing—"

"Other thing," Gignomai repeated. "I see."

"Luso wants you to be his best man," Pasi said. "Or at least to be there when we get married. He keeps going on and on about it. I'm sick of hearing him, in fact."

Gignomai shook his head. "Not possible," he said.

"Oh, you don't need to worry about that," she replied. "Luso's said, he'll put his foot down. If your father makes any fuss at all, there won't be a wedding. He told me, he's absolutely set his heart on it. It just wouldn't be right without you, he said."

"Then he's going to be disappointed," Gignomai replied. He stood up, a beautifully composed gesture of finality. "Thank you so much for coming to see me," he said. "And I wish you every happiness, needless to say. If you'd care to wait there, I'll fetch your horse."

"Don't be so stupid," she snapped, and he felt the tug of her voice; it was hard to ignore. "Stupid and selfish. One day being civil to your brother isn't going to kill you."

He turned round slowly and smiled at her. "First, don't be too sure about that, not till you've known my family for as long as I have. Second, I have no desire to force Luso to stand up to my father for the first time in his worthless life. Not over this. Besides, it's a bit late now for him to grow a backbone. He wouldn't have a clue what to do with it."

Before his brother died and left him the store, Marzo had done many things, all of them miserable, none of them for very long. He'd cut and stacked wood for the charcoal-burners, when there was still wood to cut; he'd loaded and unloaded lumber at the sawmill (he was too cack-handed to be allowed to work the saw); he'd been a striker at the forge, until he nearly smashed the smith's hand to pulp; he'd carted stone for the wall builders, and been a fieldhand in the busy season, when any clumsy idiot could find work. Many times, more often than he cared to remember, he'd been exhausted, to the point where breathing was an effort he could hardly justify. But he'd never been as tired as he felt after two hours with the Heddos, the Adrescos and the Sagrennas.

It was, he decided, a bit like trying to bale out water with a sieve. He'd tried to be positive. He'd suggested compromises. He'd asked them all to be practical. As a result, at one point, Silo Adresco pulled a knife on Desio Heddo (it was a very small knife, and Desio just laughed) and Nelo Sagrenna had threatened to burn the Heddos in their house. He'd only managed to get rid of them by promising to demand compensation for all their grievances from the met'Oc.

He pushed back his chair and stared resentfully at the bottle on the table in front of him. It wouldn't solve anything, he knew perfectly well, but that didn't stop it making alluring promises. After a short, depressing battle he gave in and poured himself a massive drink.

He was just savouring the burn when Furio came in, saw the bottle and didn't say anything in the most reproachful manner possible. "Did it go well?" Furio asked.

"Guess."

Furio sat down. "So what are you going to do?"

Marzo closed his eyes. "What I said I'd do," he replied. "I'm going to see Luso met'Oc and demand full compensation."

"Compensation? What for?"

Marzo shrugged. "Like it matters. Luso'll just laugh at me. Not to my face, though, because he's a gentleman. But that's all right. I'll have done what I said I'll do, and then they'll all know I'm useless and maybe they'll leave me alone."

"Which is all you want."

"Which is all I want." Marzo looked at the bottle, then turned his head away. "You know anything about snapping-hen pistols?"

"No. Why should I?"

"Thought your pal Gignomai might've told you something. Doesn't matter."

Furio leaned forward a little. "I saw Gig firing one," he said. "He took a shot at a tree stump, at five yards. He missed."

Marzo laughed. "That might explain why he gave me the bloody thing," he said.

"What do you want to know?"

Wearily, Marzo explained about the bullet from Heddo's wall weighing the same as the bullets Gignomai had given him. "Which means it's pretty certain Luso shot that hole in the Heddos' door," he said. "Which means, if you want to look at it that way, he caused all this aggravation, so really he should be the one to sort it all out."

"Did you tell them about it?"

"God, no," Marzo replied. "You don't want to go telling things to people like that, it only gives them ideas. Bloody Silo Adresco was on at me about a night attack on the Tabletop. Thought we could all scramble up there in the dark with muckforks and murder them all in their beds."

Furio raised an eyebrow. "Silo? He's the little short one, isn't he? Stuck a fork through his own foot once, walks with a limp."

"Quite," Marzo said. "I got the impression he wasn't actually planning on doing much fighting and killing himself. Not sure who he thought was going to do it. Just goes to show, though. You can know someone for years, and they'll still surprise you."

"I expect he was just making a noise," Furio said. "It's easy to suggest something like that when you know it's not going to happen."

Marzo drove the donkey cart to the Tabletop, but the guards wouldn't let him through. Lusomai was busy, they said, wouldn't be free all day. Marzo could try coming back the next day, but they couldn't say whether he'd be available or not. They undertook to deliver a message, but they didn't seem to be paying much attention when he told them what he wanted them to say.

"Leave it a day or so," Furio urged him. "Don't come across as too eager, or he'll think you're scared or worried about something. He's probably just playing games with you."

"I'd go back tomorrow if I were you," Teucer interrupted, though her opinion hadn't been asked for. "When he gets your message he'll be expecting you."

Marzo sighed. "Does it ever occur to anybody that I've got other things to do with my time besides running backwards and forwards playing diplomacy? I'm a shopkeeper, damn it. If they want me to be lord high emissary, then someone had better start paying me for loss of earnings."

"I can look after the store," Teucer said. "Especially if you go in the afternoon, when it's quiet."

Marzo didn't go the next day, or the day after that. In the early hours of the morning of the third day, Silo Adresco's pedigree boar was shot dead in its sty.

"The really spiteful thing," someone was saying in the store later that morning, "was killing it in the middle of the night, so by the time Silo came down and found it, the meat was all spoiled because the blood wasn't drained in time. Useless. Had to bury it under the shit heap. That's what I call a really nasty thing to do."

It occurred to Furio, who was serving at the time, that there might have been other reasons for staging the attack in the small hours, more to do with getting away unchallenged than delicate refinements of malice, but he kept his reflections to himself. After all, if Lusomai met'Oc was responsible (as everybody seemed to be assuming), it didn't necessarily follow that getting in and out unseen would be a priority. In the past, Luso had attacked openly, and hadn't seemed to give a damn who saw him.

"Maybe someone's stolen Luso's gun," he suggested. "One of his gang who's got a grudge against the Heddos, perhaps."

Marzo shook his head. "Don't complicate matters, for crying out loud," he said. "Look, it really doesn't matter whose finger was on the trigger. It was someone who lives on the Tabletop, therefore it's Luso's responsibility. That's all that matters."

"I told you," Teucer said blithely, as she folded clean linen. "You should've gone back the next day. For all you know, he could be punishing you for not going back when you said you would."

Marzo and Furio shared a look. "Sneaking about at night isn't Luso's style," Marzo said. "And I can't believe that one of his men would go and do something like this, using Luso's precious gun, without express orders. More than his life'd be worth."

Furio's eyes widened slightly. "You're thinking it could have been the met'Ousas."

"What I'm trying really hard to do is not think about it at all,"

Marzo replied. "But you don't know, do you? How far are they under Luso's control? I mean, they're guests. There's all sorts of complicated rules of honour and stuff like that. But if they're really mad about what happened, who knows what they'd do?"

"Hold on, though," Furio said. "You reckon the thing about the bullet weights proves it was Luso's gun."

"Unless Boulomai's gun shoots the same size ball, which is entirely possible. Or maybe Boulomai's gun doesn't actually work, so he used Luso's, with or without his knowledge and consent." Marzo spread both hands wide, a gesture he'd picked up from Furio's father. "It's one of those things where the more you think about it, the harder it gets. Which would be fine," he went on, letting his hands drop into his lap, "if I wasn't mixed up in it. I mean, it'd be fine entertainment and good honest fun, sitting here talking over all the possibilities, which I bet everybody else in the colony's doing right now. Difference is, I'm supposed to do something about it."

Furio grinned weakly. "Serves you right for standing for high public office."

"What we should really do is have proper elections," Teucer said. "Have a proper mayor, with clearly defined powers and responsibilities. It's times like these when you realise how important these things can be."

"What bites me," Marzo said, after they'd both ignored her for an appropriate length of time, "is how Luso went banging on about being practical and keeping the peace. And the next thing is, he's running around the place making trouble. Really, I thought he meant all that stuff he said. I mean, I'm not saying I liked the man — he's arrogant and vicious and he makes you feel like a chess piece. But I thought that when he said what matters is keeping a lid on things and not letting them get out of hand, he actually meant it. I thought we could figure out a way of living next to these people without anybody getting seriously hurt."

"It doesn't sound like Luso to me," Furio said. "If he was going to make trouble, it'd be big. Killing a pig is the sort of thing we'd do."

*   *   *

The next morning was cold and crisp, the first frost of the year. Furio hadn't slept well, and he was glad to have an excuse to get out of bed before daybreak: it was his turn to see to the horses. He was in the yard breaking the ice on the water barrel when he heard hooves clattering on the flagstones outside. He walked to the gate and put his head round the corner to see who it was.

He saw two huge men, the biggest he'd ever seen in his life. Their faces were muffled in scarves, but their sheer bulk told him who they were. He ducked back round the corner and sprinted for the back door.

Much to his surprise, he found Marzo awake and pottering in the kitchen, trying to light the fire. "Luso met'Oc's outside," he said, in a hoarse whisper.

Marzo was slightly deaf in one ear. "You what?"

"Luso met'Oc," Furio repeated, dropping the whisper. "Outside. And I think…"

Marzo didn't wait for the rest of the sentence. He dropped the tinderbox he'd been fumbling with (Marzo never had any luck with fires), swung round with an agonised look on his face, located his slippers and stuffed his bare feet into them. "Where's my fucking coat?" he wailed.

"Behind the door."

"What? Oh, right." He clawed at his head in an attempt to drag a stray tuft of hair over his bald spot, plunged into the coat like a diver and shot out of the kitchen. A moment later, Furio heard the bolts on the front door grinding back. A voice said something he couldn't quite make out. For a moment he was sure it was Gig talking. He heard Uncle Marzo reply, "No, that's fine, please come in."

"You'll excuse us for calling so horribly early," the voice went on. "Only, given the situation, we thought it'd be better not to be out and about in broad daylight."

Furio grabbed the tinderbox, quickly struck a spark and emptied the smouldering moss onto Uncle Marzo's vilely constructed pyramid of kindling. A blast from the bellows got it going. Somehow it wouldn't be right to have visitors in the house and no fire lit. Then he retreated into the kitchen, leaving the door slightly open so he could hear.

"I'm sorry to have to bother you with this," Luso said, walking over to the fire. He scowled at it, grabbed the charcoal bucket and shook a triple handful into the grate. "But I guess you're the proper person to talk to. Oh, I'm sorry, let me introduce my brother Sthenomai. Stheno, this is Mayor Opello."

Stheno grinned. "You'll be Furio's father, then."

"Uncle," Marzo said. "Please, sit down." There was more than a hint of urgency in the request. If they'd only sit down, they'd stop towering over him, and he wouldn't feel quite so much like a dog in a yard full of horses. "Can I offer you a —?" He stopped dead, realising he hadn't got anything for them to eat or drink apart from the dregs of last night's brandy. Fortunately, Luso shook his head.

"I'll get straight to the point," he said, as the chair he was sitting in creaked dangerously. It was the big, straight-backed chair with the carved arms, which nobody ever sat in because they knew the left-hand upright was cracked. Marzo wasn't prepared to guess how much Luso weighed, but it had to be considerably more than anybody who'd ever been in the house before. Unfortunately, it was too late to say anything now. "Last night, someone tried to get past our sentries. Whoever it was made a bit of a racket and when a guard went to see what was going on, he was attacked, stabbed from behind. He's all right, but only because he happened to be wearing a jack—that's a padded jacket—under his coat. Anyway, he tried to grab the attacker, but then someone else hit him over the head. We think that was the end of it, because there's nothing to suggest anybody got past the sentry-block. We're assuming the scrap with the guard made them lose their nerve and they legged it. We found the tracks of three horses, leading straight here. Of course, we couldn't follow them once we reached the town—there's so many horse tracks, you can't pick out just one trail. But whoever did it came straight back here afterwards." Luso paused, reached out an impossibly long arm, took the poker and gave the fire a sharp poke. "Now I'm sure this is all news to you, and you don't know who was involved. I'm also confident that you'll agree with me that this sort of thing needs to be stopped before it gets out of hand. I'm afraid my father takes a rather dim view of trespassing. I've told him it's probably just a couple of stupid young lads out after the deer. I'd like to think that's true. What do you think?"

Please, Marzo prayed under his breath, don't let the chair break, this really wouldn't be a good time. "You're right," he said, "it's the first I've heard of it. From what you've told me it does sound more like poachers than anything else."

Stheno made a sort of grunting noise. Luso said, "We'd both like it to be that, of course. But the fact is, we haven't had trouble with poachers for, what?" He looked at his brother, who muttered a number. "Thanks, Stheno, forty years, which is before Stheno and I were born. I seem to remember Father telling us he came down on the people responsible pretty hard."

Marzo winced. The men in question had been carpenters, but now they did odd jobs for charitably minded neighbours. Hard to do carpentry with only one hand.

"Things are different now, of course," Luso went on. "Father had his way of doing things, I have mine. I accept this isn't Home, and the traditional approach, if I can call it that, may not always be appropriate. I prefer to get along with people, if I can."

His voice was so pleasant, so sensible and reassuring—you could trust that voice, you could be sure that anything it said was obviously the right thing—that Marzo almost forgot the point he wanted to raise. Saying it seemed impossible, just as it was impossible to believe that the speaker could ever have maliciously shot someone's pig. He imagined what it must be like to be an arm or a leg, controlled by the brain, obeying without question because, after all, we're all part of the same body. So he surprised himself when he heard himself say, "Me too. I like to keep the peace. But maybe you should accept that you're partly to blame."

Luso sat up straight, as if he'd just been slapped by a girl. "Well, I suppose there's some truth in that, we haven't exactly been the best of neighbours. But you'll remember, when we spoke last, I gave you my word there'd be no cattle raiding or any nonsense like that, and I think you'll find I've kept my end of the bargain."

Marzo opened his mouth and closed it again. He knew there had to be words to say what he needed to say, but he couldn't imagine what they could be. He resolved to do his best, and hope. "With respect," he said, "I think you may be overlooking a couple of things."

Luso's eyes opened wide. "Really?"

"Please," Marzo said. "Please, just wait there."

He almost ran out of the room. Once he was in his back store room, with the door closed, he had to sit down and wait for his breath to catch up with him. More than anything else he wanted to wedge the door shut with a chair, or climb out of the window, anything rather than go back in there and call Lusomai met'Oc a liar to his face. But when he came out again a little while later, he was breathing normally again, and he had both hands tightly closed.

"We found this," he said, "in the wall of Desio Heddo's house. I was wondering if you could tell me what it is."

He knew all right. There was a blank look, then a quiver of the eyebrows. "That's a bullet," Luso said. "Where did you say...?"

"Lodged in a wall," Marzo replied, in a brittle voice. "Whoever it was shot through the door. And then there's this one." He opened his other hand, and let the thing fall onto the table, next to the flat disc. This one looked like a grey pebble, irregular, squashed at one end, rounded at the other. "We dug this out of the skull of a valuable pedigree boar belonging to a man called Silo Adresco. If you'd like me to fetch my scales, I can show you that both bullets weigh practically the same, which suggests they were fired from the same gun."

Luso looked up at him. "Somebody shot a pig?"

"You tell me," Marzo replied. "You're the expert. I don't know anything about it. I'm assuming that's a gun bullet, because it's lead and it was driven so hard it smashed a hole in a boar's skull, which is about as thick a bit of bone as you'll get anywhere. I think both of those are bullets from a snapping-hen pistol, but maybe you could confirm that for me."

Luso picked them up and stared at them on the palm of his hand. "They look like pistol balls to me," he said. "I take it you think I fired the shots."

Marzo shrugged; he overdid it a little. "As far as I know, there's three of the things in the colony. You've got one, your cousin Boulomai's got one."

"Two, actually," Luso said. "But they're half-inch bore. These are five-eighths."

"I was going to ask you about that," Marzo said. "And there's the third one, which happens to belong to me."

Stheno lifted his head suddenly. "That's open to debate," he said.

"It's all right, Stheno," Luso said. "My brother doesn't accept the notion of legitimate spoils of war," he said. "But I do, so we won't go into all that now. I didn't know you'd got it, though. I tried to buy it back, but the man wouldn't sell."

Marzo swallowed, to get his throat working again. "You'll have to take my word for it, I'm afraid, but I can guarantee that neither of those came from my gun. It's kept in a safe place, and I know for a fact it hasn't been moved."

"You can check quite easily," Luso said. "If it's been fired, it stinks to high heaven of burnt powder. Or if it's been cleaned, either it'll be starting to rust or it'll be oiled up to stop it rusting. I take it..."

"In that case, I can confirm it wasn't my gun," Marzo said. "I don't suppose you happen to have yours with you."

Luso grinned. "Well, no," he said. "Didn't think it'd be polite, for one thing. Also, as it happens I did fire the gun yesterday. I practise with it once a week."

Marzo remembered what Furio had told him: Gignomai couldn't hit a log, at five paces. "If it wasn't mine," he said, "and it wasn't your cousin's..."

"Beats me," Luso said. "And yes, I can see why you think it must've been me. All I can say is, it wasn't. When did all this happen, by the way?"

Marzo told him. He shook his head. "Sorry," he said, "but it doesn't look like I can help you there. Our place is pretty big, you know. People can come and go, and I wouldn't necessarily know about it."

"Could someone have taken your gun without you knowing?"

Stheno laughed. "Hardly," Luso said, "if they knew what's good for them, they wouldn't even try." He frowned, and Marzo desperately wished he knew what he was thinking. "Well," he said, "I'll ask questions when I get back home, but I can't promise anything. Meanwhile, we really do have to sort out this other business. I can see what you're thinking and believe me, I can understand why you're upset, but it's got to be done. I haven't come all this way to go back empty-handed."

Silo Adresco, Marzo thought. Silo, who was sitting right there a day or so ago, talking nonsense about storming the Tabletop with a few good men, and then his stupid pig gets shot. And then a few men, by the sound of it not particularly good, try and knife a guard in the dark. It was hideously plausible. He tried to think of something to say, but when the words came out, he instantly regretted them.

"We've got to be practical," was what he said.

Stheno met'Oc seemed to find that enormously funny. Luso shot him a mock scowl, and said, "Exactly what I was thinking. You and I need to find a way to close all this nonsense right down before somebody gets hurt." He paused, then added, "I'm open to suggestions."

Marzo tried to think, but nothing came. "You're sure these couldn't have been shot out of one of your other guns?"

Luso smiled. "Not possible," he said. "They're all hunting pieces, three-quarter inch bore. And they don't take bullets, they fire small shot. I suppose you could wrap the ball in several layers of cloth, but then you'd have found bits of burnt fabric at the scene. Also, I'd have known if someone borrowed one. Nice idea, but it couldn't have been."

Marzo nodded. Irrelevant, in any case. And if Boulomai's gun used a smaller bullet...He shook his head. That line of thought really wasn't helping. "You suggest something," he said.

"Are you sure? A moment ago you were telling me I caused all this."

"I really don't care," Marzo said. "I just want it all to go away. You're supposed to be good at this. Do you think you can arrange it?"

Luso leaned back a little; the chair groaned painfully, but he didn't seem to be aware of it. "It depends," he said, "on whether you can control your people. I can handle mine, but I've got to give them something. My father especially. The trouble is, he wants to believe that you don't exist. It'd suit his view of the world so much better if he could be sure you're figments of his imagination. Stuff like this only reminds him, and he really doesn't like that. I can't just go to him and say, 'Forget about it, I've dealt with it.' He needs..." Luso paused, searching for the right word. "He needs a trophy, something he could stick on the wall alongside the stags' horns and the boars' masks. Something tangible, if you follow me."

Marzo nodded slowly. "Stick on the wall" was his cue. Well, he didn't really want it anyway. "You can have the snapping-hen back," he said.

Luso nodded approvingly. "I think that'd do it," he said. "But I'm going to impose a condition of my own. You've got to tell me how you came by it."

"I bought it from Calo Brotti," Marzo said.

"Who wouldn't sell to me."

"He owed me," Marzo said, "for a new plough and share. He needed the stuff but couldn't pay cash. We did a deal. He wasn't happy."

"Thank you," Luso said. "All right, that's my end dealt with. What do you need?"

Marzo closed his eyes. "The way I see it," he said, "if I give you mine, it'll mean all the snapping-hens in the colony will be up there on the Tabletop, safely under your control. Is that right?"

"That's a good question," Luso said. "I'm not sure I'm in a position to give you a guarantee. You see, I didn't shoot either of those two balls you've got there. I give you my word on that."

Marzo looked at him despairingly, like a man drowning in a river who sees a passer-by stop, then walk away. "Tell you what," he said. "If I make myself believe what you've just said is true, and I give you the stupid gun, will you promise me there'll be no more shootings? Because there can't be, can there? Not if all the guns are in your hands, and I've got your word."

Luso closed his eyes. "I can't make that promise," he said. "Because, if I didn't do it, someone else must have. There's got to be a third gun somewhere."

"Not possible," Marzo snapped, and Stheno frowned—don't you shout at my kid brother. Under other circumstances, it'd have been funny. "How could there be? I've lived here all my damn life, my brother used to have the import concession, and now I've got it. If a snapping-hen got brought in on a ship, I'd have known about it. If there was such a thing floating about loose somewhere, I'd know."

"Maybe Boulomai brought it," Stheno said.

There was dead silence. Luso turned his head and stared at his brother, as if a voice had just boomed out from a thundercloud. "Well," Stheno went on, "it's a possibility. Strikes me it's the only possibility. We know he's got a pair of the things he wears like jewellery."

"The half-inchers," Luso said.

"Whatever," Stheno replied. "You're the one who knows that stuff. But for all we know, he could have another one, in the bigger size. Or another pair, even. Those two brought a whole load of luggage with them, and I don't suppose anybody's taken a look to see what kind of toys they've got in there. First article of faith in the met'Oc family code of conduct: don't search your house guests' stuff for concealed weapons. In which case," he went on, after a pause, "you've solved your mystery, haven't you? Oh, have you heard, by the way? Luso here's going to marry cousin Pasi. That's the girl," he explained. "Not always easy to tell them apart, of course, unless they're standing sideways."

Luso glowered at his brother, who took no notice. "I guess Stheno's right," he said. "It's entirely possible. Boulo could well have two pairs; a fancy pair for dressing up and a plain pair for actual mischief."

"Needn't necessarily be him," Stheno said to the wall. "She's quite capable —"

"Stheno."

Stheno raised a hand in vestigial apology. "Sorry, mustn't say nasty things about my future sister-in-law. But she's — well, a bit of a tomboy, that one. Also somewhat inclined to do what the hell she likes and ask if it's all right afterwards."

Luso shifted so that the back of his head was pointed at his brother. "One or two unresolved issues," he said to Marzo, synthetically cheerful. "Nothing that need concern you, and I do apologize for any embarrassment we may have caused you. But yes, he's got a point. My fiancée can be a little bit boisterous at times. I don't really see her snooping about in the dark assassinating pigs, but it's not impossible she might have fluttered her eyelashes at someone and got them to do it for her. And she does have quite a collection of interesting trinkets."

Stheno laughed. Luso clicked his tongue at him. "Well," Stheno said, "looks like I've cleared up your problem for you. And just think, Luso didn't want me to come along."

"It's the only explanation," Luso said. "Well, isn't it? And that's just fine, because when we get back, I'll have a word with my cousins, both of them." He turned and shot a quick scowl at his brother. "And, yes, I can guarantee there won't be any more gunshots in the night. On that, you have my unconditional promise."

"There," Stheno said solemnly, clapping his hands together. The noise made Furio jump and bang his head on the door latch. "Luso's word of honour. What more could anybody ask for?"

Luso swung round to say something to him. At that point, the chair collapsed.

*   *   *

Gignomai drove a cart into town two days later. He pulled up outside the store just as Furio was opening the door for the start of business. They looked at each other.

"Hello, stranger," Gignomai said. "Marzo about?"

"I'll get him," Furio replied.

"That's all right." Gignomai jumped down and landed awkwardly, yelping as his ankle went over. "Mind giving me a hand with this lot? I did my back in a day or so ago, and heavy lifting isn't going to improve it."

Furio hesitated, but he was curious. "What've you got?" he said.

"The first batch," Gignomai replied.

"You mean...?"

Gignomai grinned. "A dozen shovels, two dozen hay-forks, ten ploughshares, a dozen hay-knives, three dozen tin plates, ditto cups—"

"Already?"

"We don't hang about," Gignomai said, dropping the tailgate. "We're using oak formers for the pressings. They won't last long, but they're easy enough to replace, and it means we're in production. Later, when we've got five minutes, we can make up proper iron swages."

Furio didn't understand most of that, but he got the general idea. "We'd better get this lot inside, then," he said. "You take the back end."

They lugged half a dozen long crates into the shop and dumped them on the floor. Marzo must have heard the thumps. He came out of the back store room and tripped over a crate. Then he looked down.

"Is that...?" he said.

"Ploughshares," Gignomai said, grinning broadly. "One hundred per cent domestic product."

Marzo stared at the crate as if it was the most remarkable thing he'd ever seen, until Furio tapped him on the shoulder. "Crowbar," Furio said.

"Careful with the crates, please," Gignomai said. "I'll be needing them back. Actually, those represent our entire stock of packing cases. We decided that for now we'd concentrate on making stuff, rather than stuff for putting stuff in."

Marzo tried to prise the lid off the crate, but instead dropped the crowbar. "You do it," he told Furio. "Over-excited," he explained. Gignomai laughed, and Furio gently lifted the lid. They all stood over the crate and looked inside.

After a while, Furio said, "They just look like plain ordinary ploughshares to me."

"Thank you," Gignomai said.

"That's the whole point," Marzo said. "Plain, ordinary plough-shares. From here, you can't tell them apart from the real thing."

"They're real ploughshares," Gignomai growled. "Hence the marked bloody similarity. They fit the standard Company eighteen-inch plough. We tested them, they're fine. Only difference is, they haven't got the Company crests and batchmarks stamped on them."

Marzo didn't seem capable of standing for much longer. He grabbed a chair and sank into it. "What're you doing for steel?" he asked.

"Ah." Gignomai frowned. "Need to talk to you about that. We made these up out of the last of the scrap."

Furio looked at him. "You mean you've run out of metal?"

"Temporarily." Gignomai didn't sound too happy. "But that's all in hand. Open that crate there, it's billhooks."

The billhooks were plain, ordinary billhooks, though real enough for Marzo to nick his thumb when he tried a blade for sharpness. And the forks were ordinary forks, and the shovels were ordinary shovels. "That's amazing," Marzo said.

"That's half a year's stock," Furio said.

"At current prices," Gignomai replied. "But you're going to sell them at a quarter of that."

Marzo looked up sharply. "Am I?"

"Sure," Gignomai said. "Which means everybody'll be able to afford one. Which means you'll sell ten times as many. Do the arithmetic."

Marzo was silent for a moment, and Furio could feel a certain tension. "Depends what I've got to pay you for them," he said.

"No money changes hands," Gignomai said. "Not yet, at least. Same terms as before, until we've built up a solid market. You send us food, we send you finished goods." Suddenly he smiled. Just like his brother, Furio thought. "I can't say fairer than that, can I?"

"I guess not." Marzo was examining a shovel blade.

"Very practical approach," Furio muttered, but neither of them seemed to be listening. He left them to it and went outside to see to Gignomai's horse. After a while, Teucer came out to join him.

"Well?" Furio said.

"Well what?"

"Seems like we were both wrong."

She turned a bucket upside down and sat on it. "What makes you say that?"

"You've been in the store."

She nodded. "They've got tools and things spread out all over the floor. You can't get to the door without risking cutting your ankles."

"There you are, then."

"You aren't making any sense."

Furio sighed. "You told me—persuaded me that Gig was up to something. Apparently not. He said he was going to go away and make hardware, and that's exactly what he's done."

"Maybe that's not all he's been doing."

Furio laughed. "Teucer, he can't have had *time* for anything else. He's been working flat out all day and half the night, and he's got to sleep sometimes."

She shook her head. "He's up to something. Someone like that doesn't change his whole life just so the working man can buy an affordable shovel." She picked up a few strands of straw and bent them till they broke. "Did you talk to him about his brother getting married?"

"Haven't had a chance."

"You should," Teucer said. "Do you think he'll go to the wedding?"

"I doubt it," Furio said. "I got the impression that if he sets foot on the Tabletop he's dead."

"That's an exaggeration," Teucer said. "If he goes back, they might even patch things up."

"Still fancy him, do you?"

She looked at him, as he leaned on the handle of the hayfork. "Yes," she said, "on balance. But I don't think I'd want to marry him."

Furio barked out a laugh. "Don't suppose there's much danger of you being asked," he said.

She shrugged. "Did he ever tell you what happened to his sister?"

Furio scratched his head. "No," he said. "I gather there was a sister once, when he was a kid. I assume she died." He leaned the fork against the wall. "Why, did he ever say anything to you?"

"No. But I just wondered. Maybe he's not interested in girls because they remind him of his sister."

Furio thought about it for a very short time, which was as long as he felt the hypothesis merited. "I don't think so," he said. "I think he's not interested in any of the girls round here because none of them are grand enough for the son of the met'Oc. I think he might have had a go at that cousin of his, if she'd held still long enough."

"I doubt it," Teucer said. "No, I get the impression she and Luso-mai will be very well suited. Still, it really doesn't matter now, does it?"

Furio watched her go, then sat down on her bucket. As always when he'd said more than two words together with Teucer, he was left feeling slightly bewildered and vaguely uncomfortable. She reminded him of a character in a fairy tale, but he couldn't decide which one.

*   *   *

The news that Mayor Opello was practically giving stuff away swept through the colony like an epidemic. Since no ship had called, apart from the strangers', it was naturally assumed that Marzo was in some kind of trouble, which was forcing him to raise money by selling his stock at a loss. Deeper thinkers made a link between Marzo's presumed financial collapse and the weird project he was funding out in the savages' country, about which the colonists still knew tantalisingly little. Not that they cared particularly. What mattered was a new shovel for a turner, ploughshares for six bits, and a new pattern of tin plate nobody had seen before for half a double.

By the time the deep-country people reached the store it was all over, though that didn't stop them buying stuff, at full price, believing that what they were paying was the sacrificial discount. When Marzo eventually closed the doors on the second day, he calculated that his iron-bound cashbox now held at least a third of the coined money in the colony. He sat down in his chair behind the counter, feeling exhausted, exhilarated and more than a little scared.

Far from solving anything, the success of the first batch of home-produced goods had multiplied his problems to a terrifying extent. He now had money, more of it than he'd ever seen before (the image of Gignomai's sword came into his mind and he expelled it quickly), but he was running perilously short of flour, malt, dried foods and all the other stores he was pledged to supply the factory with. He could now pay for replacement stock with money rather than other goods (he was running low on that sort of thing; he was running low on *everything*) but that didn't help much. He'd more or less exhausted the surplus stocks of the colony, which was hardly surprising, given that they now had an extra twenty-odd mouths to feed: the sailors from the met'Ousa ship, now working at the factory. The colony's subsistence economy was so finely poised that twenty extra eaters endangered everybody.

Let them eat beef, he told himself, because there was still plenty of that. Trouble was, it was spoken for, it belonged to the Company, it wasn't his to buy or the farmers' to sell. So what? If he tendered a hundred fewer steers than he was contracted to deliver, all that'd happen would be that he'd get paid a smaller quantity of trade goods, which wouldn't matter a damn since Gignomai would be making all that stuff for him. True. But he'd have had to pay the farmers in cash and credit, and in return he'd be getting goods that would now be too expensive to compete with Gignomai's products, so he'd be stuck with them or have to sell them at a loss (pretty irony). Furthermore, most of the things Gignomai was going to make, most of the stuff people in the colony wanted, were made of iron. He'd bought up practically every piece of rusty scrap in the colony, and Gignomai had used it to make his machines and the first batch of samples. There wasn't any more. Gignomai had said that wouldn't be a problem, but he hadn't been prepared to expand on that, so Marzo felt entirely within his rights to worry.

Also, there was the inevitable fact that the colonists could only use so many shovels, spades, axes, tin plates, nails, wedges, saw-blades, knives and buckets. It wouldn't be long before everybody had all the things he needed, and then what would become of the glorious bloodless revolution? Not to mention the reaction of the Company and (in Marzo's mind, at least) its evil twin the government, when they figured out what was going on.

And that wasn't all. Practically every eager buyer who'd been through his door over the last two days had stopped to talk, the way country people do when they come to town, and there'd been one predominant subject of conversation: what did the mayor propose doing about the met'Oc, following the spate of unprovoked murderous attacks? The stories had waxed fat in the telling, and the further out people lived, the more lurid the tales they'd heard. On the second day, when the people from the eastern hills showed up, he was reliably informed that Desio Heddo had been shot dead, or at least he was dying, and the Adrescos' entire cattle herd had been slaughtered and left lying in grotesque heaps out on the pasture. You could smell the rotting meat for miles around, they said, though since most of them would have had to pass within half a mile of the Adresco house and none of them had smelt anything, Marzo wondered where that particular gem had come from, and how it had managed to survive the sharp frost of common sense. Most remarkable of all was the way that everybody, no matter how far out they lived or how rarely they saw another human face, had learned to call him Mayor Opello. Some of them were quite friendly about it, but there were clearly some who wondered who the hell he thought he was, awarding himself grand titles and putting on airs. They sort of spat the honorific at him, and scowled at him to show they weren't impressed, not one bit.

He'd done his best, of course. He'd told anybody who looked as though they might be listening (a depressingly low percentage) that he'd met with Lusomai met'Oc (they already knew that) and that they'd had a full and frank discussion about the recent disturbances, and he had the met'Oc's word that there wouldn't be any further trouble. His pronouncements were met with a mixture of awe and disbelief. Awe, because here was a man who actually talked to the semi-mythical creatures who lived on the mountain top. Disbelief, because who could trust a man who kept company with that sort of people?

After all that, the other snippet of news had come as light relief. It was weird, but he couldn't see how there was any harm in it, which made it the exception. Apparently, several families who lived near the southern border had seen parties of savages, in most cases for the first time in their lives. No big deal, they said. The savages, usually in groups of a dozen or so, men and women, had taken to standing on hilltops and other vantage points and staring at people as they went about their daily chores. Nothing hostile, no reports of any visible weapons or aggressive posturing, and if you called out to them, they took no notice—maybe they were all deaf; after all, we know so little about them—and nobody was missing any cattle or chickens, no fences had been broken down, no unexplained footmarks on this side of the border. They just stood and watched, was all.

Two days later, Furio volunteered to be driver's mate on a cartload of flour barrels headed for the factory.

"Please yourself," Marzo replied. "It's not like we're rushed off our feet right now."

Which was true. Ever since the orgy of buying, business had been painfully quiet. Just as well, Marzo made a point of saying, since we've hardly got anything left to sell. That was a gross exaggeration, but Furio couldn't be bothered to raise the issue. He left Marzo leaning on the counter doing sums on a scrap of the coarse brown paper that came wrapped round scythe blades.

It was the first time Furio had been back to the factory since his grand departure, so he wasn't expecting the noise. When he first noticed it, miles away, it was a faint, almost dainty tinkling, like a cow-bell. Once they were inside the wood, it made hearing the cart driver impossible. When they reached the factory, Furio could feel the blood pumping in his ears in counterpoint. No doubt about it, the drop-hammer was working just fine. It was, he discovered by taking his own pulse, a very slightly longer interval than a heartbeat. Maybe that was why it jarred so badly. Each time the hammer fell, it crashed on the anvil, a dampened ring, the sound of sheer weight and frustrated motion. After a minute, he found he was having difficulty with his breathing.

The carter didn't want to hang around. He pulled up the cart, jumped down, dropped the tailgate and started hauling barrels in a way that was bound to damage his back. Furio didn't offer to help. Instead, he leaned in close and shouted, "I'll stay here for a bit. You go on, I'll walk back."

"What?"

"I'll walk back," Furio yelled, but it was obviously no use. He shook his head and walked away. The carter carried on wrestling barrels.

Furio stopped by a fallen tree and tore a couple of handfuls of moss off the trunk, but he couldn't get it to stay in his ears. He looked round to see if he could find Gignomai, but there didn't seem to be anybody about. It occurred to him to wonder what the hammer was pounding, if there wasn't any metal left.

A man hurried past him, someone he didn't recognise. He shouted, but the man didn't hear, so he followed him, and was led to a building that hadn't been there when he left. He went inside.

He saw what looked like an enormous mound of clay, swelling out of the ground like a huge fungus. Its top disappeared through a hole in the roof. There was a small door, just big enough for a child to crawl through, about a foot above ground level. A two-foot-diameter clay pipe branched off the other side and disappeared through the wall. For a brief, bewildering moment he wondered if Gignomai, in an intense burst of homesickness, had built a scale model of the Tabletop, but he wouldn't do that, would he?

"It's a furnace," a voice yelled in his ear. It was too loud to recognise; he turned, and there was Gignomai, covered in dirt and soot, grinning at him. "Come on, I can't hear myself think."

He followed Gignomai out, and they walked beside the river for quite a while, then up the hill to the hollow where Furio had watched Gignomai fire the snapping-hen. At the bottom of the hollow, the thump of the drop-hammer was muffled, and Gignomai could be heard without yelling.

"Nice to see you again," Gignomai said. "How are you keeping?"

"What is that thing?"

Gignomai laughed. "It's a furnace," he said. "It melts iron out of rock. After the hammer, it's our biggest project yet."

"Does it work?"

"I bloody well hope so. We'll find out tomorrow, when we fire it up." He sat down cross-legged on the ground, and after a moment's hesitation, Furio joined him. He felt very young, sitting in the leaf mould. "You didn't answer my question," he said. "How are you?"

"What? Oh, fine. What rock?"

Gignomai pulled an exasperated face, which flowed into a grin. "That's where iron comes from," he said. "Iron ore is a kind of rock. There's a whole hillside of the stuff not two miles from here downstream. You don't even have to dig, you can wander around filling buckets with it."

Furio frowned. "You can really get iron out of it?"

Gignomai nodded. "We smash it up really small under the drop-hammer, then pack it in baskets with lime, sulphur and charcoal. There's three tons of charcoal in the bottom of the furnace already. Tomorrow we tip the ore and the lime and stuff in on top and get it burning. That pipe you may have seen leads to the big bellows we've got for the drop-hammer forge. You need to blast lots of air in to get the fire hot enough. When it's up to full heat, apparently, the whole thing'll glow red. We won't be in there with it, of course. We'll be outside, chucking buckets of water on the shed walls to keep them from catching fire."

Furio thought for a moment. "That little door in the side?"

"To tap off the molten iron when it's melted," Gignomai said. "It runs down a clay channel into a nest of about a dozen moulds, where it cools off, and then you've got a stack of iron bars, ready to make into stuff."

"Why keep it in a shed," Furio asked, "if it gets that hot?"

"Rain," Gignomai replied. "A few drops of water on it when it's good and hot, and there'd be a blast you could hear back Home. And it'd be raining droplets of iron right across the colony. Rain falling down the chimney's not a problem, it evaporates before it would hit anything, but we daren't risk it on the furnace walls. Besides," he added, "if it burns the shed down, so what? We stand well back, and once it's cooled down we build another shed." He shook his head. "It scares the life out of me, but we need it. All the iron we can use for free."

Furio looked at him. There was genuine happiness in his grin, but his eyes were cold. "You got all that out of a book, I suppose," he said.

"Eutropius' *Concerning Metals*. There isn't one like it in the world, not any more. All the commentators say building one's impossible, it wouldn't work, it'd crack and blow up. They think Eutropius dreamed it up but never tried it out."

Furio blinked. "You don't suppose they're right, do you?"

"We'll find out, won't we? If you're sitting on your porch this time tomorrow and suddenly there's a loud bang and it starts raining body parts, you'll know Eutropius was a liar. I don't think so, though. I think it'll work."

"You've been busy," Furio said.

"You could say that," Gignomai replied. "I'll tell you what, though. This beats sitting in my father's library reading law books."

Furio nodded slowly. "Gig," he said, "where's Aurelio?"

Gignomai picked up a bit of twig and crumbled it between his thumbs. "You asked me that before," he said.

"Yes. You lied to me. Where is he?"

"Third shed from the left as you come in." Gignomai jerked his head in what Furio assumed was the right direction; he'd lost his bearings some time ago. "Don't go telling anyone. His relatives are quite keen to meet him, but he doesn't share their enthusiasm."

"Is he making guns?"

Gignomai's face went blank. Then he said, "Not whole ones. Parts for the lock mechanisms. He can't start making barrels till we've got the furnace going."

"That's what you wanted the snapping-hen for," Furio said. "So you could copy it."

Gignomai smiled. "Rough copies," he said, "none of the fancy stuff. The original's a work of art, you couldn't squeeze a hair between the parts, the tolerances are so fine. I'll be happy with something much cruder, so long as it works."

Furio took a deep breath. "What do you want them for?"

"To sell, of course." Gignomai raised an eyebrow. "So that when the government sends soldiers to stop us doing all this, we can persuade them to go home and leave us in peace. If it comes to that," he added quickly. "But it might, so there's no harm in being prepared.

Also, people will be prepared to pay good money. After all, your uncle wanted one, and he's the most peaceable man I've ever met."

"Have you made one yet?"

Gignomai's face was empty. "I told you," he said, "we can't start production till we've got the furnace running. Aurelio says you need a special sort of iron for making barrels out of. You can't just weld them up out of old rubbish."

"So the one you tested..."

This time, he got a reaction. It was a little spurt of anger, quickly stifled and overlaid with a big grin. "You were watching me."

"Yes."

"You saw me..."

"Miss a tree stump." Furio nodded.

"Quite." Gignomai shook his head. "I'd always wanted to have a go with one, but of course Luso wouldn't let me. It looked so easy when he did it. You hold it out at arm's length, pull the trigger and bang! There's a hole the size of your thumb in the middle of the target. Presumably there's rather more to it. Anyway, I don't plan on wasting much time on it. Just so long as they work, I'm not fussed. That's why it's got to be guns, you see. If we make swords and pikes and arrowheads and the soldiers come, chances are there'd be actual fighting. In which case, we'd probably lose and people would almost certainly get hurt. But if they show up and we start shooting at them, they'll piss off back Home so fast they'll make your head spin. Doesn't matter a damn if we hit anything or not. They'll assume they're outmatched. All the noise and the smoke, you see. It's why Luso's so fond of the things."

"Fine," Furio said. "So that explains about Aurelio. Why didn't you tell me?"

Gignomai shrugged. "Be realistic," he said. "The whole point is that I don't want anybody knowing about it. Even my people here don't know—just Aurelio and me. And now you, of course. You're smart, Furio. How did you figure it out?"

"Why not? Why the big secret?"

"Because it's illegal," Gignomai said, with a big smile. "Not just breach of monopoly illegal, like making shovel blades. I should think it probably constitutes high treason, procuring arms for use in a rebellion, but I'd need to look it up in Father's book. Anyway, it's not the sort of thing I wanted anybody knowing about."

"But there won't be a ship till the spring."

Gignomai nodded. "True," he said. "But then cousin Boulomai shows up. It might suit him very nicely to play the good citizen and help foil a rebellion in the colonies, don't you think? Good way for him and his loathsome sister to get back home. It's what I'd do in his shoes. So," Gignomai went on, shaking his head, "hence the deadly secrecy. I had to keep Aurelio hidden where nobody would see him."

"He was in the livery?"

"You're very smart. Yes, for a while, but that was no good, obviously. Had him stashed away in an old barn on the Gimalli place, and that was a risk I wasn't happy about taking. And nobody could know about it. Not even you."

"I see."

"I'm sorry. I wish I could've told you. You've always been like a brother to me."

Lusomai and Sthenomai. "I hope you don't mean that."

Gignomai laughed. "All right, I'm sorry, I'll rephrase that. I do trust you, as much as I can trust anybody. I guess it's not in my nature." Something had changed. For a moment, Furio didn't know what it was. Then he realised that the hammer had stopped. "It's how I grew up," Gignomai went on, "always having to hide stuff, or have it taken away from me. After a bit it turned into a sort of game, I suppose: how long could I keep something hidden from those two? And it was always something really stupid, like a bird's nest or some rusty iron I'd found, or a book, or a toy sword made out of bits of shingle. But as I got older, there was a bit more of an edge to it, if you see what I mean. I was supposed to have grown out of all that, and I hadn't." He made a vague conciliatory gesture, all hands and shoulders. "So I don't tell anybody anything. It's not just you. I don't expect you to like me for it, it's just how I am."

It was a pretty good performance, Furio had to concede. The question was, to what extent was he supposed to believe it? Of course, Gignomai had a special way of lying, which involved mostly telling the truth.

"The hammer's stopped," Gignomai said.

"I'd noticed."

"I didn't. Shows I've been here too long." he stood up. "If it's stopped, it must mean something's bust. You'll have to excuse me. I've told them how to fix most things, but they pretend they don't understand."

"I'd best be getting back," Furio said. "Good luck with your furnace."

"Thanks. You won't tell anyone, will you? About the other thing. You can tell them about the furnace all you like."

The dozen or so leading citizens—the criteria for inclusion were vague and mostly consisted of being affluent enough to be able to spare the time to sit in the back room of the store during the day, when everybody else was working—gathered to discuss the forth-coming met'Oc wedding.

They hadn't warned Marzo that they were coming, and so they found him in his shirtsleeves, looking disreputable and smelling worse. He'd been digging a new soakaway for the outhouse, a job so fearsome that money couldn't persuade anybody else to do it for him. He'd been tempted to beg leave to go and wash and change, but they'd assured him they'd only take a minute or so. Two hours later, the meeting was deadlocked.

"It's about keeping the peace," said Rasso from the livery. His choice of words made Marzo want to smile. Rasso had borrowed the phrase from him and, like any man in the colony who borrowed anything, he seemed determined to use it till it fell apart before he was called on to give it back. "Ever since the mayor here had his big meeting with the met'Oc boys, there's been no trouble."

"Not yet," grunted Gimao the chandler. "Wasn't any trouble at all before the youngest met'Oc boy ran away from home. Not for a long time, anyhow."

Marzo turned his head and scowled at him. "Meaning?"

"Meaning," Gimao replied aggressively, "we get trouble when we interfere in their business, or the other way about. Long as they stay up there and we stay down here and we don't have anything to do with each other, things stay nice and quiet. Soon as they remember we exist, there's trouble."

Marzo couldn't have asked for a more succinct statement of his own deeply held belief. Unfortunately, for some reason, he was in the process of trying to argue the opposing case. That, apparently, was the sort of thing mayors did. "In the past, yes," he said. "And you know why? Because we never talked to them before."

"Whose fault was that?" interrupted Stenora the horse doctor.

"Let's not talk about whose fault things were in the past," Marzo said firmly. "Let's be practical. Lusomai met'Oc is prepared to talk to me. He even listens to what I have to say. Sometimes," he added, with a faint grin. "Take this latest thing. Someone goes poaching on the Tabletop and tries to stab one of their guards."

"So they say," Gimao muttered. "Only got their word for it."

Marzo ignored him. "Not so long ago," he went on, "there'd have been burnt hayricks and run off cattle and maybe worse. Instead, what happens? The two met'Oc boys come down here, they sit right where you're sitting now, and we talk. That's got to be progress, hasn't it?"

"Oh sure." Stenora folded his arms and glowered behind them, like the defenders of a besieged city. "That's after Luso'd been charging round the place firing off his gun and terrorising innocent folk. And what did we do about it?"

"Lusomai gave me his word he had nothing to do with that stuff."

"And you take his word," Gimao said bitterly, "over ours. And now you want to send the bastard a wedding present. Strikes me we've heard rather a lot out of you lately about what a fine man Luso met'Oc is, and you won't hear a word against him. Ever since you went into business with his brother, seems to me."

"That's garbage," Marzo snapped, so fiercely that the others stared at him. "For a start, young Gignomai's not exactly popular up there, or hadn't you heard? They chucked him out, remember. Luso came burning and stealing just because we took the boy in. So don't you try and make out I'm siding with the met'Oc just because of that."

Gimao shrugged, like a man walking through a waterfall. "That's not what I'm saying," he said, with a magnificently blank face. "What I'm saying is, you're the mayor of this town; you ought to be on our side. I'm not sure you are, any more."

"Fine," Marzo spat. "In that case, I resign. I won't be mayor, and one of you buggers can go up there and be blindfolded and shit yourself for terror next time there's trouble. No, really, I mean it. I never wanted the stupid job. I'm damned if I can remember anybody asking me if I wanted to do it. I'm damned if I know how I got stuck with it in the first place. It's been nothing but misery, and I don't want to do it any more."

"Yes, all right," Stenora said briskly, "you've made your point, and Gimao's sorry he made it sound like —"

"No," Marzo said firmly, "I mean it, I really do. I say we should do it properly and have an election and choose a real mayor. And I won't be standing."

There was an awkward silence. Then Rasso said, "Pull yourself together, Marzo, nobody's saying we don't want you to be mayor any more. And we all appreciate everything you've done, and by and large you've done a good job. That's not what we're here to talk about. We're here because you want the town to send a wedding present to the met'Oc. And we're not convinced, is all. But if we all hold our water and talk about this like sensible people —"

"It wasn't my idea," Marzo broke in. "I heard people talking about it in the store."

"You said you thought it'd be a good idea."

"I do." Marzo stopped. He'd only said that because the people he'd talked to in the store had all seemed so certain about it, and he'd agreed to put it to the town council, that entirely non-existent body. "It's a gesture of goodwill," he said. "It's polite. It's good manners. And if it'll stop the Tabletop mob coming down here in the middle of the night and shooting at people, I say it's worth doing."

"If," Gimao repeated. "Who's to say it'll have any effect at all?"

Eventually, they thrashed out a compromise. Marzo would send Lusomai met'Oc a wedding present, at his own expense, with a covering note ambiguously phrased so that it could be taken to be on behalf of the town or not, depending on what anybody wanted it to say. In return, the council wouldn't try to stop him.

"What'll it be?" Furio asked later.

Marzo shook his head. "No idea," he said. "What the hell do we have that somebody like that could possibly want?"

Teucer looked blank. "There must be something," she said.

"There isn't," Marzo replied. "I know that for a fact. Because if there was something down here that Luso wanted, he'd have ridden in with his boys and stolen it years ago."

Furio grinned. "I can think of something," he said.

"What?"

"Ten pounds of lead pipe," Furio replied. "For casting into bullets. Gig told me, they're desperately short of the stuff. Every time Luso shoots at something in the woods and misses, he sends his men to find the tree where the bullet landed and dig it out so he can melt it down and use it again. He'd be really grateful if you gave him that."

Marzo decided that Furio was probably joking. "Any sensible suggestions?"

Furio shrugged. "All right," he said, "what about ten pounds of nails? I don't know if Luso'd be pleased, but Stheno'd be absolutely thrilled. Apparently the nails they've got up there have been pulled out and straightened so many times they're starting to break. You could give him some of the ones Gignomai's started making. They're not bad, actually. I can hardly tell them apart from the ones we get from Home."

"Not nails," Marzo said, "and not lead pipe. Come on, there's got to be something."

In the end they settled on an eighteen-month pedigree steer, because, as Marzo said, nobody can ever have too much beef. He paid for it with two buckets of Gignomai's nails. It was an unpopular choice in the town, where people were saying that the met'Oc had had far too much of other people's beef already and furthermore, sending up a steer of their own free will might not be such a good precedent. As it happened, Marzo had thought precisely the same thing, but he couldn't think of anything else.

"Not very tactful, is it?" was Teucer's verdict. "If I was them, I'd be offended."

Maybe Teucer was right. The steer was returned, with a letter from Luso saying that he was deeply touched by the gesture, but the met'Oc were doing their best to get along without beef these days, and it was hardly fair to remind them of what they were missing. Marzo, stuck with a bullock he had nowhere to keep, traded it to Desio Heddo for two barrels of barley flour which, when opened, proved to be damp.

The hammer broke down. A pinion had broken in the primary drive, which meant taking the whole thing apart. Gignomai sent the partners out to collect iron ore, and did the job himself. It was a morning's work, but he didn't seem unduly dejected. As he told one of the men, it was a genuine pleasure to be able to hear himself think.

He'd got most of the job done when he came up against a seized bolt. Damp had got into the mechanism, and the nut was rusted on solid. He tried heating it with a blowpipe and a lamp, but that didn't work, and there wasn't enough room to get in there with a hacksaw. He wriggled into a gap between the frames that was rather too small for him, and set about cutting off the nut with a hammer and cold chisel.

"You've been busy."

He looked up so fast he banged the top of his head on a cross-beam. He felt a strong pulse in his scalp, and something wet dribbled down over his forehead.

"Scalp wound," said the voice. "They bleed like the devil."

As quickly as he could, Gignomai unwound himself from the machine and peered out. "Luso," he said, "what the hell are you doing here?"

"Thought I'd come and see what you've been up to."

"You can't," Gignomai replied. "I don't exist, remember?"

Luso laughed. He was wearing a magnificent hunting outfit that Gignomai hadn't seen before, but recognised instantly. "Present from our cousins?"

"It's a bit small for me," Luso replied. "I had Spetta take it out as far as she could, but sometimes when I move I hear tearing noises. What do you mean, you don't exist?"

Spetta. Always so good with a needle. "Father cancelled me," Gignomai said. "Didn't he copy you in?"

"Oh, that." Luso frowned. "All right, then, you'll have to be my imaginary friend. I didn't have one when I was a kid, so I reckon I'm entitled."

"You didn't have one because none of the imaginary people wanted to know you."

Luso's big laugh sounded like a bull roaring. "Well, you've made up for that," he said. "All your friends these days are pretend people. What the hell is this contraption in aid of?"

"It's a flower press," Gignomai said. "Don't touch that."

Too late. A worm drive component skittered off the platform and into the grass. "Sorry," Luso said. "Was that important?"

"Forget it," Gignomai said. "Get off the platform before you do any more damage. I'll come out."

Luso backed away with exaggerated delicacy, like someone miming a cat. "Presumably it's this thing that makes that unholy racket," Luso said. "You do realise, you can hear it from the Doorstep."

"Scaring the deer away? My heart bleeds."

Luso sat down on a log. He looked like he owned the place. "Yes," he said, "for which I'm much obliged to you. They've moved up from the Doorstep to Upper Room, and we've been taking them out by the dozen. We've got enough smoked venison laid up to see us right through till new year."

"Thrilled to have been of service." Gignomai looked around for something to sit on, then gave up and squatted on the ground. "Why are you here?"

Luso was examining him. "What've you been doing to yourself?" he asked. "You look like you've been in a fight every day for a week."

"Odd, that," Gignomai replied, "since we don't do fencing practice any more. No, it's just usual wear and tear, I guess."

"I hardly recognised you. You're not getting enough sleep."

"Yes, Mother."

Luso nodded. "She sends her love. I didn't tell Stheno I was coming, or he'd have done the same."

"I doubt it." Gignomai stretched out his legs. Cramp wouldn't help matters. "Why are you here?"

"To ask you to come to the wedding," Luso replied. "It wouldn't be right if you weren't there."

"Sorry," Gignomai said quickly, "can't. Too busy."

"Balls." Luso lifted his head. He was surveying the site, as though he intended to buy it. "What's that big shed over there?"

"That's for making cheese."

"Of course. Look," he said, leaning forward a little, "I know I should've stopped Father from sending you that ridiculous letter. I didn't; I'm sorry. But when you come to the wedding—"

"He'll set the dogs on me."

"No he won't." Luso scowled at something. "You have my word. I'll make sure there's no trouble. I've made it a condition of the marriage."

Gignomai stared at him, then laughed. "You've done what?"

"I told him," Luso said. "You forgive Gig, or the wedding's off. He wasn't happy about it, but he's agreed. So..."

"Forgive me," Gignomai said. "I see."

"That's how he sees it," Luso said. "You've got to talk to him on his own terms or he simply refuses to listen. You and I both know—"

"I don't have to talk to him at all. It's been wonderful, not talking to him. It's probably my greatest pleasure in life right now."

"In that case, I'm sorry for you. Listen, Gig, we've got to be realistic."

"And practical?"

"Yes, and practical. You know what this wedding means?"

Gignomai shrugged. "I'll have a psychopath for a sister-in-law. Big deal. She'll fit in well."

"It means," Luso said, "that we're going Home. Things are changing. The Revisionists are in real trouble, the economy's a mess, the Optimate tendency's on its knees and the KKA are poised and ready to jump in. The met'Ousa are right there on the front lines, it's only a matter of time. And when the KKA get in—"

"I have no idea," Gignomai said, "what you're talking about."

Luso sighed. "Yes, you do," he said. "It means Boulo and Pasi will be going Home very soon now, and we'll be going with them. The exile is nearly over, Gig. We've done our time and soon we'll be back where we belong. It's in the bag. And you're coming with us."

"Am I really?"

"You bet your life," Luso snapped. "You think I'm going to let our family go home and leave my brother behind with these savages? It's not happening. Look, I know you haven't been happy here. Understandable. There just isn't a place for you here. Back Home, it'll be completely different. A man of your energy and intelligence—"

"Thank you so much."

"Well, it's true. I always knew you were the best of us. Stheno's been squashed by his responsibilities, keeping us all fed and clothed. He's just a farmer now. Father—well, what sort of a life has he had? Back home, he'd have been First Citizen. Out here, it was just a waste."

"And you?"

"Me?" Luso grinned. "I'm your stereotypical second son, all I care about is hunting and having a good time. And keeping the peace. It's what I'm for. But you've got all the good things in our family, and you're still young enough to make something of yourself."

Gignomai was looking for something in his pockets. "You reckon?" he said.

"Fact," Luso replied. "I'll tell you something, Gig. Ever since I can remember, I've envied you. You're smart and you're brave and you don't give in. It's amazing what you've done here with nothing. God only knows what you're up to."

"I told you. Pressing flowers."

"And making cheese, yes. I don't know what you've got in mind, but just think what you could achieve back Home. Think about it, for crying out loud. You want to build factories? Well, fine. You could be the richest man in—"

"You're not going Home," Gignomai said quietly. "Not ever."

Luso was furious. "You stupid little bastard, haven't you been listening? I told you, the met'Oc—"

"It's not going to happen," Gignomai said. "Trust me."

"You don't know anything about it," Luso roared at him. "Listen to me for once in your stupid life. We're going Home. It's a done deal; it's settled. And I'm damned if I'm going to let your stupid pride get in the way of our family being where it ought to be."

"Fine. You go."

"Not without you. Not acceptable."

Gignomai shivered. The blood from his cut was trickling down his nose, and it tickled. He wiped it away with the back of his hand; there was a lot of it. He could feel the cut throbbing, as if it was keeping time with the rhythm of the hammer, substituting for it now that it was silent. "You really want me to come."

"Yes."

"Then I'm definitely not coming." He wiped his bloody hand on the seat of his trousers. "Just for once, you can't have everything your own way. Interesting new experience for you."

He watched Luso closely, expecting him to move any moment: a lunge, an attack initiated. Fencing lessons. But Luso didn't move, which surprised him.

"I've missed you," Luso said.

Gignomai felt a sharp pain in his head; the hammer, extremely strong. "Is that right?"

"Yes."

"Afraid you're running out of siblings, I assume."

It was a clumsier thrust than he'd have liked, but it made Luso shake. "That's it?"

"Yes, that's it."

Luso stood up. "You're a fool to yourself," he said. "I'll expect you to be there. Don't mess me around. Understood?"

"What're you going to do, Luso? Send your men to drag me there? Tie me to a chair?"

"The thought had crossed my mind." Suddenly Luso sighed. He seemed to deflate a little. "But I decided against. I thought I'd appeal to your better nature instead."

"Tell you what." Finally, he'd found what he'd been looking for. It had slipped through a hole in the pocket and lodged in the lining. He teased it back through the hole with his fingertips and closed his hand around it. "I may come, after all. But in case I don't, here's my wedding present for my new sister-in-law."

He started to take his hand out of his pocket. Luso froze, watching the hand, as if he was afraid it'd be a weapon. Except, if it had been a weapon, Luso wouldn't have frozen.

"Gig," Luso said.

Gignomai removed his hand from his pocket and opened it. On his palm lay a small silver brooch, mounting a single blue stone. "Go on," he said. "Take it."

He'd waited all his life for Luso to look at him like that. "Take it," he repeated. "After all, it's a family heirloom. She ought to have it, don't you think?"

Luso turned and walked away. Gignomai watched him until the trees swallowed him up, then wrapped the brooch in the foul scrap of cloth he used as a handkerchief, oily rag and emergency bandage, and stowed it carefully in his other pocket.

The Calimeo family came to town to buy rope.

Furio, standing on the porch, saw them coming up the street and darted inside. Marzo stopped him before he could disappear into the cellar.

"What?" Marzo demanded.

"They're coming," Furio said.

Marzo frowned. "Who? The met'Oc? The government?"

"Worse."

"Oh." Marzo somehow managed to slide between Furio and the cellar door. "Would you mind seeing to them? I've got to fetch something."

Portly he might have been, but Marzo could be diabolically agile when he wanted to be. Furio addressed his refusal to a closing cellar door, and then the shop door opened. He turned round slowly, and smiled.

The Calimeos were generally referred to as the Summer Cold (annoying and so very hard to get rid of). There were six of them, always together: father, mother, uncle and three juvenile daughters, or it might have been the same daughter projected back in time and observed at eighteen-month intervals. The daughters never, ever spoke. Their elders made up for it.

"What can I—?" was as far as Furio got before the torrent overwhelmed him. All three of them tended to talk at once, all on different, equally fatuous topics, none of them apparently aware that the other two were in the same room. If, as a result of the blended hubbub of their voices, their interlocutor appeared to be having trouble understanding them, they helpfully shouted. Furio fixed a smile on his face, said yes, sure, is that right at fixed intervals, and hoped very much that Uncle Marzo would meet a giant rat in the cellar, which would eat him up.

"Damnedest thing," the uncle was saying. "Them savages."

Furio blinked. "Savages?"

Infuriatingly, the uncle chose that moment to pause a fraction of second to breathe in, and Mother filled the empty fragment of time with a question, which he entirely failed to hear. She repeated it at full volume at precisely the same time as Uncle replied to Furio's enquiry.

"What savages?" Furio said.

"At East Ford." Furio strained his ears to pick uncle's theme out of the fugue. "Fifteen or twenty. Just sat there. All day. Damnedest thing."

East Ford. He tried to picture it in his mind. Seven miles or so upstream from the factory site, a flat, treeless meadow, good grazing, prone to flooding in the spring and autumn. Empty, nothing to see. Flat. You could see, or be seen, for miles.

Fifteen or twenty?

Forcibly, as though dragging a reluctant animal, he pulled the picture of the savages' camp into his mind. "Did they have livestock?" he asked. "Wagons, tents, that sort of—?"

Father Calimeo was telling him about an encounter he'd had with the met'Oc raiders, twenty years ago. They'd ridden past him on their way to somewhere else. It had been the standout event of his life. "Did they have livestock?" Furio repeated loudly. Maybe the other two were talking to people next to him, people he couldn't see. Imaginary friends.

"No, no livestock," Uncle Calimeo replied. "Just fifteen or twenty of them, men and women too. Just sat there cross-legged in the grass like they were waiting on something. Watching me. Damnedest thing."

Watching someone who didn't exist. Waiting on something. Mother Calimeo was describing a bolt of cloth she'd seen on the shelf behind his head six years ago. Either her memory was exceptionally vivid, or she could see back through time. Oddly enough, he remembered the exact same bolt: blue cotton, with a faint yellow check. Father had sold it to . . .

"Geant Poneta," Mother Calimeo said, a split second before he could. "She made it up into two shirts for the boys and a working dress for her niece, for her eighteenth. It had a double row of horn buttons."

"Can't think what they were looking at that was so damned interesting," Uncle Calimeo went on. "I was just rounding up the stock, moving them up the valley, same as I've done every year for I don't remember how long. Just sat there and watched. You wouldn't credit it."

"We want to buy some rope," Father Calimeo said loudly, as if to a deaf man, or a stranger. "Thirty ells of the hemp three-ply. Rope," he added, making a coiling round the arm gesture.

"Rope," Furio repeated. "I'll see what we've got."

"Bought some rope in here sixteen years ago," Uncle said. "Jute four-ply, damned good rope. Left it out in the rain one year and after that it was no good anyhow."

Damnedest thing, Furio thought, fifteen or twenty of them, watching. How could you watch someone you knew wasn't really there? He turned round and looked Uncle straight in the eye. "Was one of them an old man?" he asked.

"Rain gets in it, in between the strands, it starts to rot," Uncle replied. "Next thing you know, it comes apart in your hands."

"No old man," Father said. "Reckon they was all about your age. Mind, it's hard to tell with them savages."

Furio dropped the rope. "You saw them too."

"Sure I saw them. There was twenty-six."

"Fifteen or twenty," Uncle said. "No old man, though. Not as I could see."

"They were just sat there," Father said. "Watching what we was doing. I yelled at them, 'Go on, get lost,' but they just went on sitting."

Uncle shook his head. "Damnedest thing," he said.

"That's the niece over to Wellhead," mother pointed out. "Married Daso Disiano, but he died. He was a thin, short man, went bald early. You won't remember him, I don't suppose. There was a daughter."

The three Calimeo girls were sitting on a long packing case containing Gignomai-made hay rakes, only two left. They sat in a row, swinging their legs, not in time. "That's four-ply," Uncle pointed out, "not three-ply. We asked for three-ply. Three-ply hemp."

"I think we may have some in the cellar," Furio said, and bolted like a rabbit.

There was a man called Sao Glabrio, who lived at Middle Bridge. There was no bridge at Middle Bridge, though there may have been one once, and the Fesennas were always talking about building one there. Glabrio farmed in a small way: two brood sows, a small suckler herd of roundback dairy cows, a handful of goats who wandered on and off the property as the mood took them. His wife had died long since; his daughter was married to Desio Heddo. Glabrio and Heddo loathed each other and never spoke a civil word. The only member of his family Glabrio had any time for was his grandson, Scarpedino, who would inherit the Glabrio place when the time came, assuming he could be bothered with it. Glabrio didn't get on particularly well with his neighbours, either—the Biasige on the north side or the Fesennas on the south.

Not long before the met'Ousa arrived on their ship, the eldest Fesenna boy and some friends of his decided to go long-netting on Glabrio's pond. Glabrio called it a lake. It was half an acre of brown water and eight-foot-tall sedge, surrounded by bog. No use to anybody except for a few winter duck. The Fesenna boy called on Glabrio to ask his permission, which was refused. This didn't matter, since long-netting is best done at night, and Glabrio's house was on the other side of a tall ridge, so lights and noise wouldn't carry. Glabrio always did his early morning chores at the same time, in the same order, and wouldn't be anywhere near the pond until mid-morning.

The boys reached the pond at about midnight and set up the net all round the pond, hanging it from the tops of sedge stalks. Then they loosed their dogs into the pond to put up the ducks. They were good at their job. They got a dozen ducks rising up off the water, and another half dozen coming back in again. It all went pretty well, until the youngest Fesenna boy (too young, really, but he'd whined to be allowed to come) fell in the water.

It was a cold night—just right for fowling; not so good for a swim—and they all got fairly well soaked hauling the boy out again. By the time they'd done that it was about an hour before dawn, the coldest time of all. The boy was shivering and moaning, and the elder Fesenna was worried. He'd neglected to tell his mother he was taking the kid, and he had a fair idea what she'd have to say if he brought him home with pneumonia. It was a two-hour walk back home. Glabrio would still be in bed. Fesenna decided to light a fire to dry them all out.

Lighting a fire in the sedge wasn't a problem. The leaves were dry and papery and burnt hot quickly. The boys tore up armfuls and piled them on, delighting in the wild flames. One of them suggested plucking and roasting a duck for a field breakfast. They were debating the motion when a stiff wind got up.

It shouldn't have, not at that time of day in that season, but it did. The fire blew into the tall stand of sedge at the foot of the ridge, which went up like gunpowder. The boys dumped the ducks and ran.

Glabrio saw the smoke as he came out of the chicken-house. By that time, with the sun well up and the wind dropped back. It was just a tall, thin plume and he assumed it was somebody camped out on their way somewhere. Trespassing, by definition. He called up his dogs and set off, grinning, to shout at them.

By the time he got there, all the sedge on the south side of the pond had burnt down to black ash. Glabrio, who relied on the sedge for winter bedding, stood still and breathless for quite some time, then trudged miserably down the ridge to investigate. He found half a charred long-net and the incinerated bones of eighteen ducks, piled up in a heap.

He wasn't the world's greatest analytical thinker. He didn't have to be.

Melo Fesenna, the boys' father, apologised fulsomely and with a grim, strained face. He'd see to it that both boys wouldn't lie down comfortably for a fortnight, and he'd make up the lost sedge with straw and reed from his own barn. Glabrio wasn't satisfied. There was also trespass, poaching, fire-starting and reckless endangerment (neither of them knew what that meant, but it sounded ominously legal), all of which amounted in Glabrio's estimation to ten silver thalers. Fesenna, who'd had enough of his neighbour by this point, laughed in his face. Glabrio's whole place wasn't worth ten thalers, he said. He wouldn't pay such a sum even if he'd got it, which he hadn't. Two carts of reeds and one of straw, take it or leave it. Glabrio swore at him and walked away.

And there the matter festered for quite some time. From time to time, one of the Fesennas would run into Glabrio on the road or out on the boundaries. Glabrio would yell abuse, the Fesenna would ignore him, no big deal. When Melo Fasenna cut his reeds, he had two carts loaded and sent round to Glabrio's place. Glabrio wouldn't let the men unload, and threw stones at them until they drove off. When Melo heard that, he shrugged and said that'd have to be an end of it.

Around the time that the news of Luso met'Oc's wedding broke, there was a fire one night in the Fesennas' barn. All the reed went up and a good quarter of the straw, but they managed to get the animals out and save the hay. The next morning, while they were damping down, Melo Fasenna noticed something unusual about the barn door. At first glance it looked like a knot-hole, but there hadn't been such a hole in the door before, and he'd known that door for fifty years. He took out his pocketknife and probed about in the hole, and found something soft.

They had to drill it out from the back with a bit and brace. It proved to be a squashed lump of lead, about thumbnail size.

Melo looked at it for a while, then he called for his eldest son and told him to ride into town and fetch the mayor.

"It's possible," Marzo reluctantly conceded.

"Possible be damned." Melo was one of those people whose anger is slow and steady. By this time, it was starting to get good and hot. "Any fool can see what happened. He set the barn on fire to draw me out, so he could take a shot at me and kill me. Here's the hole, look." He turned round and pointed in the opposite direction. "Straight line from that clump of briars. That'll be where he was sat waiting." He stood with his back to the door. The hole was a foot higher than the top of his head. "And that's how much he missed me by. Too damn close, I reckon."

Marzo knew what the reply would be, but he had to ask. "And who would he be?"

"Scarpedino Heddo, of course." Melo closed his fist hard around the lead lump. "Everybody knows he's up on the hill these days, and everybody knows he'll have Glabrio's place when he's gone. Obvious. Glabrio went to the boy and told him to kill me, because of that business back along."

Marzo thought, If I was Scarpedino, and if Scarpedino was the sort of monster who'd kill a man because his crazy grandpa told him to, I wouldn't do it like this, because it wouldn't work, and it didn't. No, I'd have wedged the house door with a bit of plank and set fire to the thatch. "It's going to be hard proving it," he said.

"Like hell." Melo swung his fist under Marzo's nose and opened it. "What's this, then? It's a pistol ball. Who's got pistols? The met'Oc. Where's Scarpedino now? Well, is that proof or isn't it?"

As delicately as he could, Marzo lifted the lump off Melo's palm and dropped it in his pocket. "If it was Scarpedino—"

"No if about it."

"Then," Marzo went on, "I'll take it up with Lusomai met'Oc, I promise you. But you said, you didn't hear a shot fired. Those things make a hell of a racket."

"Means nothing," Melo snapped at him. "All the noise of the fire, everybody yelling, there were beams falling in. That's all my winter reed gone and a good part of the straw, and who's going to pay for lumber and time for fixing the barn? You're damned right you're going to take it up with the met'Oc, and Glabrio too. That crazy old man wants stringing up."

"I hate to say it," Furio said, "but he's probably right."

"Don't," Marzo replied, lifting the scales with his left hand. The pans danced, and he dampened them with a finger. "I've known Glabrio all my life. He's a nasty mean old man with a vicious temper. He's not a killer."

"Scarpedino is."

Marzo put the crushed lump of lead in one pan, and an unfired ball in the other. "How'd he get hold of a snapping-hen? Luso wouldn't just lend him one, and he keeps them locked up."

"In which case, Luso must've done it. Come on, which is more likely?"

The pans weren't balancing; nowhere near. Marzo frowned, laid them down and took the bullets out of the pans. "I think we can rule out Luso," he said.

"And Boulo met'Ousa?"

Marzo didn't reply. He'd laid the two bullets side by side. Even allowing for loss of metal as a result of being shot into and dug out of a door, it was definitely smaller than the unfired specimen. He looked up. Furio was looking straight at him.

"Would Boulo met'Ousa lend Scarpedino his gun?" Furio asked.

"Or Boulo doesn't lock his bedroom door," Marzo replied. He picked up the bullets and put them in a drawer of his desk. "Didn't you say you'd seen Scarpedino at Gignomai's place?"

Furio nodded. "Surprised me," he said, "but I didn't ask about it."

Marzo sat down. The bottle was empty. "If I wanted to kill Melo

Fesenna, I'd burn him in his house. It's no bother to do, most likely people would think it was an accident, and I'd be sure of getting him. Setting a fire so I'd have a shot at him, in the dark, at thirty-five yards' range; you'd have to be a bloody fool to do it that way."

Furio thought for a moment. "If you burnt the house you'd kill them all," he said. "Maybe..."

Marzo shook his head. "I don't know," he said. "If it was Glabrio, and he was mad enough to do something like this—Only he's not." He sighed. "Maybe Scarpedino's got principles," he said. "I don't know him well enough. But I don't suppose Luso himself would bank on hitting a moving target at thirty-five yards, and he practises every week. Scarpedino..."

"Didn't mean to kill Melo, just give him a good scare?"

"You aren't helping, you know." Marzo opened the lid of the rosewood box, lifted the scales and dropped them on the floor. "I want you to tell me how it couldn't have been Scarpedino, or Luso, or Boulo met'Ousa." Furio stooped, gathered up the scales and put them back in the box. "All right," he said. "The hell with who actually did what. Tell me what I'm supposed to do about it."

"Go to Luso," Furio said. "Sort it out." Suddenly he grinned. "Be practical."

"Two words I wish I'd never heard," Marzo said, sweeping the rosewood box into a drawer, "are practical and mayor. Odd, isn't it, how two little words can really screw up your life?"

"Go to Luso," Furio repeated. "He'll know what to do."

Lusomai met'Oc presented his compliments to Mayor Opello, but regretted that he was unable to meet him at that time, being engaged in preparations for his forthcoming wedding. If the mayor would care to call again in twenty-eight days' time, Lusomai met'Oc would be delighted to speak to him.

The guard had recited this with his chin raised and eyes averted, as though repeating by rote some incantation in an unknown dead language. Marzo winced, but stayed put.

"Fine," he said. "In that case, I'd like to see Sthenomai."

The guard looked at him. "You know the difference between luck and a wheelbarrow?"

"Go on."

"Pushing a wheelbarrow doesn't get you a smack on the head."

Marzo nodded. "Heard it," he said. "Now go and tell Stheno the mayor wants to see him."

The guard withdrew, and Marzo collapsed against a fortuitous tree trunk, breathing hard and reflecting that he might have been hasty in his judgement. Marzo Opello would never have dared talk to a Tabletop guard like that. If he had, he'd probably have carried his teeth home in his hat. The mayor, apparently, could get away with it.

He stayed leaning against the tree for quite some time. Then he sat down on the ground, trying to look dignified. Twenty yards away, the mule was happily guzzling the long, unmown meadow grass, a luxury it never usually encountered. It wasn't his mule, of course. He'd borrowed it from the livery. Mayor's privilege.

After a very long time, a different guard came down to him. "This way," he said.

Marzo hesitated, then said, "No blindfold?"

The guard shrugged. "Nobody said anything to me. You can have one if you want."

"No, that's fine."

Not that it made the slightest difference. Marzo had always lived in and around town, where trees were landmarks. In the first ten yards, he saw more trees than he'd seen in his whole life put together. He kept very close behind the guard so as not to get hopelessly lost.

After a long walk through the forest, uphill (his calves ached until he was sure the muscles were going to burst out through the skin), they came out into the open into a twenty-acre field of poor grass, with flints showing through. They crossed it and came to a post and rail fence. There was a gateway. The gate was off its hinges. A huge man was slowly, carefully pulling it apart. For a moment, Marzo couldn't think why then he saw that the crosswise bar had splintered, and was about to be fixed.

"Lucky for you," the man said without looking round, "I happened to be up here doing this rotten bloody job. Might as well talk to you while I work. If I'd been out the far side, you'd have had a wasted trip."

Marzo couldn't think of anything to say.

"Right." Stheno had prised off both parts of the broken rail and laid them on the ground. He took a step back and looked at them. "What can I do for you?"

"It's about the attack on Melo Fasenna."

"I see. Who the hell is Melo Fasenna?"

Marzo debated with himself whether he should go round the other side, so Stheno would have to look at him. He decided it would be the best course of action, but couldn't quite bring himself to do it. He felt about twelve years old. "The Fasennas are farmers out by East Ford. Someone fired a shot at Melo Fasenna, with a snapping-hen pistol."

Stheno turned round slowly. "Is that right?"

Marzo opened the fist in which the squashed ball lay. "We dug this out of his barn door," he said. "Someone set light to his reed store, then shot at him when he went out to see what was going on."

"Missed?"

"Yes. A foot high." He hesitated, then added, "We think it might have been your brother's man Scarpedino."

"That little shit," Stheno said. His hand dipped into his coat pocket and came out grasping a tangled ball of plaited-straw twine. "Evidence?"

"The Fasennas are on bad terms with their neighbour Glabrio. Glabrio's Scarpedino's grandfather, and Scarpedino'll inherit the Glabrio farm."

Stheno shrugged, then knelt down and started binding the two broken ends of the bar together. "Sounds like a motive," he said. "Not that that bastard'd need a reason. I gather he killed a man's wife."

"We think so, yes."

"Nasty piece of work," Stheno said, exerting an impossible force on the ends of the twine. "But he's not here."

Marzo took a moment to understand. "Not on the Tabletop?"

"Haven't seen him in a while," Stheno replied. He tied a complex knot, then stood up. "Go on," he said, "ask me why I'm trying to mend a busted gate with string."

"It's none of my—"

"Because I can't be fucked to walk all the way back to the house for a hammer and a bucket of nails," he said. "Because I've got too much to do. So I mend it with string, because string's all I happen to have on me. Makes a piss-poor job, won't last five minutes, but it's very slightly better than nothing. I can't swear you a solemn oath the Heddo boy's not up here somewhere, but I haven't seen him for a long time, and I'm pretty sure I'd have seen him if he was here. He tends to lounge around the steps of the long barn, along with the rest of Luso's thugs. It's not like they've got much else to do, except when Luso's hunting." He knelt and lifted the lashed-together bar. It sagged unhappily around the splice, but Stheno laid it in position on the carcass of the gate, and picked up a twice-fist-sized lump of flint. "Lazy man's hammer," he explained. "I suppose you're going to go home and tell everybody who comes in your store how this is the way the high and mighty met'Oc do things."

Marzo hesitated. "Not if you don't want me to."

Stheno laughed. The sound bounced back off the forward ridge. "Doesn't bother me," he said. "Might do some good if your lot knew how we really live. Just poor farmers, same as you. Anyhow," he went on, lining the bar up, "I wouldn't spit on Scarpedino if his arse was on fire, but it can't have been him if he isn't here. Setting the fire could be him, but not shooting. We'd all know about it if one of Luso's precious toys had gone missing."

"It wasn't Luso's gun," Marzo said, in a rather small voice. "We think it could have been your cousin Boulomai's. It's a smaller bullet."

Suddenly he had Stheno's attention. He put down the stone and stood up slowly. "Boulomai's gun."

"Lusomai explained," Marzo said, "that Boulomai's snapping-hen shoots a smaller bullet. I weighed this one and it's quite a bit lighter."

Stheno nodded to stop him wasting time with further details. "Boulo's got three of the things," he said, with a curious mixture of disapproval and awe. "Two half-inchers and a three-quarter. Oh, and Cousin Pasi's got one, a little wee tiny thing, shoots a ball like a pea. You'd have every right to be annoyed if she shot you in the arse with it and you found out about it."

Marzo waited for a moment, then said, "Would Boulomai have noticed if one of his was taken?"

Stheno shrugged. "No idea," he said. "He wears them as ornaments sometimes, rest of the time I assume they're in his bedroom. Boulo's got all manner of stuff in there. Probably hasn't unpacked half of it yet."

"So Scarpedino could have..."

"It's possible. Mind you, he'd need balls like boulders. Luso'd snap his neck like a carrot if he got caught." He paused and rubbed his eyes, the weariest man Marzo had ever seen. "All right," he said. "You say a barn was on fire. Anyone hurt?"

"No."

"Damage?"

"The whole winter store of reed, quite a bit of straw, and the barn'll need a lot of work with winter coming on."

"Shit," Stheno said. "Luso's stupid wedding complicates things, of course." He lifted his head and looked Marzo in the eye. It felt like carrying a hundredweight sack on your head. "Fact is, Mister Mayor, we're broke. Can't offer you money because we haven't got any. Can't offer you much in the way of goods or livestock because we'll be eating beetles before too long thanks to Luso's big day using up all our surpluses. Can't give you Scarpedino because he ain't here." He grinned, a huge expression. Marzo caught sight of the back of

his left hand; it was a mess of briar-scratches. "I don't suppose that's
what you came all this way to hear."

Marzo shrugged. "I just want to sort it all out."

"Keep the peace, I know," Stheno said. "It's a pain in the arse
Luso can't deal with it; he'd send you away with fuck-all and make
you feel he was doing you a grand favour." His shoulders sagged,
and he said, "Don't suppose you've got any suggestions?"

Marzo struggled with himself, then said, "You haven't got..."

"Anything. Take my word for it."

"In that case," Marzo said, "I'm sorry, no."

"Fine. So you've come asking politely for justice, and the met'Oc
spat in your face and told you to get lost. What do you do next?"

"Your cousins —"

"Ask them for a loan? Father'd burn the house down with his own
two hands rather than think of it. Guests, see. Also, it'd mean admit-
ting to them we're broke, and that's not an option. They know, obviously, they're not blind, but there's some things you can't say out
loud. No, forget them." He paused again, ground something out of
his eye with his knuckle. "Which just leaves my kid brother Gignomai. He's got money, hasn't he?"

It was like the time he'd put his full weight on the ice in the brook,
believing it would take his weight. "Gignomai? But I thought..."

Stheno grinned at him. "Indeed. Father disinherited him. Formal
document, grand gesture, very noble, very *us*. But what Father
doesn't know won't upset him."

"You wouldn't tell him? Surely —"

"You'd be amazed what we haven't told Father over the years.
Learnt that lesson the hard way," Stheno added with a frown, "but
that's none of your damn business. No, it's ideal. You go to my
brother and tell him to pay off this Fasenna character and we'll handle Father. Fact is..." Stheno hesitated, then seemed to reach a decision. "Things may be happening around here quite soon. You didn't
hear this, but it's possible the time's coming when you might not
have to worry about us at all. We'll be out of your hair for good. No

promises, mind, but that's what we're working towards, and it goes without saying, we really wouldn't want to screw it up for the sake of some stupid local dispute with your people. Just think about it, Mister Mayor. Wouldn't your life be so much easier if you woke up one morning and found we'd gone?"

Marzo felt stupid, as though he'd just walked into a door. "You mean, gone Home?"

"I didn't say that. In fact, I haven't said anything. But if you nagging Gignomai into parting with a few dozen thalers means not having to put up with us any more, isn't it worth the effort? Well?"

Life without the met'Oc. Marzo realised his mouth was open, and closed it. What would that be like? He had no way of guessing, because it was unthinkable. "Well, yes," he said. "No offence," he added quickly. "But—"

"None taken. Now, I'm not saying it will happen. What I'm saying is, if there's a blazing row between you and us and things turn nasty and word of it reaches Home, then I can more or less guarantee that it *won't* happen, and I'm sure that'd make you very unhappy, thinking about how you had a really great chance and you blew it." His face changed. Something that could almost have been a sly smile spread over it, like the rusting of metal speeded up. "For one thing," he said, "there'd be this place. All the timber you could ever want. Lousy with small furry animals to help you meet your fur quota. Piss-awful grazing and growing land, but somebody might want it. We could do you a deal, maybe a document of title with your name on it." Suddenly Stheno laughed, as if thinking of a private joke. "In twenty years' time, you could be us. Now wouldn't that be worth a bit of tact and diplomacy?"

Marzo thought hard as he drove home. He thought about Gignomai met'Oc, whom he'd always found pleasant and polite enough. His nephew's best friend, so he'd made a bit of an effort, like you do. And then the deal had come along—the sword, unimaginable wealth, possibly even escape from the colony, the glittering prospect of

Home, a gentleman's life in the soft, fat countryside he'd never seen but could picture effortlessly in his mind. Then the reality of the deal, putting his business on the line, wheedling and cajoling his neighbours and customers, the exhausting burden of filling carts with barrels of flour and getting nothing in return. Then the first crates of finished goods, the exhilaration, the wild dance of selling and getting money. He grinned at the thought of how exciting he'd found that. He despised himself for it. The money was just flat metal discs for all the good it'd do him, at least until spring when the ship came, but it had been glorious, the apotheosis of shopkeeping. And now the eldest son of the met'Oc was tempting him with an offer of all the kingdoms of the Earth, if only he could persuade Gignomai met'Oc to do something he'd never, ever do.

I'm a simple man, he told himself, a simple, greedy man, a small man. All I ever wanted to do was screw my neighbours a little bit on a few small deals, make a nice profit and live quietly and peacefully, keep the peace, be on good terms with everybody. A greedy man, but not greedy enough. All you ask for is more than your fair share of a pound of sausages, and some bastard offers you the whole pig.

He couldn't pretend to know Gignomai well, but he knew him a bit, enough for the job in hand. There was something going on. Gignomai was up to something. All that stuff about the bloodless revolution and freedom for the colony; it was possible, true and achievable, and Gignomai meant to do it, but only as a necessary chore of a step on the way to something else. And if Gignomai had wanted to be a member of the met'Oc, he'd never have left in the first place.

But if the met'Oc were to leave, go Home, abandon the Tabletop with its defences and its fine house, its barns and outbuildings and extensive estate of mediocre farmland—well, somebody would have to take it over, as public trustee, run it for the benefit of the people (the newly independent people; the new nation), and who better, who possibly other than the mayor? Chosen by the people, not a single voice dissenting. The obvious leader of the community, the one man who everybody trusted.

(That was going a bit far. Trusted with their lives, perhaps, quite possibly, but not necessarily with small sums of money.)

No use thinking that way, he thought, and gave the mule an unnecessary flick of the whip, which the animal completely ignored. Gignomai won't pay, and that's an end of it.

An idea emerged from his unconscious mind like the yoke from a cracked eggshell. A few dozen thalers, Stheno had said. To speak so airily of such a sum was of course the mark of a gentleman, even if that gentleman had only raised the subject because he didn't have two quarters to rub together. A few dozen thalers was still a fortune, but Marzo Opello had a few dozen thalers. If he lent the money to the met'Oc, saying it had come from Gignomai, and the met'Oc paid off the Fasennas, and the peace was kept and everybody stayed practical and realistic long enough for the met'Oc to clear off back where they'd come from...

A few dozen. Could mean anything from twenty-four to forty-eight. He winced. Then he thought long and hard about the Fasennas, the cost of lumber and day labour, and came to the conclusion that the whole thing could be done for twenty-eight thalers, no bother. Twenty-six if he could do a deal on the lumber. Twenty-five if he twisted a few arms over the labour cost. With Gignomai making nails at his factory, twenty-four.

On the other hand, he thought, do I really want all the kingdoms of the Earth?

That question troubled him for a long time: what do I really want? As opposed to what I *should* want, as a properly greedy man. The sword money should be enough, more than enough, but what if there could be more? I *ought* to want it. Do I?

There's young Furio to think of, he told himself (he knew he was lying, but he lied well enough to get away with it), and Teucer—she deserves better. They both of them ought to have the chance of going Home, making something of themselves.

Since he'd raised the matter, he thought about Teucer. Back home she could be a comfortable housewife in a comfortable house, probably spend most of her waking life doing embroidery. Here, give her a few books from the met'Oc library and in a year or so she'd be the colony's only competent surgeon.

I only want to do what's for the best, he told himself. For the colony, for my family, but most of all for me.

Furio found what he was looking for in the pile of scrap metal outside the back door of the store. It was, of course, bound for the factory, not that there was very much of it, since Gignomai had already used up nearly all the rusty and broken iron in the colony. But Uncle Marzo had sent a cart round the outlying farms in the valleys. The carters had taken two days, and come back with about a quarter of a full load.

He unearthed the nozzle of a household bellows, crumbly brown and blocked with mould and soft black dirt from under a rusted bucket. He carefully rodded it out with a bit of thin stick. Then he took the pebble and a scrap of waste cloth and made his experiment. As he'd anticipated, the pebble could be lodged good and tight. It wasn't conclusive, because he didn't really understand the science behind it, but it left a case to answer.

Getting the pebble out again turned out to be awkward; he tried driving it out using the stick and a stone as a hammer, but the stick snapped off, increasing the blockage. He wasn't quite sure how to interpret that data—either it strengthened his hypothesis or completely disproved it, and he had no way of knowing which.

Gignomai was stitching up a broken drive belt when they found him. The hammer was quiet, waiting for him to mend the belt. He looked up and said, "Well?"

"You'd better come," they said.

"I can't, I'm busy," Gignomai replied. "Can't someone else deal with it, whatever it is?"

"Not really," they told him. "You'd better come and see for yourself."

302 K. J. Parker

He shrugged, looped the half-mended belt over the branch of a tree, and followed them down to the river. There he saw a party of strangers, sitting on the ground. They were wearing long coats without pockets and absurd-looking round hats, all except one man, the oldest, whom he recognised. He hesitated, then went down to greet them.

"What are you doing here?" he asked.

The old man looked up at him and didn't smile. He looked sad, and lost. "They insisted," he said. "I had no choice." The old man breathed in as though drowning in air. "You told them you would give them snapping-hen pistols."

"That's right," Gignomai said.

"The demonstration you gave them had a considerable effect." The old man wasn't looking at him. "After you'd gone, the news spread quickly. Dozens of our people came to see. They stuck their fingers in the hole the bullet made." He frowned. "Many of them feel it was the most important thing that has happened to our people for centuries. There has been..." He shivered, "a great deal of debate."

Gignomai glanced at the other strangers. "Do they want the guns or not?"

"We now have two factions in our society," the old man went on, "those who believe, and those who do not. The former are a small minority—most of them are here with me now—but more and more of my people are coming round to their way of thinking every day. If you give them the snapping-hens, they propose to use force to make the rest of us believe. They have compelled me to be their spokesman. I didn't want to come here, but I had no choice."

Gignomai nodded slowly. "So they've decided we're real after all."

"They saw the hole the bullet made," the old man said. "They pushed down into the hole until they could feel it. They said that any agency that could do that must be real, existing in our reality, sharing our time and space." He paused, then went on, "They saw what you could do. They are afraid that unless they acquire the same power, sooner or later your people will attack them and destroy them. I told them that your people are a noble, enlightened race. I tried to explain to them about the wonders I saw in the Old Country, the beautiful way in which your people live, the magnificent houses, the well-ordered streets, the fine clothes, the books. I told them that if your people had wanted to destroy them, they could have done so effortlessly at any time in the past seventy years. A few of them may have listened to me, but most are too afraid. They refuse to take my word for it. All they've seen for themselves is the bullet hole. They said, 'If he will give us the power, we have to take it.' So," he said, wiping his nose on the back of his hand, "here we are."

"I'm sorry," Gignomai said.

The old man stared at him, hesitated for a moment, then burst out, "Why would you want to do such a thing? We were never a threat to you. We didn't believe you existed."

"You did," Gignomai said.

"I was a crazy old man," the old man replied. "I was a joke. Children came and asked me about the place where I grew up because they thought I was funny. They didn't believe what I told them."

"But it was true," Gignomai said.

The old man shook his head. "I realised a long time ago," he said, "it was all for the best. I was comfortable, and they were happy. Now you've changed everything, and these people want weapons. You do realise what they want them for, don't you?"

Gignomai nodded. "I'm sorry," he repeated. "It's just one of those things that had to be done."

The old man sighed. "I don't understand," he said. "I can see no possible benefit, to your people or to mine. Quite the reverse. Do you want my people to fight the colonists on behalf of the met'Oc? Is that what you have in mind?"

Gignomai shook his head. "That's the last thing I want," he said.

"Then it makes no sense," the old man roared at him. "You will pardon my stupidity, but I can see no advantage to be gained from starting a war between my people and the colonists. There are so many more of us than you, and your people have no weapons, only farm tools and axes. It makes no sense. Unless," the old man added, his head slightly on one side, "you aim to arm my people and then sell guns to your own people so they can defend themselves. I can believe there are human beings who would do such a thing, but I doubt very much that you would. For one thing, your people are so poor. And there must be easier ways to make money."

Gignomai smiled bleakly. "What I want," he said, "money can't buy. I really am sorry," he said, "but I knew what I was doing. If they want the snapping-hens, they can have them. At least, I can let them have a dozen. That's all I can spare right now."

The old man was looking past him, towards the factory. "You made them yourself," he said.

"That's right," Gignomai replied. "It was a lot of work. But we got here in the end."

The old man nodded slowly. "All that," he said. "Just to make the guns?"

"Mostly," Gignomai said. "There were other reasons, but that was the main one. They're good copies," he went on. "Not pretty, like the real ones my brother has. They're just a pipe clamped to a bit of wood, with a bit of a mechanism to make the spark. But they work."

The old man bowed his head. "You will have to show us what to do," he said. "If you would be so kind as to explain to me, I will pass it on to them. I promise I'll translate accurately," he added, with a faint grin. "I know what would happen to me if I didn't. I'm ashamed to say I still value my life, although I really can't say why."

"Wait there," Gignomai said, and he left them and went to the shed that housed the drop-hammer. He'd stored the finished snapping-hens under a loose floorboard. There were sixteen left. He chose a dozen and put them in an empty grain sack, along with two hollowed-out cow horns full of powder, a five-pound bag of lead balls and a handful of spare flints. He walked back and went through the loading procedure slowly and carefully with the old man, loading four of the pistols and making him load the fifth, to make sure he'd understood. Then he showed him how to prime the pan, close it and cock the hammer.

"Then all you do is point it and pull this lever here," he said. "That releases the hammer, which hits the steel, which strikes a spark, which sets off the powder in the pan. Simple as that." he handed the cocked pistol to the old man, who looked at it nervously. "If you don't want to fire it, give it to one of them."

The old man shook his head. "You do it," he said. "They need to see you do it. Otherwise..."

Gignomai shrugged, took back the snapping-hen, pointed it at a tree trunk and pulled the trigger. When the smoke had cleared, he went forward to inspect the damage. He'd missed the tree he was aiming at—it was about five yards away from where he'd been standing—and hit the one next to it. He poked his little finger into the bullet hole, up as far as the second joint.

Dalo Tavio's eldest son fell through the rotten floor of a hayloft into the firewood store below. He broke his left arm and leg, and the splintered end of a branch left sticking out from a badly trimmed log punched a hole in his face on the left side next to his nose. Remarkably, the boy wasn't killed. When his father tried to move him, the branch snapped off, leaving an inch of wood trapped in the bone. It was generally accepted that the wound would go bad and the boy would die, but the boy's mother insisted on sending to town and asking the mayor for help. If anybody knew what to do, she felt, it would be him. Tavio, who'd known Marzo Opello all his life, doubted this but couldn't bring himself to say so. Also, he vaguely remembered hearing that Opello's nephew was training to be a surgeon. He filled the cart with straw and put the boy in it, and drove straight to town, arriving in the early hours of the morning.

"Not my nephew," the mayor told him. "My niece."

Tavio looked at him as though he'd been drinking (which of course he had, but no more than usual). On the other hand, he thought, the boy will probably die in any event, and we've come all this way. "Fine," he said. "Call her."

Teucer came down in her nightdress, with two fat brown books under her arm. Tavio held a lantern over the cart while she examined the boy. He was deeply impressed at how calm she was about it, although there was something about her manner that disturbed him a little — too calm, maybe, and almost as if she was enjoying herself. She told her uncle and her cousin Furio how to lift him out of the cart without hurting him more than necessary, and she really did sound as though she knew what she was talking about. They laid the boy on the kitchen table, and Teucer carried out a closer examination.

"The leg shouldn't be a problem," she said. "The arm's an awkward break and it won't mend quite right, but I'll do the best I can. The piece of wood in his skull will probably kill him unless I can get it out."

Tavio, who'd felt mostly frozen up till then, felt as though he'd been hit across the face. But the girl was clearly something else. If he'd closed his eyes and ignored the pitch of her voice, he could have believed he was talking to a man. "Can you do that?" he asked. "Get it out, I mean."

"I don't know," she said. "Really, it's more of a woodworking problem than a medical one, and I'm not a carpenter. But there's something similar in the book. Give me five minutes and I'll look it up and tell you."

She walked away, taking a candle and one of the books into the mayor's office and closing the door behind her. There was a long moment of silence. Then Marzo Opello said, "You shouldn't judge her by her manners. She was brought up back Home; she doesn't really know how to talk to people."

Tavio said, "Does she know about this stuff?"

"From books," Marzo replied. "If you like, I can send for the horse doctor. But by the time he gets here —"

"My son's not a horse," Tavio said. "God help the man who marries her, but I think she knows what she's doing."

"He's your son," Marzo said.

Furio Opello withdrew at this point, muttering something about boiling some water. Tavio said, "Where did she get the books?"

"They came from the met'Oc library," Marzo replied. "So they should be pretty good. I tried reading one once, but I couldn't make any sense of it. She reckons she can understand them, though. She patched up young Furio when he cut himself a while back. Made a fair job of it, too. You can hardly see the scar."

Tavio sat down on a chair. "I suppose the met'Oc know all about this sort of thing," he said. "Maybe we could ask them to come out."

Marzo shook his head. "Young Luso knows a bit about cuts and bonesetting," he said, "but otherwise they do the best they can, like the rest of us. I don't think they read all those books. They're just for having, not reading. Besides, the met'Oc wouldn't come down here just to heal a farm boy."

Teucer came out of the office, with the book closed around her thumb to mark the place. "I'll need splints and bandages," she said, "and two feet of dry elder wood, rose honey, white wine, new bread, barley flour and turpentine. And someone's got to go out to the factory. I need a tool made, straight away."

"I'll go," said Furio, who'd just come in with a steaming kettle. "What do you want them to make?"

She opened the book and handed it to him. "Gignomai will be able to understand the sketch," she said, pointing to a diagram in the middle of the page. It looked like a spider on a stick. "Tell him it's got to be clean, so scrub off all the soot and firescale."

"You might as well take my cart," Tavio said. "Quicker than walking."

Furio laid the open book beside him on the box, with a glove across the page to keep the place in case a bump on the road closed it. He glanced at it from time to time as he drove, trying to make out words by the dizzy light of the swinging lantern. It was something to do with a doctor digging an arrowhead out of the head of a prince, after some battle back Home a long time ago. The diagram still looked like a spider on a stick, no matter how often he looked at it.

He heard the pulse of the hammer long before he saw the glow of the furnace. By the time he reached the factory, his head was throbbing and he could barely think. He realised he was still wearing his nightshirt, with a worn-out old stockman's coat over it.

A man walked out of the darkness and caught up the horse's head. Not anybody Furio knew. "Where's Gignomai?" Furio said.

"Asleep. Not to be disturbed."

"I asked you where he is, not what he's doing."

The man shrugged, and jerked his thumb in an undecipherable direction. Furio jumped down, taking the book with him, and made for the shack where Gignomai usually slept. He saw light under the door, knocked and walked in.

"Furio." Gignomai looked up from a book. "What the hell are you doing here?"

Furio explained. It was hard, having to shout over the noise of the hammer, and he had trouble expressing himself clearly. But Gignomai seemed to understand, and took the book from him, and moved the lamp closer so he could see the picture.

"Aurelio can make that," he said. "The awkward bit's the screwthread, but he's got a die that'll cut one easy as anything. When do you need it by?"

"Now."

Gignomai grinned. "You'll have to make do with as soon as possible," he said. "Stay here. I'll take the book with me."

He was gone for quite some time. Shortly before he came back, the hammer stopped.

"I told them to shut it down till Aurelio's finished," he said. "Can't expect anybody to do fine work with that racket going on."

"It's wonderful when it stops," Furio said.

"I don't hear it any more," Gignomai replied. "Except when it stops, and then it just feels strange."

"How can you sleep?"

"Being tired helps," Gignomai replied, and sat down on the edge of the bed, where he'd been when Furio found him. "Now then," he said, "we'd better talk about how much this is going to cost you."

That aspect of the matter hadn't crossed Furio's mind. "All right," he said. "How much?"

Gignomai shrugged. "Really, you should pay for the lost production, while the hammer's down," he said, "but what the hell. I've told them to strip down the gears and give it a good clean-out, so it's not exactly wasted time. The job itself I can do for ten thalers."

Furio looked at him, as though he was talking a language he didn't understand. "That's a fortune," he said.

"Fine," Gignomai replied. "Get it made somewhere else, then."

"You know we can't."

"Indeed. And I know you can't find ten thalers, or your farmer friend can't. I guess your uncle the mayor will just have to knock it off our slate. Which in real terms is the same as doing it for free. I don't have a problem with that, but it'd be nice if someone made a bit of a big deal out of it." He looked keenly at Furio, who wasn't sure how he was supposed to react.

"I'm sure Tavio'll be really grateful," Furio said. "Will that do?"

"So long as he tells everybody," Gignomai replied, "it'll have to. And even then, I expect Cousin Teucer'll get all the praise. Stroke of luck for her. I bet she's having the time of her life. And the boy might still die, of course, which won't do anybody any good."

Furio looked straight at him. "You've changed," he said.

"Have I?" Gignomai laughed. "I don't think so. If anything, I think I'm more myself than I've ever been. You haven't changed, though. I guess that's why you find me so disappointing."

Furio didn't reply straight away. "How long will it take?"

"You know craftsmen," Gignomai replied. "Ask them how long and they just pull faces and make noises with their teeth. If I was doing it, about three hours. But if I did it, it wouldn't work worth a damn. So," he went on, not bothering to try and hide the effort he was making, "what's been happening in town? I'm so out of touch here I don't know anything."

"I think you do," Furio said. "Talking of which, why are you going to so much trouble to start a war between your family and the colony?"

Gignomai's face was completely blank and still. "I don't follow," he said.

"You've been shooting holes in doors with those guns you've been making."

"Not me personally." His lips hardly moved. It was as though Furio had heard the words inside his own head. "I can't hit a damn thing further than three feet, not even a door. But young Scarpedino Heddo's turned out to be a natural. You guessed, then."

"I'm not stupid."

Gignomai smiled. "There's a big difference between not stupid and really smart," he said. "I always knew you were smart, Furio. Smarter than my brother Luso, even, and that's saying something."

Furio felt cold all over, as if he'd just broken the ice on the water-butt and plunged both hands in. "Why d'you do it, Gig? What the hell are you playing at?"

"How did you figure it out?" Gignomai said. He breathed in through his mouth and out through his nose, and Furio noticed that one of his hands, the one that wasn't gripping the arm of his chair, was shaking. "What gave it away?"

"Bits and pieces," Furio replied. He wasn't interested in giving explanations. "Luck, mostly. Seeing the light burning in the livery. Also, being here and watching you. And knowing you. At least, I thought I knew you."

"Probably better than most," Gignomai said.

"What clinched it was an experiment I did," Furio went on, wondering why he was still talking. Maybe he just didn't want to hear the answer to his question. "I was pretty sure the snapping-hens you were making here were the big-bullet size, but then someone shot at Melo Fasenna with a small bullet. You wanted to make it look like your cousin Boulomai, because we know he's got one of the small-bullet guns."

He looked sideways at Gignomai, who seemed to be paying close attention. "Go on," Gignomai said.

"I did an experiment," Furio said. "I got a piece of old pipe and a round pebble, small enough that it just fell down inside the pipe without sticking. Then I wrapped cloth round the pebble and rammed it down the pipe. It stayed there, of course. That's how you shot a small bullet from a big-bullet gun. You wedged it with a bit of rag."

"Luso calls them patches," Gignomai said, his chin resting on his hand. "Of course, the bullet doesn't fly straight worth a damn if you do that, but it gets there. I gather Scarpedino only missed by a hand's breadth. It'd have been bloody ironic if he'd hit Fasenna, since he was supposed to miss."

Furio waited, but Gignomai just carried on watching him, as though he was a performance Gig had paid to see. "So why are you doing it?" Furio asked. "There must be a reason, but I'm damned if I can guess what it is."

Gignomai smiled. Furio could only see half of it, because Gignomai's hand covered part of his face. "How about for the public good?"

"No."

"All right," Gignomai said, "though that's part of the reason. A very small part. I wouldn't want you to think I'm a selfish person, not that it matters particularly." He frowned, as though he'd lost the thread of what he was saying. "The reason," he said, "is quite simple. You know I had a sister?"

Furio nodded. "You used to talk about her," he said, "and then you never mentioned her again."

"That's right." Gignomai was looking over the top of his head, and he still wore the slight frown, which made him look as if he was surprised by his own words. "She died."

"I guessed it was something like that."

"My father killed her."

It was the way he said it, casually, with a vague hint of disapproval, as in, "My father wouldn't let me have a dog" or "My father sold my favourite pony." It didn't matter, but only because nothing mattered any more. "She was two years older than me. Luso caught her in the hayloft with one of his hired thugs—little more than a kid himself, about seventeen or so, a quiet lad, I remember him clearly. Anyway, Luso killed him on the spot, with his bare hands, and then he dragged my sister across the yard up to Father's study. I was in the apple tree at the time, hiding from Stheno because he wanted me to do some rotten job. I saw them cross the yard, Luso pulling on her hair and her screaming. I thought it was a game. Luso always did play rough, but we didn't mind because it was fun. She always screamed like that when they were playing."

Furio waited, unable to speak. Still the slight frown, and Furio began to understand what it meant: the tender probing of the wound, to see if it's still there.

"I think Luso realised pretty quick that he'd made a terrible mistake," Gignomai went on. "He told me once, if he'd had the faintest idea what Father was going to do, he'd have just killed the boy and buried him in the dungheap, and that'd have been the end of it. Soon as he got wind of what Father had in mind, he pleaded with him. Stheno too, to do him credit. But both of them..." He paused, and shrugged. "The trouble with my brothers," he said, "is they're both so weak. Soft as butter. All Stheno's interested in is keeping the farm going more or less as it is. Luso just wants to keep the peace and avoid embarrassing scenes. He's the mediator in our family, you might say. If one of us falls out with one of the others, Luso tries to patch things up. Always defending me to Father, or jollying Father and Stheno along when they're having one of their sulking wars. No wonder he needs to go out burning down houses from time to time. It's his way of letting off steam, I suppose, after trying to be reasonable with all us unreasonable people. Anyway, I'm prepared to accept that he tried. At least, until it became clear that if he carried on trying, Father was going to get seriously angry with him. All

Stheno did was have a shouting match, then he stormed off and didn't come home for a week. No bloody use at all. As for Mother, she pretended it wasn't happening. That's what she does. Most of the time, she acts like none of us really exist."

Furio felt the words forming in his mouth; he couldn't stop them. "What happened to your sister?"

Gignomai didn't answer for quite some time, and Furio thought he wasn't going to. But then he said, quite calmly, "We had an old woman with us, Spetta, who knew a bit of basic rough and ready medicine: she could set bones, strap up sprains, sew up wounds. I think she'd been Father's nurse. Anyhow, she always did what he told her. It wouldn't have occurred to her not to. He had a couple of the men bring down a big old chair from one of the barns. It was from Home, I think, originally. It was carved all over and massive, with big thick arms. You could jump up and down on it in heavy boots and not break it. Father had Aurelio make up steel brackets to fix the legs to the floorboards in the dining hall, so it wouldn't move an inch. Then he got two of Luso's men to tie her down in the chair. They soaked rawhide strips and bound her arms to the arms of the chair and the legs to the legs, good and tight. When the rawhide dried out, of course, it shrank. She couldn't move, you'd have had to cut the straps with a knife. Then he got the old woman to sew my sister's lips together." Gignomai closed his eyes, just for a moment. When he opened them again, they were wide, bright and clear. "And there she stayed," he went on. "She couldn't move or talk, or eat, or drink. Father didn't say anything to us, but we knew it would have been more than our lives were worth even to notice she was there. Of course we thought he'd keep here there for a day or so and then cut her loose, and then it'd be over. So we went on as if nothing was happening, breakfast and lunch and dinner, with her sitting in a chair at the table. She stank to high heaven, but we couldn't notice that either; we'd sort of got out of the habit of looking in her direction, as though she was an embarrassment. On the fourth day at breakfast, I noticed her eyes were closed and she didn't seem to be breathing. I told myself she was asleep. When I came back at lunchtime she'd gone, the chair, everything; just holes in the floorboards where the bracket-screws had been, and the next day someone had put down a rug. A while later, I found a few burnt bits of wood in the fire-pit at the back of the pigsties, where they used to burn rubbish. You could still just make out the carving on one bit. It was that chair. And that was that," Gignomai said. "And none of us ever said a word about it, not ever." Suddenly he grinned, like a skull covered in skin. "I do believe it was that, the not saying anything, that made my mind up. Otherwise, I'd just have bided my time and killed Father. It'd have been easy enough when he was asleep in his chair or from behind, reading in the library. But none of them said a word, it was as though she'd never existed, never been real." He paused, and looked down at his hands, as though checking they were still there. "Like what the savages believe," he said. "You can see why it gave me a jolt when the old man told us about it. I knew exactly what he was talking about. I think my brothers, my father and mother stopped believing in her when she died. The whole household disbelieved her away, and I was the only one who knew the truth, and they wouldn't have listened to me if I'd tried to tell them. Just like the old man, don't you think? I even started wondering if they might just possibly be right. What I mean is, suppose she never did exist, suppose she was like the imaginary friends kids make up: my imaginary sister. If I was the only one who remembered her, and everybody else believed she'd never been real..." He shook his head. "But then I talked to the old man, and he'd been through roughly the same thing, and I *knew* he was right and all the other savages were wrong. Which made me recognise it was possible. I could be the only witness, completely outnumbered, unanimous denial, and still be right." He shook himself like a wet dog, and went on, "So, anyway, I knew I couldn't stay there any more, not knowing the truth. At first I just wanted to get out. I stole the sword, assuming it'd buy me a boat ride Home and that'd be fine. I thought, if I was in a different country where nobody else knew about what had happened but me, maybe I could stop thinking about it and it'd be fine. But then you had your accident, and Teucer was about to sew you back together, and suddenly I was back there again, in the dining hall, watching the needle sinking into the skin. I knew, not a shadow of doubt in my mind, that just distance on its own wasn't going to solve anything, which only left one course of action. Which I regret, because it'll make me just as bad as Father, but really, I don't see how I have any choice at all."

Furio forced himself to look at him. It was painful, but he had to. "You want to kill your family."

"I want them dead," Gignomai replied. "I'm not fussed about striking the actual blows, that'd just be self-indulgence. I think of it more as a miserable sort of necessity. They've got to be got rid of, and I'm the only one who can make it happen. Also," he added, shaking a little, as though just released from confinement, "I don't see why I should give up my life just because of this. If I went back there one dark night and cut their throats while they slept—believe me, I've thought about it, planned it all out, route, timings, every last finicky detail—it'd all come back on me sooner or later, I'd never get away with it. If I wasn't strung up out of hand I'd have to explain, and, really, I'd rather not do that. And it'd still be murder, of course. I'm not prepared to be a martyr for justice. I stopped living when I was fourteen years old. When this is all over, I'd like to try living again. I mean, why the hell shouldn't I? It wasn't my fault, I didn't start it."

He paused and drew a huge breath, as though he'd been running. Furio felt a pain in his hand, and realised his fist was clenched so tight he'd given himself cramp. "Gig," he said, "this is crazy. You've got to give it up before it gets completely out of hand."

"Really?" Gignomai was frowning at him, thinking, Furio, don't be tiresome. "What makes you say that?"

"It's ridiculous," Furio said. "You can't just sit there calmly contemplating murder. Your own family, for crying out loud."

"My father managed it." Gignomai closed one eye and rubbed it with the tip of his finger to get rid of a bit of dust or something. "Stheno always said I was the one who took after him most. At the time I was insulted, but I'm gradually coming round to his point of view. The thing is, I can almost understand him — my father, I mean. He was faced with what he saw as an impossible situation — his daughter, a met'Oc, fucking one of Luso's scum of the earth desperados. In so far as he's capable of love, he loved her, like he does all his children. But something like that, in the situation our family's in..." He shrugged his shoulders, the old Gignomai gesture, as though he was still fifteen years old. "I expect he'd have talked about the thin end of the wedge, except he wouldn't use a cliché like that. The point being, once we start interbreeding with these people here, we're lost, we cease to exist. If he spared her, and she did it again and got pregnant — it was something he simply daren't risk. He took no pleasure in it, I'm sure. I expect he made her die that way as much to punish himself as for any other reason. He'd have to watch her dying, to torture himself for bringing her up so badly that such a thing could happen. I can understand." He twisted his head round, almost as if trying to look over his shoulder. "I can actually imagine a different me, back Home, eldest son instead of youngest, head of the family, faced with something world-destroying like that to deal with, and doing the same thing myself. Got to be practical, you see. Got to make sure it doesn't happen again, no possible chance whatsoever, so you make the deterrent so unbelievably horrible —" He stopped. It was as though he'd been trying to force his way through a dense tangle of briars, the more caught up he got the harder he pushed forward, until eventually he was so deeply trapped he'd have to be cut out. "Well, of course," he said, "of course I understand. I appreciate the need to take effective action, not to let luxuries like morality or ethics stand in the way of doing what has to be done." He looked up, and for a moment Furio saw someone else behind his eyes, someone he remembered from a long way back. "You do see what I'm driving at, Furio, don't you? You do understand."

Furio thought, I hope not, because if Gig's right, to understand evil is to become capable of it. On those terms, I'd rather be really, really stupid.

"I can see that what your father did was appallingly bad," Furio said, slowly and carefully. "I can see you can't rest till you've brought him to justice. But this isn't justice. It's murder."

And Gignomai laughed with genuine amusement, as if at a pun or a smart comeback. "That's just silly, Furio," he said. "Just listen to yourself, will you? There's no law here, there's no magistrate, no advocate general, no governor, no garrison commander. I can't just go to the proper authorities and swear a complaint before a notary. God, I wish I could. Wouldn't that be wonderful; it wouldn't be up to me, I could leave it all to someone else. Well, I suppose that's what I'm doing. I've made it the mayor's business. Your uncle Marzo, the mayor." Furio opened his mouth to speak, but it was a false impulse, he had nothing to say. "And it's not just my father," he went on, "it's all of them. They sat and watched her starve to death at the dinner table, and they didn't do a damn thing. You must be able to see it, Furio, you're not completely stupid. We've got to make sure it doesn't happen again, and there's only one way."

It was so hard to believe that Furio nearly gave up; it was like arguing with the sea. But he said, "What you're doing, the way you're going about it, the lies, all that stuff. Why not just go to the people in town and tell them the truth? Don't you think they'd see that justice has to be done?"

Gignomai gave him a look of pure contempt. "Be realistic," was all he said.

Furio was dead quiet for a moment. There had to be an argument, a way of using words to demonstrate that Gig's case was built on an enormous, glaring fallacy. There had to be one, but he simply couldn't think what it was. "You've got no right," he said. "You're going to get the people in town so angry with the met'Oc that they'll attack them, right? But your brother and his men have got weapons, there'll be men killed and injured. It's not their fight. You can't drag them in."

Gignomai's answer was cold and distant. He's right, Furio thought, he could have been a fine politician or a statesman. "I have a duty to make sure as little harm comes to them as possible," he said, "but what can I do? I didn't start it, all I can do is finish it." His voice changed abruptly. "Can't you understand I hate that it's got to be me? It'd be so easy just to say my family, right or wrong. Two evils don't cancel each other out. If I do this, I'll be just as bad as they are. All perfectly true, that's what's so horrible. I *will* be as bad as they are. I already am. All I want is for it to be over, and me as far away as possible. But I am who I am. It's mine to deal with, nobody else's. And this is the only way I can do it, so this is what I'm doing. Cut away the garbage and you'll see it's absolutely straightforward."

It was as though Furio had been tied down, and had suddenly been set free. He stood up. "Sorry," he said, "but you can't do it. I won't let you. That's all there is to it."

Gignomai looked at him. There was love in his eyes, and a kind of gratitude. "Why?"

"For your sake," Furio said. "Not theirs."

"Ah." Gignomai smiled. "I always did like you, Furio. Better than my brothers, though that's not saying much. But please, don't be a pain in the arse. Sit down and we'll go through it all again, and I'll make you understand."

"No." Furio stared at him; and into his mind came the fairy tale about the man who married a demon in disguise, and only found out what she was many years later. "You think I'm going to let you carry on with this? You must be out of your mind."

He turned and walked quickly away, not looking round, and kept on going down the path, until he could see the cart, the horse tied to a tree, the way out, escape, home. He let go of the breath he'd taken when he turned his back on Gignomai, and made an effort to release his hand, which had frozen clenched shut. He was three yards from the cart when Gignomai, who'd taken the short cut through the trees, stepped smartly and quietly up behind him and hit him on the back of the head with a heavy stick.

*   *   *

The man who knocked at the door was a stranger, a short, square man with grey hair parted down the middle. "Gignomai met'Oc sent me," he said. Marzo looked over his shoulder and recognised the Tavio horse tied to the rail.

"Have you got it?"

"Right here." The stranger handed him something wrapped in clean white shirt-cloth. It felt like a pair of fire tongs.

"Thanks. Where's my nephew?"

The man took a step back. "Are you Mayor Opello?"

"That's me."

"Your nephew's decided to stay at the factory for a few days. Gignomai met'Oc needs his help with something. He said to tell you, he hopes you won't mind, and consider it as payment for making the tool."

Marzo made him repeat the message, then thanked him and asked if he wanted to come in and have something to eat or drink. No, he had to get back, thanks all the same.

Marzo took the thing he'd been given into the store, still wrapped in its cloth. He gave it to Teucer, who fumbled as she unwrapped it. It looked convincing, but he had no idea what it was supposed to be for.

"Well?" he asked.

She was turning a knob, which raised two arms along a screw-thread. "How should I know?" she said. "I've never seen one before."

"Is it like the one in the book?"

"I think so. Let's try it out and see."

Marzo looked at the wood screw at the end of the threaded rod. He had a fair idea where that was supposed to go. "You carry on," he said. "I'll be in my office if anyone needs me."

He sat down in his chair. There was an inch left in the old bottle, and there was a new one next to it. He left them alone. He had a feeling that if he drank anything, he'd probably be sick. He pulled his stock book across the table towards him, opened it, stared at it for quite some time before he realised it was upside down. He tried to add up a column of figures, but kept losing count.

Some time later, he wasn't sure how long, he heard a terrible scream. He closed his eyes, then went back to the top of the column and started again.

The news spread quickly. The mayor's niece (nobody could quite bring themselves to remember her name, in spite of everything) had saved the Tavio boy when he'd been on the point of death by pulling a huge splinter of wood thick as a finger right out of his skull with a weird thing like a cross between tongs and a drill, which the met'Oc boy had made for her at his factory. She'd worked for six hours, they said, teasing the splinter out of the wound a shred at a time, while the boy's father and a couple of other men held him down, so tight he couldn't move a hair's breadth. It was generally agreed that the thing was a miracle, Opello's niece was a heroine and the mayor was a hero, and so was young met'Oc, who'd made the tool for nothing in no time at all. The boy was still at the mayor's place, weak, but mending remarkably quickly. Of course, they noted, she was from Home, where people were very different—that explained it and excused it, as if the mayor's niece had two heads, or wings.

In other news, the mayor's nephew, young Furio, was back at the factory, and the impression was he'd be staying there. It was generally assumed there'd been some kind of falling-out between him and the met'Oc boy, which had prompted Furio to leave the factory for a while, and which had now been sorted out. This was held to be a good thing, since the factory was marvellous and they were making good stuff there. It was even rumoured that young met'Oc was mining iron somewhere. If that was true, and the factory kept going the way it had started, it wouldn't be long before they could do without the shipments from Home. Just think what that would mean!

Furio opened his eyes and saw nothing. Then he heard the scrape of a flint, and a little orange glare in the darkness blinded him for a moment. The light gradually expanded, as a patient, methodical man lit a lamp.

"You're Aurelio," Furio said.

The face looked as though it had been rolled out and folded a few times, like the dough for making bread. The eyes were small, watery and bright. "You're Furio Opello."

"That's right." Furio wasn't aware of trying to move his left hand, not until he found he couldn't. It was attached to his right hand by three turns of good-quality cord, the sort they sold in the store for a thaler a furlong.

"I'm to tell you it's not how it looks," Aurelio said. "It's for your own good, he said."

"Leaving me tied up in a darkened room is good for me," Furio said. "You live and learn."

Aurelio grinned. "That's a good one," he said. "Also, he said to tell you, you're in no danger. When it's over, you'll be free to go." He paused, frowned. "I think that's everything," he said.

There wasn't enough light to make out whether he was armed, or if he was tied up too. "It's ten thalers if you untie me," he said, "and another ten if you stay out of my way while I kick my way out of here."

"Love to take your money, but I can't, sorry." Aurelio lifted his hands, which were tied together at the wrist. "Looks like we're stuck with each other," he said. "Cheer up," he went on, "I know the boss, this is just what he calls attention to detail. Sets a lot of store by it, the boss does."

Furio let the strength flow back out of his muscles. His back was against a wall, and he was sitting on the floor. His neck ached. "You here for your own good too, are you?"

"It's to stop me running away," Aurelio replied. "Not that I would, because I've got nowhere to go. But Master Gignomai, he likes to be sure. Always the same, ever since he was little."

Furio couldn't help grinning. "Known him long, then?"

"All his life," Aurelio replied. "Easily the pick of that family.

322   K. J. Parker

Smartest, knows his own mind, doesn't give a damn, just like his dad. Only," Aurelio added, with a crease to his face that wasn't quite a frown, "he's got that extra edge, if you know what I mean. The old man plays by the rules, always. Gignomai makes his own rules, and not so many of them."

Furio looked up, but he couldn't see rafters or the underside of the thatch, just more darkness, like a pool. "This must be the hammer-house," he said.

Aurelio nodded. "Just as well for you and me it's not running," he said. "Else we'd be off our heads with the racket. I've been a smith fifty years, I'm as near deaf as makes no odds, but that thing makes my head spin."

"Where's Gignomai?" Furio asked, but Aurelio just shrugged.

"I've been watching the shadow that crack of light under the door makes," he said, "and it was back where it started about an hour ago. Leastways, an hour more or less. I was counting, but I can't get my fingers where I can feel my pulse, so it's a bit rough and ready. Still, I'd say I've been here twenty-five hours. You, about four."

Furio looked at him. "You've been sitting there counting for a whole day?"

"Helps pass the time," Aurelio replied. "And I'm what you might call the precise sort. I like measuring things, you know where you are if you've got the numbers. That said, I lost count when they brought the food in, so the total's all askew anyhow."

"I'm sorry," Furio said. "I've made you lose count again."

"Doesn't matter. Talking's better than counting, anyway."

Furio had no idea what to make of that. He said, "You must know this shed pretty well. If I can get my hands free, what's the best way out of here?"

"Door's locked," Aurelio said, "and I think it's barred on the out-side. Windows are shuttered. You could try shinning up the chim-ney, but you'd get stuck halfway, and God knows how we'd get you down again. You're better off staying put, if you ask me. Gignomai wouldn't have left us here if there was any danger."

Furio shook his head. "I need to get out," he said. "I need to get back to town and tell them Gig's gone crazy and he's trying to start a war. If I've only been here four hours—"

"Sorry," Aurelio said. "Can't do that."

"Why?"

"Because if you try, I'll stop you."

Furio was lost for words for a moment. "After he's tied you up and dumped you here for a whole day?"

"He's the boss," Aurelio said. "He knows what he's doing. You can bank on that."

Furio stared at him for a while, but Aurelio wasn't looking in his direction. Furio leaned his head back against the wall and tried not to move his neck.

"You've been with the met'Oc how long?" he asked.

"Fifty years. Fifty-one come the spring. Got taken on when I was twelve years old, been there ever since."

It was the question Furio didn't want to ask. "Gignomai had a sister."

"That's right, yes."

"What happened to her?"

Aurelio slowly turned his head and looked at him. "She went to the bad," he said. "Master Phainomai had her killed. Tied to a chair and starved to death. Hell of a thing."

Furio could feel his heart pounding against the walls of his chest, as though he'd been running, or carrying a load too heavy for his strength. "And you stayed there, after that?"

"Nothing to do with me," Aurelio said, almost casually. "Hell of a thing, but like I said, the old man goes by the rules, even when they don't suit. That way, you know where you stand."

"Gignomai's going to kill him," Furio said. "Him and his brothers, his mother too for all I know. The whole lot of them."

"Wouldn't surprise me," Aurelio said quietly. "Got a wild streak in him, that boy, but it runs cold rather than hot, if you follow me. Good-hearted, cares about people the way the rest of them don't, but single-minded. And patient, too. That's another way he's different from the others."

Furio gave up. It was like talking to a priest; he'd interpret scripture for you, but wouldn't ever venture an opinion about the content. "I don't suppose there's a knife or anything sharp lying around, is there?"

"Bit of old broken saw-blade, came out of the scrap. That the sort of thing?"

"That'd do nicely," Furio said. "Where is it?"

"Under my foot," the old man replied. "Sorry."

So maybe Gig's right after all, Furio told himself, closing his eyes against the unnecessary light. Maybe they do all have to go. Maybe evil is a habit or a mannerism you can pick up from the people around you, without even noticing you've done it. Or maybe there's no such thing, and all that matters is to be practical. He tried to imagine the colony without the met'Oc; it was surprisingly easy to do. There'd be no more cattle raids, which would be just as well, since once the link with Home was broken and the rent quota no longer needed to be filled, the cattle would genuinely belong to the farmers, not the Company. What else? There'd be land up for grabs, for a little while — miserable land, more trouble than it was worth to plough. Whoever took it on would probably run sheep up there as a sideline. The silver, the furniture, the books — one way or another, he felt sure, they'd pass through Uncle Marzo's hands on their way back Home where they belonged. You could call it reparations, or plunder. He doubted very much whether Gig would show any interest in it. If he was bothered about wealth, he could make himself rich running the factory. Somehow Furio doubted whether anything on the Tabletop held any sentimental value for him. Quite the reverse.

In any case, Furio thought, he's got a long way to go yet. Maybe he'll fail. All he'd managed to achieve so far was a vague atmosphere of distrust, to some extent neutralised by Uncle Marzo's remarkable and totally unexpected success as diplomat and community leader. He'd need a really bold, magnificent stroke to get the colonists mad enough to attack the Tabletop, or years of slow, patient effort, like a single mole undermining a whole city.

The latest shipment was mostly shovels, picks and ploughshares, three barrels of nails, a barrel of gate hinges. Also, ten coils of wire — poor quality, Gignomai confessed, of irregular thickness and somewhat brittle, but the next batch would be better — and a new line: billhooks with steel cutting edges welded into soft iron for toughness and economy, hardened and drawn to purple to stay sharp all day, seasoned ash shafts, five dozen at a thaler a dozen.

Marzo picked one out of the straw and examined it. Still black and greasy from the tempering oil, no finish to speak of but a good, straight, well-balanced tool. From Home, three thalers a dozen if he could get them. He'd ordered twelve dozen, but there hadn't been any on the last three ships. On the other hand…

"Not much call for them," he said. "I mean, everybody's got one, and it's not as though they wear out in a hurry."

"Ah yes," Gignomai said with a pale smile, "but now people can have one and a spare. At that price, you can get one for the boy to use, and then there'll be two of you on the job and you'll get it done in half the time."

"Hedging's winter work," Marzo replied, arguing more from habit than conviction. "Time's not exactly of the essence." He wondered why he was bothering. Gignomai wouldn't lower the price — he was practically giving them away as it was — and Marzo had decided he'd take them as soon as Gignomai had told him what was in the crate.

"Fine," Gignomai said. "Tell you what I'll do. Sale or return. I'll leave them here and you don't have to give me any money until you've sold them. If they're still here in three weeks, I'll take them back and work them into hayknives. All right?"

Marzo just managed to stop himself whimpering with surprise. Achieving a deal like that without even trying was — well, disappointing. He felt almost cheated, as if his hard-earned bargaining skills had been utterly devalued. "If you like," he said, trying to sound casual. "And the same terms for the gate hinges?"

Gignomai gave him a beautiful smile. "The hell with that," he said cheerfully. "Cash in hand or I take them back with me."

Marzo nodded, relieved. Back to normal. "Two thalers five."

"Three, and I want the barrel back."

Marzo opened his book and made a show of examining the figures, though of course he knew the balances by heart. "Cash in hand for the hinges, then," he said. "You want cash for the rest of the stuff, or shall I write it up?"

"Cash," Gignomai said. "Which reminds me of the main reason I'm here. I've been thinking." He perched on the edge of the long table and folded his arms, instinctively elegant like an animal. "Seems to me it'd make more sense for us to start buying our supplies direct from the farmers, instead of going through you for everything, now we're earning money. What do you reckon?"

Marzo exaggerated the shrug a little. "That's up to you," he said. "You do what you like."

Gignomai shook his head. "No, I want us to stay friends," he said. "I worked out there can't be much margin for you in supplying us, and it's a lot of work for you, with storage and carting."

"True," Marzo said, and left it at that, in case Gignomai had something else to offer.

"In return," (*Ah*, Marzo thought) "I suggest we draw a line under everything up to now. How would that be?"

"Sorry," Marzo said. "I don't follow."

"Simple. I don't owe you anything for what I've had from you so far, and you can have the sword, sell it, keep the money for yourself. Is that a deal?"

"But it's worth—" Marzo managed to bite off the rest of the sentence, but he had an idea the look on his face would tell Gignomai all he needed to know.

"Yes," Gignomai said, "ten, twenty times what I've had from you, sure. More like fifty. So what? Back up on the Tabletop it wasn't worth anything. Down here, it means I've been able to get the job done. For you, it's a passage out of here and a nice life back Home for you and your family, if that's what you want. Amazing how one stupid bit of pointed metal can do so much good for so many people." He yawned, and stroked his throat; maybe he had a cold coming. "If you'd rather do it some other way I'm open to suggestions."

"No, that's fine," Marzo said, altogether too quickly. "Thank you. You're being very generous."

For some reason, that made Gignomai laugh. "Forget about it," he said. "Now, can we get the rest of this stuff unloaded so I can be on my way?"

Marzo was about to call for Furio to come and help, then remembered he wasn't there. "How's that nephew of mine getting on?" he asked.

"Miserable," Gignomai replied, as he crossed the porch. "He always gets a bit sad when called on to do demeaning manual labour. I left him sweeping out the wheel-house."

"He's good at sweeping," Marzo said. "He's had practice."

"I bet." Gignomai let down the tailgate of the cart. "No, he's fine. I should have mentioned it before, but I had to talk to him first about it, naturally. I want him to take over the whole of the business side, and I'll get on with making stuff. It makes sense, after all. He knows about that sort of thing, it's in the blood, and I haven't really got a clue. Where I come from, buying and selling's one of those things where you wash your hands afterwards for fear of catching something."

Marzo didn't speak immediately. Something was snagged in the back of his mind. "He's his father's son when it comes to business," he heard himself say. "And it makes good sense from my end, keeping it in the family. And after I'm gone, of course, it'll all be his anyway."

"Quite," Gignomai said, "unless you see us both out, which isn't impossible. Anyway, that's why I asked him to come back to the factory full time. He needs to get a really good grasp of everything we're doing. I don't know anything about it, but it stands to reason, you can't run a business unless you know everything about it. Right," he added, scrambling up onto the bed of the cart, using the hub of the back wheel as a stepping-stone. "This crate's the scythe blades. Careful, it's quite heavy."

No doubt about it, Gignomai had changed. For one thing, he'd grown deceptively strong, or else he'd taught himself the subtle art of lifting. Probably a bit of both, Marzo decided, as he took the strain at his end and felt something fail in the small of his back, a combination of increased capacity and the ability to make full use of what you've got. Basically, the polar opposite of the way the met'Oc did things.

"To me," Gignomai commanded, as they swung the case round to get it through the door. "Right, where do you want it?"

More than anything (money, power, respect, repose and tranquillity), Marzo wanted a rest and a chance to straighten out his back before they went outside again for the next crate. But Gignomai didn't hang around long enough to give him a chance to drop hints. He followed him into the street, and saw four men walking quickly towards him, from the East Ford side of town. He could have wept for relief and joy, even when he recognised them: the Stalio brothers from Long Cross, their son, and Nuca Emmo, their hired man. Four more tedious people you couldn't hope to meet on a summer's day, but still...

Gignomai had seen them too. He pulled a long face, muttered something about business at the livery, and vanished like snow on hot coals. Marzo put on his smile of office, and stood up straight to greet them.

"It's the savages," said Ila Stalio (fifty-seven, fat, full head of grey hair). "They attacked us."

Marzo tried to speak, but nothing came out.

"With guns," Emmo said. "They shot at us."

"But the savages haven't got guns. Nobody's got—"

"They have now." Ila's brother, Namone, was the sort of person nobody ever listened to on principle. "Ila's telling the truth, Mayor. I was there. They shot at me too."

"But the savages haven't got guns," Marzo repeated. It was the truth, and they were refusing to acknowledge it. He had no idea what to do under such circumstances.

"Me and Dad and Uncle Namone were bringing in the heifers from our long meadow," said the boy, Telo. He wasn't so bad, except he treated his father as some sort of god. "And Nuca was with us as well. We saw them, other side of the river, about two hundred yards off. We stopped and looked at them—"

"You don't see savages every day," Namone put in. "Not in our neck of the woods."

Marzo turned to the boy. "You're sure they were…"

"They had those long coats, and those dumb hats," Ila said. "They were just stood there, watching us. So we yelled at them to go away."

"We just yelled," Nuca put in. "We didn't do nothing."

"And then we heard this noise," Telo went on, "like thunder. And a split second later, there were these little clouds of smoke, where they were stood to. We didn't figure it at first."

"Two hundred yards away," Marzo said. One of them he could have handled, just about. Four was too many.

"On the other side of the river," Namone said. "Their side, properly speaking. But they were shooting at us."

"How do you know?"

Ila shrugged. "Wasn't anything else to shoot at," he said. "They were dead set on killing us, Mister Mayor, and what we want to know is, what're you going to do about it?"

Marzo couldn't feel his feet. It was a strange feeling, as if he'd been sitting still too long. "But the savages haven't got guns," he said for the third time. "Nobody's got guns except the met'Oc. Everybody knows that."

"Why would the met'Oc be shooting at us?" Ila said. "Besides, they were savages. No question about it. You can always tell. It's the way they stand, dead still."

Marzo drew in a long breath, as if he knew it'd have to last him for a while. "You'd better come inside," he said, and led the way into the store. There he found Gignomai, unloading gate hinges from the barrel.

"What's the matter?" Gignomai said. "You look like the world's about to end."

"Maybe it is," said Ila mournfully, "if the savages have declared war on us."

"What?" Gignomai looked as though he was about to laugh.

"Tell him," Marzo said, and when the four of them had repeated their story, practically word for word but arranged for different voices, Gignomai sat down on a crate and covered his mouth with his hand.

"It's not possible," Marzo said. "It can't be. Where the hell would they get guns from?"

"From my family," Gignomai said.

Marzo was standing beside him, looking sideways down at him. At that moment a connection formed in his mind, and he asked himself: if Gignomai is planning on Furio taking over the business, why would he give me the sword, knowing perfectly well that it means I'd be able to take us all, Furio included, back Home? It was, he admitted to himself, a strange time to be thinking about that sort of thing, and it was wrong of him to give it mind room when the worst crisis in the colony's history might be about to break, but somehow, he couldn't shift it from his thoughts, so he missed what Ila said to Gignomai. But he heard the reply.

"On the contrary," Gignomai said, "it's just the sort of thing Luso would do. In fact, he's talked about it to my father, at least twice, to my certain knowledge. I was there at the time."

"Why?" Nuca said. "It doesn't—"

"Think about it," Gignomai said. "An alliance between the

met'Oc and the savages, to drive the colonists out, or wipe them out—whichever's easiest, I suppose, though extermination would be the more logical course. Vacant possession of the entire colony, and a labour force to work the land once the primary objective's been achieved. Really, just like back Home, where families like ours used to have whole armies of tenants, or serfs, or whatever you choose to call them. I know it's been at the back of my father's mind for a long time, but he doesn't have the energy. When Luso suggested it, he said no because he reckoned Luso was too young and inexperienced to pull it off. Now that he's getting married, though, he needs property of his own, a dowry." He shrugged. "It's a stupid idea, of course. There aren't enough of the met'Oc to wipe out the savages once they've done their side of it; it's much more likely to be the other way about. I can only guess that Boulo figures he can bring in reinforcements from Home. It's just the sort of thing they'd come up with: a little pocket empire of their own with slaves to work the fields. And what else could we have to offer that'd tempt the met'Ousa into a marriage alliance?"

Marzo had been trying to grasp some relevant fact that had been floating out of reach in the confusion of his mind. He caught it at last, and said, "But Gignomai, your people only have about five guns between them. They haven't got enough to go giving them away to—"

Gignomai laughed. "That was true when I left," he said. "But it's obvious, isn't it? They've been making the things. It's not all that difficult, I believe. Luso told me once, if you can make a door lock and you can make a piece of pipe, you can make a snapping-hen. Luso's got two or three men up there who'd be able to do it. And how many would you need? Two dozen? Three? Suppose it takes a day to make one. In a couple of months, you'd have enough for a small army."

Marzo felt as though his head had just been plunged under water. "They could do that?"

"I'm sure of it," Gignomai said. "All it'd take would be the need to

332   K. J. Parker

do it. And if you think about it, that'd explain a lot of what's been going on around here lately."

"The attacks," Ila said. "Fasenna, and the Heddos."

Gignomai nodded. "Softening you up," he said, "getting you all nice and scared, reminding you of who's got the real power around here. While my dear brother's been pretending to play nice with the mayor here, they've been getting ready to make their move. I imagine that what happened today was a bunch of savages who couldn't wait till the agreed date before trying out their new toys." He looked at each of them in turn, then shook his head. "And you wonder why I left home," he said. "Trust me, my family are capable of anything."

Even then, a part of Marzo's mind was fussing over the inconsistency of Furio and the sword. "There's no proof, though, is there?" he said. "I mean, it's all just your guesses."

"Fine." Gignomai glared at him. "You give me another explanation that fits all the facts." He sighed, and went on, "I've been worried for some time that they might be up to something like this. Before I left, Luso was away for three days. Said he was going hunting on the west side, but there weren't any deer out there, I'd been there myself, and he didn't take the dogs, so what he was hunting I don't know. When he came back, he and Father shut themselves away in the study and had a long, long conversation about something, but I never did find out about what. And Aurelio—who used to be our smith—thrown out on his ear to make way for a new man. Want to hazard a guess what the new man was good at? And before they got rid of him, they had him working for a whole week just making files. Files, for heaven's sake! We use up one every ten years. But if you're going to be making a lot of small, intricate metal parts, you could well want a boxful of sharp new files." He shrugged. "Little things like that. But put them all together…"

Marzo felt like he was standing on a rotten floor, but he couldn't think straight. "All right," he said. "Ila, Namone, I want you to go round all the houses and tell everybody to come here. Get them to send the boys to all the nearest farms. We need all the people we can get. I'm damned if I'm going to make a decision on something like this without as many people agreeing with me as possible."

Three hours later, the store was packed with forty or fifty men pressed shoulder to shoulder, and Marzo and Gignomai sitting in the middle of the room on a rostrum improvised out of the newly delivered packing cases. The Stalio brothers had told their story once again, and Gignomai had offered his interpretation, with further circumstantial evidence of the met'Oc's long-standing preparations. He'd taken off his coat because of the closeness of the room; under it he wore a fine linen shirt, torn and stained with oil, rust and millstone slurry. Marzo was disconcerted to see how thin he was: skin and bone with ropes of muscle.

"That's about it," Gignomai said, and the room was extraordinarily quiet. "But I'd like to add one thing. It's not strictly relevant, but I think it's something you ought to know." He paused, as if allowing time for objections, then went on, "I expect some of you have been asking yourselves why I left home in the first place. Well, I'll tell you. When I was fourteen years old, my father murdered my sister. He'd found out she was seeing a boy, one of my brother Luso's gang. He didn't approve. Luso killed the boy—I'm sorry, I never knew his name, it wasn't the sort of detail my family regards as important—and my father had my sister tied to a chair and sewed her lips together. She stayed in the chair, in the dining room, till she starved to death, and nobody lifted a finger to help her. That's my family, gentlemen, that's the sort of people they are, so if you were thinking that no one could bring themselves to do the sort of thing I've been talking about, think again. Also, you might care to consider this. Maybe I'm wrong, about my family arming the savages and sending them against you. Maybe there's some other explanation, and I'm doing them a grave injustice. Well, so what? They did my sister a grave injustice seven years ago. I didn't study law, like my father wanted me to, but I have an idea that the lawful penalty for murder is death, and they've had it coming for a long, long time. I'm a met'Oc, I was born one, I've still got most of their shit in my head:

honour, pride, perfect disdain for the lower orders. I try and fight it but it'll probably always be there. When Luso ran off your cattle and stole from you and burnt your barns, I thought, well, they're just farmers, it doesn't matter. I admit it, I'm sorry for it, but I just let it happen and didn't lift a finger. When they killed my sister, I didn't lift a finger. But I think the time's come for a better way of doing justice round here. I think it ought to start right now. I've been absolutely straight with you, I've told you something I never thought I'd tell anyone, because I believe you have a right to know. You can say I'm all eaten up with wanting revenge on my father and my brothers and you'd be right—that's me. But if you're in two minds about doing something about the met'Oc, because you're not sure they're guilty as charged, all I'm saying is—don't be. That's it."

During the long, intimidating silence that followed, all Marzo could think of was that if Gignomai was serious about the business, and having Furio to run the trading side, why would he make it possible for Furio to go Home? It made no sense. Look at him, he's a real met'Oc. He can make them do and think whatever he likes; he's got the touch, like his brother. Like both his brothers. Only when they do it to you, you know. They want you to know. Gignomai makes you believe it's inside yourself, and that's scary.

And what about the bloodless revolution and the new republic? He wants shot of his family, he wants shot of Furio and me. So who would that leave here?

"Well?" Gignomai said.

It was as though he'd smacked every man in the room across the face. They looked at him, suddenly and painfully aware they had no choice now, they had to make the decision. Telling them about his sister had dragged them all across the line. If they kept quiet now, and started to slip away, then nothing would be done, nothing would ever be done, because he'd be disgusted with them, he'd leave them, to the savages and the met'Oc and the government, and presumably the wolves and the bears and all their natural enemies, with nobody but Marzo the mayor to lead them. He's got them, Marzo thought.

The hook's in their lips, the halter's on, he can pull them along by their pain, *and he lied to me.* He had no call to go doing that.

And if he lied, then where's Furio?

He knew, in that moment, exactly what he had to do. He had to get to his feet, denounce Gignomai as a liar and a deceiver and quite possibly a man with his eyes on a crown. How he'd convince them he had no idea, but it had to be done. He thought, I'm a short, fat, middle-aged man who wants nothing more out of life than to sell things to people for slightly more than they're worth. I shouldn't have to do this. But he felt the beginnings of movement in his knees and back, which told him he was about to stand up (and if he stood up, he'd have to speak, and if he spoke, he'd have to tell the truth).

Under his feet, the packing case rocked ominously. If I stand up, he thought, I'll tip the case and go flying arse over tip, possibly break an arm, definitely never live it down.

He stayed where he was.

"Well?" Gignomai repeated, and the pressure in the room was more than flesh and bone could stand. It tried to vent itself through Rasso the liveryman, who said, in a voice as slim and fragile as an icicle, "What do you think we should do, then?"

Gignomai waited a heartbeat or so before answering. "Go up there," he said. "Flush them out. If needs be, kill them. It's the only way. I'm sorry, but there it is."

"We can't do that," someone said, deep in the pool of faces. "They've got weapons. They live in a fucking castle. We'd be slaughtered."

Gignomai didn't smile as he answered, but Marzo knew him well enough by now to recognise the faint light in his eyes, the firmness of the line of his mouth. Inside, he was grinning like a skull. "No," he said. "You think I'd suggest it if there wasn't a way? We can take them, I promise you. I can tell you how. That's not the question. The question is, do you want to?"

There are silences that mean yes, and silences that mean no. This one was unambiguous.

"That's easy said," Rasso replied. He was having trouble with his words, like a drunk. "What makes you think we can take out your family without a whole lot of us getting killed?"

"Because I've thought about it," Gignomai replied, quiet and calm, just right; tall and skinny, like a spider on a stick. "I've given it a lot of thought over a long time. Also, we've got two wonderful advantages that'll make it easy. I can tell you about them if you're serious, otherwise I'll keep them to myself."

There was a terrible silence, then someone said, "Go on."

Gignomai nodded, acknowledging the formation of the contract. They all saw him, and nobody could have been in any doubt about what that slight movement meant. "First," he said, "I know a way of getting up there without being seen. It's not guarded. It's well away from anywhere Luso posts guards. They don't know about it; nobody does, except me." He paused for a moment, then said, "It's how I escaped. Twice. And I know Luso hasn't found out about it, because I've been back to look. If he'd found it, he'd have blocked it up. He hasn't. They don't know."

It was the performance of a miracle—sand into flour, water into wine. They looked at him, and Marzo knew what they were thinking: that's one, what's the other?

"The other thing," Gignomai went on, "is my brother Luso's wedding. If we go up there while the wedding's going on, they'll all be in the house, every single one of them. They'll be drinking and dancing, playing music. We could walk up to the front door shouting our heads off and they wouldn't know we were there. We can take them all together, too pissed to fight, all the weapons in the racks in the armoury. Believe me," he added, with a perfect smile, "I wouldn't dream of taking you up there if I thought there was a chance in a million you'd have to fight. You're not fighters. That's a good thing. I grew up among fighters, and it's not a good thing to be. You're better than that, and I'm not going to turn you into the sort of people we're going there to get rid of."

"What about your brother?" Rasso said. "I don't see him coming quietly."

Gignomai's face was suddenly dead. "Leave him to me," he said.

"That's easy to say—"

"I can guarantee it," Gignomai said. "By the time you're on the Tabletop, I'll have taken care of my brother. That's the whole point. I can tell you exactly when the wedding's going to be, because the only thing they're waiting for is me. Luso's said, he won't get married unless I'm there. So, I'll go to the wedding. And Luso won't be a problem. You have my word."

His word, the met'Oc word. Marzo thought about Luso, of the bond between them. He was nice to me when he didn't have to be, he thought. He gave me his word, but Gignomai deceived me. And Furio...

Suddenly he felt very cold. Furio was missing, but he had no doubt at all in his mind that Gignomai knew where Furio was. Not a business partner, then. A hostage. He lifted his head, and found that Gignomai was looking at him. He looked away, and at that moment someone called out, "Mayor, what do you reckon? Should we do it?"

As if the whole weight of the building was resting on his neck. Marzo knew exactly what he ought to do. Whoever it was had given him the chance. All he had to do was say no, and he could stop it right there.

"I'm not your bloody mayor," he said. "I wish you'd stop calling me that. If you want a mayor, then bloody well elect one. I quit."

Someone laughed, presumably thinking he was making a joke.

"What do you think?" Gignomai said quietly.

At that moment, Marzo hated Gignomai more than anyone else he'd ever met. He knew what had to be done, and what he'd just said was a lie. By negotiating with Luso met'Oc, trying to help, do the best he could, and never losing sight of the fact that respect and popularity would do business in the store no harm at all, he'd accepted the ridiculous, idiotic title and everything it implied. Now, for Furio's sake, he was going to have to do the wrong thing. And wasn't Gignomai clever? he thought. He's given me Furio as an excuse, so I can do what I do best and be weak.

"I think it's got to be done," he said. "Now, or later. Now would be easier. If we leave it, people are going to get killed. And if Gignomai's telling the truth about what they did to his sister, I don't think we need to bother ourselves with the rights and wrongs." He looked at the faces. He knew all of them, he'd known them all his life, and he was betraying them to the met'Oc sitting next to him. "I'm not your fucking mayor, but I think we should do it, yes. I really don't see where we've got a choice."

There was a moment when the lock tripped and the hammer fell. Someone said, "But what are we going to do for weapons? We can't just go in there empty-handed, no matter what he says."

Gignomai smiled this time, and lifted his foot and stamped it lightly on the packing case under him. "In this box," he said, "there's five dozen quality billhooks. You won't find a better weapon anywhere." (And Marzo understood, and cursed himself for being a fool.) "Right now they're the property of Marzo here, but I'm sure he wouldn't mind giving us the loan of them. And if you want a little bit more to make you feel better, there's knives and axes, and I know some of you have bows. We'll be better kitted out than Luso's men, I promise you."

Marzo felt himself nod helplessly. It was as though the command that made his head move came from Gignomai, not himself. Sale or return, he thought. I really should have seen it coming.

After that, it was mostly practicalities, tedious military stuff which Marzo found both terrifying and boring at the same time. Once he was satisfied that he wasn't expected to play a part in the great plan of campaign, he disengaged himself from it and fixed his eyes on the corner of the room, letting his mind drift while Gignomai instructed his troops. So the end of the meeting took him by surprise, and the room began to empty in silence. It wasn't long before he was alone with Gignomai, the two of them sitting on the piled-up boxes, like emperors without an empire. He looks shattered, Marzo thought, hardly surprising, bearing in mind the performance he'd just given. But he'd been expecting to see a buzz, a gradual winding down from feverish intensity of feeling, and instead, Gignomai looked as though he'd just spent a day shovelling gravel.

Gignomai turned his head and looked at him. "The trick'll be," he said, "getting down from here without dislodging the boxes. Slow and very careful is my suggestion."

Marzo felt his face twitch but kept the laugh squashed down. He stood up defiantly and walked down the cases as though they were stairs. It'd have been fine if the penultimate crate hadn't skipped out from under his foot and shot him onto his backside on the floor.

A moment later Gignomai was bending over him. "You all right?"

Marzo had jarred his spine and his head was hurting. "Fine."

Gignomai stretched out his hand to help him up. He could have refused to take it. "Thanks," he muttered, as he regained his feet, and Gignomai let go. He had nothing else to say.

"For what it's worth," Gignomai said, "I'm sorry."

"Well." Marzo tried putting his weight on his front foot. His ankle twanged like a harp string. "That's all fine and splendid, but it doesn't change anything, does it?"

"No. Never claimed it did. But I'm sorry." Gignomai was about to walk away, but hesitated. "Furio's fine," he said.

"He'd better be."

"He's my best friend."

Which sounded ridiculous, like Death having a wife and children, and a dog.

Aurelio, formerly smith to the met'Oc, had an extraordinary, inhuman, incredible, unnatural ability to stay awake. Throughout their joint captivity—Furio had no idea how long it lasted; the only unit of time was the Meal, presented at wildly irregular intervals—the last thing he saw before he drifted into sleep and the first thing he saw when he opened his eyes was the old man's insufferable eyes, watching him like an elderly, patient cat at a mousehole. Saying things, shouting them, had absolutely no effect. No matter how he pleaded, yelled or threatened, Aurelio continued to watch over him like an all-seeing, powerless god, and his foot stayed firmly planted on the fragment of saw-blade which was, as far as Furio could see, the only way out of there.

He'd considered other options, but none of them held any realistic prospect of success. Even if he managed to overpower Aurelio (a fight in a darkened room between two men with their hands tied together; he had no idea how that would work, but he had a shrewd suspicion that Aurelio the blacksmith, though more than twice his age, was probably stronger than he was, and almost certainly knew more about fighting dirty), in doing so he'd make a hell of a racket, and that would bring the guards. His only chance was to get the saw-blade out from under Aurelio's foot while the old man was sleeping, and the old man never slept.

Like Marzo and Gignomai's sword, he thought, all I need to get out of here is one miserable artefact.

He was dreaming. In his dream, he was back in the store, except that the store was this room he was confined in, and he was tied to the chair he was sitting in, and the chair was clamped to the floor with brackets Aurelio had made, and Teucer had sewn his lips together, scolding him for being a baby when he winced as the needle sank into his skin, and Gignomai and Uncle Marzo and the old savage, and Aurelio, of course, were all sitting in the dark watching him, waiting for him to die. He tried to struggle against the utterly immovable rope that bound him to the chair when the rope suddenly gave way, and he fell forward onto the floor, and realised he was awake.

Next to him, two inches from his nose, was the toe of Aurelio's boot. Between the boot's sole and the floor, he could see a little grey strip, no more than a sixteenth of an inch wide, metal crystallised by fracture. He craned his neck, keeping his body as still as he could, and saw Aurelio's head lolling forward on his chest, his eyes shut.

Glory and wonder, the old bastard had finally nodded off.

Furio considered the tactical position. If he tried to shift Aurelio's boot off the saw-blade, and he got it wrong and the old man woke up, with Furio's nose less than a finger's length from the toe of his steel-capped boot, the outcome could well be distressing, anything from a broken nose to concussion and a fractured skull. On the other hand, the opportunity was too good to waste.

He wriggled his tied at the wrist hands across the floor until his fingernails were resting against the sewn-down welt of the boot. Then, horribly afraid, he used the fingers of his left hand to raise the boot off the floor, proceeding by slow multiples of the width of a strand of a spider's web. His nerve failed by the time he'd lifted the boot an eighth of an inch, but in theory that ought to be enough. With the tips of his bruised, crushed right-hand fingers, he pecked and scratched at the bit of saw until he felt it come loose from under the old man's foot. He pulled it towards him — it proved to be considerably longer than he'd imagined it would be — then lowered the boot, gentle as a mother finally getting her baby to sleep, until its whole weight was once again resting on the floor.

Victory.

But don't celebrate yet. He inched and edged and squirmed his way back onto his chair, looked quickly to make sure Aurelio was still asleep, then began the difficult, painful and exquisitely awkward job of sawing through the ropes around his wrist with a sliver of saw-blade wedged between the pads of his left and right index fingers.

The saw-blade was largely blunt, and its teeth were widely spaced, just fine for rip-sawing rough lumber into planks, but nearly useless for nibbling through hemp rope. By the time he finally got there and the ends of the severed rope fell away to the floor, he'd ripped open his fingertips on the blade's serrated edge, and gouged several caverns into his wrist and the heels of his hands with the sharp, fractured end.

The sense of achievement, though...

No time for fooling about. He flexed his newly released hands, like a man working his fingers into tight new gloves, then sat in the chair again, shuffled about to find the least uncomfortable position, and drew his hands together in his lap, so that nobody would guess just by looking what he was up to.

He sat motionless and quiet. Aurelio, still asleep, didn't stir.

An infinity of time later, a guard came in with a wooden trencher bearing the usual stale bread and grindstone cheese. Furio made himself wait till the man was close enough for him to smell butter on his breath, then kicked with both heels against the man's shins. The guard yelped, of course, but Furio was out of the chair and squeezing his throat before he had time to draw breath.

Furio had no idea how to kill a man with his bare hands. It turned out to be one of those things you can pick up as you go along.

He hadn't meant to do it. Right up to the point where the struggling stopped, he hadn't even thought about the man as a man at all, just as an obstacle, a really difficult and awkward problem he didn't know how to deal with, a writhing, twisting, horribly strong thing that'd be the death of him if he relaxed his grip for a moment. Then it went still; then it started jerking again; then there was a revolting smell. Then he let go, and the dead man slithered down him, down his chest and his leg, and slid onto the floor like a drunk's discarded clothes. Furio jumped back, horrified by its touch, and realised he'd just killed someone.

Which makes me...

But he didn't have time for that. It occurred to him, as he observed the thing on the floor not moving, that no matter how deeply asleep he'd been, Aurelio must've woken up with all that going on. He turned and looked at the old man, his head still slumped forward, and thought, Oh. Then, to be sure, he stretched out two fingers and touched the neck. No pulse.

Furio had never seen a dead body before.

The most important thing, so essential that it blotted out all other considerations, was to get out of there, before the dead men crowding in on him changed their minds and woke up. The door was ajar. He was through it and out the other side before he knew it, and found himself in blazing, glaring light, stunned and helpless for a

good, long five heartbeats. Then he sprinted across the clearing for
the nearest line of trees. If anybody saw him, they didn't do anything about it. He ducked behind a waist-thick oak and slumped
down onto the wet leaf mould.

I didn't mean to. The skin under his fingers had been warm. It had
been fear and horror that had given him the strength to squeeze. He
knew from experience that he'd probably strained one hand. Neither of them would be any good the next day, when they'd had a
chance to stiffen up; he wouldn't be able to make a fist for a week. *I
didn't mean to,* he told himself. It sounded pathetic. It had been a
stranger, one of Cousin Boulo's crew, who'd gone to give two men
something to eat, who'd died because he was in the way. Some
reason.

Time to go, urged a voice in his head, but he couldn't move. Com-
munications were out between his head and his legs; orders weren't
getting through. It was a bit like the way you feel in bed on a very
cold morning—you know you've got to get up and go outside and
feed the pigs, but you can't quite make yourself do it, even though
you know perfectly well that the longer you leave it, the later you'll
be and the more you'll have to hurry for the rest of the day to make
up. He reasoned, I escaped from there because I've got to get to
town and tell them that Gignomai's gone off his head, he's cooked
up an appalling scheme to start a war. I've escaped and it's cost a
man I didn't even know his life. If I don't go, what an unforgivable
waste that'd be, like killing a chicken and then not eating it.

The opposing view said, Gig had a reason, a bad one, but very
strong. You just killed that man because he was an impediment.

In the distance, he saw two men walk from the foundry to the
store shed. The voices in his head went quiet while he considered:
nobody had any reason to go in the hammer-house, not till it was
time for the prisoners' next meal. Yes, but someone's going to miss
the man I killed. How long, before they find I've gone and come
looking? Can't afford to sit here a moment longer. He stayed where
he was.

Deliberate murder, he thought. The colony had its own way of dealing with that on the extremely rare occasions when it happened. If there were adult males in the victim's family, they took care of it; if not, there were always neighbours. It was always done quickly, with a rope whenever possible, but if the murderer was liable to make a fuss, then anything would do—an axe or a big hammer or a knife. It was generally considered not to be murder, provided you made no effort to conceal the body. There had been two feuds in the colony's history, both long since resolved. People still talked about them: the South Room War and the Sesto War. The general consensus was, nothing like that should ever happen again. And now, of course, they had a mayor, who'd be sure to see justice done.

In spite of everything, the thought of it made him grin.

Not deliberate murder: heroic action, justified force. In an ideal world, he'd have smacked the man on the point of the chin and he'd have gone out like a snuffed candle and woken up an hour or so later with a splitting headache. But instead he'd died. Gignomai, on the other hand, had been at great pains not to hurt anybody. He'd shot bullets into doors, which don't bleed or die. For some reason, Furio got the impression that he'd just lost the argument.

For the first time, he thought about the old man, Aurelio. For the first time, he realised that he hadn't seen the old man eat anything, or drink anything. He'd been so hungry he hadn't bothered to look, and so bored that eating the food was the absolute highlight of each time period. Or maybe he had a weak heart, or perhaps it was a stroke, brought on by confinement, fear, lack of sleep. People don't just die, but, yes, sometimes they do.

I've got to make a move, he told himself.

When he stood up, his legs proved to be treacherously weak. He staggered, just managed to fling his arms round the tree, steadied himself and hung on tight, like a child clinging to its mother. The thought of climbing the rather steep hill was miserably daunting. I didn't mean to, he told himself for the third time, and it sounded even weaker now than before. Legs stiff, one step at a time, he walked away up the hill.

Luso grabbed Gignomai, pinning both his arms, and crushed him till he couldn't breathe. His fingers lost the strength to hold the strap of the bag he was carrying, and he heard it hit the floor with a bump.

"Leave off," he whispered, with the very last wisps of air in his lungs. "You're suff—"

"Sorry." Luso let go and Gignomai reeled backwards, dragging in air. His throat was raw, as it had been the few times in his life when he'd completely exhausted himself. "I'm just so pleased you came," he heard Luso say. He'd have replied if he could, but he had other priorities.

"You've lost weight," Luso went on, clamping a massive hand over his right shoulder. "God, you're a bloody skeleton. When Mother sees you, she'll have a fit."

Indeed, he thought, death by starvation. Enough to upset anybody. "I'm fine," he wheezed. "At least, I was, before you started strangling me."

He looked his brother in the face, and saw happiness, and love. "So," he said, "how's it been around here while I've been away?"

Luso laughed, a brief, intense roar, abruptly cut off. "Guess," he said. "And guess who's had to take the brunt of it. I ought to smash your face in, after what I've been through."

Gignomai grinned feebly. "Father wasn't happy, then."

"You could say that." Luso let go of him, and smiled instead. "And of course it was all my fault. Apparently I was responsible for your moral welfare. He wouldn't even speak to me for a week. For crying out loud, Gig, what the hell made you do a thing like that?"

Gignomai took a step back; it brought him up against the wall. "We can talk about that," he said, "or we could keep our mouths shut and thereby not spoil your wedding. Up to you, really."

"Fine." Luso held up his hand, which meant it was decided. "You're right. You're here now and that's all that matters. Bloody hell, though, it's good to see you again."

"I'm not staying," Gignomai said.

"Whatever. We'll talk about it later."

"No," Gignomai replied. "We'll get it straight right now, or I'm leaving. After the wedding, I go. Agreed?"

"If you say so." You couldn't beat Luso down in an argument like this. It was like fencing with him—you lunged, and he simply wasn't there. "Now, for God's sake, let's find you something to wear, instead of those rags. And a bath. When was the last time you had a bath?"

"This morning, actually."

"You mean you waded about in the river for two minutes. Not the same thing, and you know it."

The hand was on his shoulder again, propelling him out of the room. It was like being a dog on a lead. "So," Luso was saying, "was she worth it?"

"I beg your pardon?"

"The girl. No, don't do the gormless stare, it must've been some girl, in the town. I'm guessing it's Opello's niece, the smart one from Home. Well? Any good?"

"You're an idiot, Luso," he said, and got no further, as his brother accidentally on purpose steered him into a door frame. He banged his chin. It hurt.

"Anyway." Luso guided him through the door. "Let's talk about something really important. Where's my present?"

"What?"

"My wedding present, you half-wit. Even a no-good waste of space like you wouldn't show up to a wedding without bringing a present."

"Actually, I did," Gignomai said, and that was enough to stop Luso in his tracks.

"Did you?"

"Yes," Gignomai said. "It's in the bag I brought, but you made me drop it. If it's broken..."

"Gig, I was just kidding." Luso was looking at him, a curiously subdued, puzzled look. "I never expected—"

"Well, I brought you something. At least," he went on, "it's not for you and it's not mine to give, and I know for a fact you've got one already. But it's the thought that counts."

He could see the thought take shape in Luso's mind, and made a bet with himself: would Luso say it, or just wait? He lost the bet.

"It's the sword," Gignomai said. "You know, the one I—"

"But you sold it to Marzo Opello," Luso said, "to pay for the supplies for your factory."

Gignomai allowed his eyebrows to lift. "You really are going to have to tell me how you know all this stuff, Luso. Anyone would think you've got someone in town keeping an eye on me."

"You stole it back."

Gignomai shrugged. "I reckon the true ownership of that stupid thing is such a grey area, it really doesn't matter any more. I just thought it might be good politics to return it, that's all."

Luso beamed at him. It wasn't the diplomatic smile; it was the real thing. "Thanks," Luso said. "It's appreciated."

"He's been going on about it, I take it."

Luso rolled his eyes. "You could say that, yes. Actually, I can just about put up with the gross betrayal of trust speech, all I do is look solemn and nod occasionally. But the been in our family for seven generations speech is starting to get on my nerves, because anybody with half a clue about swords can tell just by looking at it, it's simply not that old. But what the hell." He grinned, a huge grin, a sunburst. "Best present I could've asked for, little brother. Thanks. Now," he went on, renewing his grip on Gignomai's shoulder, "clothes. And a bath. And then, I guess, we'll have to go and see Father."

Some time later, he closed the door of his old room and lifted the lamp, letting the light soak into the shadows.

The stupid thing was, he'd never really thought of it as his, not when he'd lived and slept there, perched next to the window just before dawn, waiting for the first glow of light so he could carry on reading a stolen book where he'd left off the night before (a lamp or candle would show light under the door; his father had a suspicious and sharply analytical mind). He'd never dared think of it that way, just as he'd never considered his clothes or his shoes to be his own. He'd been issued with them, like a soldier's kit. They were liable to be inspected at any time, without notice, and he would be held to account for loss, damage or neglect. The only property he'd owned had been junk salvaged from the sheds and barns, things Stheno had lost or forgotten about, or couldn't be bothered with, and which Gignomai had lovingly renovated, modified, converted to his own use: a small knife slowly, painfully ground out of a worn-out file; a pair of sacking leggings to keep mud off his trousers; a derelict coat thrown over the harrow to keep off the damp, which he'd surreptitiously worn for a year until Father saw him through the window and ordered the offending item confiscated and burnt. As a boy he'd always thought of Furio as fabulously, obscenely rich, and of his house as a sort of royal treasury.

His room, accordingly, shouldn't have hurt. The memories should have been resentments, further arguments to support his case. It shouldn't have felt, it had no right to feel, like home. Force of habit, he told himself. Perhaps a released prisoner would get a little misty-eyed, revisiting his old cell. For the room to argue that he belonged here was an insult. He lowered the lamp a little to cast light on the small, straight chair in the corner. His sister used to sit there, when he was small, when she heard him crying in the night and came to shut him up before he woke Father, to tell him stories, to make him laugh. He summoned her, chief witness for the prosecution, and dutifully she came, but she was faint, a forced recollection of the memory of her that had haunted him lying in that bed, looking at those rafters. The truth was, she'd died too long ago, and he'd been too young at the time. He let her go, no further questions, in case the other side found out she was an unreliable witness.

He put down the lamp and sat on the bed. It was, he remembered (he hadn't given it any thought since he'd left) a moot point whether his sleepless nights here had had more to do with the lumpy, compacted mattress than the unquiet spirit of his murdered sister. Same thing, in a way: the mattress woke him up, the ghost kept him from getting back to sleep. Query, therefore, whether a comfortable bed would have made a difference, back then, when he was still red-hot under the hammer and capable of taking a shape.

But, he reflected, easing off one savagely uncomfortable borrowed shoe, he'd learned a thing or two since then. This room wasn't the forge any more, and the bed was too lumpy for an anvil. Just because the memory was no longer sharp didn't mean it had never happened. The chair in the corner was a scar, to mark the place where the wound had been.

Stupid, to let his old room upset him so much, when he'd made himself so cold and hard that the hammer glanced off and the file skidded. Yet again, his mind turned back to what the crazy old savage had said, about the quaint beliefs of his misguided people. The old fool had known all that stuff was mere nonsense, but had been shocked and dismayed when the snapping-hen disproved it. Why? he wondered. Why would the old man have minded being proved right, after a lifetime of being considered insane for trying to tell people the truth? He frowned, aware that he'd missed the point. Look at it rationally, he told himself. One man says one thing, everybody else believes otherwise. What possible value can there be in a truth that chooses to manifest itself to one outsider only? Justice, of course, doesn't work that way. As far as justice is concerned, truth is defined as the shared opinion of the majority of twelve jurors, and that criterion is reliable enough to hang people by. Therefore, for the purposes of a court of law, the old man was crazy and the others were right, at least until Gignomai met'Oc shot a goat.

But Gignomai met'Oc is a notorious deceiver, plotter, contriver and traitor, so his evidence can't carry too much weight. Disregard his evidence, and the case collapses. Therefore, the old man must be wrong and the accepted view must prevail; therefore, the savages share the country with images from the past and the future but not the present, with people who aren't really there at all. Imaginary friends.

Such as my sister, Gignomai thought, for whom I seek to achieve justice (a jury of one). She's still here, in that chair, and I'm still here, in the bed, which accounts for my discomfort here, being torn in half between the present and the past, one place, two times. A touch on the trigger, the fall of the hammer, makes no difference really. She'll always be here, no matter what I do, and all I can reasonably expect to achieve is to disturb the peace.

So, which is it? he demanded of himself, justice, revenge, spite, a blood sacrifice to appease the angry spirit of his imaginary friend? Yes, he replied.

He put the shoe back on. It pressed on his instep and cut into his heel.

Gignomai had drawn a map, a remarkably accurate one. Even so, finding the place wasn't easy. They walked right past it three times, staring up at the hole in the sheer cliff face without seeing it, until the sun came out for a moment and cast a faint shadow on a crease in the rock, faint and alluring as make-up under a woman's eye.

They stood and considered it for a while. The advance party had brought a long ladder, and half a dozen scaffolding poles, rope and an assortment of tools, loaded on a couple of donkey carts, along with packed lunches and a small barrel of cider, and the billhooks, still in the crate. They looked as if they were off to mend someone's roof.

Needless to say, the ladder was just too short, so they unhitched the donkey from one of the carts and stood the ladder on the bed, its feet secured by wooden battens nailed to the floor. Nobody wanted to be the first to go up.

"Don't look at me," Marzo said. "I'm too fat, for one thing."

No arguing with something so self-evidently true. Eventually, the

youngest Fasenna shrugged his shoulders and scrambled onto the
cart. They handed him a trowel and a hoe with the shaft cut down
to ten inches, and he began to climb. Nobody could bear to watch as
he disappeared into the hole, dragging himself up by his hands and
elbows, his feet dangling uselessly, so that he looked like a dead
mouse in a cat's mouth.

Marzo was thinking about Gignomai's description of his escape.
As far as he could remember, Gignomai had slithered down a lot of
the way, because of the steepness of the gradient. Climbing up would
be an entirely different proposition, not so much danger of getting
hopelessly wedged, of course, and young Fasenna had the advantage
of knowing that the shaft really did go all the way through.

After a disturbingly long time, during which there was nothing at
all to see, Fasenna's toes poked out of the hole, then his legs, waving
wildly, feeling for the top rung of the ladder. When at last he got
down, his hands and face were a horrible mess of grazes and cuts.

"Can't cut it," he said, feebly brandishing the bent hoe; he'd abandoned the trowel. "Rock. Hammer and a cold chisel."

Another uncomfortable silence. Then Ilio Jacolo, who was a bit of
a stonemason when he needed the money, muttered, "Oh, for crying
out loud," pulled a lump hammer and three chisels out of the tool
bag, and slowly climbed up out of sight. They couldn't see him,
either, but at least they could hear the soft, woodpecker taps, and
from time to time, gravel and small stones dropped out of the hole
and rattled on the bed of the cart.

"Does he have to make so much noise?" Rasso demanded, loudly.
"If we can hear it, so can they."

"Gignomai said they'd all be at the house," Marzo replied.

"Yes, but what if he's wrong?"

Marzo shrugged. "Then we're in trouble."

Jacolo came down eventually, brown with stone-dust with a gleam
of red showing through on his skinned knuckles, turning the dust to
mud. "Just give me a while," he said, and flopped on the ground, his
back to the cart wheel, and fell asleep.

Marzo looked round. He really didn't want to be the man who gave the orders, but someone had to do it; the supply of volunteers had dried up completely. "What we need," he said, giving the Grado twins a long, thoughtful stare, "is someone who's used to working up ladders."

The Grado twins were the colony's best thatchers, only using their slender, miserable tongue of land between the river and the marshes to grow reed. They took it better than he'd anticipated. Also, Marzo noted with approval, they'd brought their gloves.

Piro Grado went first, with Gelerio close on his heels. They were short, slim men, with forearms like legs, used to working fast because they were paid by the job, not the hour. Chips and stones rattled on the cart-bed like hail, and the rest of the company began to relax, the way you do when finally someone who knows what he's doing takes charge and gets on with it. Everybody except Marzo, of course. He was watching the sun. The simple fact was that, when Gignomai drew up the plan, he seriously underestimated how long it'd take to widen the hole enough for the company to get through. Since Marzo didn't actually know what Gignomai had in mind—you leave that side of things to me, he'd said, and they'd been delighted to let it go at that—he couldn't tell what ill-effects the delay would have: whether the worst of it would be Gignomai waiting impatiently for them on the doorstep, tapping his foot, or whether they'd all end up walking into a lethal trap. He wondered, as mayor, if it was his duty to share his misgivings with his fellow citizens, but decided against it. One thing he was absolutely sure about: if they gave up now and went home, they'd never come back and try again, not if Luso and a thousand armed savages burnt a farm a day and nailed their victims' heads to every tree in the colony. And the job had to be done; he knew that now—he believed. Cattle raids and bullets in doors were one thing. People were used to putting up with that sort of nuisance, just as they were used to rooks trampling down the barley and the water-troughs freezing over in winter. But the savages—that was, of course, a different matter entirely. Anybody insanely irresponsible enough to unleash a force that powerful had to be stopped and put down.

Piro Grado's head appeared in the hole, upside down. "We're through," he called out. (How the hell was he doing that? Must be hanging by his toes, like a bat.) "We've cut steps where it's too steep to crawl. We're going on ahead."

There was a moment of shocked stillness, as sixty men who'd secretly believed the passage would prove impassable and the mission would be called off were suddenly faced with the prospect of going through with it after all. Piro's head had already vanished back up the hole. Nobody wanted to go up the ladder, but everybody knew they couldn't just abandon the Grado boys. There was still, of course, the awkward matter of who was going to go up first. Marzo was just about to talk himself into believing it had to be him when Gimao the chandler, who'd had unnaturally little to say for himself so far, sang out, "Here goes, then," and scampered up the ladder like a twelve-year-old picking apples. Marzo would've been at a loss to know what to make of it if he hadn't met Gimao's eye, as he stooped to pick a billhook out of the crate. Sheer blind terror, the sort that makes you do the thing that's freezing you to the marrow, just so it'll be over and done with.

The thing is, Marzo thought, we're supposed to be the aggressors. We shouldn't be terrified like this, we're predators, we're the ones starting the fight. Suddenly he grinned, and people standing next to him must have wondered what the joke was. I don't feel the slightest bit like a predator, Marzo thought. I couldn't be Luso met'Oc if I practised for fifty years.

They were scrambling up the ladder now, grimly quiet, concentrating on what they were doing, and a whole new motivation had taken hold of them, the desperate urge not to show themselves up in front of their neighbours and friends. Seeing the looks on their faces, Marzo understood. All the causes and dangers and injustices in the world wouldn't be enough to force a civilian up a ladder into a narrow tunnel leading to a war, not even if the alternative was fire in the night and the charred bones of their children in the ashes in the morning. But fear of shame would be enough to make them do anything, and that trigger had been pulled as soon as Piro Grado had told them he was going on ahead. Ridiculous, Marzo couldn't help thinking. Completely stupid, he thought, as he put his foot on the first rung of the ladder and hoped like hell that nobody could see he was shivering.

Furio limped into town, too preoccupied to wonder why there was nobody about in the middle of the day, and headed straight for the store. He found Teucer in the main room. She'd cleared everything off the long table, which she'd dragged into the middle of the room. She was sharpening a filleting-knife on a fine whetstone.

"There you are," she said. "You missed the meeting."

"What are you doing?" he asked.

"Getting ready," she replied.

She'd pulled out another, smaller table. It was neatly piled with rolled-up strips of cloth, tin basins, various incongruous tools— pliers, a hacksaw, a spread-out roll of needles. "What's all this junk for?" he asked.

"Like I said," she told him, "I'm getting ready."

And three books: two closed, the third open and face down, to mark the place if she needed it in a hurry. "What's going on?" he asked.

"You don't know."

"If I knew…"

She frowned. Such inefficiency. "Uncle Marzo and Gignomai and a load of other people have gone to fight the met'Oc," she said. "I'm not entirely sure why, they wouldn't let me listen. I think it's because the met'Oc have given guns to the savages so they can attack us."

He stared at her. "Gignomai—"

"He made a speech," Teucer said. "He said something about his sister, but I couldn't hear enough to make any sense of it. Anyway, they've all gone off, so I thought I'd better make a few preparations, in case anybody gets hurt." There was a sort of wild hope under her flat, calm voice that turned his stomach. After all, what better chance could she possibly ask for?

"When did they leave?" Furio asked.

She shrugged. "Five hours ago, more or less. They've gone to the Tabletop. They took a couple of carts full of tools and Uncle's long ladder. I'm guessing Gignomai's going to show them the place where he got out, when he ran away."

Furio stood perfectly still. I have no idea what I'm supposed to do now, he thought. Five hours. How long would it take him to run to the Tabletop? Not that he was capable of running that far; he'd be lucky to make it at a slow hobble. But there were horses in the livery. Of course, Rasso would most likely have joined the posse, so the livery would be closed for business, so he'd have to break in and steal a horse, which was against the law. "Are you going after them?" he heard Teucer say. It was one of her flat questions; she might just as well have been asking him what he fancied for dinner.

"I don't know," Furio replied. "I mean, what use would I be?"

"Gignomai's your friend. I'd have thought you'd have wanted to help him."

No point in even starting to explain. "Do you happen to know if Rasso was with them? You know, at the livery."

"I heard his voice," Teucer said, "at the meeting. So presumably yes. Why?"

She'd finished with the oilstone and was stropping the blade on one of Uncle Marzo's belts. You'd need the finest possible edge for surgery. He shivered. "Thanks," he said, and made for the door.

"You've hurt your ankle," she called after him. "Want me to take a look at it?"

He fled without answering and hobbled and skipped as quickly as he could down the street to the corner, where the livery stood. The main gate was closed and the bar was down, but there was no padlock in the hasp. No point stealing a horse in the colony, where everybody knew every horse, pony, donkey and mule by sight, along with who owned it. He chose a short-legged chestnut cob, purely because it was closer to the ground than any of the other horses, so less far to fall. He knew how to tack up a carthorse, but he'd never put on a saddle before. He was a lousy rider at the best of times.

He led it outside, lined it up with the mounting-block, climbed the two short steps and put his foot in the stirrup. "Nice horse," he said.

The first ten yards were fine, then the saddle slipped. He dismounted, and tightened the girth, which had been plenty tight when he'd put the saddle on. Bloody thing must've been holding its breath, he rationalised. He led it back to the block and tried again. Gripping the pommel of the saddle with the fingers of both hands, he nudged firmly with his heels. The horse carried on ambling, like a prosperous citizen taking a turn round the square after dinner. He kicked harder, and harder still. The horse broke into a grudging trot, which threatened to hammer his spine into his head like a nail.

The earliest version of the met'Oc wedding ceremony to survive dates from the reign of the Sixth Emperor. Inscribed on four bronze shields installed on the central pillar of the north transept of the New Temple, they are largely illegible on account of corrosion and the extremely archaic script in which they are written, but a transcript made in the fifteenth year of the Twenty-First Emperor survives in the archives of the Studium. The version generally used, up to the family's exile in the ninth year of the Fortieth Emperor, was the Seventh Revision, compiled on the orders of Lambanomai met'Oc on the occasion of his eldest son's wedding to Anser, youngest daughter of the Nineteenth Emperor in the last year of his reign. The Seventh Revision requires that the bride be brought in procession from her father's house, preceded by twelve Knights of Equity on white horses and accompanied by ninety halbardiers, who will in due course comprise her honour guard during her first three years of married life. The groom meets her on the steps of the White Temple, escorted by the Senate and the heads of the six Departments in military dress and representatives of the Studium, the Hospital and the three Orders Martial. The bride is permitted to wear the customary costume of her family, but the groom must be dressed in his formal regalia as Count of the Stables and Chaplain Domestic. The ceremony is conducted by the City Patriarch, assisted by the Provost of the White Temple, the bride's family chaplain and the met'Oc Chaplain-General. After the ceremony it is optional, but customary, for the groom's honour guard to distribute gold angels, struck with the groom's head on the obverse and the bride's on the reverse, to the crowds in Temple Square. These coins are recognised as legal tender by a special Act of Senate.

The met'Oc in exile used the Ninth, or Emergency, Revision for the wedding of Lusomai met'Oc. Dating from the sixth year of the Twenty-Second Emperor, it was compiled by government draughtsmen on the orders of the Senate to facilitate the wedding of Thanomai met'Oc to his cousin Passer as he lay dying in his tent after the Battle of the Field of Roses, thereby ensuring the smooth transition of the family honours and properties to Passer's brother, Lanthanomai, who served as Steward Regent until Thanomai's son by his previous marriage came of age. Since the Ninth Revision, of necessity, provided for a morganatic marriage, the terms were amended for Phainomai's wedding. Copies of the amendment were sent to the Senate for ratification, but no reply was ever received.

In the third book of his *Commentaries on the House Law of the met'Oc*, a copy of which, in his own hand, was lodged by met'Oc sympathisers in the Studium archives at some point before his death, Phainomai met'Oc came to the conclusion that the validity of the Ninth Revision depended on the groom being entitled to the status of *sun hoplois*—that is to say, on active service as a commander of forces in the field, and therefore exempt from the formal requirements of certain aspects of matrimonial, property and testamentary law. Phainomai argued that the second son of the met'Oc in exile was, by virtue of his position as House Constable, inherently and permanently *sun hoplois* until such time as his elder brother succeeded to the family honours, maintaining that the perilous nature of the met'Oc's existence, surrounded on all sides by potentially hostile neighbours, meant that the Constable's service was, in theory and often in practice, continuously active. Nevertheless, quite possibly under pressure from Boulomai met'Ousa to ensure the irreproachable legitimacy of the marriage, Phainomai formally invested Lusomai met'Oc with an active commission against the colonists and the savages before allowing the bride to be admitted to the Great Hall for the public part of the ceremony.

To reflect this, the full-strength house garrison paraded in the courtyard throughout the ceremony. Lusomai protested about this, expressing grave concern about leaving the Gates and Doorstep unguarded. His father overruled him, citing the case of Coptomai met'Oc in the reign of the Fourteenth Emperor, whose commission in the Fifth Vesani War was retrospectively invalidated because two regiments of his army were not present in the encampment when Coptomai assumed his command. Phainomai's interpretation was supported by Boulomai met'Ousa, referring to the practice of his own family, and Gignomai met'Oc, who also drew attention to the fourth section of the *Dispensations*, concerning commencement and transfer of commands. Lusomai gave way with his customary good grace, and ordered the muster of the garrison.

He had to stand on the raised platform at the far end of the Hall, next to Stheno and Boulo. He could see the back of Luso's head, and beyond that the faces of the two dozen or so farmhands and servants standing on either side of the strip of faded blue carpet along which the bride would walk. Off to the left, Father was waiting in the cheese store to make his grand entrance. He saw his mother in the front row. They'd let her have a chair to sit in. He couldn't see from where he was standing, but he doubted the chair legs were fastened to the floor.

Someone had made an effort. The sconces in the walls (no longer used; they made do with tallow candles these days) were draped with swathes of ivy and fir branches. Someone had knotted a rope of wild roses, twenty feet long, and looped it through the crossbeams of the roof, too high to be properly seen unless you stood with your head right back. It looked ridiculous and faintly sad, like children dressing up as people from history, using their imaginations but having to make do with what they could find in the hedgerows or the dressing-up basket.

His mother was staring at her feet. He hadn't seen her for months. If she'd looked up at him, it must've been when he was looking the other way. Stheno's boots were black and shiny with the stuff they used for blacking the fire-irons. He only had the one pair, but they'd come up really well. As for Boulomai, he looked like the rich kid at the party who doesn't fit in. His parents have had a proper costume made for him, while all the other kids are wearing painted paper armour and old sheets. There were oil-stains on his sash where a snapping-hen pistol usually rested, but he hadn't felt the need to come armed to his sister's wedding. He was picking at the buttons on his tunic sleeve.

"Hello, Cousin Boulo," Gignomai said quietly.

"Gignomai." Boulo frowned, looking straight ahead. "Thanks for coming back. I know how much it means to your brother."

"Well." Gignomai glanced sideways at him. Less to Cousin Boulo than meets the eye. "This is the sort of occasion when the whole family needs to be together. It's just a shame my sister couldn't be here."

"I didn't know you had a sister."

"She's away at school," Gignomai said, "back Home, under a false name. That's why we don't talk about her in front of strangers. But you're family. I guess the rule doesn't apply." He was about to add, "Ask Luso about her; he's got lots of stories," but bit the words back. No point, and no need. Forgive me, he mouthed silently, as the nail forgives the hammer. But Boulo was still looking dead ahead, and didn't notice.

The Ninth Revision was silent on the subject of appropriate music, so Father had given orders for the house musician to play a solemn air on the rebec until the arrival of the bride, at which point he was to strike up the met'Oc march. This was his debut performance (he usually worked for Stheno, doing odd jobs) and he was out of practice, or just not very good. The rebec was two hundred years old and had belonged to an emperor's daughter; its soundbox was cracked and two of the strings had gone soft.

I must watch all this, Gignomai told himself, and make sure I remember. This time tomorrow, I'll be the only one left, and I have a duty to posterity to bear witness.

The double doors at the far end of the hall opened, and the bride came through. At least, there was a figure dressed in a great swathe of material, and he assumed she was in there somewhere. Gignomai frowned slightly. He knew the contents of every trunk and box in the store rooms, the sculleries and the barns. He'd have noticed enough fine white silk to cover a hay-rick. She'd brought it with her, then, her wedding dress, and presumably not just on the off-chance. She looked lonely and barely human pacing slowly up the Hall. He guessed she was taking her time so as not to tread on the trailing excess of hem and end up flat on her face. It could just as easily have been a bear under all that veil, but nobody here had that sort of sense of humour.

Eventually she halted, like a ship drifting into harbour on a flat wind. Beside him Stheno coughed loudly, whereupon the cheese-store door opened and Father came out. He was an extraordinary sight, in the full formal court dress of an Elector of the Empire, complete with brocaded gown, wig and sword. He walked painfully, taking short steps. The costume was his father's, and Phainomai was several sizes bigger. He looked like a man wearing his wife's clothes for a bet.

Even in the Emergency Revision, the words of the ceremony were in the old language. There was a speech to begin with, a general address that lasted for as long as it takes to pluck a chicken. Then Luso was allowed to take two steps forward. He and Pasi knew their lines reasonably well, though since nobody in the room except

Father could understand what they were saying, it didn't matter terribly much. Cousin Boulo kept his eyes tight shut until the last response had been given, then breathed a long sigh, which Gignomai assumed was relief. He knew how he felt.

Next came the reading of the settlement, and Gignomai stood up a little straighter, paying close attention. As her dowry, Pasi brought with her substantial estates in the northern and eastern provinces, together with the rents of three market towns and the benefit of four advowsons, and a number of turnpike roads, a merchant ship and a share in a mercantile consortium, a street of shops and two inns in the City. In return, the met'Oc settled on her a whole county in the southern province, a bell foundry, the benefit of government contracts in perpetuity to supply lumber, rope and chain to the Navy, the met'Oc town house and, very much an afterthought, all honours and possessions currently enjoyed by the met'Oc overseas. The deed was signed by Father, Luso and Pasi (a tiny pink hand struggled out of the cloth to take the pen), and sealed by Father with the Great Seal, after three goes at getting the wax to melt.

That's it, Gignomai thought, that's the fall of the hammer: going once, going twice, sold and delivered. He felt an unsettling flow of strength seep into his arms and legs, as though a lever had been thrown to connect him to the drive-shaft. He'd lost track of the time, but it didn't really matter. If they had to wait, so what?

His original plan had simply been to pretend to pass out, but he'd decided against it. Father was quite capable of leaving him lying there until the ceremony was over. So much simpler just to walk out, quickly, stepping in front of Boulo rather than Stheno, since his brother might make a grab and stop him. Even so, it proved extraordinarily difficult to make himself do it. You'll be in so much trouble later, yelled every instinct he had. But there wouldn't be a later. He took the first step, and the rest followed. He saw Father look round at him with murderous fury on his face; Boulo even took a step back to let him pass. Luso, the only one who might conceivably have guessed, was mercifully preoccupied.

Out through the side door into the boot-and-hat room, through that and into fresh air. The first thing he did was glance up at the sun, but it was masked in cloud. He had no idea what the time was. He looked back to make sure nobody was following him, then walked quickly across the stable yard, pushed open the rickety gate and broke into a run.

Even then he couldn't help grinning, thinking of himself as a boy, slipping out to go and meet his common friend from town. Different friends would be waiting for him this time, but it hardly signified. He was glad there wasn't enough time for him to linger and take a last look, which he knew he would have done, had it been possible.

He'd drawn them a map, but he wasn't expecting them actually to be there. He was, therefore, pleasantly surprised to see them—they were doing their best to keep out of sight, but they stood out like blood on snow—though the incongruity of their presence offended him before he'd had a chance to adjust his attitude. They had no right to be here; trespassers on private land. That's all right, he told himself firmly, they're with me. They're my guests.

"What the hell took you so—?"

"Quiet," he snapped, and whoever it was, someone he didn't recognise, fell silent as abruptly as though he'd had his throat cut. "The wedding's in full swing, they're all inside except the garrison, and they're standing to in the courtyard."

"That's not what you said," Rasso interrupted; he was terrified. "You said they'd all be in the house. We can't—"

Gignomai rolled his eyes. "Can't you read a simple map? The courtyard's inside the main wall. The hall's right next to the wall. We can secure all three doors of the hall without anyone in the courtyard noticing, and we'll block the yard gate so the garrison won't be able to get through. They'll just have to stand there and watch; they won't be able to do a thing." He turned his head and looked for Marzo, and found him. "You brought the stuff I told you?"

Marzo nodded. "Hammers, nails, a couple of saws. That's what you said," he added. "Isn't it?"

"That's fine." Gignomai stopped to take a deep breath, like a diver who expects to be under for a dangerously long time. "Right," he said, "follow me."

He led them back the way he'd just come, and it felt all wrong. They were all scared half to death, as though he was leading them out of the fire and the slaughter, not in to start it. Luso'd wet himself laughing if he could see them, he thought. Some army. But there was nobody about, not in the home meadow, not in the stableyard. They filled the yard; there was barely enough room for them all. He thought what Luso would be able to achieve with his hanger, among so many frightened men, so tightly packed together. He didn't really care, but the thought disturbed him.

"All right," he said. "This is the side door, ten of you here, there's planks and battens in the woodshed just over there. Ten of you round that side, you'll find the kitchen door. You four, shoot the bolts on the yard gates, then get back here. The rest of you with me, round the front."

They emptied the woodshed of suitable lumber and divided up into their three contingents. Gignomai didn't look back. He'd put Heddo in charge of the kitchen door and Rasso (yes, but what harm could he do?) would deal with the side. He led his party, forty strong, with Marzo right behind him trying to keep up, round the corner to the main gate.

"Double doors," he said, "so we'll need at least a ten-foot plank." He chose one from the selection they offered him, and took a hammer and a fistful of long nails, his own make, from the factory. "Soon as we start hammering they're going to realise something's going on, so we need to wedge the door first. It opens outwards, so there's no problem. Then we just get the nails in as quick as we can, and that's the job done."

He looked at them, and although they were white with fear, he could see they believed him. None of them had taken the trouble to look up and see the great first-floor bow window, the only weak point in his plan. He herded his party closer together. If anyone dropped anything out of the window it'd hit someone, but they wouldn't be able to jump out and expect to survive. That was the best he could do.

He chose a good solid fence post and wedged it under the head-sized iron knocker on the left door. On the right side he had to make do with jamming a section of rafter under the bottom edge of the hinge. Shouldn't matter. It'd take Luso a second or two to figure out what the hammering meant, and six, seven more seconds to run to the door. Plenty of time to knock in a couple of nails.

He put one nail in his mouth, the other stayed between the fingers of his left hand. With his right, he lifted the hammer. He nodded, and two men lifted the inch-thick oak plank and presented it level across the door, just above the knocker. He touched the point of the nail lightly to the wood and swung the hammer.

The sound of the blow was like Luso's gun going off in the early morning, lifting the crows out of the trees, hitting the edge of the wood and bouncing back. He hit hard, counting the seconds under his breath. One nail home. He spat the other one into his hand, fumbled it, positioned it and hammered. He paused for a moment, just long enough to hear hammer blows from the other side of the house. Then he drove in four more nails, two each side, as easily as if he'd been doing this sort of thing all his life.

"Finish up," he snapped, pushing the hammer at the man standing next to him. "Three more planks." As he turned away, he heard the thump of a fist on the other side of the door. They'd be shoulder-charging it in a moment or so, but the plank was in and should hold. He strolled across the yard, pausing to pick up a bit of stick from the woodshed, to the small hay barn. Plenty of loose straw on the floor. He picked up a fat handful and wrapped it carefully, tightly round the stick.

Father had always been mortified that the met'Oc should live in a thatched house. His father had tried to make tiles, or have tiles made, but the river clay wasn't the right sort. It cracked when you fired it. Father had had his eye on the slate beds down by the coast

for many years, but obtaining enough slate would have meant trading with the colonists. The house stayed thatched.

Gignomai had stolen a tinderbox from the kitchens rather than
use his own, which had come from Marzo's store and didn't work
very well. He watched the spark drop into the moss and blew on it
gently, like a boy blowing in a girl's ear. Such a little thing, a spark,
like an idea. He watched it bud and flower, then touched the straw to
it and wandered back to the gate.

"What are you doing?" someone asked. He didn't answer. He felt
and savoured the moment as it sank in, as they figured it out for
themselves, were properly horrified, and did nothing.

He fancied he could hear Luso's voice, but it was hard to tell
over the noise of the hammers and the thump of bodies slamming
against the other side of the door. It was shaking with every impact,
but the met'Oc had built their doors of ply, to resist axes, sledge-
hammers and battering-rams. It was the posts wedged against the
doors rather than the planks nailed across them that were taking,
and resisting, the strain. Gignomai was surprised at that, but it all
came to the same thing. He walked backwards a few steps until he
could see the top ridge of the roof. Then he swung the torch back
and threw it as hard as he could.

It was better this way, he thought. He had no particular interest in
watching them die, no furious need to taunt or harangue them, to
let them know how he felt. He was quite content to communicate
with them purely through fire with the minimum possible contact.
When it was all over, there'd be nothing left to speak of, just anony-
mous bones that could just as easily be some farm worker as his
brothers or parents. It'd be like coming home from a long journey to
find your family had all died while you were away—upsetting, but
all over. Gignomai had no time for people who enjoyed revelling in
their emotions.

The torch pitched just short of the top ridge, rolled a little way
and came to rest. It flickered, for a moment Gignomai thought it was
going to go out, but the thatch all around it began to smoke, and

then to burn. He'd chosen his spot with care, directly over the north wall of the library. As soon as it burned through, fire would fall on Father's desk, where there were always loose papers, and on the old, dry books of genealogy, history, house law. The heat would shatter the windows, letting in the brisk southerly breeze. The polished oak floor, fanned by the crossdraught, would burn through and drop floorboards and rafters into the hall below, while the fire would carry down through the cricks and beams of the house and collapse the walls. By then, of course, the smoke would have—

"Just a moment," someone was saying. "The women and the farm hands. How're they going to get out?"

He looked past the face that had just spoken. They were all looking at him. "They can't," he said.

"But that's—" The speaker, someone he knew by sight from over East Reach, had a stunned look on his face. "You can't do that. It's murder."

Gignomai did Luso's shrug, all lazy shoulders and straight back. "Fine," he said. "If that bothers you, you can pry off those planks and pull out the props. Go on, there's still time." He waited. Nobody moved. "Of course," he went on, "you'll have to apologise to my brother for spoiling his wedding, and he might not be in a mood to listen. But if it bothers you that much, go ahead."

Nobody moved. Gignomai remembered nobody moving the first time, when Father had his daughter tied to a chair. They'd known something bad was about to happen, the moment had come and passed and moved on, but nobody could quite bring themselves to be the first to speak, and the moment moved on a little more as Father beckoned to the nurse and she stepped forward with the needle and thread, and nobody moved then either, or spoke. Now, this time, he looked round for somebody to move, or say something. They all looked at him, but nobody said anything or did anything, and the only sound was the crackle of burning straw and the thumping of a fist on the inside. He tried to remember if Father had said anything. He rather thought not, and so decided to say nothing himself. The moments came and went and moved on, and Gignomai couldn't help thinking, Like Father, like son. Same act, different reason, same outcome. At least I said something this time, he comforted himself. It's them standing still and quiet while the thatch burns. Very clearly he could see inside their minds: any moment now, someone else would do something or say something, any moment now they'll rip down the planks and let those people out of there, and the met'Oc would come tumbling out, coughing and blind, weak as baby rats in a nest, and we'll take away their weapons and tell them not to do it again, and they'll have learned their lesson and everything will be fine. There's still time (there had still been time, right up to the time she died, and then there was no time at all) for someone to do something, but not me. Not me standing up to the man in charge, the last of the met'Oc, and getting my throat cut for it.

He heard the crack of timber. Soon the first burning beam would fall on the paper.

To take his mind off the passage of time, he considered the doors. Six planks had been nailed across, a fistful of nails each side. But Luso was in there, a clever, strong, resourceful man. "Get another half-dozen planks and nail them longwise," he said. "Better safe than sorry."

Four men jumped to it. They looked happy to be doing something, rather than just standing around. The man who'd spoken earlier came close. He was short, and Gignomai had to lean forward to hear him, because for some reason he was whispering, "I thought we'd light the thatch and just guard the doors," the short man said, "and as they came running out—well, we'd let the women and the farm hands go."

Gignomai nodded gravely. "And cut down the met'Oc with our billhooks."

The short man didn't answer. His face was twisted with fear and something else—shame, Gignomai guessed. "I didn't think we were going to kill *all* of them."

"All right," Gignomai said. "We can do it that way if you want, there's still time. You want to prise off the planks, be my guest. You may need to talk it over with the others, but I won't stop you."

The short man stared at him as though he'd spoken to someone he thought he knew, who had turned out to be the Angel of Death in a big, floppy hood. "Sure?" Gignomai said. "I mean it. You go right ahead and take down the planks and let Luso out, and I promise I won't interfere."

The short man took a long step backwards, and Gignomai lost sight of his face in the crowd. One man, he thought, and too scared when it came to it, but better than us. Not better enough, though. The four men came back with more planks, and a bucket of rusty nails they'd found on the windowledge. Those who had hammers kept themselves busy for quite some time.

Smoke, Gignomai thought. In a house fire it's the smoke that kills everyone. It's a well-known fact. Must be filling up by now. Maybe they were all dead already. He smiled, thinking of the first time Stheno had tried to make charcoal. He had been too impatient, and kept pulling the rick apart to see what was happening inside, with the result that the air got in and burned most of the wood to ash. He wasn't about to make the same mistake. In fact, there wasn't any reason why they should hang around waiting. It made much more sense if they all went home and came back in the morning.

He heard a woman scream. He had to think for a moment before he could place the voice: Dorper, she worked in the kitchen; a big mound of a woman who talked in grunts; she'd run away from the colony twelve years ago because her husband beat her up. He speculated whether, if he could talk to Luso, maybe they could arrange something, a truce, safe passage for the women, at least. Just the sort of thing Luso might agree to, given how marinaded in honour and proper conduct he'd been all his life. But it was his parents and brother in there, in that furnace with him, and his wife. Honour might just slip his mind at the sight of a door opening. Besides, Dorper worked in the kitchen. She could've smuggled out a few crusts of bread in her sleeves or her apron pocket, or used a small paring-knife to cut through his sister's stitches. He apologised to her under his breath, but that was as far as he was prepared to go.

He heard the glass in the bow window above his head shatter. As he lifted his head to look, he saw a blur, something falling, a man. He should have broken his neck, but he landed with his heels on young Fasenna's shoulders. Fasenna crumpled, going down like a nail driven into wood by a hammer. The jumper stood up, and some fool lifted a billhook at him. With a movement so smooth you'd have sworn they'd rehearsed it together for hours, the jumper twisted the billhook out of the man's hands, took a neat step back and swung at the fool's knee. There was a sound like someone driving in a fence post, then a crack as the jumper twisted on the hook handle to free the blade, which had sunk two inches into the fool's kneecap. The fool dropped, his mouth moving, both hands round his knee. He twisted on the ground like a landed fish. Nobody else moved, of course.

"Luso?" Gignomai said.

The jumper took a pace sideways and backwards, fencer's foot-work. His head was bald and bright red, and his face was more or less melted away, but he wore burnt rags that had once been Luso's wedding costume. His boots were still smoking. Gignomai knew him by his size, the remains of the clothes and his footwork. He shortened his grip on the billhook shaft and, like a shape-shifter in a fairy tale, became the low guard for polearms, straight out of the coaching manual.

Gignomai glanced past him, afraid that someone might be stupid enough to try and stab Luso in the back. Such an attempt, he knew, would not end well for the attacker. But the half circle of colonists standing well out of Luso's reach were quite still, all desperately hoping that the eyes in the back of Lusomai met'Oc's head wouldn't notice them so long as they didn't move. Luso shifted his guard from low to middle. His left eye was opaque and half closed.

"What're you going to do, Luso?" Gignomai asked. "Are you going to kill us all?"

(Which he could, of course. He had the strength and the skill, and the colonists were far too scared to fight, too frozen to run. There were technical exercises in Luso's books that covered the single-handed slaughter of a section, a platoon, a company. The skill, according to the books, lay in achieving the slaughter using the minimum number of handstrokes.)

Then Luso spoke. He said, "Gig? Are you all right?"

Coming from a man half burned away, it was a ludicrous thing to say. "I'm fine, Luso," he replied.

"You got out in time."

"Sure." Gignomai couldn't feel scared any more. He realised, with a deep, sick feeling, that Luso had been worried about him; hadn't yet figured it out. "I got out before the fire started. I started the fire."

Luso shivered, but it wasn't the pain. "Don't say that, Gig. Not funny."

"I started the fire." He said it like a child almost, like a child taunting his elder brother from some place of safety, halfway up a tree or down a hole too small for a nearly grown-up to crawl into. "I planned it all. I brought them here. I came to your wedding so I could burn you all to death." He tried to look at Luso's face, but he couldn't help watching the billhook blade. Too many hours of weapon practice: always watch the blade, not the man. "It was all me, Luso. So, what're you going to do about it?"

And the forty or so men Luso had his back to just stood there and did nothing, while he faced a sharp edge, unarmed and unarmoured. I don't care what happens next, Gignomai realised, whatever happens is just tidying up loose ends.

"You fucking bastard, Gig," Luso said. "What did you want to do a thing like that for?"

It was as if he'd borrowed Luso's bow and lost his favourite arrow, or galloped his favourite horse over the stones and lamed it, as though it was some act of thoughtless stupidity, but no malice. Gignomai sighed. He'd have to spell it out, then. "He tied her to a chair and sewed her mouth up, Luso," he said, patiently, as to an idiot, "and you just stood back and didn't do anything. All of you. So…" He shrugged. That just about covered it. What more needed to be said? "What're you going to do?" he repeated. "Up to you. I really don't mind."

And that, he knew as he made himself look away from the sharp edge and into his brother's one good eye, was no more or less than the truth. There was no anger left. Still, he thought, I'm also here as a witness. We might as well have the facts, while there's still time. "Father?" he asked. "And Stheno?"

"Dead," Luso said. "Stheno was trying to cut a hole in the roof, and a rafter fell on him. I was in the library, trying to beat out the fire. When I went down to tell them it was out of control, Father and Mother were dead in the smoke. So I thought…"

"You came to find me," Gignomai said. "To see if I'd made it." He waited, to see if he could gouge a reply out of the melted face. No chance. "And your wife? Your brother-in-law?"

"Smoke," Luso said. "They're all dead, except me."

"It would be you, wouldn't it?" Gignomai shook his head. "Well, you're the head of the family now, Luso. You'd better make your mind up."

Luso looked at him, and Gignomai realised that he didn't understand. He still didn't understand. But being left alive is worse, for him. Serves him right for being too awkward to die. "Well?" Gignomai said, and Luso opened his hands, letting the billhook fall. It missed his feet by an inch or so and clattered on the flagstones. Then, slow, sad and weary, Luso turned his back on him and walked away. The colonists parted to let him through like an honour guard.

Gignomai counted ten steps. Then, from his inside pocket, he took the miniature snapping-hen pistol, the last one Aurelio had made, no bigger than an outstretched hand, three-eighths bore, one-inch barrel. He drew back the hammer until the sear snicked into place, then levelled it, looking down the stupid little barrel at the middle of Luso's back. He was fifteen yards away by now, an unreliable shot with a full-sized pistol, let alone a toy, and so far, Gignomai had never managed to hit what he'd been aiming at, not even at five yards. He concentrated, and pulled the trigger. The puff of white smoke from the pan blinded him for a moment. When it cleared, he saw that Luso had stopped. He was trying to turn round when he fell, like a sack of grain dropped from the hayloft door. He made an untidy pile of limbs on the ground.

Gignomai put the pistol back in his pocket and walked away.

He met Furio on the track leading down to the Doorstep. He was out of breath, plastered with mud all down his left side, and limping. Gignomai, who knew the signs, gathered that he'd recently fallen off a horse.

"Hello," he said.

Furio stopped dead, shying like an animal. Energy seemed to drain out of him. "Hello, Gig," he said. He'd seen the smoke from the house and soot on Gignomai's face and clothes. "It's all over, then."

Gignomai nodded. "You missed it. Not that there was much of a show in the end."

"What have you done?"

Gignomai felt his shoulders drop. He felt aimless with nothing left to do, no hurry. He could spare the time to stop and chat. "We nailed up the doors and set fire to the house. My family are all dead. Your uncle's still up there, with the people from town. They don't need me any more, so I thought I'd go on."

A grin cracked Furio's face. "You make it sound like a barn dance."

"Hardly."

Furio took a few steps back until he bumped up against a tree. He leaned back on it. "I was going to stop you."

"Thought you might try," Gignomai said. He found a tree of his own to lean against. He felt painfully weary, as though he'd been stacking cordwood. "Sorry."

"I killed one of your guards," Furio said.

Gignomai winced. "I'm sorry," he repeated.

"You shouldn't have done that to me." It was a reproach, but a half-hearted one. "It's your fault—"

"Agreed." Gignomai shrugged. "I knew that if anybody was going to try and do something, it'd be you. I cheated. I couldn't allow you to restore my faith in human nature."

Furio let that one go. "Is my uncle all right?"

"No casualties on our side," Gignomai said—he regretted his choice of possessive pronoun, "at least, not when I left. Luso's thugs weren't in the house when we torched it, but I imagine they'll be realistic. After all, there's only twelve of them."

Furio was clearly shocked. "Twelve?"

"That's right." Gignomai nodded, grinning. "That's all we could afford to keep. Luso always made it seem as though we had at least fifty. He was clever like that. I don't anticipate any trouble. They're not heroes. I expect Marzo'll sort something out. He's a practical man."

Furio's eyes were still wide. "What about your cousin's men? I take it you killed Boulomai too."

"Unfortunately," Gignomai said. "But his people are my people now, I can handle them. They're making good money. And they never liked Boulo much, anyway."

"So that's…" Furio sagged at the knees and slid down his tree, ending up squatting awkwardly on the ground, "everything pretty much covered, then," he said. "You've done well."

Gignomai closed his eyes. "I'm sorry," he said. "It's given me no pleasure, believe me. I just wish it could've been someone else, not me."

Furio looked straight at him. "Is that right?" he said.

"Yes, as a matter of fact. If I could've chosen which side of the door to be on, I wouldn't be talking to you now."

Furio sighed. "I don't believe—"

"Suit yourself," Gignomai said, indifferently. "Fact is, I was just as guilty as the rest of them. I didn't do anything when they sewed up her mouth."

Furio pursed his lips. "You were just a kid."

"Could've sneaked down there at night with a small knife," Gignomai replied. "I knew how to get past the guards. I could've brought her here. Of course, it'd have meant war between Luso and the town, but that wouldn't have been my fault. No, I'm every bit as guilty as Stheno or Luso, or my mother. And there's today's work to take into account, as well. Still," he went on, "someone had to do it, and nobody else was going to. Really, all I can say is, I'm very sorry."

"Sorry," Furio repeated. "That makes it all right."

"Of course not. Nothing's going to make it *right*. Still, it's done now. And I'm left over, at the end." He looked up. "I gave Luso a fair chance," he said. "He could've killed me where I stood. But he just walked away."

"You said he's dead."

Gignomai nodded. "I shot him," he said wearily. "In the back, naturally. Only safe way."

Furio let out a long breath. "How very practical of you," he said.

"Well, I did my best. Really, I did," Gignomai said, with just a flicker of animation. "I faked all the attacks on the colony without actually hurting anybody. Using the savages was a pretty good idea, you must admit. I knew they'd want to fire those guns at someone, but they wouldn't dare come close. It'd have been a miracle if they'd hit someone. And I really did work hard to make sure there was as little risk as possible, just now, up there. Considering what I had to do and what I've achieved, it could've been a hell of a lot worse."

Furio took a moment to reply. "You're a clever man, Gig, nobody's going to argue about that. I just wish—"

"Yes," Gignomai said. "But I've said I'm sorry. Unless you can think of something else I can do, that's about it, isn't it?" He smiled. "Don't be shy," he said. "I'm open to suggestions."

Furio closed his eyes. "If I'd made it in time, what would you have done?"

"Nothing," Gignomai said. "I guess I'd have had to let you talk to them. But I made sure that wouldn't happen. It was cheating, yes, but when it's important, you cheat. I'm sorry it had to be you. For what it's worth, I feel very bad about the way I've treated you."

"That's all right," Furio said reluctantly. "I mean, in context, it really doesn't count for very much."

Gignomai straightened up. "What are you doing to do now?" he said.

"I suppose I'd better go and find my uncle," Furio replied. "He'll be worried about me. Does he know...?"

Gignomai nodded. "I'm pretty sure he guessed," he said. "I sort of implied you were a hostage. It was necessary, at the time."

Furio started to say something, thought better of it. "He'll be relieved I'm all right," he said. "You know, he's not a bad man, really. He does his best."

"He's a better man than me," Gignomai said. "Not that that's saying a great deal." He waited for a moment, then added, "Are you going to tell them?"

It was clearly a question Furio had already considered. He shook his head. "What'd be the point?" he said. "It's done now. It'd just make everybody feel really sick and guilty. And besides, you were right. About your sister, I mean. It was justice."

"Oh," Gignomai said. "That."

Furio smiled. "Does it feel like you thought it would? Do you feel...?"

"Disappointed?" Gignomai shook his head. "I was never in it for the fun of it," he said.

That seemed to satisfy Furio. Gignomai was mildly surprised. He'd expected more of him. "What about you?" Furio said. "What are you going to do?"

"I thought I'd go over to your place," Gignomai replied. "It's where they'll end up, after they're done here. They can crown me or lynch me if they want to. I just want to make myself easy to find."

"I thought you'd go back to the factory."

"No," Gignomai said. "If your lot come for me with a rope, my people would probably defend me. Last thing I'd want." He moved away from the tree. "Maybe Teucer can find me something to eat," he said. "I'm starving."

He walked away a few yards.

Furio said, "What you did. It was justice."

He stopped but didn't look round. "You know," he said, "I've had about as much justice as I can take. From now on, I intend to adopt a more practical approach."

"I killed a man today too," Furio said. "For a moment there, I'd actually forgotten about it."

"Ah well." Gignomai turned slowly round. "It's not often commented on, but when you stop and think, mercy is the biggest injustice of them all."

Furio looked startled for a moment, then grinned. "If you say so, Gig," he said.

He didn't go to the store after all. He got as far as the edge of town, where there was a tall chestnut tree beside the road. He sat down under it, realising he was still wearing his ridiculous wedding clothes, with the boots that rubbed his heel. There was quite a substantial blister, and he hadn't noticed it. He closed his eyes and fell asleep.

When he woke up, it was just beginning to get dark. In the distance, he could see a body of men approaching from the direction he'd come. He breathed in deeply and got to his feet. No peace for the wicked. He walked briskly into town, and was sitting on the store porch with his feet up when Marzo and the war party trudged up the road.

Marzo was black with soot; he looked comical. He had a roll of cloth under one arm. "We were looking for you," he said.

"I left early," Gignomai replied, lifting his feet off the other chair. "Well, you've found me. All done?"

Marzo nodded. The war party had come to a halt behind him.

They looked worried. Mostly they just wanted to go home, but they were afraid of splitting up.

"What happened to Luso's men?" Gignomai asked.

"They saw reason," Marzo said grimly—just the way Luso would've said it, Gignomai noted with approval. "I told them; You want to make something of it, now's your chance. They counted heads and decided to be realistic." He pulled a sour face. "You might have told us—"

"You wouldn't have believed me," Gignomai replied. "You'd have thought I was lying about the strength of Luso's forces to persuade you to attack."

Marzo shrugged; he wasn't convinced, but it was a plausible excuse. "I gave them a choice," Marzo said. "We'd string them up, or they could go and join your lot at the factory. They'll be reporting to you in the morning."

"Thanks ever so much," Gignomai said. "Just what I need, my own private army."

"If they don't show up, you tell me," Marzo said.

"Of course."

Marzo sighed, seemed to deflate, as if he'd been possessed by some outside force, which had now left him. "Well," he said, "I think that's about it for today." He turned to address his troops. "You might as well all go home," he said.

"What about the savages?" someone asked. "They're still—"

"We can round them up and slaughter them like sheep in the morning," Marzo snapped. "Go home. That's an order."

First one, then in twos and threes, they broke up like melting ice and drifted away. Once they were a safe distance from the store, they started talking in low voices. Marzo hauled himself up onto the porch, then collapsed into a chair. "I'm worn out," he said. "It's been a hell of a day."

"Where's Furio?"

"He'll be along in a minute," Marzo said, his eyes shut. "He and a few of the others loaded all Luso's men's weapons on a cart. They're dropping them off at the livery. Wanted to bring them here, but I said no. This is a store, not the town dump." He frowned. "Talking of garbage and junk," he said, and unrolled the bundle of cloth he'd been carrying. "Found this," he said.

It was the sword, or what was left of it. The cast hilt had melted away, leaving the bare tang. The blade had warped into a curve in the heat. A good blacksmith might be able to make a dozen or so nails out of it.

"Sorry about that," Gignomai said. "I needed a wedding present for Luso."

Marzo looked at it, then dropped it on the floor. "Looks like we won't be going Home after all," he said.

Gignomai grinned at him. "There's no Home any more," he said, "not for any of us."

"I guess not," Marzo said. "Serves me right, I suppose. I should never have listened to you in the first place."

"It'll be fine," Gignomai told him. "In case you've forgotten, we now have the factory. All the stuff you can sell. You won't do too badly."

"Neither will you."

Gignomai made no effort to contradict him. "Nor will Furio," he said. "This colony belongs to the three of us now. And it's worth having, too. You'll have me to thank for that."

Marzo hesitated, then nodded. "I don't get you, though," he said. "Was it just revenge? You could've done it a simpler way, I'm sure, a clever man like you."

"Why should a man have only one reason?" Gignomai said. "This way, I did what had to be done, for justice, and something good will come out of it. Justice and something good; they don't usually go together."

Marzo looked at him, suddenly hopeful. "You think it'll work?"

"Freedom for the colony, you mean?" Gignomai smiled, and nodded. "I don't see why not," he said. "It's a business decision, after all. If the Company can't make money here, they'll give us up as a bad job. A garrison of five hundred pikemen to keep us in order would be very expensive. Especially," he added, "with people shooting at them all the time."

Marzo frowned. "I thought all the guns were on the Tabletop," he said.

"I can make them," Gignomai said. He thought he saw a flicker in Marzo's eyes, which would mean he'd said too much, but if he had, so what? "Give me three months, there'll be a matchlock or a snapping-hen for everybody in the colony who wants one, free of charge, compliments of the mayor. Then nobody need worry about the savages, or the Company, or the government."

Marzo thought for a moment, then said, "Cheap. Not free."

Gignomai laughed. "All right, then, cheap. Very cheap."

"Fairly cheap," Marzo amended. "Like all the other stuff from the factory. I always reckon, people don't appreciate stuff unless they have to pay for it."

Like justice, Gignomai didn't say. In the end, nobody had paid too dearly for it, but it most certainly hadn't been free. "We'll have to talk about that some time soon," Gignomai said, "when we're not so bloody tired. I suggest a realistic approach."

"Practical," Marzo grunted. "After all, we're practical men, right?"

Which was only fair, Gignomai had to think. If I turn into my father, Marzo can turn into Luso. "You know," he said, "I think that when we're free and independent, we ought to have more civic leaders as well as the mayor. I think we should have a Justice of the Peace."

Marzo looked at him, then burst out laughing. "But that's ridiculous," he said. "You can have justice, or you can keep the peace. Can't have both."

Gignomai found that he was laughing too. Fine joke. "Unrealistic, you think."

"Impractical."

There was something on Gignomai's face, something wet. If it had been anybody else, he could've sworn it was tears. "I never liked

Stheno much," he said. "But Luso was different. It's a pity that torture was his way of showing affection."

"He was always polite to me," Marzo said. "He didn't have to be. A real gentleman, you might say."

When Furio came home, not long afterwards, he found them laughing helplessly. He looked for a bottle, several empty bottles, but couldn't see any.

Gignomai slept at the store that night, at least, he occupied a bed. As he lay in the dark, he tried to convince himself that what he'd seen, or believed he'd seen, was real: the house burning, Luso lying face down on the ground. He tried to persuade himself that the Tabletop was uninhabited now, that the house was a ruin, the family dead, no guards on the Doorstep, no distant thump of a shot far off in the woods. He closed his eyes, and he could see them all as sharp as midday, which made it impossible to believe the wild hypothesis. The only one he couldn't see was his sister, who'd died young. He had no idea where the tears came from.

The next day, there was a meeting at the store. The main room was crowded, but perfectly quiet. Everybody knew they had to be there, but nobody wanted to speak.

Marzo had fixed up a platform out of empty crates. There were two chairs on it. At Gignomai's suggestion, the legs of the chairs had been fixed to the crates with brackets—just bits of scrap iron sheet bent at right-angles and punched with nail holes—so there was no danger of overbalancing and falling into the crowd.

Marzo stood up. He could feel the crate he was standing on wobbling under his weight, so he made sure he kept his feet still. He said that what had just happened was something that had to be done (he didn't expand on that), and now it was done and over with, the important thing was to look forward. He told everybody about the factory, and what it'd mean to all of them: cheap tools and hardware, which meant they wouldn't have to buy those things from

Home any more at crazy prices that kept them all permanently poor. In fact, with the factory making nearly everything they had to have, did they really need ships from Home at all? Ships, he said, that didn't just bring stuff, they took stuff away—practically every steer raised in the colony, and what did they get in return? He didn't answer his own question.

Some of them might be worried about what Home might do if they told the ships not to bother coming any more. Well, that was a fair point. They paid rent for this land they worked so hard, to a bunch of rich lords far away across the sea who'd never been here, who wouldn't last five minutes here if they did come. That was the other thing that kept them poor, he said, rent, and the Company trade monopoly. They could carry on as they were, and be poor all their lives, keep the peace, close down the factory, keep the law, be good. Or, there was another way. It would mean taking a risk. The government might send soldiers, men with pikes and swords— though he didn't think they would, it'd cost them more than they made out of the colony, and where was the sense in that? But suppose they did, what would happen then?

He paused for a moment, letting the fear sink in. Then he said, Gignomai met'Oc, who started up the factory, has figured out how to make guns. He's promised (and I believe him, Marzo said, looking unimpeachably solemn) that he can make enough guns to arm every man who's prepared to fight. The point being that the government troops don't have guns. They have long spears and swords. Most of them have never even seen a gun, or heard one go off. Now he couldn't promise that at the first volley the government troops would turn tail and run back to their ships so fast a greyhound couldn't keep up with them, though he was pretty sure in his own mind that'd be the likely outcome. He made no promises about things outside his control. No. It all depended on what they, the men of the colony, wanted, and what they were prepared to do to get it. A few days ago, maybe, he wouldn't have made this suggestion. But since then, a lot had changed. The men of this colony had taken on the met'Oc and their guns, in their impregnable fortress, and they'd won, and all of them had come home safe. So, he asked them to consider, if they could beat the met'Oc, why not the government?

Sooner or later, he said, they were going to have to fight. The savages still had the guns the met'Oc had given them, and one thing he was absolutely certain of was that the government wouldn't be sending any troops to protect the colony from the savages. Like it or not, the old days were gone; like it or not, they had no choice but to fight someone, sometime. So, if they had to fight, why not fight the people who were making their lives a misery, draining all the wealth out of the colony, taking it all and giving nothing back? Maybe, he said, they'd never fought up till now because they'd had nothing to fight with, or maybe it was because they'd had nothing to fight *for*. But that, Marzo said, was back then. This was now, the day after the battle of the Tabletop, the end of the past, the beginning of the future. Well, he said, they might like to think about that. It was entirely up to them, of course, but he knew which way he'd choose to go.

One last thing, he said. It had been a great privilege and honour to be their mayor, but whatever they chose to do, there'd be hard times ahead. They needed the right man to lead them, and a middle-aged storekeeper wasn't that man. Accordingly, with deep regret but knowing he was doing the right thing, he was resigning the office of mayor, and he invited them all to join with him in electing the right man for the job, an educated man, a man who'd already given proof of his energy, resourcefulness and commitment to the future of the colony, the man who'd built the factory that would make their future possible, a man born and bred to lead: Gignomai met'Oc.

Nobody moved, or said a word.

Then Marzo said, "Does anybody want to vote against Gignomai met'Oc as mayor?" He waited: one, two, three. "Carried unanimously," he said. "Gignomai met'Oc is your new mayor."

Gignomai sat perfectly still in his immovable chair, and kept a straight face. He couldn't have said a word if he'd wanted to. He felt as though his lips were sewn together.

"You could have warned me," he told Marzo, when the people had gone home, and they were dismantling the platform.

Marzo shrugged. "Being around you for a while, I guess I learned a thing or two. Besides, I thought you'd be pleased."

"You thought that."

"Ah well." Marzo put a claw-hammer to the nails securing his chair to the brackets. "I'm out of it now, thank God. You started it, you can see it through. Like I said," he added spitefully, "born and bred to lead."

Gignomai smiled, a lolling, death's head grin. "Justice," he said.

"Just being practical," Marzo replied. "You're the right man for the job. You've got the knack of twisting people. We need a man like you."

"And that's why you did this to me. Nothing to do with punishing me for whatever it is you think I've done."

Marzo smiled. He was determined to enjoy this moment, no matter what. "Why should a man have only one reason?" he said.

Five Years Later

When they found him, Gignomai was in the hammer shed, stitching a broken drive belt back together. He gave them his sourest what is it now look, but they took no notice.

"Someone here to see you," young Heddo said.

"Tell him to get lost, whoever he is."

"You ought to come," the Fasenna boy said, "in case there's any trouble."

Gignomai sighed, and left the unmended belt drooping from the pulley. "Fine," he said. "Since nobody around here seems capable of doing anything except me. Who and where?"

"Out front," Heddo said. One question answered.

It was the old man. Gignomai hadn't seen him since before the Burning. In fact, nobody could remember the last time they'd seen any of the savages, though that didn't stop fools and time-wasters like Rasso from harping on about them at council meetings. He looked very old and frail now, leaning on the arm of a tall, square young woman in one of those ludicrous long coats. The way he didn't react when Gignomai walked up to him suggested he'd gone blind.

"Hello," Gignomai said.

"Gignomai met'Oc."

"Right here," Gignomai said. "Can you see me?"

That made the old man laugh, for some reason. "Clearly enough," he said, apparently to an invisible person standing two yards to Gignomai's left. "There's no need to shout, by the way. I'm not deaf."

Gignomai smiled. "I am," he said. "Spent too long close to the big hammer. I guess it makes me talk too loud, I'm sorry. I'm…" Amazed you're still alive. "Glad to see you."

"I had to come and say goodbye," the old man said. "Could somebody fetch me something to sit on? I find standing very difficult these days."

Gignomai grabbed an empty crate that happened to be about the right height, and guided the old man down onto it. The square woman took a dozen steps back, until she was hard to see among the trees.

"Going somewhere?" Gignomai asked.

The old man nodded. "We all are," he said. "My people, I mean. We're moving across the eastern mountains."

"Are there mountains in the east?" Gignomai asked.

The old man laughed. "You have no idea about this country," he said, "about how large it is, or how it's made up. The furthest my people have ever been is fifty days' ride from here that's about a thousand Imperial miles. Beyond that point the grasslands give way to scrub, and in the distance, nothing but sand and desert, as far as the white-topped mountains that block the view."

"You're going there?" Gignomai asked, astonished.

"Good heavens, no." The old man smiled. "Only as far as the near mountains, about twenty-six days' ride. Between them and the far mountains is a great plain of tall, dark grass, through which two great rivers run side by side. We've decided to go there," he went on, "to get away from you."

"Oh," Gignomai said.

"We believe," the old man went on, "that we will be safe there for some time. Should you cross the near mountains, we will either go north, where the winters are hard but the pasture is excellent in summer, or south, where there are further plains as far as the eye can see. It may take you several hundred years before we run out of land to escape into, depending, of course, on how quickly you breed. And in two hundred years, who knows? Things may be different."

Gignomai thought for a while. Then he said, "Why are you going? We're no bother to each other."

"My people think differently," the old man said, wriggling a little to get comfortable. "When you showed us the snapping-hen pistol, some of us, as you know, took it as proof that what we've always believed was untrue. They started believing in you—that you exist, here in the same world and time as we do—and from there it was only a short step to seeing you as an intolerable threat. At first, they wanted to attack you, kill you all and burn your houses to the ground."

"You persuaded them not to," Gignomai said.

"On the contrary." The old man lifted his head proudly. The gesture would have worked quite well if he hadn't been facing a tree instead of the person he was talking to. "I urged them to wipe you out without fear or mercy. After all, I'd seen this place, and heard what you did to your own family up on the flat hill. I told them, I had been to your country and seen your beautiful city, I knew that your people are exceptionally wise and immeasurably strong. Our only chance, therefore, was to kill you all and hope that would persuade your people that this place is too dangerous, considering the sparse returns they'd be likely to get from exploiting it."

"I see," Gignomai said. "Well, I'm glad they didn't listen."

The old man grinned. "Many of them did," he said. "More than a thousand, at one point. There would have been enough of us, if we'd come at you suddenly and unexpectedly. Fortunately, the other faction prevailed. They believe in you, because of the snapping-hen, but their solution is to move away. They maintain that there's no point defeating an enemy if, in order to do so, you turn yourself into him. Once I'd thought it through, I could see that they were quite right. So, we're leaving." He lowered his chin onto his chest and sat quite still for a while, until Gignomai wondered if he'd fallen asleep. "I've been teaching them your language," he said suddenly, "And everything I can remember about Home. Quite a large number of our young people are very keen to learn."

"Really?" Gignomai said. "I thought you all wanted nothing to do with us."

"We study you," the old man said mildly, "the way a doctor studies a disease. If we know about you, we can do everything we can to stop ourselves becoming like you. That's their argument, at any rate. Personally, I believe you are a contamination that should be avoided at all costs. As evidence of my view, I offer myself. I hold myself responsible, you see."

"Responsible?" Gignomai asked. "What for?"

"For you," the old man said. "The time I spent in your country filled me with such a longing for all the wonders and beautiful things I saw there that I couldn't resist meeting you, when you first came to find us. As a direct result, you showed us the snapping-hen and changed us for ever. My fault. But they will insist on pestering me to teach them, and I do so love to speak your language and hear it spoken. So I teach them, and risk making matters infinitely worse. Which is why," the old man went on, lowering his voice and turning his head, as though looking round for eavesdroppers, "I have a very great favour to ask you, if you wouldn't mind. I have no great hopes that my ruse will succeed, but it might just delay the inevitable for a little while, which would be something."

"What can I do for you?" Gignomai asked.

"You can tell them," the old man said in a loud, hoarse whisper, "that the savages have told you that beyond the near mountains there's nothing but desert, burning hot by day and freezing by night. You have this information from an unimpeachable source, who had also told you that the savages have contracted a terrible disease—caught from your people, I would suggest. Something you've become immune to over the years, but which is wiping us out by the thousand. In a desperate attempt to save ourselves, we are migrating to the desert beyond the mountains, believing that the extremes of heat and cold there will halt the progress of the disease, or at least slow it down. To all intents and purposes, you can tell them, we no longer exist, as far as your people are concerned." He paused for breath, and said, "Will you do that for me? As a very great favour?"

"I think it's the least I can do," Gignomai replied gravely.

"Thank you," the old man said. "If they believe you, there's a chance that in time your people will forget about us, at least until we meet again, and any stories that might still be told about us will be held to be impossible legends, echoes of folk tales you brought with you from Home. For our part, we will try and believe that you never existed, and that I'm mad and never did cross the sea. Really, it would be for the best, if you think you could manage it."

"I've never exterminated a whole nation before," Gignomai said.

The old man looked very solemn and wise. "If anybody can do it," he said, "you can."

Two days later, a dot appeared at the seam of the sea and sky, which gradually grew into a ship. By the time a man with keen eyes could distinguish the sail from the hull, the Council had met in emergency session and ordered out the militia. Runners scampered off to the nearest farms, while the militiamen who happened to be in town at the time, some two dozen of them, ran to the big shed on the quay and dragged out the cannon. When they judged the ship was just out of range, they fired a single shot which, much to their surprise, pitched no more than twenty yards off the ship's port bow, lifting a great plume of water, like a leaping dolphin.

The ship dropped anchor immediately and ran up a flag, which nobody could see clearly enough to identify. The cannon was reloaded, and the touch-hole was covered up with someone's hat, to make sure it wasn't accidentally lit. Maybe half an hour later the ship lowered a boat, which began the long struggle to shore. The cannon crew covered it until they were quite sure the thing hanging off its keel was a limp white flag.

Just to be on the safe side, the militia fired their guns in the air as soon as the boat was close enough for them to see the faces of the men in it. The boat's crew backed water frantically, stopped, and brandished the white flag. Furio, who'd just arrived to take charge, beckoned them to come in closer. When they were within shouting range, he called out, "That's close enough," and signalled to his men to level their guns.

A man stood up in the prow of the boat, waving his hat. They weren't from the government, he shouted, it wasn't a Navy ship. They were merchant seamen employed by the met'Ousa, with a message for Phainomai met'Oc. They were unarmed (at this point, all the oarsmen raised their hands, an eloquent but meaningless gesture) and they had no hostile intentions. Furio thought for a moment, conferred with the cannon crew, and beckoned to them to come ashore. He may simply have forgotten to tell his men to stop pointing their guns at the men in the boat.

The boat came in and threw out a line. Someone handed his gun to his neighbour while he tied the boat up. The hat-waver came ashore; the rest of the crew stayed where they were.

"What's the message?" Furio said.

The messenger looked doubtful. "I take it you're not Phainomai met'Oc."

"That's right," Furio said. "I'm a captain in the militia. You can answer my questions, or you can turn right round and go home. Up to you."

The messenger thought for a moment, and looked at the muzzles of the guns, and said, "The met'Ousa just want to know how Master Boulomai met'Ousa and Mistress Pasi met'Oc are getting on," he said. "It's been five years since they heard from them, and—"

"They're dead," Furio said. "I'm sorry."

The messenger's eyes opened wide. "Dead?" he repeated, as though the word was unfamiliar to him.

"There was a fire," Furio said, "at the met'Oc house. The entire family died, no survivors. It was a great tragedy. I'm sorry. Please pass on the Council's sympathy to the met'Ousa."

"That's—" The messenger stopped, as though uncertain of what he was allowed to say. "That's unfortunate," he said. "Perhaps I might be allowed to address the Council? I'm sorry, I'm not entirely clear how things work here now."

Furio smiled. "That's all right," he said. "At the moment, we're pretty much making it up as we go along. You'd best come and talk to the Chief Justice."

"The Chief…?"

"My uncle," Furio said. "He's also the Secretary of State for Foreign Affairs. Or he will be," Furio added, "once I've told him. This way." He paused and looked over the messenger's shoulder. "Are your men all right staying there, or would they rather come up to the store for a beer?"

As it happened, the Council was still in session when they reached the store, although Marzo had done his best to shoo them out. Accordingly, he and Furio took the messenger into the back office, leaving the Council to mind the store.

"I told him," Furio said, "about the fire."

Marzo's face didn't move. He could have been a statue of himself, raised by a grateful nation. "Dreadful business," he said. "Five years ago, practically to the day."

The messenger sat down and laid his hat in his lap. "That complicates things," he said.

"Oh?"

The messenger nodded. "You did say all the family died in the fire?"

"That's right," Furio said firmly. "Boulomai and Pasi, Phainomai and Passer met'Oc, and their three sons."

"Ah." The messenger picked up his hat and let it drop. "I don't suppose you have any way of knowing the order in which they died. You see, it could make a huge difference."

Marzo's eyes flashed, but Furio just looked bewildered. "What possible difference could it—?"

"To who inherits," the messenger said. "I might as well tell you, there was another reason why my employers sent me at this precise point in time. You see, there's been a change of government back home. Quite a drastic one, in fact. I won't bore you with the details, but the practical effect is, the faction to which the met'Ousa belong is pretty much running things. One of the first things they did was issue a general pardon to the met'Oc."

Furio opened his mouth, but said nothing. Marzo's lips were pressed tightly together, as if he was strangling a smile. "I see what you mean about complicating things," Marzo said eventually. "This pardon..."

"Includes a full restoration of all the family properties and honours," the messenger said. "To include accumulated income and compensation. So you can see," he went on, looking down at his hands, "why it'd be really helpful if it's possible to establish who died when. Assuming," he added quickly, looking up at Marzo, "that the wedding actually did take place."

"Oh yes," Marzo said. "I can vouch for that. I was there."

The messenger nodded, plainly relieved. "In which case," he said, "you can see for yourself how matters stand. If Lusomai died before Pasi, she would have inherited any interest he might have had in the met'Oc estates. Since she died childless—at least, we're assuming..."

Marzo nodded briskly.

"In that case," the messenger said, licking his lips, "her next of kin and legal heir would be her father, Nicomai met'Ousa, assuming she had anything to leave, I mean, which depends..."

"On who died when," Marzo said, "exactly." He folded his hands and looked down at his fingernails, as if he'd got the answers written on them in tiny letters. "So, from your people's point of view, the ideal situation would be, Phainomai dies first."

392 K. J. Parker

Furio coughed gently. "Actually, if Passer died first."

"Sorry, yes. Passer dies first, so her marriage settlement passes to Phainomai, her husband. Phainomai dies next, and Sthenomai immediately inherits as eldest son. But he dies next, unmarried, and Lusomai inherits."

"Pasi's still very much alive at this point," Furio said helpfully.

"Of course, yes," Marzo said. "And Boulomai?"

The messenger shrugged. "Not really particularly relevant," he said.

Marzo nodded. "That's all right, then, we can forget about him. Now, so long as Luso dies before Pasi, does it matter particularly if Gignomai...?"

The messenger nodded. "If the younger brother survives the widow," he said, "there would, under intestacy law, be an equal division of the estate. However, if Gignomai predeceased..."

Marzo smiled warmly. "Which he did," he said. "Luso, then Gignomai, then Pasi last of all."

The messenger's eyebrows went up. "You'd be prepared to certify that?"

"As Lord Chief Justice," Marzo said, "sure. In writing. We made a thorough investigation of the scene, and found incontrovertible proof that the deaths took place in that order. There's a report somewhere," he added, with a vague wave of his hand toward the stack of paper on the windowsill — receipted bills from the factory, as it happened. "You don't mind if I don't dig it out right now, do you? We're a bit behind on our filing, to tell you the truth."

"No, that's perfectly all right," the messenger said quickly. "All I need is a signed certificate from the Chief Justice."

"Lord Chief Justice," Furio murmured, as Marzo uncapped his inkwell and reached for the nearest piece of paper, turned it over and found it had been written on already and scrabbled about until he found a blank sheet.

"Of course," Marzo said, as he wrote, "there are certain implications. I'm sure I don't need to explain."

The messenger shrugged. "Just to clarify," he said.

"Of course." Marzo laid his pen down carefully. "You see, it occurs to me that this certificate I'm writing for you now won't actually mean anything in a court of law, for example, unless your government recognises its validity."

The messenger blinked. "I'm sorry? I don't quite..."

"Oh, I think you do," Marzo said. "Let me make it easy for you. If your government recognises that this colony is now an independent state, with the right to appoint its own officers, such as the Lord Chief Justice, for example, then this certificate is a valid instrument and can be relied on in a court of law. But if your government doesn't recognise us, and reckons we're still just a bunch of rebels, then this piece of paper is worthless and no use to you whatsoever."

The messenger nodded, very slowly. "I think I see what you're saying," he said.

"Now obviously," Marzo went on, "you're just a messenger, you haven't got the authority to recognise us as an independent nation. But it seems to me, if the met'Ousa take their inheritance claim to court, and the court accepts this as a valid certificate, then by implication, the court, and the government it represents, must also be recognising our independence. In other words, if your met'Ousa want the met'Oc money, we want this country for ourselves. Now that's fair, isn't it?"

The messenger hesitated for quite some time. "There's also the matter," he said, "of the met'Oc assets in this country. We were led to believe that these assets were quite substantial. Land, a house."

Furio and Marzo looked at each other. "I'm afraid you may have been misled," Marzo said. "The house burned to the ground, along with all the contents."

"I see," the messenger said quietly. "The land."

"Death duties," Furio said. "Just about covered what was due. It's now in public ownership."

"Of course," the messenger said, in a rather brittle voice. "You might just certify that as well, if it's no trouble."

"No trouble at all," Marzo said, and picked up his pen.

Later, when the messenger had gone back to his boat and was halfway across the bay, Furio said, "Do you think we ought to tell him?"

Marzo shook his head. "Better not," he said.

"I think we should," Furio said.

"Better not," Marzo repeated firmly. "Justice is all very well, but my job's keeping the peace. Besides, Gignomai belongs to us now. The less any of us dwells on the past, the better for everyone."

Furio looked at him, then nodded. "Yes, Lord Chief Justice," he said.

There was a particular kind of weed that grew well in ashes. It grew fast and tall, and was so bitter that even the rabbits and goats left it alone. It had a thick brown stem and a wispy pale red flower, and the site of the met'Oc house was covered in it, so that nothing was visible apart from the patch that Gignomai kept clear, where the bay window used to overlook the gates of the hall. There, to the remaining stub of wall, he had fixed five iron plates, with the names of his parents, brothers and sister, including all their titles and honours. It was his custom throughout his life to lay lavender blossom under these plates on the anniversary of the Great Fire, as it had come to be known.

On the fifth anniversary, he met Marzo coming up the track as he was coming down. Marzo was carrying a sheaf of flags and wild lilies, the kind that grew on the riverbank a couple of hundred yards upstream from the ford.

"Paying my respects to your brother," Marzo said. Gignomai didn't ask which one. He grinned.

"It's a free country," he said.

Marzo pulled a slight face. "You?" he said.

"Same sort of thing." In his left hand, he held the brush hook he'd been using to cut back the fire-weed. "I'm sure Luso would appreciate it," he said.

"I doubt that very much," Marzo replied cheerfully. "Still, he's got no say in the matter, so I can do what I like."

Gignomai smiled, then the smile faded, quickly and completely. "I hear there was a ship yesterday."

"That's right." Marzo leaned against a tree. He was short of breath from the climb. "The lads put a ball over her bows. Turned out they didn't want to land here after all."

Gignomai nodded. "Scarpedino tells me you had the captain over at your place for a while. Council was in session, too, so I heard."

"Coincidence," Marzo said. "Nice man, their captain. I sold him a few bits and pieces, just to keep my hand in." Which was true. All the met'Oc's gold and silver plate had melted in the fire, but gold and silver nuggets, even with chunks of slag and cinder in them, were still worth good money, and one day there'd be other ships. "We'd have sent down to you, only we knew you were busy, and we didn't really want the ship hanging about any longer than necessary."

Gignomai dipped his head to acknowledge the validity of the reasoning. "They didn't need to take on water, then, or anything like that."

"They didn't ask," Marzo replied, "we didn't offer. I've got lads out watching, in case they try and put in down the coast some place. And I've put a guard on Boulomai's ship down at East Bay. Doesn't do to leave valuable stuff just lying around when there's strangers about."

"That's all right, then," Gignomai said. "No big deal."

"No big deal," Marzo confirmed. "How's Teucer, by the way? And the kid?"

Gignomai didn't like it when Marzo called young Luso "the kid," but Marzo never seemed to take the hint. "Oh, they're fine," he said. "Last time I looked."

Marzo pulled a sad face. "Things are still...?"

"We keep out of each other's way," Gignomai said.

"It's a shame, though, really," Marzo persisted. He could tell Gignomai wanted to be on his way, so he was determined to spin the conversation out a little longer. "She was really quite keen on you at one time, I always thought."

"Maybe," Gignomai said. "But we both knew what we were getting into. I needed an heir, for the family name and all that garbage. She wanted a husband so she could own property and generally have a life. So long as there's plenty of broken arms and bashed heads for her to fuss over, she's happy enough. And making money, too," he added with a grin. "Not sure I could afford to have her patch me up, the rates she charges. Chip off the old block there, I reckon."

"Thank you," Marzo said sincerely. "Coming from you, that means a great deal."

"Well," Gignomai said, injecting a little briskness into his voice, "I mustn't keep you. I expect you've got a lot to do. Give my best to Furio. Haven't seen him at the factory for a day or so."

"His youngest is teething," Marzo said, "poor bugger hasn't been getting quite as much sleep as he's used to. Of course, you'll know all about that."

Gignomai gave him a cold look. "Not really," he said. "We put Luso out to a wetnurse when he was at that stage. If there's one thing I can't be doing with, it's being woken up in the middle of the night."

"Me too," Marzo said. "Nothing more annoying, specially if you have trouble sleeping. Wouldn't suit me, though, sending the kid away like that. Still, it wouldn't do if all families were alike. I'll tell Furio you asked after him."

"Remind him I want a dozen men up here, day after tomorrow," Gignomai said. "We're re-opening the old clay pit, remember?" He sighed, and looked round. "Only thing worth having up here any more," he said.

"Oh, I don't know," Marzo said. "I heard somewhere you've got a nice flock of goats up here these days, and some pretty good pigs coming on, too."

Gignomai shrugged. "It's rubbish land," he said. "Goats and pigs is all it's good for, Stheno always said. He nearly killed himself trying to grow wheat up on Redside. That's all briars and nettles now," he added.

"No luck finding a tenant?"

"Who'd want to pay rent for that when there's all the good land you could ever want on the other side of the river, rent free?" He shook his head. "No, I don't think I'll be bothering with this lot any more after this year. I'm too busy, and what I'd get off it wouldn't pay the men's wages for working it. Might put it down to coppice some time, if I can make the effort. You can never have enough charcoal, after all."

Marzo smiled at him. He considered saying that it had always been a good spot for burning things, but he didn't want to push his luck. "That'd probably be best," he said, "if you can keep the deer out. But who knows, your kid might turn out like his uncle, and then you'd be all right."

Gignomai rewarded him with a faint grin. "Actually," he said, "there's not nearly as many deer up here as there used to be. Luso put a lot of effort into managing them, culling the weak bucks, that sort of thing. Also, the farmers shoot them, which doesn't bother me at all," he added brightly. "Means we'd be in with a chance if we do decide to plant it out with coppice. We'll have to see how we go, though. Can't see how I could spare the manpower any time this year, the way things are at the factory."

Marzo put on a sympathetic face. "I heard the hammer was down again yesterday."

"Bloody thing," Gignomai said, with feeling. "Looks like the foundations have completely broken up, what with all the pounding they get. So that means dismantling the whole thing and starting again from scratch, which'll mean at least a week's lost production. If I had the energy I'd build another one, so at least there's be one running when the other breaks down."

"Good idea," Marzo said. "You ought to do that."

"It's time," Gignomai said sadly. "That's the problem. Never enough time to get things done, so you're always slipping behind.

Then, when something breaks, you're screwed." He laughed quite suddenly. "I'm starting to sound just like Stheno," he said. "Still, I'm beginning to understand how he felt, poor bugger. He never did have it easy, my brother."

"I'll let you get on," Marzo said, and headed on up the hill, whistling.

After he'd finished at the Tabletop, Gignomai didn't go back to his house in town. He rarely went there these days—usually only when he had to preside at a council meeting, or deal with some other form of official business. He told anyone who asked that it was because he didn't like being around all the sick people who came to see his wife. It was a shame nobody believed him, because it was partly true. Instead, he walked back to the factory, where he slept on a mattress in the tiny back room of the drawing office. When he remembered about food, he ate in the canteen, usually after everybody else had gone back on shift. A woman came down from town once a month with clean, ironed, folded clothes for him to wear. Most of them were still folded when she called again. It was, people said to him, a strange way for the richest man in the colony to live, at which point, he would smile politely and change the subject.

To his surprise, he found Furio waiting for him in the drawing office, sitting on the high draughtsman's stool, staring at the plans he'd been working on for the improved iron furnace. They were upside down.

"I never could make head nor tail of your drawings," he said.

"Don't see why not," Gignomai replied, throwing the brush-hook into the corner of the room and taking off his hat. "I taught myself to read this sort of thing, so you could do it too, if you wanted."

Furio smiled at him. "Can't be bothered," he said. "Presumably it all means something to you, and that's all that matters. What...?"

"The new furnace," Gignomai said. "Been having a bit of trouble joining the flue to the chimney hood. But I think I can see how to do it." He pulled the paper gently out of Furio's hand and laid it down flat on the desk. "What brings you here?"

It was always interesting to watch Furio trying to bring himself to tell a lie. Sometimes he struggled so hard that you really wanted him to succeed. The nearest thing to it that Gignomai had ever seen was a very old man pushing a very heavy wheelbarrow halfway (and no further) up an impossibly steep, narrow ramp.

"Five years," Furio said, giving up the attempt.

"Ah." Gignomai nodded. "You want to talk to me about what happened five years ago." He shrugged, and sat on the edge of the long plank table. "Go ahead."

"We've never talked about it. I think it's about time."

"Sure," Gignomai snapped impatiently, "fine. Like I said, go ahead. You know your trouble, Furio? You're incapable of taking yes for an answer."

But Furio wasn't going to be rushed, flustered or bounced. Maybe Luso could've done it, in his prime, but Gignomai wasn't in his league. He folded his arms and looked so solemn that Gignomai wanted to laugh. "I never told my uncle," he said.

"I know. But he's guessed quite a lot, I think. At least," Gignomai went on, scratching the back of his head, "he's got a number of theories, and he sort of tries them out on me by needling me, ever so gently, every time we meet. Never goes too far, but always keeps up a slight, continuous pressure. I don't mind," he added, "I reckon he's earned the right."

"He worries," Furio said, "about what he did, what he was party to. Actually, he's asked me direct questions, once or twice."

"And you said?"

"Don't be so bloody stupid, or words to that effect. But it's like the way you ask a kid if he's done something, when you know he's done it. He wouldn't have asked me if he wasn't sure in his mind he knew the answer."

Gignomai smiled. "Your uncle is a shrewd man," he said, "but a pragmatist."

"Oh, sure." Furio shrugged. "He'd never pass on his suspicions to anybody else, he's too deeply implicated himself. He likes the way things have turned out. I'm just saying, I didn't tell him. In case you were wondering."

"Never crossed my mind," Gignomai replied. "You had your chance to turn me in, and —"

"I missed it. Because I was held up, killing a man."

Gignomai acknowledged that with a slight movement of the head and shoulders. "Not your fault."

"I'm grateful to you, actually," Furio said. "I never had to make the choice: intervene, or stand by and say nothing. You were kind enough to spare me that."

"Least I could do," Gignomai said. "After I'd used you, like I used everybody else. I'm not proud of that. In fact, I'm not proud of anything I've done, ever." Furio raised an eyebrow, so he went on, "Motive, you see. Always motive. It's like when someone's born particularly tall or very handsome — good things to be, and people will always like you for them, but you don't deserve the admiration because you had no part in it. You were born that way. Same with me, in a sense. I reckon I don't deserve blame or praise for what I did. Something happened when I was a kid that demanded that action be taken. For various reasons, I was the only one who could take that action. I did what I had to do. I did bad things and good things. I don't think we need to go through the bad things; the good things gave us independence, and a somewhat better life for the people of this colony. I didn't intend the good things any more than the bad. They were incidental by-products. So, no pride, no guilt." He grinned. "In theory, anyway."

Furio looked at him for a moment. "Is that why the richest man in the colony lives in a hut and eats cold porridge twice a day?"

Gignomai laughed. "That's incidental too. I live here because it's on site, I eat what I eat when I eat because I haven't got time for anything else, I'm too busy."

"Why? You don't need to be."

"Oh come on," Gignomai said. "Who else could run this place?"

"Only you," Furio said. "Only the last of the met'Oc. Is that it?"

"Partly," Gignomai said (he surprised himself with the admission). "Mostly because it needs doing, I'm good at it, there's nobody else and I haven't got anything better to do. Motive, you see. Always motive."

Furio sighed. "Motive doesn't matter a damn. Only what happens matters." He stood up, as if he'd decided to make that his exit line, then he must have changed his mind. "Which is why I've never said anything, about what you did."

"Oh," Gignomai said. "I thought it was because we were friends."

"Really?" Furio scowled at him. "You didn't bloody well treat me as a—"

"No," Gignomai said, and although he didn't raise his voice, it was as though he'd shouted. "No, I didn't. But you're a better man than me. I expected more from you than I'd ever expect from myself." He smiled again, and said, "Also, you didn't have that one great big important thing you had to do, not like me. You had a choice. Makes a difference, that does."

Furio was still looking daggers. "Sorry if I disappointed you."

Gignomai's turn to frown. "Is that it," said, "or were there other issues you wanted to explore?"

There was a brittle moment, then Furio shook his head. "What the hell did you marry Teucer for, anyhow? You never could stand her."

"That's overstating it," Gignomai said mildly. "But I needed to marry someone."

"To acquire a legitimate heir, yes, I know. But Teucer."

"Back Home," Gignomai said, "there used to be a fashion among the monks of the Studium for wearing hair shirts under their sumptuous robes of velvet and ermine. The reasoning was we don't give a damn what people think about us, we certainly don't make a show of our true piety, so we dress up like spoilt rich kids and let everyone believe we're effete and corrupt. But underneath, we're who we are, and it's good if it itches, it helps concentrate the mind. And when a monk died and they peeled off the thousand-thaler shell, they'd find the body was rubbed raw with sores and abscesses, but they were sworn to secrecy, on their immortal souls, and nobody ever knew." He smiled pleasantly. "Teucer keeps me raw under the met'Oc," he said. "But don't tell a soul."

Furio looked at him. "You're..."

"Crazy?"

"Incorrigible," Furio replied. "Never occurred to you to wonder what sort of a life she has, being your hair shirt."

"True," Gignomai said calmly. "Well, no. First, when I asked her she could've said no, and she didn't. Second, because she's married to me, she can be a doctor, which is what she really wanted."

"By-products."

"Yes, of course." Gignomai shrugged. "I try and keep the inconvenience to others as slight as possible, but I do what I have to."

"What gives you the right?"

Gignomai grinned suddenly; he looked about twelve years old. "I'm a met'Oc," he said. "We were born with the right, along with the responsibility. If I could've chosen my parents, I'd have been a merchant's son, probably, I'd have made a fortune by the time I was twenty-five, and spent the rest of my life playing at being a country gentleman. No such luck. You, on the other hand..."

"Screw you, Gig."

"You, on the other hand," Gignomai persisted, "would have made a splendid met'Oc. Not in exile, maybe, but back Home you'd have done well. Noble, honourable, principled. You'd have been a great First Citizen. And if you'd been my father's youngest son, you wouldn't have sat still and done nothing." He looked away for a moment, then back again. "And none of this would've been necessary. Ironic, don't you think?"

"And we'd still be ruled by the Company."

"Well, yes," Gignomai said. "It wouldn't have occurred to you to break the law."

Furio thought for a moment. Then, "The hell with it," he said. "Serves me right for raising the subject in the first place."

"Agreed," Gignomai said. "A mistake you won't make again."

Furio smiled weakly. "Agreed," he said. "But there's one thing..."

"Oh for crying out loud. What now?"

"If the men who laid out the dead monks were sworn to secrecy, like you just said, how come you know about it?"

Gignomai laughed out loud, with relief that was almost joy. "Because the monks couldn't resist telling someone," he said, "because if *nobody* knew, what'd be the point?"

On his way home, Furio stopped off at Gignomai's town house, or the doctor's house, as everybody else thought of it. Teucer was sweeping up in the big room she used as a surgery.

"Oh, it's you," she said, when the maid showed him in.

He asked after young Lusomai, who was fine, thank you, and after Teucer herself, who couldn't complain (a lie if ever he'd heard one). Then he stood looking nervous for a while, until Teucer asked him what he really wanted.

"Why did you marry Gignomai?" he asked.

You could ask her things like that, but there was a price to pay. She could ask you things like that right back. "It's a marriage of convenience," she said. "I got all this. Back Home, I'd have spent my entire life planning meals and embroidering cushion covers."

"The real reason," Furio said.

"Because I love him," Teucer replied.

When Furio had gone, and he was sure he was alone, Gignomai unbuttoned his shirt halfway down and slipped his hand inside. With his fingertips, he gently encountered the texture of the coarse horsehair vest he'd worn for the last five years. It had been the only thing he'd taken from the house, just before he slipped out to join the colonists and start the fire. It had belonged, of course, to his father, who had worn it ever since he ordered his daughter's death (and nobody had known, except for Passer, his wife, and Gignomai, who'd watched him undress once through the key hole), only once taking it off, as custom prescribed, for the day of his son's wedding, but leaving it neatly folded by his bed, to put back on as soon as the ceremony was over.

Teucer had asked him about it, once. He said it was for warmth, because he had a weak chest. She knew he was lying, but didn't say or do anything, at which point, he knew she was well suited to be a met'Oc.

He rebuked himself for the indulgence, which was a sort of pride, and buttoned up his shirt to the neck.

extras

orbit

meet the author

K. J. PARKER is a pseudonym. Find more about the author at www.kjparker.com.

introducing

If you enjoyed
THE HAMMER,
look out for

THE FOLDING KNIFE

by K. J. Parker

Basso the Magnificent. Basso the Great. Basso the Wise. The First Citizen of the Vesani Republic is an extraordinary man.

He is ruthless, cunning, and above all, lucky. He brings wealth, power, and prestige to his people. But with power comes unwanted attention, and Basso must defend his nation and himself from threats foreign and domestic. In a lifetime of crucial decisions, he's only ever made one mistake.

One mistake, though, can be enough.

On the morning of the day when Basso (Bassianus Severus, the future First Citizen) was born, his mother woke up to find a strange woman sitting at the foot of her bed.

Her husband was away somewhere on business, and the

servants slept downstairs. The woman was dirty and shabby, and she was holding a small knife.

"Hello," Basso's mother said. "What do you want?"

Over the woman's shoulder, Basso's mother could see that the skylight had been forced. She was shocked. It had never occurred to her that a woman could climb a drainpipe.

"Money," the woman said.

Basso's mother assessed her. About her own age, though she looked much older; a foreigner, most likely a Mavortine (blonde hair, short, fat nose, blue eyes); there were always Mavortines in the city at that time of year, seasonal workers. She was wearing the remains of a man's coat, several sizes too big.

"I'm terribly sorry," Basso's mother said, "but I don't have any. My husband doesn't let me have money. He does all the…"

The woman made a strange grunting noise; frustration and annoyance, all that work for nothing. "I'm sorry," Basso's mother repeated. "If I had any money, I'd give it to you." She paused, then added, "You look like you could use it."

The woman scowled at her. "What about downstairs?"

Basso's mother shook her head sadly. "All the money in the house is kept in my husband's iron chest," she said. "It's got seven padlocks, and he carries the keys about with him. The servants might have a few coppers," she added helpfully, "but it's nearly the end of the month, so I doubt it."

The woman was holding the knife rather than brandishing it. Basso's mother guessed she'd used it to work open the skylight catch. It was a folding knife, an expensive item, with a slim blade and a gold handle; the sort of thing a prosperous clerk would own, for sharpening pens.

"If you're that hard up," Basso's mother said, "you could sell your knife. It must be worth a bit."

The woman looked at it, then back at her. "Can't," she said.

"If I went in a shop, they'd know it was stolen. I'd be arrested." She gasped, then burst into a noisy coughing fit that lasted several seconds.

Basso's mother nodded. "So jewellery wouldn't be much use to you either," she said. She was feeling sick, but managed to keep her face straight and calm. "All I can suggest is that you help yourself to some decent clothes. The dressing room's next door, just there, look."

The woman was looking at her, considering the tactical implications. "Shoes," she said.

Basso's mother wasn't able to see the woman's feet. "Oh, I've got plenty of shoes," she said. "I think a pair of good stout walking shoes would be the most useful thing, don't you?"

The woman started to reply, then broke out coughing again. Basso's mother waited till she'd finished, then said, "I'm sorry about the money, but at least let me get you something for that cough. How long have you had it?"

The woman didn't answer, but there was an interested look in her eyes. Medicine clearly didn't feature in her life. Basso's mother pushed back the sheets and carefully levered herself out of bed and onto her feet. She didn't bother putting her slippers on.

"Rosehip syrup, I think," she said, waddling across the room to the table where her apothecary chest stood. She took the key from the little lacquered box and opened the chest. "There's a jug of water on the stand beside the bed. Would you mind?"

The woman hesitated, then brought the jug. Her feet were bare, red, nearly purple; quite disgusting. "While I'm fixing this, have a look in the shoe closet. It's just there, look, on your left."

Not that the woman would be able to read the labels on the bottles. Basso's mother poured a little dark brown syrup into a glass and added water. "Here," she said, "drink this."

The woman had already pulled out two pairs of boots; she

was clutching them, pinched together, in her left hand. The knife was still in her right. She hesitated, then threw the boots on the bed and took the glass.

"When you've drunk that," Basso's mother said, "I'll ring for some food. When did you last have anything to eat?"

The woman was staring at her, a stupid look on her face. Basso's mother counted under her breath. On five, the woman staggered; on seven, she flopped down on the floor. Usually it was at least ten before it had any effect at all.

Later, Basso's mother decided she must have given her too much (understandable, in the circumstances). Also, the woman may have had a weak heart or some similar condition. It was sad, of course, but just one of those things. Basso's mother paid for a coffin and a plot in the public cemetery. It was, she felt, the least she could do.

Whether the shock induced early labour the doctors couldn't say. In the event, there were no complications and the baby was perfectly healthy, though a little underweight. Basso's father had bars fitted over the skylight. A better catch would have done just as well, but he was that sort of man. Basso's mother tried not to notice the bars, but they were always there in her mind after that.

The woman must have dropped the folding knife when she fell over, and knocked it under the bed. A maid found it and put it away in a drawer. Basso's mother came across it some time later and decided to keep it; not quite a trophy, but not something you just throw away. Besides, it was very good quality. When Basso was ten years old she gave it to him. He knew the story that went with it, of course.

Back home his name was seven syllables long, but here, in the army of the Vesani Republic, he was Aelius of the Seventeenth Auxiliary, the youngest captain in the service, kicking his heels in barracks in the City when men with half his ability were shipping out to the war in charge of a battalion. He was checking supply requisitions in his office when a flustered-looking sergeant interrupted him.

"We've arrested a boy, captain," the sergeant said.

Aelius looked up. "And?" he said.

"He beat up a sentry."

The culture of the service demanded that enlisted men addressed officers as rarely and as briefly as possible. Aelius thought it was a stupid rule, but he observed it rigorously. "You'd better bring him in," he said.

A boy, sure enough. Fourteen rather than fifteen, Aelius decided, mostly on the evidence of the face; on the tall side for his age, but still only a kid. "And this child assaulted a sentry?"

The sergeant nodded. "Broken arm, broken jaw, two cracked ribs and knocked out a couple of teeth, sir. Unprovoked attack. Two witnesses."

The boy didn't seem to have a mark on him. Correction: skinned knuckles on his left hand. "This boy attacked a grown man for no apparent reason and broke his jaw," Aelius said. The boy was looking past him, at the far wall. "Well?" he barked. The boy said nothing. "I'm talking to you."

The boy shrugged. "I hit that man, if that's what you mean."

Aelius nodded slowly. "Why?"

"He spoke to my sister."

"And?"

The boy frowned. "He made a lewd suggestion."

Aelius managed to keep a straight face. "So you beat him up."

"Yes."

Aelius looked sideways at the floor. Bringing charges was out of the question. A soldier of the Seventeenth beaten to a jelly by a child; they'd never live it down. The face was vaguely familiar. Not a pleasant sight: his nose was a little concave stub, and his enormous lower lip curled up over his upper lip, smothering it. "What's your name?"

"Arcadius Severus."

That made Aelius frown. The boy wasn't dressed like a gentleman's son, but he had a formal name. The voice was completely nondescript, and Aelius hadn't been in the Republic long enough to distinguish the subtleties of class from a man's accent. Harder still with a boy with a tendency to mumble. "That's a big name for a kid," he said. "Who's your father?"

The boy felt in his pocket, produced a copper penny and held it out on his palm, heads upwards. "*He* is."

No wonder the face was familiar. "Sergeant," Aelius said, "get out."

As the door closed, Aelius leaned forward across his desk. The boy was watching him, to see what would happen next. He wasn't afraid, he wasn't smug. That alone was enough to confirm that he was who he said he was. "What kind of lewd suggestion?" Aelius asked.

"None of your business."

Aelius shrugged. "Fine," he said. "All right, you can go."

The boy turned towards the door, and Aelius rose smoothly to his feet, snatched his swagger stick off the desk and slammed it against the side of the boy's head, hitting him just above the left ear. He went down, started to get up, staggered, recovered and got to his feet.

"Can I go now?" the boy said.

Aelius nodded. "I think that makes us all square," he said. "Do you agree?"

"Yes," the boy said. "Yes, that's fair."

Fair, Aelius thought. Not the word he'd have chosen, but surprisingly appropriate. "Then go home," he said. "And maybe you'd like to think about the relationship between the military and the civil authorities. Ask your dad; he'll explain it to you."

Outside, the boy's sister was waiting for him. She was flanked by two sentries; not physically restrained, but held in place like a chess piece that can't move without being taken. "It's all right," the boy said. "They let me go."

She said something to him as they walked away. He couldn't make out the words—his ears were still ringing from the blow on the head—but he didn't really need to. His sister wasn't happy at all.

"You won't tell Father," he said.

She scowled, then shook her head. "I ought to."

"I settled it with the captain," the boy replied. "You'll only make trouble."

She made a tutting noise, like a mother reproving an infant. "They'll know something's happened when they see you like that," she said.

"I fell out of a tree."

Scornful look. "Since when did you climb trees?"

He grinned at her. "That's why I fell," he said. "Lack of experience."

"I'm sick of covering up for you," she said, walking a little faster. It cost her disproportionate effort, because she would wear those ridiculous shoes. "I'm always having to lie for you, and I've had enough. Next time…"

"Oh, that's wonderful," the boy said. "It was all your fault anyway. If you hadn't been making eyes at that soldier…"

(Which he knew was a lie; but a lie he could pretend to believe, thereby putting her on the defensive.)

"That's just rubbish," she snapped. "And you're stupid. I've got a good mind to tell Father what happened. It'd serve you right if I did."

She didn't, of course. As it turned out, there was no need for anybody to say anything. The First Citizen and his wife were out for the evening at a reception, and off early the next morning for the state opening of the Assembly. Undoubtedly the servants noticed his scabbed knuckles, and when the ringing in his ears didn't go away, they quickly learned to talk to his right side or speak a little louder. He had no trouble hearing his father, because the First Citizen's voice was plenty loud enough, even at home, and his mother never had anything much to say for herself at the best of times.

Six months later, the boy's father lost the election and was replaced as First Citizen by Didius Vetranio, whose father had been a sausage-maker. That is to say, Didius Maesus had owned a twenty per cent stake in a slaughterhouse where they made the best-quality air-dried sausage for the export trade, along with a large number of other sound investments. As far as the boy's father was concerned, that made him a sausage-maker. He sulked for a month, then bought a ship — ridiculously cheap, he told anybody who'd listen, the most incredible bargain — and cheered up again. His good mood lasted five weeks, until the ship sank in the Strait of Essedine with a full cargo of pepper and saffron.

"Fucking disaster," the boy overheard his father telling one of his business associates (a small, dried man with hollow cheeks and a very sharp nose). "Eight hundred thousand, and that's without what that bastard gouged me out of for the ship."

The little man frowned. "Borrowed?"

"Six hundred thousand." The boy's father sighed. "Unsecured, which is a blessing, I suppose, but it puts me where I squelch when I walk. Bastard had no business selling a ship that wasn't seaworthy."

The little man thought for a moment. He was a study for a major sculpture, *Man Thinking*. "You need capital," he said.

"Yes, thank you, that had in fact occurred to me already." The boy's father took a peach off the top of the fruit dish, bit off a third and discarded the rest. "You wouldn't happen to ..."

"No."

A slight shrug; no harm in trying. "Looks like marriage, then," he said. "That or mortgage the vineyard, and I'd be reluctant to do that."

The little man nodded. "Which one?"

"Oh, the boy," the boy's father said. "I've already done a deal for the girl, but it's a long-term job, I'd hate to spoil it by rushing it along. The good thing about children," he went on, "is that when you run out you can always make some more. Friend of mine used to say, a man of good family carries his pension between his legs. No, I had an offer for the boy only last month, but of course I was flush then and told them to stuff it."

"Good offer?"

The boy's father leaned back in his chair and let his head droop forward. "It'd be enough to see me out of this mess, and a bit left over, but that's about it. On the other hand, it'd be cash up front on betrothal, with the real estate settled till he comes of age. I could borrow against the realty, invest it, pick a winner, clear off my debts with the profit and break off the betrothal. It's a thought," he added defensively, though the little man hadn't said anything. "No, I suppose not. I have an idea my luck's not at its best and brightest right now."

The little man folded his hands in his lap. "None of this would've happened if you'd insured the ship," he said.

"Yes, well."

But the little man was like a little dog that gets its teeth in something and won't let go. "How much have you got left, Palo?"

A long sigh; and the boy saw that look on his father's face, the one that meant he was about to answer quietly. "Not enough," he said. "Oh, I've got assets to show for it, land and good securities, but either they're tied up or they're long-term. Like the brickyard," he said, rubbing the sides of his nose with both forefingers, like a man just waking up. "I've put a lot of money into that. Fifteen years' time it'll be a gold mine, but if I sold it now I'd be screwed. Actual ready cash..." He shook his head. "Hence the short-term unsecured loans, which are eating me alive, of course. And I spent a lot of money on the election, of course, and that was a joke. Beaten by a sausage-maker, very funny, ha ha. Makes you wonder why you ever bother in the first place."

The little man coughed, a strange noise, a bit like a bone breaking. "I never could see the point in running for office," he said. "I've always had better things to do with my time. People talk about the contacts and the influence, but I don't see it myself. Personally, I prefer to concentrate my energies on business."

The boy's father grinned. "With hindsight, I tend to agree with you. Still, your circumstances are a bit different. You could always afford the best senators money could buy."

A very slight shrug, to concede an inconsequential point. "The offer for your son."

"Quite." (The boy shifted to ease the cramp in his leg and banged his foot against the leg of a table. Fortunately, neither man heard.) "Malo Sinvestri's daughter. Could be worse."

"The Licinii have done very well in bulk grain," the little man said. "You have those warehouses down by the weir standing empty. Presumably your intention—"

"Actually, I hadn't thought of that." A suddenly cheering-up lilt in his father's voice. "Thanks, Galba, that puts quite a nice edge on the deal. Of course, I'd have to use proxies."

"Licinius doesn't know?"

"Why should he?" A short laugh, like a hammer on an anvil, or a bell. "Not in my name, you see, so not on the register. It'd be worth it just to see the look on Malo's face."

On the day of the betrothal ceremony, he wasn't well. He had an upset stomach, ferocious stabbing pains between his navel and his groin that made him twist like a dancer.

His mother didn't appear to believe him. "Don't be stupid," she said. "This is a serious occasion. It's not something you can get out of by pretending you're ill."

He couldn't answer immediately. When he'd got the use of his mouth back, he said, "Tell you what, you can come and inspect the contents of my chamber pot. Will that do you?"

"Don't be—"

"That's evidence," he said. "Solid proof. Well, maybe not solid. For pity's sake, mother, I'm not *well*. I can hardly stand upright."

His mother's look held the unique alloy of pity and contempt she reserved just for him. "Well, you've nobody but yourself to blame," she said, dipping her hand into the linen pocket she wore on her belt and taking out nine plum stones. "You don't even *like* plums," she said.

He nodded. His mistake had been throwing the stones out of the window, instead of burying them in the midden. Attention to detail. "Oh, I like them," he said, "but they don't like me." A particularly sharp spasm put him out of action for a while, and then he said, "It doesn't alter the fact that I'm not well enough to stand through a long formal ceremony. Unless you want me to make a spectacle of myself in front of all those people."

His mother shook her head. "I haven't told your father about these," she said, moving the plum stones a little closer to his nose.

"You don't have to go to the ceremony, I'll send a note to say you're ill, but I'll tell your father the truth. It's entirely up to you."

He breathed in deeply. "All right," he said. "What do you suggest?"

She nodded briskly. "I'll get you some medicine," she said.

Her words coincided with yet another spasm, so the face he pulled was submerged in a greater reaction. His mother collected medicines, rather in the way a boy collects coins or seals or arrowheads; one or two genuine pieces, along with a whole load of junk. "Thanks," he said, "but I think I'll be —"

"Stay there," she said, and a few minutes later she came back with a little blue-glass cup. "Drink this," she said, "it'll get you through the ceremony."

The last attack had left him gasping for air. "Does it work?"

"I don't know," his mother replied, "I've never tried it myself. The man said it's a miracle cure, but I've never dealt with him before. You don't have to take it if you don't want to."

He took the cup and stared into it; off-white sludge, like the scum on top of new cream. "What is it?"

"The man said it's a special sort of clay dust," his mother answered blandly. "Apparently there's a magic mountain in Sigaea, which is the only place in the world this stuff's ever been found. It's mined by an ancient order of monks exclusively for the Imperial court, but somehow this man managed to get hold of a jar." She shrugged. "You never know," she said. "Anyway, drink it if you like. It might do you good."

Remarkably, it did. At least, it stopped up his bowels like a cork for three days. It didn't do anything for the pain, but he handled that himself, and if any of the guests at the betrothal noticed anything, they didn't mention it. In a way, he was almost glad of it, since it gave him something else to think about apart from the bride and her family. The latter would have scared the life out of him if he'd been in any fit state to care; several huge men, tall, broad and fat, with close-cropped beards that came up to the tops of their cheekbones, and tall thin women who looked at him and shuddered. His father was extremely subdued, which was unnerving, and sober, which was unprecedented. He couldn't see his mother most of the time, because she had to sit on the far side of the temple with his sister and the other women, but he could feel her eyes on him like a bridle. As for the bride, she was muffled up in veils like a beekeeper (what's the matter, he thought, is she afraid I'm going to sting her to death or something?) so she registered with him as little more than a shape in a gauze mist and a small, sullen voice that mumbled the words after the priest. But when she first saw him, she stopped dead in her tracks, the way a horse stops when it sees something it doesn't like, and no amount of booting and spurring will get it to shift. Her father and uncle whispered something to her, "What do you think you're playing at?" or words to that effect; she whispered back, and then her father put his hand between her shoulder blades and shoved so hard she nearly fell over. An auspicious start, he couldn't help thinking; not that he blamed her in the least. He owned a mirror. It was a small comfort to know there was someone who was even more wretched about the performance than he was, but the pain in his stomach was the only thing he could think about.

The priest got his name the wrong way round: Bassianus Severus Arcadius. On the way home, he asked if it was still legal. His father assured him that it was.

*